What People Are Saying about
Sarah, My Beloved and Sharlene MacLaren

As I've come to expect from her, Sharlene MacLaren writes an engaging story with characters I'd like to call my friends. Through this tale of faith and the journey to triumphing over grief, she paints a beautiful picture of what home can be, when it's made by people willing to open their hearts to each other and to the Lord. I can't wait to see what's waiting for me next in Little Hickman Creek.

—Roseanna White, Christian Review of Books

Sharlene MacLaren makes you feel right at home in Little Hickman. With charming, down-to-earth characters and back drop, I felt like a lifelong resident. Curl up in your favorite chair and prepare to be transported to a simpler time. A delightful addition to the Little Hickman Creek Series.

—Teresa Slack,
Author of the award-winning Jenna's Creek Novels

Sarah, My Beloved is a keeper! Sharlene MacLaren has written an engaging historical romance that will keep you turning the pages and reliving scenes from the Callahans' lives long after the back cover is closed. Watch for this author when you want just the right touch of detail and depth mixed with humor and meaningful emotion brought to a satisfying ending.

—Mildred Colvin,
Author, winner of Reader's Choice Award

Sarah, My Beloved is a fresh take on the "marriage-of-convenience" plot, with wonderfully fleshed out characters. Sharlene MacLaren weaves a touching story that grips the heart, and leaves the reader satisfied, yet wanting more.

—Deborah M. Piccurelli, Author, *In the Midst of Deceit*

This faith-based story reveals how a blended family can move from fractured to whole. For an absorbing read, get to know the Callahan clan and visit Little Hickman, Kentucky, through author Sharlene MacLaren's keen words.

—Cathy Messecar, Author, *The Stained Glass Pickup*

A mail-order bride and a marriage in name only are tucked flawlessly inside a historical novel you won't want to put down. Sharlene MacLaren has done it again.

—Molly Noble Bull,
Author of *The Winter Pearl* and *Sanctuary*

Sarah, My Beloved is a charming addition to the Little Hickman series. MacLaren writes with a colorful voice that will keep the reader turning pages. Filled with dynamic dialogue and likeable characters, this books is one you won't want to put down. A satisfying read for those who love a gentle romance.

—Lacy Williams,
Reviewer for Armchair Interviews
and the Christian Suspense Zone

Sarah, My Beloved is a delightful addition to the Little Hickman Creek series. Red-haired and strong-minded, Sarah is a match for any man, even Rocky Callahan. A heartwarming story that hooked me from page one. Sharlene MacLaren has done it again.

—Barbara Warren,
Author, *The Gathering Storm,* Jireh Publishers
Blue Mountain Editorial Service

Little Hickman Creek Series

Sarah

My Beloved

Dedication

To my darling husband, Cecil,
the inspiration behind my writing…

And the true love of my life.

(You had me with that first kiss.)

Little Hickman Creek Series

Sarah
My Beloved

Sharlene MacLaren

WHITAKER
HOUSE

SARAH, MY BELOVED
Second in the Little Hickman Creek Series

ISBN-13: 978-0-88368-425-2
ISBN-10: 0-88368-425-X
Printed in the United States of America
© 2007 by Sharlene MacLaren

1030 Hunt Valley Circle
New Kensington, PA 15068
www.whitakerhouse.com

Library of Congress Cataloging-in-Publication Data

MacLaren, Sharlene, 1948–
Sarah, my beloved / Sharlene MacLaren.
    p.   cm. — (Little Hickman Creek series)
Summary: "Following God's leading, mail-order bride Sarah Woodward arrives in Little Hickman Creek, Kentucky, and enters into a marriage in name only with Rocky Callahan to help him raise his orphaned niece and nephew"—Provided by publisher.
    ISBN-13: 978-0-88368-425-2 (trade pbk. : alk. paper)
    ISBN-10: 0-88368-425-X (trade pbk. : alk. paper) 1. Mail order brides—Fiction. 2. Orphans—Fiction. 3. Kentucky—Fiction. I. Title.
    PS3613.A27356S27 2007
    813'.6—dc22   2007024006

1 2 3 4 5 6 7 8 9 **WH** 13 12 11 10 09 08 07

Chapter One

January 1896

*I*t was the nicest, pertiest weddin' I ever did see." The woman's high-pitched voice soared across the room.

"You're right, Mrs. Warner. Never saw a sweeter couple," another woman chirped in reply.

"And so in love," someone twittered.

"Why, the bride fairly glowed."

"Indeed."

The ceaseless nattering of female voices forced twenty-seven-year-old Sarah Woodward to find a hiding place in a far corner behind a bolt of purple gingham in Winthrop's Dry Goods. Her presence in the store had gone undiscovered since she'd entered ahead of the others and while the owner was in the back room. Too embarrassed to show her face now, she longed to disappear between the slats in the worn wood floor. After all, the aforementioned bride should have been *her*.

It seemed a cruel twist of fate that the man she'd agreed to wed by means of the Marriage Made in Heaven Agency out east, and had traveled halfway across the country to meet up with, had fallen in love with the town's schoolteacher before Sarah even had the chance to lay eyes on him. She should have known better than to seek the assistance of a mail-order bridal service for the sake of adventure, never mind that she'd felt certain God had led the way.

7

Of course, the man had been a gentleman about it, apologizing profusely for the mix-up in communication. His message to halt the proceedings had not reached her in time, and he had offered to pay her for her trouble, namely sending her back to where she'd come from—Winchester, Massachusetts.

Naturally, she'd refused his offer of compensation. She didn't want his money. Besides, she wouldn't go back to Winchester—not as long as Stephen Alden, attorney-at-law, lived there. The man seemed bent on marrying her, and it was truly the last thing Sarah wanted.

It wasn't as if her heart had broken over the news of Benjamin Broughton's plans to wed another. She scarcely knew the man. No, it was more regret than heartbreak, regret that her plans had failed. After all, without the benefits of a marriage license, Stephen would still consider her open territory—might even chase her down—and she couldn't have that.

Lord, there has to be another way, she'd prayed in earnest that first night she'd arrived in Little Hickman, Kentucky, and learned that her trip had been in vain. But if there was another way, He had yet to reveal it to her.

"And to think that poor Woodward woman traveled all the way from Massachusetts to marry Benjamin," someone tittered.

Sarah's throat went dry as she covered herself more fully with the bolt of cloth, praying no one would notice her. So far, her luck had held, but if the women didn't vacate the place soon, she felt certain she was in for more humiliation. As if she hadn't already taken the prize in that department.

The ring of the cash register's drawer opening floated through the air.

"Yes, it's a shame she made the wasted trip," said one woman. "Of course, what would one expect? Imagine! Calling on a marriage service to procure a husband. It's beyond me why any woman would resort to such measures. It makes one wonder."

A round of concurrence rose up amid all the yammering.

"Mighty pretty thing, she is. Looks like she comes from wealth," said Mrs. Warner, the only woman whose voice Sarah recognized.

"Yes, doesn't she?" agreed one. "She wears such fine clothing."

"But that hair," rattled another. "Seems to me she ought to do something about that awful mass of red curls!"

Sarah instinctively seized a fistful of hair and silently rebuked her mother for having passed it down to her. It was true. Her thick, unruly, garnet-colored mane had been akin to a curse. For once, she would like to walk into a room and not feel the stares of countless eyes—as if she'd grown two heads and three arms.

"I agree. It looks like a ball of fire most of the time. Even hats don't seem to cover the worst of it." Sarah recognized that particular voice as belonging to the proprietor, Mrs. Winthrop, a woman seemingly determined to discover everyone's biggest fault.

Sarah swallowed hard and adjusted her feet, still ice-cold from her walk from Emma Browning's Boardinghouse. She waited for the small gathering of gossipy women to disperse, taking care to keep her head down and her eyes on her leather tie-up boots.

About the time she thought the last woman had made her purchase, the bell on the door tinkled softly, indicating the arrival of a new customer. At the door's gaping, a blast of cold winter air skittered past Sarah's legs, generating an unexpected shiver that ran the length of her five-foot, five-inch slender frame.

Voices stilled at the newest customer's arrival, making Sarah crane her neck in curiosity. Careful not to make a sound, she peered past aisles and shelves crammed with stitching supplies—everything from embroidered tapestry to threads, scissors to needles, and luxurious velvet to sensible cotton. With interest, she surveyed the source of the women's sudden hush, thankful that the Winthrops' large inventory made hiding easy.

Looming in the doorway, looking uncomfortable if not overtly out of place, was the man Sarah instantly recognized as the uncle of the two young children she'd come into town on the stage with three weeks ago. Alone and forlorn, the poor little urchins had lost their mother to some fatal lung disease and been shipped to an uncle who, she'd learned later, didn't want them. Her heart had gone out to them almost immediately, for she knew how feelings of rejection could play upon the psyche of a small child.

Although she didn't know the man, and certainly didn't care to, she'd surely wanted to give him a piece of her mind. How could anyone deny small children the affection due them, particularly when the subjects were family members who had just lost a loved one?

Her blood had boiled then, and it fairly simmered even now. *Lord, forgive me for despising someone I don't even know.*

"Afternoon, ladies," came the cavernous voice of the powerfully built man, his shoulders so broad it surprised her that he'd passed through the door without having to shift sideways.

A woolen cap pulled low over his head shaded his eyes, making their color imperceptible, but failing to conceal his granite-like stare. Black hair, gleaming in the light, wavy and unkempt, hung beneath the cap's line, skimming the top of his collar. A muscle clenched along his beardless, square-set jaw, automatically triggering a response from Sarah to recoil. Why did he have to show up now, when she was already eager to flee the dry goods store?

"Why, Mr. Callahan, I don't believe you've ever graced our store with your presence," said Mrs. Winthrop, her buttery tone making Sarah grimace. "What can I do for you?"

"I'm lookin' for some fabric for my niece, Rachel," was his curt reply. "She needs a new dress or two; warm, serviceable ones, mind you. I'm also needin' someone to sew them. I was hopin' you could make a recommendation."

"Oh my! Well, a seamstress for hire is something we dearly lack in this town. Most make do with their own meager talents."

"Well, I don't happen to be too handy in that department," Mr. Callahan snapped, his tone indicating his lack of amusement at the situation.

"Yes, well, I have a few ready-made dresses in stock if you'd care to look. Or you could place an order if you'd like to glance through a catalog. What size would your niece...?"

"I could have gone to Johansson's Mercantile if I'd wanted a ready-made dress," he cut in, fingering a piece of woolen material under Mrs. Winthrop's nose. "But I'm not of a mind to pay for such an unnecessary extravagance. That's why I came here—seeing as you have so much cloth in stock." His eyes scanned the place, and for a heart-stopping instant, Sarah feared he'd spotted her lurking in the gingham. But then his gaze traveled back to Mrs. Winthrop.

"Oh, I see." Mrs. Winthrop's hand went to her throat, no doubt offended by the mention of her competitor, Eldred Johansson. The other women each took a step back, feigning disinterest, but Sarah knew better. They wouldn't be leaving the premises until Mr. Callahan did, for fear of missing the excitement. And neither would they be offering any help by the look of them.

"How are your niece and nephew?" Mrs. Winthrop asked, folding her hands at her waist, her chin protruding.

"Rachel and Seth are surviving just fine," he replied in a gruff tone.

"It was a shame—about their mother," Mrs. Winthrop offered.

"My sister, you mean," he said.

"Of course," Mrs. Winthrop answered. "It must have been a shock to—well, everyone."

"Not a shock, no. She'd been ill for some time. Now, what about that seamstress?" His curtness seemed to add an icy dimension to the already chilled room.

"Well, as I said, I don't happen to know of anyone off-hand."

"Any of you sew?" he asked the women, turning an assessing eye on each of them.

"I stitch for my family, but I'm afraid I'm quite pressed for time right now, what with all my youngins runnin' every which direction," one woman answered while nervously fingering her parcel.

Mr. Callahan nodded and looked to the other two women.

Both shook their head. "I'm afraid I can barely make do with my own pile of mending and darning, Mr. Callahan. You'd best order somethin' ready-made." This from the woman referred to as Mrs. Warner.

"Well, since I don't intend to spend the extra money on such a frivolous expense, I 'spect my niece'll have to make do with what she has, holes or not."

Sarah's blood had fairly reached its boiling point when she stepped forward, her camouflage no longer important. "I can sew," she stated calmly despite her inward seething. Perhaps it was her hasty prayer for self-control that kept her from throttling the man the second she came out of hiding. A little girl who'd just lost her mother deserved a new dress. How dare he call such a purchase an extravagance?

"Well, saints above, M-Miss Woodward," Mrs. Winthrop stammered. "W-where—?" Her eyes went round while the other women similarly gaped. Shamefaced and clearly mortified, they began a hasty retreat toward the door, filing out one by one, failing even to proffer a respectable good-bye. Icy air snaked into the room with the open door, adding to the already cold atmosphere Mr. Callahan had ushered in by his mere presence.

"You say you can stitch a dress?" Mr. Callahan asked, his eyes—a piercing shade of blue Sarah noticed now that she had the chance to see them up close—coming to rest on Sarah's face, then carefully sweeping the length of her.

Determined not to allow the man's intimidation to ruffle her, Sarah replied, "I said I can sew, didn't I?"

"But can you stitch a dress for a girl?" he asked with a good measure of impatience.

Under his scrutiny, she felt her neck muscles go stiff. "I've never made a child's dress," she admitted begrudgingly, "but I've made plenty of other things. I expect with proper measuring and planning I can make her a fine dress."

He gave her another hasty once-over. "You make what you're wearin'?"

She looked down at the blue satin gown peeking out from under her long cashmere coat. Her mother had purchased it for her as a gift before taking ill a year ago. It had been her final gift from her. An unanticipated wave of sadness threatened to divert her attention but she hastily regained control of her wobbly emotions.

"No, but I've fashioned some of my own clothing."

"Really." He tipped back on his heels and gave her a disbelieving look. "You don't appear to be the sort who would stoop to such menial tasks."

Taken aback, she prayed for the right choice of words. "I'll have you know there is nothing menial about sewing. It's a fine hobby and one that does a great deal to alleviate stress, Mr.—" The man was nothing if he wasn't a dolt.

"Callahan. Rocky Callahan." He tipped his head a little by way of a greeting, and she noticed that one corner of his mouth curved slightly upward. "But then you already knew that, didn't you, Miss—?"

"Sarah Woodward," she put in, deciding to ignore his impudence. "I met your niece and nephew on the stagecoach a few weeks back, and I saw you take them away."

No point in trying to hide the fact that she'd noticed him. She wouldn't admit to having watched him, however.

"I assumed you were the uncle in question," she added. *But not because you overflowed with love and compassion.*

He glanced at Mrs. Winthrop, who hadn't moved from her place behind the counter. Receiving a red-hot glare from him, she took up a bundle of papers and moved to the back room, expelling a loud gasp of air on her way. "I'll let you know about the fabric," he called after.

Once again turning his dark gaze on Sarah, he said, "You're the woman Ben Broughton sent for."

Sarah's stomach tightened. The last thing she intended to do was discuss her personal reasons for coming to Little Hickman.

"I suppose you would need to alleviate some stress about now," he said with a mocking grin, making Sarah's back go straight as a pin, her chin jut with resolve. "Must have been a bit of a shock to travel all that way and then find the man you came to marry had set his cap for the schoolteacher."

"I'll need to measure your niece—is it Rachel?" she asked, trying her best to ignore his callousness.

He pointed a thumb over his shoulder. "She's out on the buckboard if you've a mind to measure her right now."

"You left her sitting in the cold?" Sarah exclaimed. "And the boy as well?" Picking up her skirts, she scooted around his broad frame to see out the window. Sure enough, two unfortunate little souls sat huddled together high on their perch, plainly cold by the way they both hugged themselves. "They're freezing."

"I asked them if they wanted to come inside," he said, moving up behind her at the window to fix his eyes on the children. "They both refused."

"What is wrong with you?" she asked, whirling around to face him, no longer thrown off balance by his tough exterior.

15

"The wind is brisk today, cold enough to bite off the tips of their little noses."

"I told you I invited them in," he said, as if that should fix the matter.

"Well, you should have insisted." Without waiting for his retort, she went to the door and flung it open. "Come in out of the cold," she called over the wailing winds.

Like lifeless statues, the pair sat rigid. Finally, the boy gave his sister a hopeful look, but she rewarded him with a slow shake of the head.

"Please come in where it's warm," Sarah called again, lowering her voice so that it sounded less demanding. Again, the boy looked to his sister, his bare little fingers finding a place to warm themselves between his skinny legs.

"They're not wearing mittens," Sarah hissed in disbelief.

"I couldn't find them when it was time to leave. The girl is absentminded. I've no idea where she put them and neither does she. I figured it would teach them both a lesson to go without."

"What? How old is she, six, seven? What do you expect?"

"She's seven, and I expect some level of responsibility," he answered.

His impertinence angered her so that she made a huffing sound before traipsing out into the frigid air and coming face-to-face with the poor little imps. Eyeing them with equal amounts of compassion and firmness, she looked from one to the other. "Hello, Rachel and Seth. My name is Sarah, and I would like you both to come inside now. I'm to make a dress for you, Rachel. Isn't that nice? If you'll please come inside I can measure you."

The child turned cold eyes on Sarah and folded her arms in front of her. "I don't need no dress," she stated.

"Just the same, you should come inside. It's bitter cold today."

"Is it going to snow?" asked the boy, his teeth clattering as he spoke. His sister knocked him with her elbow, indicating he wasn't to ask questions.

"It certainly feels cold enough," Sarah replied with a smile. "Do you like snow?"

He nodded readily but, at his sister's silent admonition, chose not to elaborate.

"Do you remember me? We rode into town together on the stage."

A simple nod was all she got from Seth. Rachel remained bravely staunch. "Ar mother died," she said simply.

"I know, and I'm sorry. Did you know my mother died about the same time as yours? If you come inside we can talk about it."

Rachel's cold stare intensified. "I don't want to talk about it."

"Fine then, we won't. I do need to measure you, however, so it's best you hop on down. You might help me pick out the cloth as well. How would that be?"

Only slightly intrigued by that notion, the girl looked at the doorway from where her uncle waited, his dour expression matching hers. "Ar uncle hates us," she declared.

Sarah digested the girl's words and planned her response with care. "I don't think he hates you." Her hasty glance backward confirmed that he couldn't hear them over the whistling wind.

"Well, it don't make no difference anyway," Rachel clucked. "'Cause we don't like him neither."

Sarah shivered and offered a hand to the angry child. Begrudgingly, she took it, jumping to the hard earth below and taking care to keep her frown in place. Next, Sarah held her arms out to the boy, who went to her with no prodding, his icy fingers clinging to her neck until they stepped inside and Mr. Callahan closed the door behind them.

At the pinging of the door's little bell, Mrs. Winthrop appeared around the curtained doorway. Sarah set Seth's booted feet on the floor. "Have we made a decision on the fabric yet?" she asked.

"Not yet, Mrs. Winthrop, but I would appreciate a tape measure if you have one," Sarah said. "I need to take Rachel's measurements."

"Yes, of course." She headed for a drawer near the cash register, pulled out a long cloth tape, and then hurried to deliver it. She seemed anxious to be rid of them.

After removing Rachel's coat and tossing it to the side, Sarah saw why the girl needed dresses. This one was tattered beyond repair, the hem hanging crooked with holes in the sleeves and a three-cornered tear on the back of the skirt, revealing a portion of her petticoats. Stains from lack of washing had fixed themselves down the front. To make matters worse, the material was nothing more than thin cotton, wearing and fraying at the edges. Sarah cast an eye at Mr. Callahan and hoped he read her disapproving look. If he did, he didn't let on. Instead, he shifted his weight from one foot to the other while she measured, as if to communicate his agitation. The act only made Sarah want to dawdle.

Once finished measuring, they moved to the various bolts of cloth, Mrs. Winthrop following on their heels. Mr. Callahan and the boy remained standing near the cash register. Sarah steered Rachel in the direction of the warmer weaves, the girl's eyes seeming close to bursting at the variety of colors and patterns. Finally, her gaze landed on heavy, rose-colored, brushed cotton. Grubby fingers came out to judge its texture. Sarah watched in silent pleasure as the girl's expression went from hesitance to sureness.

"You like this one?" Sarah asked.

A simple nod of the head was Rachel's response. Had she never had the opportunity to choose before? Moreover, had she never owned a new dress? By the looks of the one she wore, it was a hand-me-down, perhaps previously worn by more than one girl. Sarah's heart squeezed at the notion, for she couldn't begin to count the number of brand-new dresses she'd owned in her lifetime.

Mrs. Winthrop removed the bolt and hurried to a long table where she laid the material out to prepare for cutting. "Do you need thread?"

"I believe I have plenty of color choices back in my trunk. I'll check my supply before purchasing," she said. The woman looked across the table at Sarah, clearly intrigued.

"Fine," she managed, taking up with the huge piece of cloth.

Just then, Mr. Callahan approached, the young boy on his heels. "How soon before you finish the dress?" he asked.

"I've nothing better to do with my time. I should think I'll finish it in the next day or so."

He lifted a dark eyebrow and then removed his woolen cap before running long muscled fingers through his thick mass of black, wavy hair. "Nothing better to do, huh? You staying over at the boardinghouse?" he asked, his bottomless voice resonating off the walls.

"Yes." It was best to keep her answers short, she determined.

"And how long will that last?"

Bemused, she angled him a curious stare. "What sort of question is that, Mr. Callahan?" Mrs. Winthrop's hand movements slowed, as if she wanted to make certain not to miss a beat in the conversation.

"A simple one. You came here to marry Benjamin Broughton, right? Since that didn't pan out for you, I was curious as to how long before you go back to wherever it is you came from." A shadow crossed his face, indiscernible in nature.

She hid her anger beneath a forced smile. "Not that it is any of your business, sir, but I shall remain in Little Hickman indefinitely. I sold most of my possessions while still in Winchester. To return now would be most futile."

"Winchester?"

"Massachusetts. Just outside of Boston."

He cocked his dark head. Sarah found she had to crane her neck to see his face, making her believe his height exceeded six feet. "No family or friends up there?"

"Friends, yes, but none worth staying for," she confessed, immediately put out with herself for divulging such personal information. As if that weren't enough, she added, "My parents are both deceased and I have no siblings."

To that, he gave a perfunctory nod. "How long you staying at Emma's place?"

She couldn't help the little huffing sound that slipped

past her lips. What did he care where she resided and for how long? "For the time being," she offered. "In time I hope to…" It wouldn't do to mention that her financial resources sat in a trust fund back in Boston, awaiting her marriage as per her mother's final will and testament, so she buttoned her lip and left the sentence unfinished.

Creased brow raised, mouth slightly agape, he waited for her dangling sentence to reach its conclusion. "What? In time you hope to what?"

The children had wandered away out of boredom and were looking at various items around the store. Finished cutting the fabric, Mrs. Winthrop carried it to the cash register and feigned busyness, then took up a writing utensil to jot some figures.

"Find some suitable place in which to live," she finished, miffed at herself for being so forthright.

"In Hickman?" He grunted in disgust, trailing it with a cold chuckle. At that, Mrs. Winthrop gave a mighty sniff, causing both adults to turn their gazes on her. Hastily, she resumed her figuring. Mr. Callahan looked down his nose at Sarah. "In that case, you might be lookin' a while. You'll not find much finery in these parts, lady, and from the look of you, you've been conditioned to enjoy life's finer offerings."

His mocking manner unnerved her, the way he perused her from top to bottom, as if she were some piece of furniture he'd been pondering buying and couldn't quite determine whether it would mesh with his older pieces.

"I'll have you know I'm quite adaptable, sir!"

As if he had good reason to disbelieve her, he gave a half-nod. "No need to be snappish," he chided. Then, with a twist of his head, he glanced at the children, who'd wandered to the back of the store. "Don't touch anything," he ordered. At the harsh tone, his niece and nephew jolted to attention.

"Now who's the snappish one?" she asked, sticking out her chin.

Clearly irritated, he ignored the remark and moved to the cash register where he pulled out a sheaf of bills from his pocket. Sarah examined the roll of greenbacks from where she stood.

A palpable tightwad, that's what he was.

Mrs. Winthrop stated her price, and Mr. Callahan frowned. "You sure about that? Seems high to me."

"It's extremely reasonable, Mr. Callahan," Sarah inserted. Mrs. Winthrop's shoulders relaxed with gratitude.

"Oh, fine," was his annoyed response. He passed the proprietor a single bill, then waited while she made change. Once she slipped it to him, she gathered up the paper parcel containing the rose-colored material and handed it over to Sarah.

"Bring Rachel by Emma's tomorrow afternoon," she ordered. "I should be ready for her first fitting by then."

"Tomorrow?" His brow gathered into a frown. "Don't know as I'll have the time tomorrow."

Rather than react, Sarah merely gave her head a little toss. "Well, I can't put the finishing touches to the dress without first fitting her."

His broad shoulders shrugged impatiently. "Oh, all right—tomorrow."

"Good." Then to Rachel, she bent just slightly and placed a hand on her tattered wool bonnet. "See what you can do about finding those mittens, okay?"

The girl nodded, her expression bleak. Sarah smiled at both unfortunate waifs. Clearly, they needed some love and attention.

As to the man, he deserved nary a glimpse backward as she tugged open the heavy door and marched out into January's harsh gale.

Chapter Two

*E*at your eggs," Rocky told his five-year-old nephew the next morning.

"He don't like eggs," his sister said in his defense.

"I didn't ask you," Rocky said, matching Rachel's obstinate stare from across the table. "I'd appreciate it if in the future you would let me discipline your brother in the manner in which I see fit—without your help."

"He don't need discipline," she stated, her tone cold and firm.

"Every kid needs discipline," he argued, swallowing a forkful of eggs before going for a bite of bread and then a swig of hot coffee. His nerves had worn to the point of shredding. Arguing was the last thing he desired right now, but it seemed to be Rachel's favorite pastime on any given morning.

"Is Grandma coming over today?" Seth asked, his nose just inches from his plateful of eggs.

"Not this morning."

Worry filled up Seth's face. "Who's gonna watch us?"

"You two will have to make do on your own while I tend to the chores in the barn. I should be done in a few hours."

"Why can't Grandma come?" Seth asked in his usual, high-pitched whine.

"Your grandpap's not doing well today, so she's stayin' home." Rocky pushed back from the table and winced at the sound of dirt grinding beneath the chair legs. It'd been a while

24

since his house had had a good cleaning. "Eat your eggs," he repeated, standing. But the gloomy-faced boy refused even to lift his fork.

"Ar mama never made him eat what he don't like," Rachel mumbled into her plate.

"Then she spoiled him."

"No she din't," she cried, blue eyes brimming with wetness.

Rocky looked from the blond waif to her brown-haired, brown-eyed brother. If he started giving in to them, there'd be no end to what they'd get away with. His own parents had made him clean his plate after every meal. Why should it be any different with these two? True, he wasn't their actual parent, but he was their uncle, and now their legal guardian. He was doing the best he could.

Sighing heavily, he looked at the boy. "You're not to leave the table until your plate is cleaned. Is that clear?" The boy gave a silent nod.

Somewhat satisfied, Rocky turned on his heel and reached for his coat hanging next to the door.

"You're mean," Rachel said, her pert little chin sticking straight out, her narrow shoulders poking upward.

"I've been called worse," he said, sticking his arms through the sleeves, buttoning up, then going for his hat and work gloves.

He gave Rachel an assessing look. "If I should discover that you have eaten his food for him, I will tan your hide, young lady."

Jumping to her feet, she bellowed at the top of her lungs, "You're not my papa!" Clear resentment shone in her eyes.

"No, I'm not," he replied. *Your papa is dead, but if he were alive, I'd gladly give you back to him right about now.* Several more words sat on the tip of his tongue, words he chose not to use. At the door, he inhaled sharply. "After you clean up the kitchen, see that you find both sets of mittens. I want them on your hands before we ride into town today."

Even Nell's spirits had deteriorated. As soon as Rocky pulled the stool up beside the milk cow and stuck a pail beneath her teats, the cranky beast planted her front hoof into his kneecap. "Typical woman," he snorted, rubbing his knee and readjusting himself on the stool. "Polite one minute, crabby the next."

Nell shifted her footing and mooed, her tail swishing to match her mood. Rocky gave her time to settle her nerves, glad when she finally allowed him to take up the routine morning task of emptying her milk bags. While he milked, he thought about his pathetic situation.

He wasn't fit to foster two kids he barely knew, let alone understood. Sometimes he wondered if he even liked the pair, particularly after mornings like this when all they'd done was have a shouting match. Of course, Seth didn't shout. No, he counted on his sister to do that for him. So far, the kid hadn't even picked out his own clothes in the morning without his sister's approval. Rocky wondered about handing off this whole business of parenting to Rachel. She seemed to want the job.

He thought about the uneaten eggs. Was he wrong to insist that Seth empty his plate? Or was he asking too much of a five-year-old? The pair had landed in his home under dire circumstances—orphaned, no less—but that didn't lessen their need for discipline and certainly didn't give them license to run all over him. He was their guardian now, and as such, he expected them to follow the rules, even though they didn't seem accustomed to obeying.

A mild curse slipped past his tongue. Shoot, he knew nothing about raising girls, particularly this one, and to make matters worse, his mother's earlier promise to help him seemed too much for her to fulfill.

"Your father hasn't been well since Elizabeth's passing," she'd said just yesterday, her shoulders wilting in worry. "The children make him nervous."

Rocky had fought down his own concerns. "Ma, you promised if I agreed to take these kids, you'd lend a hand as needed. Well, I need help."

Gray, watery eyes held him in their grip, their underlying circles darker than usual revealing untold weariness. "I'm doing the best I can, son. These times are not easy for any of us."

Ashamed, he'd put an arm around her slender shoulders and tugged her to him. "Okay, don't worry about it. I'll work somethin' out."

To that, she'd given a fragile smile. "God will work it out, Rocky. It's time you took your hands off and let Him work."

But how could he take his hands off when the only person he truly trusted to handle his problems was himself?

As if to scold him for his thoughts, Nell slapped Rocky in the face with her tail, dampening his disposition even further.

"Walk in love, as Christ also hath loved us."

The words from some ancient passage in Scripture hit him like a wagonload of bricks. It'd been a long while since he'd thought about the Bible. Hester had been adamant about reading from it every night at the supper table.

Of course, the habit had died with her.

Without warning, the image of that feisty redhead he'd met just yesterday materialized from nowhere. Tall and slender, she'd resembled a porcelain doll: thick curls the color of burnished copper, eyes like sapphire marbles, her fine attire making her a shining example of wealth and fastidious fashion.

What had driven her to require the help of a bridal service? The question tickled his brain. Moreover, why would she choose to stay in a town where she obviously didn't blend in— particularly after discovering the man she'd traveled several hundred miles to meet was betrothed to another?

He thought about his good friend, Ben Broughton. The man must have been desperate—two children needing a mother; Ben, an overworked farmer with little time on his hands to meet their physical and emotional needs. Understandably, he'd felt driven to send for a mail-order bride. But what would drive a woman to agree to marry a man sight unseen?

The cynic in him might have found the situation almost laughable if he had not recognized himself in the scenario, equally in need of an immediate solution to his growing problem. What did he have to offer Rachel and Seth? With each passing day, it became more apparent just how lacking he was when it came to his parenting skills.

A woman would contribute a whole new dimension.

Shoot. If he got up his nerve, he might propose to Sarah Woodward himself.

***

Sarah checked the clock on the wall in the parlor of Emma's boardinghouse, where she'd set up her sewing project with Emma's permission. Mr. Callahan and the children could be arriving anytime, she determined, taking up the dress and inspecting it once more. It had turned out better than expected with its lacy collar and fancy buttons, which she'd torn off one of her own dresses. What did Sarah need with shiny gold buttons? A little girl who'd recently lost her mother would appreciate them far more. It may have been impractical on her part, but no matter; she felt compelled to make the dress as pretty as possible.

In the event the dress didn't fit perfectly, she'd kept plenty of excess material in the seams and hem; but if she'd measured correctly, any adjustments should be minimal.

"Let's have a look," said an apron-clad Emma as she entered the room, pretty as a picture despite her tousled look. If Sarah had learned anything about the young proprietor, it was that she never wasted a second of her day. If she wasn't busy scrubbing or dusting, she was in the kitchen preparing a meal or baking some delectable dessert.

Sarah held the rose-colored dress up for Emma's examination.

"Now that's a mighty fine little dress," she said, her Kentucky twang drawing out each word. "What little girl wouldn't give her right pinky finger for a dress like that?"

Sarah laughed. "You do have a way with words, Miss Emma."

The blond, blue-eyed landlady gave a cheerful smile, showing bright, straight teeth and a dimple in her left cheek. She was the kind of woman men fell over, but it hadn't taken Sarah long to discover Emma wasn't about drawing attention to herself, particularly attention of the male variety. If anything, she wore aloofness like a coat of armor, and any man fool enough to attempt to remove it might very well pay for the act with a wounded ego. "I got no use for men," Emma had told Sarah one night while the two sat at her kitchen table sipping hot tea. "They're more trouble 'n a wagonload of snakes."

Of course, Sarah couldn't argue the point, since she was of the same mind. Hadn't she left Winchester to escape Stephen Alden's clutches? The man had been obsessed with her since childhood, and neither her mother nor Stephen's had helped matters any by encouraging the relationship. "He's such a fine young man, dear," Carmen Woodward had said from her sick-bed. "And bred with solid Christian principles. Successful men like him don't come along just every day. He'll make you a wonderful husband."

"But I don't love him, Mother," she'd argued. *His kisses do nothing for me, Christian or not. Besides, I'd always play second fiddle to his career.* "I believe God has a better plan for me."

"Better? Nonsense. What could possibly be better than Stephen?"

Thankfully, the conversation had ended when Carmen's doctor arrived. Her mother had been weak. Discussing Stephen's negative points wouldn't have solved a thing. Besides, Carmen had blinded herself to all but Stephen's finest attributes. Years of family solidarity didn't die easily, the two families having traveled from Europe to America together when Stephen and Sarah were still in their cradles.

"How did you learn to sew like that?" Emma asked, bringing Sarah back to the present.

"My nanny taught me," Sarah said, the admission slipping out before she'd had the chance to consider Emma's reaction.

 30

"You had a nanny? My, my, so it is true what folks are saying."

Curious, Sarah's gaze shot up. "Just what are folks saying?"

"That you come from good stock." Emma giggled. "Money, in other words."

Of its own accord, her face pulled into a frown. "Why would they think that?"

Emma laughed again, but not disparagingly. "Honey, either you are just plain naïve, or you truly haven't noticed that most folks in these parts don't wear cashmere and silk. You wear it like second skin, as if you were born in it."

"It's all I have," she replied almost sorrowfully.

"Don't apologize. I find your garments quite breathtaking. You shouldn't mind the folks of Little Hickman. They're mostly friendly, just not used to fine things—unless you count the very astute and proper Mrs. Iris Winthrop," she said with a wink.

Sarah planted a hand across her mouth to smother a chuckle. It didn't take a genius to see the woman placed a great deal of importance on fancy attire. The difference between her and Sarah was that while Sarah didn't require expensive things, Mrs. Winthrop appeared to thrive on them.

Emma's gaze traced a path to the window. "I see Mr. Callahan has arrived in town. Looks like he's stopping off at Johansson's before coming here. Those two little ones sure are a pathetic pair. Too bad about their mama."

Sarah's chest rose unexpectedly and she fought the urge to look for herself. Whether she anticipated Rachel's reaction to the dress or seeing Mr. Callahan again, she couldn't be sure.

The notion of the latter rankled. Yes, the man was irrefutably handsome, but his brutish personality required an overhaul. There was absolutely no reason she should be attracted to him, unless it was the fact that he was Stephen Alden's complete opposite.

"He is a difficult man to like," Sarah said, trying to make her tone appear neutral. Taking up the little dress, she folded it carefully and placed it in her lap.

Emma walked to the window and pulled back the lace curtain. "He's been through some rough times," she muttered while rubbing her index finger across the sill to check for dust. Sarah had strong doubts she would find as much as a speck of it the way she was forever cleaning the place. Briefly, she wondered what it would be like to rise every morning with a bent for scrubbing everything in sight. Living the life of luxury had kept her from worrying over such matters.

"What do you mean?"

"You haven't heard?" Emma turned to face Sarah, tucking her hands into her apron pockets. "He lost his wife to smallpox a few years back, and his son just last spring to some awful fever. He's been alone since then—that is, till them little ones came into the picture."

"But that's terrible," Sarah said, wincing to learn of his loss. Knowing it seemed to put a different slant on things.

"He used to be God-fearin', but from what I hear he's quit goin' to church altogether. 'Course, I'm not one to talk," Emma admitted with a smirk.

Sarah thought it interesting that Emma would bring up the subject of church. "Would you care to elaborate?"

"Don't need it," she answered with a flick of the wrist. "I

figure God's fine for some folks, but I'd rather make my own way. 'Sides, I'm too busy most Sundays to give church much thought."

Rebuilding the burned-down schoolhouse, which had doubled as the town's church, was all people could talk about these days. "Perhaps you'll give it a try once they erect the new building come spring."

"Pfff. Can't imagine that will make much difference to me," she remarked. "I don't hold much importance for religion and such."

Emma turned and gave another lazy glance out the window, strands of her golden hair falling out of its tight little bun, slender shoulders straight, a quiet strength about her. "Especially when it don't seem to lessen all the heartache that's out there. Take those little ones, for instance," she said in a voice so low Sarah had to strain to hear her. "Where was God when their mama was lyin' on her deathbed? Seems to me it would've been just as easy as not for Him to let her live."

Making a turn, she strolled across the room to sweep her finger over the fireplace mantel, again coming up clean, no doubt. Next, she made her way to the tall bookcase with the glass doors and did the same thing, sweeping a clean finger over the top edge. "And what of Rocky's wife and son—and Ben Broughton's first wife, who died while giving birth to their second child? And then there was that awful schoolhouse fire and the death of that young man. All senseless events, and that's just Hickman." Emma shook her head, sadness evident. "Where was God then?"

From what she'd heard, a delinquent boy had started the schoolhouse fire in his attempt to avenge his anger at Liza

33

Merriwether Broughton, Little Hickman's teacher. His futile effort had resulted in his own death. One could hardly blame God for that. The other matters, although tragic in nature, were results of living in a less than perfect world, where the hardships of life seemed to take their toll on the human body. Emma wanted to know where God was, and Sarah might have told her He was right there in the middle of it all, ready and able to help ease the burden, but she doubted Emma was open to that. Besides, now was not the time for arguing particulars. Instead, she feebly offered up a few words.

"Some things are just plain hard to understand, Emma. But I do know this: God takes some of the ugliest of situations and makes them turn out right in the end. Take Benjamin, for instance, now happily married to the lovely Miss Merriwether. That never would have happened had Liza failed to accept the teaching job last summer."

Folding her arms, Emma fixed Sarah with a curious stare. "You don't appear too bitter about that matter, considering it was *you* Ben was supposed to marry."

Sarah couldn't hold back the tiny spurt of laughter that bubbled forth. "It was plain to see from the moment I bounded off that stage that Benjamin Broughton had already handed off his heart to another. How could I fault him for something over which he had no control? Besides, he'd tried to enlighten the agency about his change of plans, but the message failed to reach me in time."

Emma tapped a finger to her lips. "So I suppose you would say that God will eventually turn even that misunderstanding into something good?"

"If I trust Him, yes," Sarah stated, if nothing else, wanting to be clear on that one thing.

With uplifted chin, Emma glanced out the window, then sauntered toward the kitchen. "Rocky and those youngins are headin' this way. I think I'll go get a plate of cookies ready."

"Don't make any fuss," Sarah called after. "They won't be here long."

"Nonsense," Emma replied. "Anyone can see by the look of those children that they haven't had any sweets in weeks. Wouldn't hurt to try sweetenin' up that Rocky Callahan either."

***

"You two mind your manners, now," Rocky told the kids as he helped them from the rig and ambled up the walk toward Emma Browning's front porch. Neither had a word to say in response. After breakfast, Rocky had discovered Seth's eggs at the bottom of the waste barrel, and so he'd made him sit on an overturned crate in the corner. Of course, the whole thing had made Rachel madder than a hornet on a hotplate, and she'd threatened not to speak to him for the rest of the week—which should have pleased him, but didn't.

The fact was, he had no idea how to handle the rascally pair.

Emma Browning met them at the door. Dressed in an old work dress and worn apron, strands of blond hair falling to either side of her smudged oval face, she was a pretty woman despite her indifference. Nice looks aside, she managed to maintain a good distance that few ever bridged. Utterly self-sufficient, Emma made it clear she had no use for men. In fact, to Rocky's knowledge she'd never even had a beau, although she was pretty enough to warrant a second glance.

35

"Come in," she invited. "Miss Woodward has been expecting you."

Rocky pulled off his hat while stepping over the threshold and glanced across the room at Sarah. She was standing and wiping her hands on the front of her apple-green satin skirt; a long-sleeved white blouse, buttoned to the neck and tucked in at the waist, accented her stately appearance. Striking hazel eyes, framed by her thick, wine-red locks, gave him a quick assessment before moving over the children with an approving look.

"My, my, who do we have here?" Emma asked, bending over the children.

When both remained silent, Rocky nudged Rachel in the side. "I'm Rachel," she said, jumping to attention. "And this here is my brother, Seth."

A warm smile played around Emma's mouth. "I'm pleased to meet you both. My name is Emma Browning," she said, extending a hand. "Miss Woodward told me yesterday what fine children you are."

Rocky's eyes made a quick path back to Sarah and found her beaming—not at him, of course, but at the impish pair. If anything, she took great pains not to bestow him with anything resembling friendliness.

Rachel and Seth stood straighter than little fence posts, shedding wary glances from Emma to Sarah. Again, he gave the girl a healthy nudge. "What do you say to Miss Browning?"

The girl quickly took the hand Emma offered. "It's nice to meet you, ma'am." Without prompting, Seth followed suit, a tiny grin lifting up the corners of his mouth when Emma shook his hand in greeting.

Sarah's full, green skirt made a rustling sound as she ambled across the room, a cascade of pink material—Rachel's dress, no doubt—hanging over one arm. Upon reaching him and the children, she touched a finger to Rachel's chin and gave it a gentle lift. He thought he saw Rachel's eyes dart to the flowy, pink fabric.

"I'm happy to see you're both wearing your mittens today," Sarah said, pleasant as could be. Of course, Rocky didn't miss the rapid, searing glance intended just for him that followed the smile. If he could have said something in his defense, he would have, but the truth was he felt like a heel for having forced them out in the elements yesterday with nothing on their fingers. As easy as it'd been to locate the mittens today, under a folded blanket in Rachel's room, he could have helped find them yesterday and saved them all the hassle.

"I have an idea," Emma said, looking from Seth to Rachel. "How about you two give me your wraps and then come with me to the kitchen and help me with the cookies and milk? When we come back Miss Woodward can show Rachel her new dress."

Seth's eyes lit like two firecrackers. "Cookies?" he asked, finding his voice. Even Rachel's usual somber mood allowed a modest smile before she cast Rocky a questioning look. As soon as he nodded his consent, they handed over their winter gear to Emma and followed her to the kitchen.

When the trio disappeared, Rocky turned his gaze on Sarah. "You finished the dress, then?"

She nodded, and he noticed a red lock coming loose from its high bun. It dangled at the side of her face, one long, fiery ringlet. "It's a rather simple dress, so it didn't require much time," she stated, holding it up for his inspection. It was the color of faded roses, a soft-looking fabric that his fingers itched to touch, but he didn't. It appeared to be complete save the hem and the bottom of the long sleeves. Even the neckline, round and ruffled, was finished to perfection, and the buttons, gold and shiny, made a straight path down the front, stopping at the gathered waistband. At first glance, he thought it quite pretty—as dresses went. Not that he was any kind of expert on female attire.

"The next one should go even faster now that I know what to expect."

He lifted a brow. "The next one?" As far as he knew, he'd only purchased enough material for one dress.

"Yes, now that I have her measurements down pat and I've fashioned an easy enough pattern. I have several dresses for which I have no use. With a little snipping, I should be able to stitch another dress quite simply—or maybe even two."

He should have been grateful for the generous offer, but instead it rankled. He might be a bit tightfisted, but he was by no means needy. "I'll not have you ripping up your own clothes for the sake of the girl. One dress should do her for now. And by the way, I intend to pay you for your trouble. How much do I owe you?" He reached into his pocket and drew out his roll of cash. Sarah's eyes narrowed.

"I meant no offense."

"None taken. How much?" he asked, more brusque than necessary.

"I have no set fee since I'm not accustomed to sewing for others."

"I see." If he'd had a knife, he might have cut the tension

 38

between them. "Are you going to suggest a fair amount?"

"I would think most any sum would appear unseemly to you, Mr. Callahan," she returned with a sharp tone. "After all, you considered the price of the material above reason."

Snappish little woman. "I've never bought fabric before," he said in his defense. Hester had, of course, and he'd never quibbled over prices then, but he wouldn't mention that. What had turned him into such a self-centered galoot?

Seconds of wasted silence ticked away while Rocky stared down at his wad of bills. "Would one dollar suffice?" he asked, glancing up.

A deep frown furrowed her pretty brow. "That seems excessive. How does fifty cents sound?"

Oh, he rued the day his sister had willed him her children and put him in this awkward position. A month ago, he never would have imagined himself standing here debating a fair price for stitching a little girl's dress, let alone with someone as fetching as the infamous Miss Sarah Woodward from Winchester, Massachusetts.

"Fine," he said, hauling out the necessary coins from his pants pocket and handing them over. In the exchange, a smooth hand brushed against his callused one, the brief touch managing to jangle his nerves to their limit. And to think he'd actually entertained the thought of asking her to marry him. Imagine living under the same roof with someone as enticing— correction, as utterly exasperating—as Sarah Woodward.

Self-control would be the order of the day, that and large doses of staying power.

As if she'd read his very thoughts, she quickly stepped away from him, tucking the coins into her skirt pocket, then nervously fingering a red curl before tucking it behind a diminutive ear. Outside, bitter winds whipped around the corners of the building. Sarah wrapped her arms about herself, her perfectly manicured fingernails digging into the folds of her tiny, belted waistline, nails that had undoubtedly never seen a trace of dirt beneath them, much less planted a single garden seed. With anxious eyes, she peered toward the kitchen, as if willing Emma and the kids to come walking through the door. What *was* taking them so long?

"The dress is nice," he finally conceded, realizing his foolishness in delaying the compliment. "Can you cook as well?"

Her jaw dropped open in shock. Truthfully, he'd surprised himself with how the question shot out of nowhere.

"Pardon?"

"Cook—can you cook?"

Her green eyes scalded him with intensity. "Actually, I'm a fine cook. Why do you ask?"

Yes, why? "Curious is all. I can't quite picture you sweatin' over a cookstove—or cleaning, for that matter. And yet that's exactly what you would have found yourself doing had you married Benjamin Broughton. That and tending to his two daughters. Have you ever taken responsibility for small children, Miss Woodward?"

Her ginger-colored eyebrows rose in curiosity as her face puckered with clear irritation. "I think that is none of your business, Mr. Callahan."

"How disappointed were you when the arrangement didn't work out?" he pushed, unsure himself where the inquiry was leading, but having an inkling. And for just an instant, he questioned his sanity. "Did you feel desperate—thwarted—

uncertain of your future? Were you depending on Ben to lend you a sense of security?"

Openly confused, if not confounded, she gaped at him. "I believe I'll go check on Emma. Perhaps she..."

Just when she would have escaped, he grabbed her by the wrist and stopped her midstride. Flecks of gold shimmered in her blue-green eyes when she met his gaze. "Don't you want to hear my proposition?" he asked, surprising himself with his raspy tone.

She yanked her hand from his grasp, but stayed rooted in place. "Just what are you talking about, Mr. Callahan?"

Tonight he would probably walk into the barn and invite Nell to give him a kick, but he had to ask the question.

"What would you say to gettin' hitched with me instead?"

Chapter Three

"You want me to marry you?" Sarah managed to ask through stiff lips. Her mouth felt dry and parched. *Swallow*, she told herself. Water, that's what she needed. Or some of Emma's iced tea—in the tallest glass she could find.

Mary, Queen of Scots, he wasn't serious.

He produced a tremulous smile. "Why not? You obviously wanted a husband, and I need a wife. It seems a simple exchange. For keeping house and taking care of the kids, you could have a place to call your own. It's not much, mind you, probably nothing like what you're accustomed to, but it's better than staying holed up in a boardinghouse with a bunch of undesirables. You said yourself you sold all your possessions before coming to Kentucky and that you wanted to settle eventually. You seem to like Rachel and Seth, and they—well, they'll get used to you," he said.

"In other words, you want a maid, or perhaps a slave better describes your fancy." Rivers of disgust ran through her veins. Had she really appeared so desperate that he thought she'd accept any proposal to escape her situation? Perhaps she should have gone back to Winchester after all—even though she'd felt so strongly about coming to Kentucky.

Dear God, have I completely misread Your will for my life?

"Rest in the Lord, and wait patiently for him: fret not thyself..." Although the psalmist's words brought comfort, they didn't bring her closer to an answer. In the meantime, a man she didn't know—didn't like, for that matter—stood before her with an offer of marriage.

"Miss Woodward, a slave is not free to come and go. You, on the other hand, may leave if the arrangement doesn't suit you."

"The 'arrangement'? You make this sound like a business deal."

He lifted one dark brow before issuing a bland smile. "Correct me if I'm wrong, but isn't that what you were working out with Benjamin Broughton? He paid for your arrival in Kentucky in return for your consent to marry."

Brought to shame, she had little to say in her defense—except for one thing. "Benjamin Broughton is a Christian man."

His mouth twisted into a mocking smile. "I'm not exactly a heathen."

"You certainly don't strike me as a joyful person, Mr. Callahan. When was the last time you attended services?"

His expression went from cynical to somber as he shifted his stance and stuffed his hands into his deep pockets, his blue gaze going flat with recollection. "I once called myself a Christian, but those days have escaped me."

"There, you see?" She turned away from him, but he stepped in front of her, blocking her passage with his rockhard frame.

"If you're worried that I'll interfere in your faith, you can rest assured I pose no threat." The faintest glint of humor etched across his face. "Who knows? Maybe you'll even persuade me to see things differently."

That alone brought her near to caving in. Marriage, after all, would solve the problem of her inheritance.

Not that she had any great plans for the money.

Perhaps an even greater sense of pleasure would come in showering Rachel and Seth with large amounts of love and affection. Heaven knew Rocky Callahan wasn't capable.

Dear Father, what am I thinking?

But her heartfelt prayer went unfinished when the kitchen door swung open and Emma, Rachel, and Seth crossed the threshold, each with a tray in hand, one carrying a plate of cookies, one with five tin cups, and the third a tall pitcher of fresh milk. It wasn't iced tea, Sarah mused, but it would suffice to wet her arid throat.

Emma's face lit with concern. "Are we interrupting anything?"

"No." Sarah's smile didn't quite reach her eyes when she looked at the threesome. "Mr. Callahan and I were simply enjoying mindless chatter." She glanced at him. "We're quite done." She put quiet emphasis on that last part.

Rather than view his reaction to that, Sarah walked across the room and turned her attention to the children, as one cookie after another slipped down their open gullets. They sat stiff-backed on the edge of the sofa and ate cookies with as much manners as could be expected. She herself couldn't have swallowed one morsel if her life depended on it. She did, however, sip at the cold milk while she watched.

Out of the corner of one eye, she dared to snag a tiny peek at Mr. Callahan. Still standing where she'd left him, he'd dropped his hands to his sides and, like everyone else, was watching Rachel and Seth. Either he was deeply regretting

44

his ridiculous proposal, or he was peeved at Sarah for brushing him off. Either way, his glum expression signified his sour mood.

When it looked like the children's appetites had slowed, Sarah went for the dress, holding it up for Rachel's perusal. The little girl released a breathy gasp. "Oh, it's pretty," she said, something in her countenance holding leashed delight, as if she wanted to explode with it but knew the risks of letting go. She met Sarah in the middle of the room. "May I touch it?" she asked in a near whisper.

"Honey, you may do more than that," Sarah said. "You may try it on. I'll need to know where to put the hem."

"Oh." Rachel seemed awestruck by the notion of actually putting on the garment. Her fingers traced a slow pattern up and down the skirt as if to memorize its every detail. Slowly her eyes went to the shiny, gold buttons, and Sarah heard another quick intake of air.

"Do you like it?" she asked.

A tiny nod told her she did. "Mama never could afford me a new dress before."

Sadness crawled under Sarah's skin. Not for the first time she thought about the countless dresses packed within her trunk and Rocky's rebuff when she'd offered the material from one of them to fashion Rachel another dress.

One dress should do her for now. Anger, new and righteous, sprouted wings and flew about the room. "I'll make you another if you like," she announced. She felt the man's eyes come to rest on her, but she resisted the urge to look at him. Her uplifted chin should tell him that she meant to do it with or without his approval.

"Can you make me somethin', too?" asked Seth, his slender body molded into Emma's side in the overstuffed chair they shared.

Oh, Lord, these children need so much.

"Seth, mind your manners," Rocky said, his brows knit together in a frown. "It isn't polite to ask for gifts."

Feeling especially bold and driven by the child's strong sense of need, Sarah blinked her eyes and said, "Of course I can make you something. Or perhaps I'll buy you a toy. How would that be?"

"A toy?" asked Seth. It was the most she'd heard from the little boy since first meeting him.

"You don't need a toy," Rocky said, seemingly making every effort to deflate his tender spirit.

In preparation for a showdown with Mr. Callahan, Sarah prayed for strength. Then, drawing back her shoulders, she leveled the beastly man with her best glare. "Every little boy needs a toy, Mr. Callahan. And since I stitched his sister a dress, all the more reason the toy should come from me."

Matching her glare, he stretched to his tallest, which in Sarah's estimation meant nearly reaching the ceiling. "The girl had need of a new dress, Miss Woodward. A toy is no necessity."

Sensing the growing tension in the room, Emma rubbed her hands together and stood, plastering on a cheery smile. "Rachel, how about I take you to the back room so you can try on this lovely dress?" she suggested. Rachel jumped to her feet. "Seth, you come too," Emma added. "I have a job for you in the kitchen."

The boy crawled off the couch and took Emma's hand. Rachel took the other, and the three left the room.

And in an instant, Sarah and Rocky were alone again.

***

Rocky stewed on the way to the barn later that night. Naturally, the children had sulked all the way home, his boorish attitude rubbing off on them, and vice versa. Even Rachel, although she loved her new dress and had hugged it close to her chest on the drive back, had remained grim and sour-faced. No doubt she would be sticking to her promise not to speak to him for the remainder of the week. Well, fine.

Cold night air chewed through his thin coat. He must remember to bring his heavier jacket out of the shed come morning. A blanket of clouds hid any trace of a winter moon, and if his guess were right, snow or sleet would come before midnight.

He dragged in a shivery breath before entering the barn. Nothing had gone as planned, particularly after the ridiculous scene he'd caused with regard to Sarah's offer to buy Seth a toy. In reality, he supposed she was right; one good turn deserved another, even though the concept went against his principles. As far as he was concerned, human need always overruled one's wants and wishes.

He thought about the spirited redhead who'd challenged him. No doubt, if she didn't before, she surely now considered him a pigheaded oaf, not to mention argumentative and self-seeking. No wonder she'd turned down his offer of marriage after he'd brought the matter up once again before leaving.

Oh, she must be laughing into her pillow about now, just imagining sharing a house with the likes of him. For crying in a bucket! He could barely stand himself. What would ever make him think anyone else would want to live under the same roof with him?

***

Sarah stood at her bedroom window, watching as townsfolk hurried from place to place, winter winds keeping most from dawdling in the streets as they might have been inclined to do on a warmer day.

Exactly one week had passed since Rocky Callahan's proposal of marriage and her rejection of the offer. Since then, he'd failed to mention it again, despite the fact she'd seen him twice more. The first time was when she'd presented Rachel with another dress, this one, to Rocky's utter chagrin, fashioned from one of her own gowns. The second time, she'd delivered an eight-inch toy soldier to Seth. She'd wondered how she was going to manage giving the gift to him, and was thankful when she'd spotted them coming into town just yesterday. Hurriedly, she'd gathered up the toy along with her skirts and met them on the street.

As usual, Rachel had appeared sullen, but she managed a weak smile from her high seat when Sarah came into view. Taking great pains to avoid eye contact with Mr. Callahan, Sarah had approached the rig before any of them descended and handed Seth the wrapped package. He'd torn into the brown paper like a hungry pup, throwing aside the string that bound the package and letting out a yelp of joy at the sight of the uniformed doll. Even Rachel had looked on with interest, smoothing out her long coat as she shifted herself in the seat to get a better view. Peeking out from the coat's frayed hem was one of the new dresses.

 48

"Look, Rachel, it's a soldier. He gots a rifle in his hand. Look, Uncle Rocky!" To that, he'd stuck the doll under his uncle's nose, and—wonder of wonders—the man had smiled, albeit halfheartedly.

Mr. Callahan gave a low chuckle. "What do you say to Miss Woodward?" he asked.

"I was gittin' to that," the boy said, half annoyed. It seemed to Sarah that each time she saw Seth, he was a bit more talkative, even confident. "Thank you, Miss Woodward. I never had no soldier doll before."

Sarah had laughed, joy welling up from deep in her chest. "You're very welcome."

"I'm wearing the pink dress today, Miss Woodward," Rachel offered, diverting Sarah's attention, her voice not much more than a whisper. She lifted up the bottom of her coat.

Sarah had nodded and given the girl a ready smile. "So you are. And it looks fine on you."

Up to now, Mr. Callahan had remained glued to his seat, a mere observer, his gaze intent on watching her, she knew, but hers intent on the children.

"I appreciate, ahem, the work you've put into the dresses," he'd said, clearing his throat mid-sentence. With that, he drew out an envelope from his jacket pocket and reached across the children to hand it to her. "Here's your payment. Since you insisted on using fabric from one of your own gowns for the second dress, I had to guess as to its worth."

How was it this man could stir her ire faster than a blustery breeze could move the grass in a meadow? Could he not see she'd intended the dress as a gift? She ignored his outstretched hand and stood the straighter. "You employed my services on the first dress, sir; the second dress was a labor of love."

He had kept his hand extended, his eyes narrowed in irritation, waiting. "Just the same, I'll not be beholden to ya."

She'd put her hands to her hips, the icy air at her ankles forcing her to prance about. "I wouldn't expect you to be, sir. I didn't make the dress for *you*." A hurried glimpse at Rachel revealed the child's quivery, pursed mouth, a dignified attempt to keep a giggle from erupting. Sarah might well have seen the humor in the situation herself if it hadn't been for her utter crossness with the big brute.

"There's someone here to see you."

Sarah whirled about at Emma's voice coming from her open bedroom doorway.

"Didn't mean to frighten ya," Emma said with a tiny grin, taking a slight step back. "You looked mighty lost in thought."

"I was just—yes, lost in thought." Putting a hand to her mussed hair, she chanced a peek in her cracked mirror above the dresser stand. After a day of cleaning and sorting through items yet unpacked, she looked a sight. "A visitor, you say? Who is it?"

Emma shrugged. "I've never seen the man before."

Sarah's heart lunged. "I've a gentleman caller?"

Emma's brows knit together in a frown. "A rather short, thin fellow, but well-manicured. He's wearin' a fine suit and bowler hat. I would imagine his arrival in town drew a few curious stares."

Stephen Alden. She'd been wondering how long it would take him to discover her exact whereabouts. How many folks had he questioned before narrowing down her location? Prickly heat crawled past her neck and up her face. Would he never give up? Oh, why had her mother placed the stipulation of marriage on her inheritance, and why did Stephen have to be the appointed legal representative to her estate?

"Are you all right, Sarah?" Emma asked, stepping inside the room to touch Sarah's arm.

"I'm fine. It's just…I'm not quite ready to face him."

"You know him, then?"

Sarah nodded and gave a deep sigh. "He's an old family friend—bent on marrying me, I'm afraid."

Emma gasped. "Oh my. Is that why you came to Little Hickman? To escape him?"

Sarah laughed weakly. "In a sense, I suppose. I had hoped he wouldn't follow me."

"Shall I send him away?" Emma asked.

It was a tempting thought. Tossing back her shoulders, she muttered a silent prayer. "No, I'm afraid that would be my job."

She found Stephen gazing out the window in the parlor onto the muddy street, his wool chesterfield topcoat draped over one arm, his hat secured in his other hand. "Hello, Stephen."

At the sound of her voice, he turned to face her. Although they came within a few months of being exactly the same age, Stephen appeared years older with his mousy, waxed brown hair, cut short and parted in the middle. A slim moustache, turned up at the ends, covered his weak upper lip. Rather short in stature, he stood only an inch or two taller than she did, and his build, although not effeminate by any means, lacked absolute masculinity.

As if his expensive-looking, chocolate-brown jacket and matching trousers, cream-color ruffled shirt, and silk bowtie were not enough to announce his copious wealth, he wore two fancy breast pins attached by a solid gold chain, which, judging from its length and weight, appeared sufficient to use at a hanging.

"Sarah, darling," he said, meeting her in the middle of the room, aiming to kiss her on the mouth but making it only to her cheek when she tilted her face. "I'm delighted to hear you didn't marry after all. Am I to assume you've come to your senses, then?"

"How did you know I hadn't married?" she asked, ignoring his question.

He threw back his head and laughed. "I'm a lawyer, remember? It's very easy for me to obtain legal information. With the wonderful invention of the telephone, I put my assistant to work to determine what, if any, weddings had taken place in this desolate town and discovered your intended husband married another—the town's schoolteacher, to be exact."

"Yes, well, he tried to reach me before I'd left Massachusetts, but regrettably our wires crossed."

His mouth moved into a tight smile. "Ah, is that so? Well, I would say you are quite fortunate not to have married a stranger. Perhaps now you will reconsider marrying me."

"I'm sorry if you traveled all this way in the hopes of changing my mind, Stephen."

"Our parents, rest their souls, always believed we were meant to be together. Are you willing to go against their wishes?" he asked, his expression desperate if not bordering on angry.

"Our parents were misguided, Stephen. I care for you as a friend, but I cannot marry you."

"But you were willing to marry a stranger." His murky gray eyes drilled into her as he shifted his weight from one foot to the other.

It was difficult to explain her draw to Little Hickman, Kentucky. All she really knew was that when she'd seen the posted sign back in Massachusetts advertising a Christian groom, she'd felt an indescribable pull to respond to the ad. Yes, it would represent escape from the possessive clutches of Stephen Alden and his unremitting pleas for her hand in marriage, but it would also mean adventure, exploration, and new beginnings.

"But as you can see, I didn't marry him."

"Then I see no reason why you shouldn't come back home to marry me. You've been here four long weeks. I should think that long enough for realizing your error."

"Massachusetts is no longer home to me, Stephen."

He made a grunt of disgust and waved his arm. "Surely you don't consider this—this mud hole home. Why, even the name itself, Little Hickman, signifies a primitive, crude lot of people." He gave her body a quick sweep of the eye. "And look at you, Sarah. If I didn't know you better, I'd say you're fast becoming one of *them*." He rubbed a thumb across the under part of her cheek and frowned. "You've even a smudged face," he clucked.

She laughed. "I've been cleaning."

"Cleaning." He scoffed at the word, as if it held little meaning for him; truth be told, it didn't.

"The people of Hickman are not so primitive," she said in their defense. "Perhaps a few are crude, but I'm learning that

53

most are very nice. There are daily newspapers, a handy wire service, and even a telephone. Why, they even have a Sears and Roebuck catalog service. It's located in the—"

"Sarah, Sarah." Stephen's frown grew tenfold. "You've grown up in high society. You cannot convince me a town of this caliber would make you happy for any length of time. You've lived a very cultured life. Where are the theatres, the ballrooms, the elegant hotels?" She stopped herself just short of telling him Madam Guttersnipe's place was just up the street, doubting he'd see the humor in that.

"God sent me here for a reason, Stephen." That buttoned his lip for the time being. "It's difficult to explain, but I feel as if He's put me right here in the middle of this town for a specific purpose. I've felt it from the beginning. Yes, the original agreement I made with Mr. Broughton didn't pan out, but it hasn't discouraged me from staying on. Truthfully, I don't miss the conveniences of city life. Besides, I enjoy Miss Emma's friendship, and there are others..." She wouldn't mention little Rachel and Seth, how her heart had melted upon first meeting them. Their uncle, well, he was another story altogether.

"But that's ridiculous. What would you have people think, that you've become a missionary? 'Sarah Woodward Leaves Lap of Luxury to Minister to the Villains of Kentucky.'" He harrumphed. "There's a headline for the *Boston Globe*."

She didn't appreciate his mockery, but then he'd always been good at it. Even as a child, he'd ridiculed her for her uncommon faith. Oh, she believed Stephen was a Christian, but he had always been more passionate about working for the almighty dollar than for almighty God. Where Sarah's heart beat for people, Stephen's beat for money and success.

"Perhaps God's reasons for sending me here are mission oriented," she replied with conviction. "No matter, I'm here to stay, and I don't care what people might think."

His colorless eyes flashed with impatience. "What about your inheritance? Even missionaries need money for accomplishing their goals."

She cringed. "So it comes to that, does it?" He'd always placed great importance on wealth. No doubt, that was the driving force behind his desires for marriage.

"Let us be realistic, Sarah. You cannot obtain possession of your properties until you marry. Your mother clearly stated in her will—"

"That I marry, yes, but she did not state that I must marry *you*, Stephen."

"No?" He reached into the inside pocket of his jacket and withdrew a folded piece of paper.

"What is that?" she asked, suddenly filled with unexplained jitters.

"Read it and see for yourself."

She took the feather-light paper from his hand and unfolded it. Her mother's shaky handwriting covered the page.

My Dear Stephen,

My days on earth are numbered, and I fear that leaving my only daughter behind will be devastating for her. Please see that she is well cared for, Stephen. I know that I can trust you to wed her when the time is right. You will be doing me an eternal favor if you see to her needs in this manner.

Yours very truly,
Carmen Woodward

Unstoppable tears rolled down Sarah's cheeks as she refolded the missive and handed it back.

When he should have been remorseful, Stephen wore a look of satisfaction. "So you see, Sarah? It is not only necessary that we wed, it is our duty." He leaned in close so that she felt his hot breath on her cheek. "You do want to fulfill your mother's final wish, don't you?"

Sarah's shoulders dropped as anguished emotions tugged at her senses. How should she respond to something like this? Worse, how could she say no to him now?

***

Rocky stomped purposefully through the mud-spattered streets toward Emma's boardinghouse. He'd fully intended to ignore the finely dressed chap he'd overheard inquiring at the post office as to Sarah Woodward's place of residence. After all, what business was it of his who visited the feisty woman with the burnished red curls who'd turned down his generous offer of marriage? However, curiosity, if not outright suspicion, prohibited him from disregarding the incident.

Something about the stuffy-looking character had disturbed him—his outlandish show of affluence, perhaps. Usually a good judge of character, Rocky had him figured for a finagler, cunning and shrewd as the day was long.

On the front porch, he spotted Sarah through the window facing the weasel directly. Without thought of what he intended to say, he entered the house, knowing it to be a public establishment. As soon as the bell above the door chimed, Sarah and the snobbish fellow both looked up. Sarah's eyes instantly widened, while the man's were indifferent.

"Hello, Sarah," Rocky said.

"Mr. Callahan," she said stiffly.

The ill-mannered lout made a grunting noise. "You know this farmer?" he asked, his eyebrows rising until they nearly disappeared under the hairline on his low-lying forehead.

"We've met, yes," she answered, straightening herself with dignity. "Rocky Callahan, meet Stephen Alden."

Rocky might have stepped forward to offer a hand, but instead he waited to see if Alden would make the first move. When he didn't, neither man moved. They simply nodded stiffly.

"How are Seth and Rachel?" Sarah hastened. Her eyes held some unspecified emotion, but the evidence of tears was more than clear.

"They're fine," he answered flatly, shooting Stephen Alden a withering glance. "They're with my mother," he added.

"That's nice," she replied, her eyes traveling back to the sourpuss at her side. She appeared distraught, but Rocky knew so little about her that it was difficult to determine what was going on. Suddenly, he had an outrageous idea.

"Of course, Rachel has been her usual obstinate self and Seth is just plain gloomy most of the time, refuses to make a single decision without his sister's say-so. Naturally, neither one of them listens to a word I say."

He gauged her reaction, noting that all-too-familiar look of ire blossom out on her rose-hued cheeks. Satisfied, he continued, "Seth rarely eats a thing, and his sister seems to think I should spoil him by making only what he enjoys. Since that's not about to happen, I think the kid has lost a pound or two."

"What?" Now apprehension accompanied the ire, and

he prided himself on his fine tactic. "He can't afford to lose weight, Mr. Callahan. He's such a small boy as it is."

"I'm not given to spoiling the kid," he answered in a harsher tone than needed.

By now, Stephen Alden, whose gaze had trailed back and forth, looked sufficiently perturbed. "Who is this—this brackish boar, Sarah—sweetheart?" Rocky noticed he made a point to add the endearment, almost as an afterthought.

"Someone who proposed marriage to her last week," Rocky supplied for her. "I was coming back to see if she'd had a change of heart."

Sarah looked as shocked by the declaration as he was himself. In fact, until now, he hadn't planned to say it. After all, he wasn't dying to marry the obstinate female, but he couldn't deny his need for a wife, either, and Sarah seemed the most likely candidate. When this cad had presented himself at the post office, the notion that someone else might be vying for her hand had put a regular thorn in his side.

The fellow scoffed and Sarah paled. "Preposterous!" he declared. "Sarah's marrying me, aren't you, Sarah? In fact, all that's needed now is to set the date." Alden drew her up beside him in a possessive clutch, and suddenly Rocky wanted nothing more than to knock the bum on his skinny little biscuit.

"Is that so?" asked Rocky. "Rather sudden, isn't it?"

The fellow gave a hard, cold-eyed smile and hugged her closer yet. "Sarah and I are old acquaintances, so it comes as no shock that we would marry." Sarah offered up a pathetic smile. "Our families traveled together to America from Europe. Of course, the trip wasn't that memorable for either of us since we were mere babes."

Sarah shifted, and Rocky could have sworn she tried to put distance between them, but the shyster's hold on her shoulder kept her cemented in place.

"Strange that she would accept a proposal from you when she traveled all the way from Massachusetts with the intentions of marrying someone else entirely," Rocky stated.

"Yes, well, stranger yet would be the notion that you might consider yourself worthy of marrying her," the fool said, accompanying the remark with a snide laugh.

"Stephen, please…" It was Sarah's first attempt at clearing the mounting cloud of instant dislike between the men.

"Well, it's true, darling, look at him," Alden said, wrinkling his nose. "Imagine—you marrying a farmer." Rocky had all he could do to keep from whacking the little man. One blow would probably do him in, he reasoned.

"When is this wedding, Sarah?" Rocky asked, looking to her for the answer.

"I—well, actually…"

"No need to fret over the date just yet," Alden hurried to say. "I'll stop by again later, Sarah—when we can discuss this matter in private."

Just then, Alden pointed her toward the stairs, giving her a little nudge in the back, as if she were his child who needed direction.

"Stephen, unhand me," she ordered, withdrawing from his clutches, clearly perturbed, if the scowl on her face were any indication.

Rocky felt a wave of relief course through his veins. *Ah, this was the Sarah he remembered meeting last week, mulish and self-sufficient.* "I'm not going to marry you," she announced flatly, folding her arms across her chest in a defensive gesture. "I'm sorry."

The stubby little snoot put his hands to her shoulders, but she promptly disengaged herself from them. "But of course you are, Sarah," he muttered through his tight jaw. "It would be a great disservice to your mother if you—."

"I'm sure my mother had her reasons for writing that letter, but I'm also certain that in the end she would have wanted me to be happy." Her eyes regarded him carefully.

Shoulders dropping a fraction, he shook his head. "Give me one good reason you should decline my offer."

"Because…" Sarah's gaze drifted from Alden to Rocky, as she hauled in a monstrous breath. "I'm marrying Mr. Callahan," she announced, pointing one long finger straight at Rocky.

"What?" Stephen's face bulged red with pent-up air, his tone just short of a polecat's screech.

Rocky felt his jaw drop as the impact of her words registered. On the one hand, he was relieved; on the other, beside himself with panic.

A wife? She was going to marry him after all?

Did she know what she was saying, or should he give her time to reconsider? No, Alden could snatch her up in the interim. Besides, Alden didn't deserve her. Not that he himself was much of a catch.

Hm. More than likely, neither one of them deserved her.

Chapter Four

"*H*e has two children desperate for a mother," Sarah said in hushed whispers to the harried Stephen Alden. "I can be that person."

"Sarah," he hissed through his teeth, craning his neck forward so that his head came within an inch of her own. "If it's children you want, I'll be more than happy to provide them." Stephen's hands fairly trembled when he squeezed her upper arms, and some part of her actually ached for the man she couldn't bring herself to love wholeheartedly. She'd always appreciated him as a friend, but unfortunately, her feelings stopped there.

Not that she carried any torch for Rocky Callahan, mind you. No, it was his niece and nephew who touched her heartstrings.

Stephen ranted while she tried to catch her bearings, grasping only the tail end of his musings when he said, "I'll be tied to a fence post before I'll allow you to go through with this sham, Sarah Woodward. Good grief, you don't even know this—this gulley-jumping hayseed."

"I'll let that remark pass, Alden," Rocky stated, stepping forward, "—except for maybe that part about your being tied to a fence post. Now that I wouldn't mind dwelling on for a bit."

Sarah's back straightened with the knowledge that she'd nearly forgotten he was in the room, so bent had she been on explaining her position to her childhood friend. One corner of Rocky's mouth shifted upward. He'd removed his hat some time back and now held it in both hands, spinning it slowly. His gaze traveled from Stephen to her then back to Stephen. Clearing his throat, he looked Stephen square in the eye.

"I'm not an ogre, Alden, as much as you'd like to think I am. I'm a farmer, yes, but not destitute. I have need of a wife, and since Sarah came here with the intentions of marrying, and her intended married another, I have given her an offer of marriage. I believe Sarah has stated her wishes. You'd do well to leave it at that."

Stephen glowered with anger. "Oh, you'd like that. I don't know what game you're playing, Callahan, but you'll not have the woman that our parents intended should go to me."

"You make her sound like a piece of property," Rocky stated coolly, his ice-blue eyes flashing.

A grunt emitted from Stephen's throat. "I traveled a great distance to locate Sarah, and I don't intend to return to Massachusetts empty-handed. She's coming with me."

Rocky continued his approach, stopping within inches of Stephen, his face slanting downward since he was considerably taller and brawnier. "Perhaps you didn't hear the lady. She doesn't want to marry you," he emphasized, his staunch look enough to make Sarah rethink her decision.

"Oh, stop it, both of you," she intervened, coming between them and putting one hand on each of their chests, instinctively noting which of the two had the sturdier one.

Lord, give me a clear head, she prayed.

Her future was vague at best, but something had told her from the start that coming to Little Hickman would unlock the mystery. *Trust* was the key, despite the fact she didn't entirely trust Rocky Callahan. "**It is better to trust in the Lord than to put confidence in man**," the Lord reminded.

"My mind is made up," she issued, preparing herself for Stephen's next outburst. "I know what our parents' wishes were, Stephen, but I cannot in good conscience marry you."

"You would marry a man you don't even know in favor of me? How does your conscience allow for that?"

"It is what God is saying I should do," she replied, straightening.

"That's hogwash! God would not have you marry someone you don't know."

"How can you be so sure? Have you been asking for God's direction in your life, Stephen, studying His holy Scriptures?"

The question must have rankled, for a huffing sound spewed from his chest as he suddenly took up his coat, stuffing his hands into the sleeves and then wrapping his woolen scarf about his neck, his actions jerky and rough. In one final move, he plunked his bowler hat on his small head. "Studying the Scriptures is the job of ministers, not the layfolk," was his curt response.

Avid learner that she was, Sarah could not agree, but this was not the time to argue. "Where are you going?"

"I'm heading into Lexington. Do you think I would stay in this godforsaken town?"

"And then?"

"Then I shall go back to Massachusetts. If you are so bent on marrying this fool, there's not much I can do to stop you, is there?"

Rocky cleared his throat and something like arrogance

skittered across his face, making Sarah want to give him a swift kick in the kneecap. "But what about the fence post idea, Alden? I was looking forward to that," he had the gall to jest, his upturned lip adding fuel to the fire between the two men.

"Now, see here," Stephen started.

"Would you excuse us, Mr. Callahan?" Sarah quickly interrupted, fixing Rocky with a stern look.

At once, he snapped to attention. "Oh, no problem. You two say your good-byes. Nice meeting you, Alden," he said, grinning from ear to ear and heading for Emma's front porch, plopping his wool cap securely in place as he walked across the room.

Once the door shut behind him, Stephen mumbled, "Ding-blasted country boy."

"Will I see you again?" Sarah asked, ignoring the remark. Although Stephen Alden could be snobbish, he was still a life-long friend, and she hated ending matters on a sour note.

He gave her a hard look that also contained the tiniest measure of tenderness. "We'll see." Snatching up a tiny strand of her hair, he rolled it between his thumb and forefinger. "You can contact my assistant, Herbert Austin, if you need anything, Sarah. Your mother's documents are in safe hands. I will dispense them and your assets upon your request." She could see he was making every effort to hold his wounded emotions intact.

She shrugged, and he dropped both hands to his sides. "I don't have need of them just yet," she replied. "I'm not marrying so that I may obtain my properties, Stephen. I'll let you know when I decide to lay claim to them. In the meantime, they may sit there and collect interest—or *dust*, for all I care."

He shook his head in disbelief. "You're really something, Sarah Woodward. You have all that money, and no place to go with it. Look at you, holed up in some filthy, dust-ridden town, about to marry a farmer you don't even know, all because of some penchant to carry out an assignment from God. All I can say is I hope you know what you're doing."

His words stung, but she recognized them as a cover-up for his disappointment. After all, he'd thought his trip to Kentucky would be sufficient to convince her to marry him. Little had he known it would only drive her in the opposite direction.

"Thank you for coming to see me," she said, granting him a weak smile. "Try not to worry about me."

Wistfulness stole into his expression. "I could have made you happy, you know."

"I know you would have tried," she replied.

Leaning close, he brushed her cheek with a light kiss. "Good-bye, Sarah."

"Good-bye."

And just like that, Stephen Alden walked out the door and out of her life—and Rocky Callahan walked in.

***

The wedding was a small affair, attended only by Emma, Sarah's witness, and Benjamin Broughton, who stood as witness for Rocky. Besides the witnesses, a small crowd of guests made up the informal gathering. They were Liza Broughton, Benjamin's new wife; Rocky's mother and father, Frank and Mary Callahan, whom Sarah had not met until just before the ceremony; and, of course, a grim-looking Rachel and an inquisitive Seth. Mr. Callahan's living room, small though it was, served as the meeting room. Although she'd had little time to peruse her surroundings, Sarah's first impression of the house was that its stark appearance reminded her of a flowerless garden. She decided a few rugs, some cheery wall hangings, and bright new curtains would add a pleasant, cozy touch. Perhaps she could enlist Rachel's help in decorating.

After some persuasion, Jonathan Atkins, the new minister, had agreed to wed the couple on short notice. His argument that a courtship should precede the marriage would have made sense to anyone else, but to Rocky and Sarah his advice fell on deaf ears. Both had determined that the marriage should go on. They had to think about the children. The time for getting to know each other would naturally follow.

Sarah didn't know what Rocky had told the man to convince him, but when they both emerged from the back room of the preacher's small farmhouse, Jonathan Atkins gave Sarah a brief smile and a nod of approval. The wedding date was set for Thursday, a mere two days away.

Now, dressed in a coral silk gown, Sarah stood beside Rocky, holding tightly to a small bouquet of dried flowers and praying that the ceremony would hasten along. Her heart took a giant leap when Reverend Atkins asked her if she promised to love, honor, and obey her husband.

Love? She'd always supposed she would marry for love, had even dreamed of it. Now look at her. Still, she couldn't deny the overwhelming sense that she was doing the right thing, that God Himself had brought her to this point. She'd experienced His peace amidst the uncertainty, and no one could take that away from her.

Out of the corner of one eye, she chanced a hasty peek at her groom. Clad in black, he looked more appropriately attired for a funeral than a wedding, particularly when she sought out his expression and found the clear-cut lines of his profile surly and stern. He hadn't even gifted her with a single smile the entire morning, which greatly perturbed her.

Despite all that, she couldn't deny his handsome looks. Tall and well-muscled, his mile-wide shoulders filled up the coat he wore, and although Sarah was of medium height, she felt small in comparison. Thick, black hair, needing a good trim, fell in wavy disarray over his damp forehead, while his taut, square-set jaw clenched. He was nervous, of that she was certain—perhaps even regretting his decision to marry.

"Miss Woodward?" the preacher asked, stealing her from her moment of reverie. "Do you take this man?"

"Oh, yes—I do," said Sarah, jumping to attention, aware of Rocky's impatience when he shifted his brawny weight from side to side. Her eyes caught his and held for just the briefest of times, and she visibly shivered under his cold stare. *Oh, Lord in heaven...*

When the reverend coached the couple to kiss, Sarah objected with a curt shake of the head, but her groom ignored her silent protest and hastily turned her into his arms, planting a hard, insensitive kiss square across her lips, leaving her breathless and dizzy on her feet. Just as quickly, he released her, set her back from him, and granted her the first of an attempted smile. "Hello, Mrs. Callahan," he murmured, one eyebrow slightly arched, his tone mysterious.

Rounds of congratulations followed, as the few guests came up to wish the couple well. "I'm happy for you, Sarah. I hope that we can be friends." Liza Broughton, the woman who'd replaced Sarah as Benjamin's bride, smiled while squeezing Sarah's hand. Petite, pretty, and exuding warmth and kindliness, she was impossible to dislike.

"Thank you," Sarah returned. "I shall look forward to it. Would you pay me a visit one day soon? I'm afraid I'll need some help decorating." She looked around the small farmhouse and whispered, "As you can see, this place needs some freshening up."

Liza giggled and wrinkled her nose. "You should have seen Benjamin's house when I first moved in. At least this house appears clean enough."

Sarah nodded her agreement. "I heard his mother came over and gave the house a good cleaning."

"Lucky you. I understand that Mr. and Mrs. Callahan are fine Christian folks. Rocky's father is ailing, from what Benjamin tells me. Poor man."

Sarah glanced across the room to find her new husband engaged in conversation with his father, a shorter version of his son, weathered and frail-looking. Only briefly did Rocky's eyes meet hers before she quickly averted her gaze, the impact of what had happened mere moments ago only now beginning to register in her mind.

Oh, Lord, I am a married woman.

Emma, Jon Atkins, and the elder Mrs. Callahan stood in the center of the room exchanging polite conversation, their hands wrapped around glasses of punch as they visited.

Rachel and Seth hovered quietly in a far corner, Rachel in her usual morose state, Seth naturally following her lead. Sarah frowned at the pair, wondering how she would go about reaching them.

"They've suffered a great deal," Liza said, seeming to read Sarah's mind.

Sarah worried her lower lip. "Yes. And I've a feeling it's going to take some doing to bring them both around."

Liza placed a comforting hand on Sarah's silk-covered arm. "I've no doubt you are just the person to do it, Sarah. I don't know you as well as I would like, but from what I've seen, you are a woman of understanding and compassion. I believe the children will sense that."

"I appreciate that. Now if I can just figure out how to go about it."

Liza gave a reassuring smile. "Don't worry. God will provide the answers."

Just then, Ben came alongside Liza and pulled her tightly against him. "What sort of nonsense is my sweet little wife filling your head with, Sarah?" He was an attractive man, tall and strapping like Rocky, but with a gentler, kinder look about him. His dark eyes sparkled as they danced from Sarah to Liza.

Sarah laughed. "Actually, your wife was filling me with words of wisdom."

Arched brows rose in question. "Ah, on being the perfect wife, I presume."

Sarah laughed, as did Liza. "Not quite, but I'm sure she could give me some fine pointers."

It seemed odd, if not ironic, to be talking to the man she'd intended to marry and not to hold ill feelings. After all, he'd as much as made an oath to her when he'd sent for her by way of the Marriage Made in Heaven Agency. Of course, he'd also attempted to stop the proceedings, and he would have,

69

had it not been for the agency's failure to keep the business running. No, she held no animosity toward the young couple. How could she begrudge them the love they so obviously had for each other?

"I'm sure you and Rocky will do just fine without any pointers," Ben said, nodding at her groom, who was now engaged in conversation with the young minister. "He's a little reserved right now, but he'll come around."

It embarrassed Sarah to be talking about her new husband, but she was curious. "Have you known him long?"

"A good share of my life. We grew up together, attended the same school, and," he took a breath and leaned in closer, "got into our share of trouble as boys, I'm afraid." He threw his head back and let forth a peal of laughter. "As we grew older and both married," he gave his new wife a penitent look, "we did things together as couples. He was a different man back then, full of life." His faraway expression gave way to a trace of sadness, but he quickly brightened. "I'm certain your marrying him is for the best. He's a good man."

Sarah longed for his confidence. "Right now, I'm mostly concerned for the children."

All three cast their eyes on Rachel and Seth. The youngsters hadn't moved from their spot in the corner. "They seem extremely quiet," Ben said.

"And very scared," Liza added. "I still remember when they got off the stagecoach several weeks ago. The children and I were watching from the classroom window. I swear Rachel and Seth's eyes were big as boulders when they first arrived."

"Yes. I rode with them from Toledo to Lexington, and I don't think they spoke more than five sentences the entire ride, although I did my best to coax them into conversation. They clung to each other, frightened as a couple of baby birds who'd just been forced from their nest."

Just then, Rocky approached from behind, making his presence known with a slight brush of his hand in the center of Sarah's back. She gave a jolt then prayed her husband hadn't noticed. "Am I interrupting?" Rocky asked the small gathering.

"Not at all, friend," offered Ben, giving a warm smile and pulling his wife snugly up against him. "We were just talking about the children. They're looking a little glum today."

Rocky glanced in the direction of Rachel and Seth and frowned. "They're quite the pair. I don't know what goes on in their heads, and I'm clean out of ideas as to what to do with them. The girl is downright cranky. I'm hoping my wife will have some fresh insights." He presented Sarah with a genuine smile, revealing straight, white teeth.

"I'll do my best," she promised.

"I'm afraid my sister failed to teach them proper manners. Ma says they're just being kids, but I'm not so sure," Rocky said. "Truth is, I'm not used to girls, particularly sassy ones."

Benjamin laughed and gave his pretty wife a sideways glance. "I know what you mean, Rock. I've had to learn firsthand how to live with a sassy female." To that, Liza slapped him playfully on the arm, which brought a round of laughter from everyone present.

"What's so funny over here?" asked Jon Atkins. The handsome young minister approached, Frank and Mary Callahan coming alongside him, and then Emma.

"We were just discussing how difficult my wife is," Ben said.

71

Liza turned cautioning eyes on him. "Oh, stop it. We were not discussing anything of the kind." Although her tone denoted scolding, her eyes held bounteous amounts of love. It was clear the two were used to good-natured badgering. Sarah could almost feel a twinge of envy for their outward show of intimate camaraderie.

"If anyone has a right to complain, it'd be Liza," Jon said. "What do you say, Rock?"

"I'd agree with that. Ben Broughton has always been a stubborn mule as far back as I can remember." Everyone chortled, including Liza.

"Hey now," Ben cut in, "let's be fair."

"Fair's got nothin' to do with it. We're speakin' facts," Rocky continued. "Remember the time we three thought to take the trip down south by way of the Mississippi? Jon and I were bound and determined to pack plenty of supplies, whereas Ben here thought it best to pack light and live off the land."

"We couldn't have been more than fourteen," Ben said with a hearty grin.

"We left in the morning and were home before nightfall, hungrier than coons," said Jon, recollection showing in his clear blue eyes. "Weren't too smart, as I recall. We didn't take enough blankets and hadn't planned on rain. Came back wetter than skunks swimmin' upriver."

"Why don't I remember anythin' about this trip?" asked Mrs. Callahan, her squinty blue eyes revealing fine wrinkles at the corners.

"Well, Ma, we figured it best not to tell our parents. We didn't plan on being gone much past three weeks. Figured you'd hardly miss us," Rocky said in a joking tone.

"I'd've missed ya come morning when it was time for the milkin'," said the elder Mr. Callahan, his grey eyes glinting with humor, his voice craggy with age.

Everyone laughed. Sarah noted that Rachel and Seth had approached the circle of adults and were snuggling up on either side of their grandmother. The roundish woman pulled them up snugly against her, taking the time to smile down at each. Only Seth returned a hint of a smile, his face disappearing in his grandma's full skirts. It was clear they loved her and she them.

As the celebration waned and folks had had their fill of conversation, food, punch, and cake, Mother Callahan suggested that Sarah and Rocky open their wedding gifts. Although the idea of gifts seemed somehow superfluous in view of their contrived marriage, Sarah obliged the group by accepting each gift with enthusiasm. There was a linen, flower-print tablecloth with silver napkin rings from Ben and Liza, a pair of silver salt and pepper shakers and matching sugar bowl from Emma, and a cake basket, ice cream knife, and full set of cast-iron pans from Sarah's new in-laws. Lastly, Jon presented them with a large family Bible. "It's beautiful," Sarah exclaimed upon taking the lovely leather-bound edition from its box. Even Rocky reached across her and stroked the fine leather. "Thank you, Jon," he murmured solemnly. "We didn't expect you to give us a gift since you already did us the honor of performing the ceremony."

"I gave the same gift to Ben and Liza a few weeks back. Wouldn't want to leave you out. You are to fill in the family tree as you add new members to your family," he said. "You can see that I've already included both your names at the top." There was a definite hint of mischief in his eyes as Sarah's face went from pale to crimson in the space of a few seconds. Would there ever be more to their family than the two of them and Rachel and Seth? It seemed unlikely since they'd both agreed that this would be a marriage in name only.

Emma broke the moment of awkward silence. "I'm sorry to break up this party, but I must be getting back to my boardinghouse. I have a couple of vacancies that I need to see to."

"And I have a Sunday sermon to prepare," Jon said. "I expect I'll see you all at the Winthrop's lovely home for services this coming Sunday?"

Sarah glanced at her unresponsive husband then answered for both of them. "I cannot guarantee that we will make it this week, but you may count on us thereafter." To that, Rocky scowled, although she doubted anyone else had caught his wrathful look. Sarah couldn't help but wonder what had so embittered his heart toward God. Yes, he'd lost his wife and son, but others suffered losses and didn't automatically wrap themselves in bitterness.

The guests said their good-byes, making their way to the door after offering their final good wishes to the newly married couple, Rocky going before to open the door for them and to see them out.

Mary Callahan hugged Sarah tightly, then pulled back and rewarded her with a pleasant smile. "You are to call on Frank and me very soon, and, of course, bring the children."

"Thank you. I'm sure I'll need your advice from time to

time." Sarah noted how both Rachel and Seth hung on the skirts of their grandma, refusing to let go.

"You'll do just fine," she whispered, then, leaning in, added, "The children will grow to love you, as will my son, you'll see. Now that you're here, their hearts will heal."

Sarah felt a burden of responsibility. Was her mother-in-law expecting more than she was able to give?

"I appreciate that, Mrs. Callahan."

The woman's seasoned face creased into a sudden smile. "Please, if you wish, call me Mother or, at the very least, Mary. I know you lost your true mother just recently, so perhaps it won't come natural, but just so you know—I'll think of you as a daughter—particularly since I just lost my own dear girl." A faraway look swept across Mary's face and Sarah's heart went out to her.

Just then, Frank Callahan approached, looping his arm through his wife's. Deep lines etched his weathered forehead and the corners of his eyes, revealing years of squinting at Kentucky's punishing sun. He wasn't as tall as his son, but his broad shoulders, now sagging from age, revealed his former strength.

"Welcome to the family, my dear," he said, his mouth turning up in a kindly smile. "I 'spect my Mary has already invited you for supper next week." He arched a white eyebrow and winked.

Mary Callahan giggled. "I've given her an open invitation for now. We'll save the formal invite for later. Don't want to overwhelm the poor girl right off."

Mrs. Callahan bent to hug the children then set them to the side to whisper something in their ears. Both gave solemn nods. Frank tipped back on his heels and waited for his wife. "They miss their ma somethin' fierce," he muttered, pulling on his white beard.

Sarah's throat tightened at the sight of the forlorn little imps. "These things take time," was all she could manage.

Chapter Five

*S*arah stared at one lone spot on the ceiling, pulled the scratchy wool blanket up under her chin, turned over on her straw mattress, and breathed in the scents of musty walls and dusty curtains. It was well past midnight, but her mind was still too cluttered with thoughts of her wedding day for sleep to come.

She glanced out the single window of the small room that had once belonged to Rocky Callahan. Although she'd insisted she could sleep on the sofa, which she'd discovered during the course of the evening wasn't bad, save the spring that jutted from its center, he'd insisted a woman needed her own place. It seemed he'd fashioned a spot for himself out in the barn, for when night fell, he gathered up his bedroll, a book, and a couple of other items, mumbled a solemn good-night, and headed out the door.

The cabin, while cozy enough, needed a good scrubbing. Of course, her mother-in-law had tended to the surface cleaning prior to the wedding, but when Rocky and the kids had given her a tour of the little house, she'd noticed rugs, bedding, and windows treatments all in need of an overhaul. She hoped her husband wouldn't mind when she handed him a list of wants for fixing up the place.

She could use her own money, she supposed, but she wanted to accustom herself to depending on her husband.

Besides, what would he say if he learned of her large inheritance? Their marriage arrangement was precarious at best. Telling him he'd married a very wealthy woman might sting his ego or even give him cause for sending her back. From all appearances, Rocky Callahan was a man of strength and great pride. *I won't be beholden to ya,* he'd stated. That being the case, she could hardly picture him accepting so much as a dime of her inheritance.

Rocky. She tried his first name on her lips and liked the feel of it. Still, it would take practice before it came off sounding natural to her.

While she lay there contemplating, the scuffle of tiny feet scampered past her doorway—a mouse?—and she pulled her blanket up closer, shuddering. A wealthy city girl, she could not abide the notion that a wild creature, no matter how small, roamed free within the confines of her home.

In the space of a few days, her life had changed dramatically—from a wealthy, pampered socialite to a farmer's wife. If nothing else, the house alone demonstrated her drastic shift in status. Whereas her home in the heart of one of Winchester's prestigious neighborhoods was spacious and airy, with windows aplenty, this little house stood alone amidst acres of rich, rising farmland, boasting only two small windows on either side of the front door, one in each of the two bedrooms, one over the kitchen sink, and another one overlooking the back.

Built of whitewashed wood slats and a primitive shingled roof, the house had a small front porch as its only welcoming feature. The yard and various outbuildings—a large barn, two sheds, and a chicken coop—made up the cabin's surroundings, along with the rich, grassy hillsides, framed by a large whitewashed fence, undoubtedly intended for her husband's livestock.

A town of this caliber will not make you happy, Sarah. She winced and turned on her side, swallowing past the hard, dry lump in her throat and trying to ignore her need for the necessary. She'd never used an outdoor facility before moving to Kentucky, her home in Massachusetts having three separate bathrooms: one on the main floor, and two on the second.

Releasing a weighty sigh, she yanked back the wool comforter and sat up. After getting her bearings, she snagged her velvet dressing gown from its nearby hook and hastily slipped into a pair of warm shoes. Next, she lit the little kerosene lamp beside her bed and crept to the doorway, hoping not to come face-to-face with the mouse she'd heard earlier.

The house was dark save for the glow of remaining embers in the centrally located fireplace. When burning at full capacity, the fireplace kept the house warm and cozy. Now, however, even with her long robe wrapped snugly around her nightdress, Sarah felt the grip of winter's chill.

She passed through the living room and the kitchen and had just put her hand to the back door when a voice halted her. "Going somewhere?"

To say she was surprised to find her husband standing mere feet away was putting it mildly. Cold shock better described her emotion as she whirled to face him, her hand going to her heart in an attempt to slow its rapid pace. "I—c-couldn't sleep," she managed. "I thought you were in the barn."

"I didn't mean to scare you." The moon's reflection traced the outline of his powerful body, making him appear dark and dangerous, even though she felt certain he wasn't. "I came in to feed the fire," he said in a gravelly voice. "Sorry to disturb you."

"You didn't disturb me." A long moment of silence made her awkwardness increase. She cleared her throat. "It seems silly for you to walk from the barn to the house to feed the fire when I could just as easily tend to it."

"No need," he answered, his face coming into view as he stepped closer. "You have your chores and I have mine. I'd just as soon keep it that way."

"I see." The gruff manner in which he spoke went against her grain, but she managed to keep her tongue from retorting. There would be time enough later for discussing household tasks. In the meantime, she had more pressing needs. "Well," again, she cleared her throat, "I have need of the outdoor facilities."

"Ah, and you think you can find your way?"

"I'm sure I'll manage." It was embarrassing enough to have been caught unawares, but to be standing here discussing her basest of needs was downright humiliating.

"It's a tricky path at night, a few dips here and there. You'll need a light so you don't twist an ankle on your way out. I should have told you where I keep the lantern." He stepped past her, his wool coat brushing against her velvet sleeve. The simple touch created a strange stir in the pit of her stomach. He opened the cabinet nearest the door and retrieved a lantern and a box of matches. Turning the wick up slightly, he struck a match against the rough wall, inserted the burning stick inside the globe, and ignited a low flame. That done, he handed her the lantern. "I'll walk with you."

"That's entirely unnecessary," she balked, her face heating with embarrassment.

"I don't mind."

"I wish to walk alone."

"Don't be mulish," he said. "Don't worry, I'll keep my distance once you go inside."

Now she was mortified. "I'm not worried, and that is precisely why I choose to walk alone."

In the lantern's dim light, she saw a muscle clench along the strong line of his jaw. Just then, she felt his hand seize her elbow as he escorted, or rather pulled, her out the door.

"What do you think you're doing?" she shrieked into the icy night, suddenly unconcerned about the children waking. "I told you..."

He stopped midway down the trail, yanked the lantern from her hand, and stared down at her. "And I told you I would take you. Now be quiet, woman, or you'll wake the bears."

"The bears?"

"Yes, the bears. Most are hibernating in their dens, but a few will wake up about this time of year, hungry for a bite to eat."

"Bears?" she repeated.

"And wolves—famished ones," he said with emphasis.

"Wolves?"

But he didn't say another word, just hauled her along toward the little shanty at the rear of the yard, holding the lantern in front of them.

Indeed the path was narrow with several gullies and rises, and she had to admit to being thankful for his presence. Once he'd even had to catch her by the arm when she started to stumble. She felt certain the words *I told you so* were fighting to get past his mouth, yet he restrained himself.

"I'll wait here," he said, stopping a short distance from the little building and handing the lantern back to her.

Without a word, she took the final few steps.

After tending to her needs as quickly as possible, shivering the entire time, she pushed open the heavy wood door, which slanted and squeaked on its hinges, and frowned. And when she meant to close it quietly, gravity pulled it shut with a loud thump. "That alone should wake the bears," she murmured.

The tiniest hint of a smile washed across his stern face. "I've been meaning to fix that," he answered quietly.

***

The first signs of daylight struck a straight path through Sarah's bedroom window. It was either that or the sounds of pans clanging and banging in the kitchen that woke her with a start. The first thing she did was open her eyes and stare at the blank wall she faced, familiarizing herself with her where-abouts. When the realization struck her that she was freshly married and waking up for the first time in her new home, she leaped out of bed. *Fine way to start a marriage*, she thought, especially after his comment last night about wanting to stick to the chores intended for each of them. She supposed the cooking chore fell to her. Already she'd failed.

Racing across the small room to her yet unpacked trunk, she threw on the first dress she could find, a full-skirted, purple satin gown she'd purchased two years ago. It was the perfect day dress for Winchester's social circles, but undoubtedly ill-suited for Little Hickman. Bell-sleeved and decorated with a dipped sequined collar and lovely pearl buttons, it seemed an unlikely housedress. Perhaps she would shorten the sleeves later and replace the buttons with something more sensible.

She ran to the door, then stopped dead in her tracks after skimming her fingers through her mass of auburn curls. Muttering to herself, she backtracked for a brush and quickly ran it through the tangled mess, then yanked a silver comb off the nearby dressing table and, after twisting her hair into a thick knot, wedged it firmly in place. Pinching her cheeks for color, she mumbled in disgust, "Oh, phooey, if he doesn't approve of my appearance, he can just look the other way."

She took a deep breath for courage and opened the door. He stood in front of the stove, stirring something. Bacon and eggs? Whatever it was, it smelled wonderful, and her stomach growled right on cue.

She didn't want to stare, but since his back was to her, it gave her the perfect opportunity. His black hair, yet uncombed, fell just over his shirt collar. As if he sensed she watched, he swept a large hand through the loose strands, then went back to tending the unidentified concoction.

Feeling somehow guilty for watching, she quietly stepped forward. Without so much as a turn of his head, he mumbled, "I see you finally decided to get up."

So this was how he greeted his wife on the morning after his wedding. Refusing to be intimidated, she swallowed a dry lump. "Good morning."

"Is it?"

"What are you making? It smells wonderful."

"Breakfast."

She chewed her lower lip. "I see that." She stepped up beside him, fully aware of his daunting presence, and looked into the fry pan. As she'd supposed, he was scrambling eggs on one side of the large pan and frying several strips of bacon on the other. A mound of fried potatoes lay warming on a hot plate beside the pan, covered with a thin towel.

"It looks delicious."

"How did you sleep?" he asked, ignoring her compliment.

"Quite well." Quite terribly, actually. She wasn't accustomed to a straw mattress, having always slept on downy feathers, but she thought it best to keep that tidbit of information to herself. To make matters worse, she'd been cold most of the night. Of top priority today was finding herself another blanket. She wondered if the children also shivered but were too afraid to let their uncle know. "And you?" she asked.

"Fine." It seemed her husband was a man of few words. Well, she would just have to find a way to make him talk.

"Have you seen anything of the children yet?"

"They don't usually rise until they smell breakfast."

"I see. Then I suppose they'll be appearing most any minute. Will they need help with dressing?"

"They haven't yet." He reached into the cabinet above the stove and brought out some plates from behind a dusty curtain. She made a mental note to take down all the curtains that covered the cupboards and wash them first chance she got.

"I see. Shall I set the table?"

"Suit yourself," he said, walking to the little square table. "You'll find forks and spoons in that drawer by the stove.

Hester always kept it..." He halted mid-sentence, his entire body seeming to go stiff. Since his back was to her, she couldn't determine his expression.

"Hester?"

"Uh, my wife," he said flatly.

"It's all right if you mention her," Sarah said. "I'd like to hear about her."

"It's not necessary."

"I'm sure you must miss her deeply." *And your son*, she thought.

When he didn't respond, just laid the plates on the table, she let the matter go. There would be plenty of time later for discovering his past.

She pulled open the drawer, noting that she had to use force, and counted out enough spoons and forks, all tarnished and mismatched, for the four of them. There was no semblance of order for how they were stored, so she had to dig in the small wooden box to find each utensil. She made another mental note.

Once they'd set the table, Rocky poured the food onto a large white platter and brought it to the table. "I'll see that the breakfast is taken care of from now on," she stated, straightening a napkin beside one of the plates then clasping her hands together at her waist.

His back to her, he reached for the coffee pot on a back burner. "You do drink coffee, right?" His question implied she'd be foolish not to.

Actually, she hated the stuff, but she supposed she could learn to adjust to its bitter taste. "Of course," she replied. "About the meals..."

"I understand that you must have been exhausted this morning. Don't worry about it." He poured coffee into two mugs, picked them up, and brought them to the table.

She glanced at the clock on the wall. It wasn't quite seven. Exactly how early did he expect her to rise every morning? She opened her mouth to ask the question just as Rachel appeared in the doorway, sleep still evident in her large blue eyes, her hair a shambles.

"Good morning, Rachel," Sarah said, walking over to the girl. "Is your brother up yet?"

Rachel shook her head. "He don't get up till I wake him."

"I see." She peeked past the girl and noted her brother still sleeping snugly in his narrow bed, blankets stacked atop him. It pleased her to know that he appeared warm and cozy.

"Did you sleep well?" Sarah asked, noting another narrow cot opposite her brother's, blankets drawn up, signifying the girl's attempt to make the bed. It wouldn't be long before the children would need separate rooms. She wondered if Rocky had considered that.

"You best wake up your brother," Rocky said. "Breakfast is cooling fast."

Rachel nodded and rubbed her eyes.

"I'll go with you," Sarah offered, following the child into the little square room.

***

Breakfast was a tranquil affair; the only sounds were the clanking of fork against plate and Sarah's occasional throat clearing between chews and swallows. Only sporadically did she glance up, and that was to smile at the children. It seemed that Rocky's failure to encourage her earlier attempts at conversation had earned him a measure of peace and quiet.

For the most part, Rachel and Seth behaved themselves; Seth even attempted a couple bites of eggs when Rocky cast him a warning glance. The boy must have sensed that his uncle was in no mood for fighting on this first morning with his bride. Even Rachel had very little to say, astonishing in itself. She'd been especially quiet throughout the wedding ceremony and reception, but he'd figured that by morning she'd be back to her usual irritable self.

Rocky rested curious eyes on the new Mrs. Callahan. She was clothed in some kind of glimmery, purple getup, and he tried to imagine her ever doing a stitch of work in it, or even working at all. Dainty features, gracefully carved, made up her perfect oval face. She had a streamlined little nose, straight and charming, a genial, soft-looking mouth, a gentle chin, and sparkling blue-green eyes that even now twinkled under a somewhat solemn expression. He wondered what she was thinking as she continued to eat in silence.

When she looked up and caught him watching, her long auburn lashes swept down over rosy cheeks, giving her the appearance of innocence even though he'd seen her downright outspoken side. Had she any notion of the life that awaited her? Hickman was a place where dirt seemed a natural ingredient at every meal, and blood and sweat mingled with the drinking water. How long before she pulled up stakes and headed back East, tossing out the ridiculous notion that God had called her here for a reason? It would be nice to think that God had seen fit to bless him with a wife, and a pretty, refined one at that, but heaven knew God didn't owe him any favors.

87

"Do you like eggs, Miss Sarah?" Seth's voice broke the blessed quietness.

Sarah gave the boy a thoughtful look and set her fork on the edge of her plate. "Actually, I do, but I don't think I was fond of them as a child. I had to learn to like them." With that, she picked up her coffee mug and took a sip. She grimaced after swallowing, then set the cup down. It didn't seem to Rocky that she'd ingested more than an ounce of the dark brew.

Seth leaned forward, his chin just coming to the rim of his plate, where his yet unfinished eggs had been neatly pushed to the other side. "Did your mama and papa make you eat 'em?"

Sarah's face flooded with softness. "No, no, they didn't force me. I think if they had I would have wound up hating them all the more." With that, her gaze veered toward Rocky. Was there a challenge hidden somewhere in her depths?

Her shrewd manner unnerved him. What could he say that wouldn't make him out to be the bigger fool? He pushed his chair back and heard the grating squeak of wood against wood.

"Are you finished?" Sarah asked, touching a napkin to her chin.

"I am," he answered pointblank, standing.

"Then it would be thoughtful to excuse yourself."

Now he stared at her, disbelieving. "What?"

She continued dabbing then faced him head-on. "If you want the children to mind their manners, you'll need to set the example."

"You expect me to..."

"It won't destroy you to say excuse me, Mr. Callahan," she urged with a hint of a smile. When he flashed a look across the table at Rachel, he found her grinning like a Cheshire cat.

He paused a moment longer, having already stood to his feet, the fingers of both his hands steepled on the table. He pushed the chair out of the way. "Oh, all right, excuse me. How is that?"

"Not very sincere, I'm afraid, but it will do. Perhaps you will have improved by the noon meal."

Rocky felt his temper rise but knew his need to restrain himself. Outright anger would only give her an additional reason to lecture. He started to walk away, but halted when his wife rebuked him for having forgotten to push his chair under the table. Biting back a reply, he stepped over to the stool, bent to pick it up, and placed it under the table. "Will that do?" he asked with clear sarcasm.

She smiled, her straight teeth glistening against the light of the kerosene lamp in the middle of the table. "Absolutely," she replied.

He walked to the far side of the room, yanked down his hat from its nail, threw on his heavy wool barn coat, slipped into his boots, and then made for the door, thinking to escape as quickly as possible. When he opened the door, a blast of winter wind smacked him square in the face.

"Oh, Mr. Callahan," her voice trailed across the room, warring with the brisk winds, "when shall I expect you for the noon meal?"

His hand still on the doorknob, he pivoted. "How about—noon—Mrs. Callahan?" He had all he could do to force back a sarcastic tone.

Her auburn locks, pulled back into a knot and secured with a shimmery silver comb, rebelled against the severe style, their curly wisps falling helter-skelter about her glowing cheeks. Obviously flustered, she attempted to pull a few strands behind her ears. "Yes, of course, noon. Perhaps it is the evening meal I'm wondering about."

"I can't say for sure on that. We'll talk about it later."

Once again, he attempted to exit, knowing that the brittle air had already made its way into the little cabin. "Oh, Mr. Callahan, what is it you want to eat?" she asked.

Now he gave a heavy sigh. "You decide that, but keep in mind I'll be good and hungry." Before taking another step, he asked, "You think you can manage without me?"

An irate expression crossed her face. "Of course. I'm not a helpless balloonhead."

Dewy grass, iced over from the frigid temperatures of the night before, crackled beneath his boots on his trek to the barn, echoing through the frozen, bracing air. Solid maples and oaks, naked of all leaves but for the few remaining brown ones that still clung to the ends of skinny branches, lined his narrow, well-worn path. They stood like giant unarmed soldiers against the bleak sky, idle and indifferent.

Balloonhead? Her flowery vocabulary sometimes made it impossible to hold back the grins, but far be it from him to let on she amused him.

Raw cold forced Rocky's head down. It seemed the only thing missing from this frosty Kentucky morning was the snow. So far, the white stuff had missed the entire upper region of the state, despite raging blizzards on all sides. Would their luck hold out, or did the dark, overcast skies and stirring winds warn of impending dire weather? Only time would tell.

Familiar barn smells bombarded Rocky's senses as he drew near the door and pushed it open, its hinges squeaking in protest. "Mornin', all," he muttered in routine fashion, snatching up a clean milk pail from a nearby shelf.

The sounds of bleating, impatient cows and hungry horses greeted him, stomping hooves against boarded walls or clomping hoofed feet into grungy straw, their way of scolding him for not coming sooner.

"Have a little patience," he murmured. "There's only one of me. First comes the milking, then the mucking out of stalls. After that, you'll all get your bellies stuffed."

On cue, they settled into a peaceful contentedness, having recognized the familiar drone of their owner's voice.

Yanking down a bridle that needed mending from a nearby nail, Rocky hitched it over one shoulder and headed across the barn toward the milk cows. He threw the bridle down on his workbench, then walked to Mary Lou. "You first, girl," he muttered. Some time ago, he'd established an order for milking, and there was no question the animals all knew it.

He led Mary Lou out of her stall and into the milking aisle, where he tied her to the milking post. "Hey there," he greeted absently. In answer, she gave a low moo and allowed him to situate her. Once done, he went about making himself comfortable on his trusty stool.

A couple of barn cats approached on schedule, one of them mewing out a chorus in hopes of coaxing Rocky into filling their dish with fresh, warm milk. The one he'd dubbed Rainbow for its multicolored coat began its usual rubbing up against his ankles. The gray tom hung back in his usual shy manner, deciding it best to let the calico do the begging for both of them.

He loved this aspect of farming—the camaraderie with the animals, the trust and allegiance they'd all formed with one another. Unlike his home, the barnyard held no expectations, no rules for uprightness or good manners. It hadn't occurred to him that once he married he would need to change his behavior in order to set an example for the children. Asking to be excused from his own table when he was finished eating seemed a bit much. He scowled in remembrance at the way his new wife had reprimanded him.

What other rules of etiquette did she have hidden up those purple satin sleeves?

Chapter Six

S arah spent the entire morning scrubbing floors, washing down kitchen shelves, scouring the sink, and taking down curtains to prepare for laundering. She put Rachel to work at the table, polishing mismatched silverware and gave Seth the job of counting and sorting canned goods in the lean-to off the small kitchen. Neither child appeared opposed to working once Sarah appointed them jobs. In fact, they seemed thrilled at the prospect, chattering nonstop as they worked.

"You don't grump at us like Uncle Rocky," said Rachel.

"Yeah, he's grouchy most of the time, 'cept when it's bed-time for me and Rachel," Seth supplied, peeking his head around the corner at both of them.

Sarah managed a smile. "Your uncle has much on his mind," she answered, temporarily averting her gaze from the floor, but not slowing her scrubbing motion. She'd long since shed her satin gown in favor of something more practical—a yellow cotton chemise with three-quarter length sleeves and belted black skirt. She longed to don a pair of men's pants for all the stooping and bending she was doing but doubted Rocky would approve. Her hair, now knotted more securely at the top of her head, still refused to stay completely put. Evidence of that were the stubborn strands that continually fell across her face, blocking her vision.

"Why does he have to be so mean to us?" Rachel asked.

Sarah looked up from her stooped position on the hardwood floor. "In what way is your uncle mean to you?" If he were truly mean to the children, she would find the underlying cause and see what she could do to alleviate the problem. On the other hand, if they objected to his sternness, there was little she could do unless the man softened.

"He don't never laugh or smile," Seth offered, giving Rachel little chance to answer the question Sarah had directed at her.

Sarah eyed Seth with sympathy, deciding to ignore his poor grammar for now. "Well, perhaps he hasn't had much occasion to do either. Maybe we'll have to see about changing that."

The boy wrinkled his nose. "How would we do that?"

"He don't even like us," Rachel interjected.

"I'm sure he loves you both. It's just that—well, he's had some difficult things happen to him along the way."

"Like what?" Seth's eyebrows shot up in question. It appeared to Sarah that he'd ceased his job of counting and sorting cans.

"Well, his wife died a few years back of a bad disease, and then his little boy died less than a year ago."

"Nobody ever told us he had a little boy," Rachel said. "How come nobody ever tells us anything?"

"I imagine most folks figured you two had enough sadness to deal with."

"No wonder he don't like us. We probably remind him of his other family," Rachel said. The child's insightfulness came as a surprise.

"Well, I wouldn't worry about that. It's been a big adjustment for all of you. It will continue to take time. And now, besides your uncle, you have me to get used to."

Neither commented on that, so Sarah continued scrubbing, noting with satisfaction how the floor had lost its dullness. Underneath the layers of dirt and grime, there emerged a lovely pine floor. Of course, it could stand a good polishing, but at least it would appear much brighter than before without all that dirt.

"How come you married Uncle Rocky?" Rachel asked after several minutes of comfortable silence. The question set her back.

"I suppose I felt compelled to help him raise the two of you," she offered. "Mostly, though, God led me to marry him."

"Do you like him?" Seth asked, peeking around the corner, a can of peaches in hand.

Sarah felt her mouth turn down in the corner. "Well, I suppose I do, although I don't know him very well."

Rachel giggled, and the sound reminded Sarah of a babbling brook, warm and free. She doubted the child had had much occasion for laughter since arriving at her uncle's farm.

"What's so funny?" she asked, blowing several strands of hair off her face in order to see the girl.

Between spurts of continued laughter, the child replied, "You look silly."

Sarah could only imagine. Crawling across the floor like a giant bug, hair falling every which direction, soiled clothing damp and grimy. Was it any wonder she laughed? As if on cue, Seth joined in, his mirth a contagious mixture of giggles and glee. She had no choice but to enter into the merriment.

At the height of their hilarity, the door blew open and in its wake stood Mr. Callahan, his wool cap pulled down over his furrowed brow, his mouth a straight line that revealed not the slightest hint of amusement. Large, booted feet spread wide in the open doorway; he resembled an ornery bear awaiting his dinner.

"Mercy me, Mr. Callahan, you frightened us," Sarah managed, arranging herself on the floor so that her legs folded beneath her, certain she looked anything but womanly. Glancing at both children, she detected fear in their eyes. Hastily, Seth scooted back to his can-sorting job in the lean-to and Rachel made quick work of polishing a spoon. Did he always greet them with a sour look?

"Nice to see you're having a grand time," he muttered, closing the door behind him and strolling across Sarah's clean floor, taking care to step around her, but nonetheless leaving a trail of clay from the door to the kitchen sink. It took all of Sarah's reserve to hold her temper under lock and key.

"You're early for lunch, Mr. Callahan," she said, placing her damp hands in the lap of her grungy black skirt.

"Just stopped in for a drink of water." He forced the pump handle up and down a few times until clear water ran from the spigot. Then he thrust a tin cup under the stream, brought it to his mouth, and drank his fill. Afterward, he plunked the cup onto the spotless sink she'd spent an hour scouring.

"You can call me by my first name, you know," he said, turning to face her, arms folded across his massive chest.

She thought about that. "Your formal name seems more suitable—at least until we get to know each other better."

"We're married, Sarah. Rocky will do just fine."

It made her shiver the way her own name rolled off his tongue so nonchalantly.

"Fine," she answered. "I'll do my best to remember that."

He permitted his eyes to roam around the room. "Appears you've been busy," he said, his tone guarded. Far be it from him to extend a compliment, Sarah mused.

"The children have been a very big help."

"As well they should," he said.

Ignoring his mood, she continued, "Seth has been working in the pantry, and as you can see, Rachel is polishing the silver. So far we've scrubbed floors, scoured the sink and cabinets, and washed a few drawers."

Rocky nodded, this time showing a measure of approval. "It hasn't looked this good since Hester..." Sarah knew he regretted having mentioned his former wife yet again in her presence, and because of it, she didn't prod him to continue. Would he never cease to think of her? Three years seemed ample enough time for him to get on with his life. "What have you done with all the curtains?" he asked.

She glanced at the bare windows. "We took them down to launder. They were full of dust, Mr.— uh, Rocky." His name did not roll off her tongue nearly as easily as hers did his.

"I see. Well, carry on, then. I'll be in the barn." He pushed himself away from the sink. "I'll be back at noon. This afternoon I'll be heading out to the north field to repair a fence line."

Suddenly, Sarah brightened. "Perhaps you would enjoy taking Seth with you. I'm sure he could be of help, and it would do both of you good to spend some time together."

A mysterious expression swept across his face. "I think not. Farming is man's work."

"But how else will he learn if you don't teach him? One day he'll be a man himself and—"

"Sarah, I'll thank you not to intrude."

His harshness set her back—but not for long. "Intrude? That was not my intention." She jumped to her feet, knowing she looked a sight but caring little. "I was merely suggesting it might be good to begin teaching the boy small tasks. He's not too young, in my opinion."

"In your opinion?" Rocky slipped an eyebrow up, whether in amusement or disapproval she couldn't say. "Already you're an authority on child rearing?"

"Of course not," she shot back, angry at his refusal to take her seriously. "It's just that I'm sure Seth would rather spend time with you than with Rachel and me. We will be working in the house most of the day."

"Taking the boy along would only slow my progress," he alleged. At this, his gaze trailed to Seth, whose saddened eyes seemed not to affect Rocky in the least. Then to Sarah, he added, "I have an agenda to keep, and since there's only one of me, I haven't time for wasting it on babysitting."

"Babysitting? Is that what you call it?"

"I'm not a baby!" Seth wailed, jumping down from his little stool in the lean-to and making a beeline for his room.

Equally upset was Rachel, who slammed down the fork she was polishing to follow in Seth's trail, making a point to shut their bedroom door with a bang.

Rocky glared at Sarah. "Now look what you've done," he said, his forehead knit together in a cavernous frown.

"Me! I did nothing but recommend you take Seth with you to the field. You're the one who broke his heart by suggesting he'd be nothing but trouble."

"Don't be dramatic. The boy will survive, and I didn't say he'd be nothing but trouble."

"You implied as much."

"It's not my problem if he chose to see it that way."

Without forethought, she inched closer, matching her husband's angry glare. "How dare you treat an innocent five-year-old as if he were a bother? Does it not occur to you that your nephew could use some male attention?"

His eyes flashed in their usual show of impatience. "Does it not occur to you that I have a farm to run? If the boy starts tagging along with me, I won't accomplish a thing in the way of work. I have fences to mend, soil to till, machinery to repair, animals to feed." He threw up his arms. "How am I supposed to do all that and still keep watch over a child?"

"Why don't you hire someone to help you if you're so overwhelmed? I'm sure you can afford it," she replied, surprising even herself with her forthrightness.

Now his eyes blazed with more than impatience. "I'm sorry to report that I haven't a great deal of wealth. Disappointed?" He leaned in close enough to touch her cheek with his hot breath, close enough to kiss her. Nervously she looped a loose strand of hair behind her ear and felt her back go ramrod straight.

"Certainly not," she replied. "I couldn't care less about your money—or lack thereof."

"Really? It's obvious you're accustomed to far more than what I have to offer you." She quivered when his eyes roamed the length of her. "In fact, I daresay you haven't broken a sweat till today." When he would have touched a finger to her damp brow, she angled her face away.

"My only concern is for the children," she hastened. "Your hiring help would free you up for giving them your attention."

Best to stay on track, she mused, much as she'd like to counter his crudeness.

His well-chiseled chin jutted forward as he cast a hurried glance at the closed bedroom door. "They have you to look after them now."

She shook her head. "I'm not enough for them. They need a father."

"Pfff." His firm mouth tensed, the clear-cut lines of his profile sharpening. "They seem to have fared fine without one up till now."

Goodness, but he was a hard-boiled rattlebrain, and she might have told him so were it not for her Christian witness. My, but it was hard to rein in her temper where Rocky Callahan was concerned. Several practiced breaths later, she raised her chin and brushed her hands on her soiled skirt. "I've work to do," she muttered.

For a change, he stood stock still, his only movement a twitching nerve that spanned his square-set jaw. "As do I," he finally replied. At the door, he paused and turned. "I expect when I get back the children's moods will have brightened."

And just like that, he disappeared from view.

When the ancient clock on the wall struck twelve, neither child's disposition appeared much improved. Although Sarah had coaxed them from their room, they hadn't smiled once, even though they'd both complied when she'd asked them to set the table, fill the water glasses, and take the two rugs by the door outside for a good shaking. This time, when her husband entered, she would insist he remove his shoes. It was the least he could do if she was to keep a tidy house.

When Rocky came inside, however, he bent to untie them

 100

of his own accord, kicked them off, and then shoved them up against the wall with his stocking-covered foot. Once done, he perused the place in silence, eyed each child with a guarded look, then fixed his gaze on Sarah. "Something smells mighty fine," he muttered, shaking off his coat and hanging it on the hook.

"I made a hearty chicken soup and baked some biscuits. I added a few vegetables to the broth. I hope you don't mind."

"Why should I mind? Anything you fix will be better than what I've eaten lately." He took a long breath, glanced once again at the silent children, then crossed the room and headed for the sink. As he passed in front of her while rolling up his sleeves, the scent of barn and animal wafted through the air.

"Isn't there a pump outside where you could wash up?" He paused midway between her and the sink and gave her a questioning stare, so she hastily added, "After today, of course."

"There is, but it's winter. I prefer to wash up inside until warmer weather sets in, if you don't mind."

"I suppose that will be fine, then. Thank you for removing your shoes at the door."

For the first time, a slight smile made its home on his mouth. "I've decided not to risk any more of your wrath today." He pumped a steady stream of water from the faucet and washed his hands, grabbing a nearby bar of soap and working up a good lather before rinsing them. Sarah stepped forward and handed him a dry towel. He gave her a look that flickered with a hint of warmth. "Thank you."

She relaxed her shoulders and returned a shy smile. It was a start.

***

His new wife was a good cook. Funny, he hadn't expected it of her. Oh, he'd known all along she'd be good to the children, but the fact she could cook and clean was a nice bonus.

After a painfully quiet lunch, during which both children watched him with suspicion, he pushed his chair back and suppressed a belch, inwardly knowing Sarah would balk if he indulged himself.

"Are you finished already?" she asked, dabbing her spotless chin with a napkin. The children looked up when Sarah spoke, Rachel's face holding a perpetual frown.

Rocky viewed his wife from across the table. She'd changed out of her drab black skirt and yellow blouse into a vivid blue gown that served to lighten her hazel-colored eyes, and had even piled her wandering locks of burnished, wine-red hair back into a tight little bun. Had she primped in the hope of pleasing him? Well, she needn't have bothered, he ruled. No matter how pretty she might be, he wasn't about to start lavishing her with attention.

"Yes," he replied, setting his napkin beside his plate. When he would have stood, it occurred to him she was waiting for his formal request to leave the table.

Irked, he gave her what truly must have been a scathing look. "Uh, excuse me. Please."

The smile she gifted him with was as wide as the whole state of Kentucky, and for reasons unknown to him, it tugged at a cold, dark place in his heart. "You're excused," she said, pulling back her shoulders in a show of pride.

Irritated with himself for wishing he could make her smile

 102

last, he stood up, then took a moment to glance at Seth. The boy watched him with wariness, his light brown eyebrows puckered, his mouth turned down into a pout.

How else will he learn if you don't teach him?

"You want to come with me, kid?" he asked, dumbfounded when the words rolled off his tongue.

"Me?" Seth squealed. Brown eyes, the color of dark chocolate, grew to twice their normal size. "You mean it?"

"I don't want you thinking we'll be making a habit of it, especially once planting season arrives."

The lad's back went straight as a trusty oak. "All right."

One day he'll be a man. Rocky gave his head a mental shake. "Come on then. We don't have all day."

At that, the boy pushed back his chair and leaped to his feet. "Yippee!" he yelped.

"Wait. Aren't you forgetting something?" he asked.

Confusion shaded the boy's expression and he stood stock-still. "Huh?"

Smothering a grin, he nodded from Seth to Sarah. "You best ask first if you may be excused."

"Oh, yeah." Seth looked at Sarah, impatience seeping from his very pores. "Can I go now?"

Her gentle laughter rippled through the air, putting Rocky in mind of a warm brook on an August afternoon. Swallowing hard, he shoved the annoying simile to the back of his head.

"Of course," she replied, her sparkling teeth gleaming. "I suppose Rachel and I can manage without you for the rest of the day. What do you think, Rachel?"

Rachel wore a hint of a smile, but chose not to respond, just gave a slow nod. Rocky took it as a sign of approval.

Well, what do you know? The girl was coming around.

The hard, cold earth refused to give under Rocky's weight as he and Seth trudged past the barn and other out-buildings just minutes later. The pair's hot breath formed puffy, white wisps of vapor as they hurried down the path, Rocky having to slow his steps for the eager five-year-old's smaller ones.

Hungry chickens in search of seed picked greedily at the dry, icy ground. "Go inside, ya dumb birds," Rocky mumbled at them. "There's plenty of food in your coop."

Seth giggled. "They're dumb, ain't they, Uncle Rocky?"

"Aren't they," Rocky corrected. "Don't say 'ain't.' And, yes, they are pretty stupid."

"Why do you gots 'em if they're so dumb?"

Rocky glanced down at Seth and found the boy's head turned toward him, his face filled with sincere curiosity. "I *have* them because they give us tasty eggs. 'Gots' is not a word, Seth."

"I don't like eggs."

Rocky repressed a grin. "So you've said. Well, you like to eat chicken, don't you?"

"I guess."

They walked up a steep incline, neither speaking again for the next several minutes, as they made their way to the first fence line needing repair. "We'll stop here," Rocky said, hauling his tool strap off his shoulder and bringing out what items he would need for repairing the fallen board.

Seth seemed to size up the damage to the fence. "How'd it get broke?"

"One of the cows kicked it last fall. I figure she was stung by a couple of wasps when she got curious about that nest down there."

Rocky pointed at the ground. Seth's eyes followed a path to the destroyed nest now lying deserted on the ground just under the fence. Obvious interest had the boy bending over it, his eyes filled with nervous excitement. "I never seen one before," he cried.

"Yeah? Well, look your fill. It's harmless now."

Seth immediately took the gray creation in with greedy eyes and, before Rocky could stop him, had his hands on the thing, gingerly picking it up. "Can I take it home and show Rachel? She never seen one neither."

"Is that a fact?" He'd known his sister Elizabeth had lived in the city with her two kids, but had she never taken them to the country? It seemed hard to believe that the boy had never laid eyes on a simple hornets' nest. "Suit yourself," he replied, hauling out his hammer and a handful of nails. While Seth scrutinized the nest inside and out, Rocky looked on.

Without warning, a picture of his son flashed across his mind. Joseph would have been five, not much different in size from Seth and certainly no less inquisitive about life. If he thought about it long enough, he could see similarities in the boys—the color of their hair and eyes, and, at times, even the sound of their voices. In fact, the resemblance was almost eerie, so much so that looking at Seth now made him ache inside.

"Put it down for now and hold this board for me."

The boy laid the worthless nest beside him and took the board Rocky handed him. It wasn't particularly heavy, but he huffed with all his might to hold it steady. "That's right," said Rocky. "Now hold it still while I put this nail in place."

The two worked companionably, Seth firing question after question at him, most pointless in nature. "Why is that board crooked?"; "How far over that hill does the fence go?"; "When will it be warm again?"; "Who lives in that house down there?"; "How strong are you?"; and the clincher, "Do you like Sarah?"

Rocky managed to answer each one but the last. That one he simply disregarded until Seth brought it up again. He might have known the scalawag wouldn't let it go.

"I suppose I like her," Rocky finally admitted.

"Sarah says she married you so she could take care of us."

"That's right."

"And she said God told her to do it."

"Yeah?" Rocky nudged the boy on the shoulder and urged him to a spot further down the hill, bee's nest tucked under an arm, where another repair job waited. The boy complied but kept up his chatter. Since when was he such a babbler? Not two weeks ago, Rocky'd been hard-pressed to get the lad to put two words together. Now all of a sudden he was spouting off about anything and everything.

God told her to marry him? Highly unlikely, but a nice thought anyway. Sarah's coming along when she did was a stroke of luck—nothing more. Of course, he didn't really believe in luck, but neither did he believe in divine intervention—at least not anymore. Perhaps he had at one time, but that was long ago, before he'd lost his Hester to a terrible disease and then, more recently, his beloved son.

Plain and simple, the notion that God had led Sarah to Little Hickman for the sole purpose of marrying him bordered on impossible.

Chapter Seven

*T*he days passed in steady succession. Sarah found herself falling into a routine of sorts, rising early to prepare breakfast and rouse the children. After breakfast, she and the children washed the dishes together, and then, while they tended to their assigned chores and Rocky headed for the barn, she scrubbed more floors and shelves and dusted and polished more furniture.

Never had she worked so hard or had the aching muscles to prove it. Even her once beautifully manicured nails showed signs of wear and tear. It seemed that every time she moved a chair away from a corner or a table from its long-held home, she discovered more dirt. It made her wonder what, if anything, her husband had done to keep the place clean once his wife had passed on. Had he counted on his elderly mother to tend to all his housekeeping chores?

Around-the-clock maids and hired cooks had been a way of life for Sarah, so taking to a broom and dust cloth didn't come naturally. Still, a keen sense of satisfaction filled her being at the end of each day when she at last fell atop her bed of straw. She was learning how to keep a tidy house, and, although it may have seemed an easy undertaking to some, it was a great accomplishment, to her way of thinking.

You'll never accustom yourself to this mud-hole town, Sarah. You've been pampered your entire life.

Stephen's words came back to sneer at her more than

107

once, usually when she found herself crouched on the floor or stretching for something on a high shelf. Usually she brushed the remembered criticism aside, but some days were tough, particularly since she'd received little affirmation from her husband. Most mornings he greeted her with half a smile and an occasional "Mornin'." She wanted to ask him how she was doing, but at the risk of rejection, she kept her mouth shut.

Another matter of distress was the children. They had been more than helpful with the chores, even eager, although neither one had smiled much since that first day. Sarah was beginning to wonder what it would take to draw them out of their cold, dark shells. Although Rocky had taken Seth with him the day he'd tended to the fence, he'd failed to invite him again, and the boy's disappointment was clear whenever Rocky set off for his afternoon duties.

Rachel, although seemingly willing to help around the house, quickly took her leave when her jobs were finished. She was an avid reader, but while Sarah was thrilled with her uncanny ability to decode even the most difficult words, it worried her that the child used her books as a means of escape.

Sarah had taken to her Bible like a starving child every morning before rising, desperate for promises from the Lord that would sustain her, keep her encouraged, and fill her with tidbits of wisdom as to how to help this dismal household. Today she'd read from the book of James a passage she'd long ago memorized. **"If any of you lack wisdom, let him ask of God, that giveth to all men liberally, and upbraideth not; and it shall be given him."** She'd certainly needed those words this morning and had drawn comfort from them. Now, however, some ten days into her marriage, as she watched a despondent seven-year-old bury her face in a volume of *Little Lord Fauntleroy*, her small frame curved into a rickety chair, she wondered what had happened to that dose of promised wisdom.

"Are you enjoying the book?" Sarah asked while washing a couple pairs of Seth's denim trousers, taking care not to speak too loudly since the youngster had crawled up on the couch next to the woodstove and fallen asleep. It appeared to be a lazy afternoon. Bitter winds blowing in from the west whistled around the little cabin, seeming to send out some kind of admonition.

Rachel looked up from her wobbly perch, her spindly legs tucked under her long dress, bare feet sticking out at the hem. Sarah made a mental note to fit the girl with some more new dresses. Her wardrobe was painfully meager in comparison to Sarah's, and the realization produced guilt in the pit of her stomach. How could she have let the matter go untended? It didn't take more than a few hours to stitch a simple dress. Maybe she would even fashion a few pairs of pants for Seth, even though it did seem his wardrobe wasn't nearly so scant.

"I like it fine," Rachel responded glumly.

Sarah left the soaking denims in the basin and crossed the room to where the girl sat. Once there, she hovered over her to peek at the book. It appeared she'd read nearly three-quarters of the novel already.

"You're an excellent reader, Rachel."

"My mama taught me even before I went to school."

Sarah noted a distant look creep across the child's face. She hadn't pushed the girl with regard to her deep loss, but then neither had she spoken of her own. Some nights, as she lay in

109

bed, the tears flowed freely from her own profound sorrow. She could only imagine the grief a mere child felt at the loss of a loved one. It must be akin to losing a part of one's soul.

"She was very smart to have exposed you to books at so early an age, but then you are very smart to have learned so quickly."

Rachel's expression turned even more introspective. "Mama always said I was smart. 'Course, so did Mrs. Riley."

"Mrs. Riley?"

"She was my second-grade teacher in Columbus, Ohio."

"I see. Is Columbus a large city?"

"I guess. We lived in a big building in the city, but we didn't go nowhere 'cause we was poor."

Sarah's heart lurched at the simple statement. "Was the school big where you attended?"

She nodded her head slowly. "There was an upstairs floor with lots more classrooms."

"It sounds like the school I attended in Winchester."

Rachel's eyes found hers. "Winchester?"

"Yes, it's where I grew up."

"Oh."

More quiet moments followed. "Do you miss your friends in Columbus?"

"I didn't have that many. Mama wouldn't let me visit no one. I do miss my school, though, and Mrs. Riley."

A tragic fire had destroyed Little Hickman's schoolhouse shortly after Sarah had arrived, forcing the town to cancel classes until the men of the village erected a new building. Talk was that the work would begin in the spring, provided sufficient funds came in. Already the townsfolk had held a bazaar to raise money, and more activities were in the works. Sarah intended to get involved in the efforts herself once she felt more settled.

"You will attend school here in the fall," she said, hoping to cheer the girl's spirits.

"I don't know none of the kids here."

"*Any* of the kids," she carefully corrected. Rachel was indeed intelligent, but it appeared her manner of expression needed improvement. "You will make friends easily once school starts. Perhaps you would enjoy meeting the Broughton girl. She is just about your age, I believe. We could drive over there one day soon if you like. Her stepmother has invited us to come anytime."

"What's her name?"

"Lili, I believe. Yes, Lili. Her parents attended our wedding festivities. You remember Mr. and Mrs. Broughton."

Rachel nodded. "I guess. My grandmother told me everyone's name, but I forgot."

Sarah smiled. "Everything has been so new for you. I imagine it's hard for both you and Seth to make such an adjustment."

At this, the girl stuck her head back in her book, so Sarah took this as a signal to change the direction of their conversation.

"Can you tell me about the book you're reading?" Sarah asked.

"I found it up there." Rachel pointed to the dozens of books tucked side by side on the bookshelf beside the fireplace. "Uncle Rocky has lots of books."

"I've noticed. I dusted behind every last one of them,

remember?" She recalled that Rocky's Bible appeared to have accumulated the most dust of any book there, and the realization had saddened her.

At last, the girl smiled, reluctantly. "And I helped."

"Yes, you did, and I appreciated it very much. Now, back to the book."

"It's about a poor little boy from New York named Cedric. His papa dies and it's very sad. But then he finds out that his grandfather in England is very rich, and so he moves there with his mama. His grandfather is very mean and grumpy, though, like Uncle Rocky. I think Cedric might become the king or something, but I haven't got that far in the book yet."

Sarah smiled at the simple description. "I remember the book, but I was much older than you when I read it."

Rachel's expression perked up. "Did you like it?"

"I enjoyed it a great deal."

"Did Ceddie become king of England?"

"Not exactly, but oh, I can't tell you how it ends, sweetie. That would spoil the whole book. You might not want to read it if you learned the ending ahead of time."

Rachel grew thoughtful again and her large blue eyes went misty. "Sometimes I wish I knew how things were gonna turn out ahead of time so I could be ready for them."

Sarah's heart turned over with Rachel's straightforward pronouncement. Such a carefully thought-out statement for a mere child.

"I think it's best that we don't know. Life would be much harder, I think. God knows all of our tomorrows, honey, and He wants us to trust Him."

"I believe in God. My mama taught me to love Him."

 112

"I'm glad to hear that."

Again, the child's eyes traveled back to the book, but it was apparent by the way she stared at the page that she wasn't truly reading.

"Well, I suppose I should finish washing Seth's trousers."

Just as Sarah headed toward the sink, Rocky came through the door, his face reddened from the cold, his wool cap pulled down low on his forehead, almost, but not quite, shielding his dark eyes.

Sarah checked the clock on the wall. It was mid-afternoon. "Are you finished early with your chores?" she asked, searching his expression for a hint of warmth, but finding none.

"Need to make a run into town for some supplies," he answered.

It'd been nearly a week and a half since Sarah had laid eyes on another human being besides Rocky and the children. The prospect of a trip into town on the buckboard, regardless of the cold, suddenly thrilled her. "Oh, may we come along?"

"I don't think it's a good idea. The weather is turning."

"I promise we won't be any trouble."

Just then, Seth started to wake up. He sat up and wiped his sleep-filled eyes. "Can we come, Uncle Rocky?"

"I didn't say you'd be any trouble," Rocky clarified, giving Sarah an impenetrable look. They'd spoken little over the past days, and Sarah thought him a difficult man to read. She'd never known anyone to be so somber. "It's the weather that worries me."

"But it'd be so nice to get out of the house," Sarah said, hating that she had to beg.

Now his blue eyes seemed to pierce straight through her.

"I guess you have been holed up here. I take it you're not used to seclusion."

Not knowing how to take the comment, she remained silent but hopeful.

"Well, I'm leaving in a few minutes. Can you all be ready?"

"Of course," she cried, finding it impossible to hide her excitement.

He walked across the room to the glowing fire. "Think I'll warm up a bit before I go out and hitch up the team. It's getting mighty cold out there. Everyone dress warm. Something seems to be brewing in the west. Storm clouds are moving in."

Sarah caught a glimpse of concern in his tone but chose to ignore it on the chance he might change his mind about allowing them to accompany him.

"Come on, Rachel," Seth squealed, running past his sister. "We gotta hurry an' get ready 'fore Uncle Rocky leaves us."

Rocky watched the lad scoot off the couch and run for his coat. A hint of a smile crossed his face, the kind that betrayed pleasure.

My goodness! Was he actually mellowing?

***

The four of them sat huddled together on the long seat atop the open buckboard. It was a cold, bumpy ride into town, but with the children squeezed in between Sarah and Rocky, Sarah occasionally grabbing hold of the side bar for security's sake, Rocky thought they managed quite well. Sarah had thrown a fleecy quilt over the children's laps and bundled them up from top to bottom so that little more than their eyes and noses saw the light of day. It was a far cry from the day Rocky had made the kids take the two-mile trek into town mittenless. He still felt haunted by Sarah's words of admonishment when she'd discovered what he'd done.

Out of the corner of one eye, Rocky studied his wife. A few curly locks of red hair had escaped her blue wool bonnet to blow in the wind and curl around the exposed part of her pale neck. He didn't doubt she was pretty enough to be pictured on the front cover of one of those newfangled ladies' magazines Hester used to drool over if ever they took an extended trip into Lexington and happened onto a bookstand.

How long before she announced her plans to leave Little Hickman? It wasn't that he wanted her to go, or even that he regretted marrying her, but how in the world could a man like him ever satisfy a woman of her caliber? It was clear she'd been pampered. Hadn't Stephen Alden, the cad from Boston, said so himself? Even the clothes she termed her "work clothing" looked too fine to wear around the house. He ought to offer her some of Hester's old dresses, although he doubted they would fit. Hester had not had the height or full curves his new wife possessed.

Icy winds whipped around the wagon like a tiger on the run, sending loose branches and dead leaves in every direction. A shiver ran the length of him when a clap of thunder sounded in the distance. He hadn't been warm since the day he married, his room in the barn offering little in the way of warmth or comfort. In fact, he wondered how much longer he could survive out there. What they needed was a bigger house. He yanked at his collar and stole a glance at the children and Sarah, huddled close together to ward off the worst of the elements.

"It's not much farther," he said into the wind, wondering if Sarah had heard the thunder.

"Fine," she answered. "It will be nice to see some different faces."

"You saying you're growing tired of us, Mrs. Callahan?" he asked, snapping the reins to step up the team's pace. The horses snorted in response but readily obeyed.

Sarah looked over Rachel and Seth's covered heads and caught Rocky's eye. "I certainly did not say that, Mr. Callahan," she retorted, her teasing tone mixed with tartness. If she'd heard the thunder, she didn't let on, and he wasn't about to bring it up, least of all let her see his growing concern. Experience had taught him how quickly the air currents could turn in these low-range mountains.

He turned his face into the driving wind and concentrated on steering the wagon toward town.

Their first stop was the post office. Although Rocky had wanted to make it a hasty one, before he'd had time to explain, all three of them piled off the wagon faster than a litter of frisky pups. He sat with gaping mouth and watched as one by one they dismounted. From the ground, Sarah stared at him. "Aren't you coming?"

He pulled the brake and looked at her. "I'm coming. It's just that I had no idea how anxious you all were to see the inside of the post office."

She threw back her head and giggled. "Right now, I'd be happy to see the inside of Madam Guttersnipe's Saloon—just see it, mind you."

He couldn't help but chuckle. The thought of her so much as going near the place made quite a picture in his head.

Madam Guttersnipe's Saloon was a place of disgrace, one that the majority of the townsfolk would just as soon see go up in flames.

Although he had to admit to imbibing more than once in some of his weaker moments, particularly after his son's passing, he'd since gotten a handle on that particular aspect of his life, having determined alcohol didn't mix well with his blood. Last fall he'd started home in a drunken stupor and gotten himself lost. It wasn't until nearly five in the morning that he discovered he'd traveled several miles off course. The horses had been exhausted from the bumpy, unfamiliar trail, but he'd fortunately found a portion of Little Hickman's winding creek, been forced to allow the horses to drink, and in the meantime, slept off the rest of his drunkenness on a riverbank. His behavior had appalled him, and so he determined then and there to cease with all drinking.

John Holden, Hickman's postmaster, greeted the four with a hearty smile.

"Well, if it ain't the Callahan family. Good to see ya'll in town, even though it's a might cold outside."

"Good afternoon, Mr. Holden," Sarah said, a smile accompanying her greeting. Rocky felt his back go stiff at the free use of the word *family*—as if they were a cozy bunch. He sneaked a look at Rachel and found the girl frowning heavily.

"Thanks, John. Any mail?" he asked.

The man put a finger to his chin. "Well, let's see here. I do believe there was a parcel fer yer missus."

"Oh?" Sarah asked, suddenly perking up at the news.

John left the counter and returned with a large package.

117

"What on earth?" she asked.

Rocky reached over the counter to retrieve the box wrapped in brown paper and addressed to Mrs. Sarah Callahan. He looked at the return address and frowned. Written neatly in the top left-hand corner was the name **Mr. Stephen Alden, Attorney at Law,** along with his return address.

The nasty little twit had sent his wife a package!

"Well, looks like your beau is having a hard time letting go of you," Rocky muttered.

"What does he mean, Sarah?" Rachel asked.

"Don't be silly," returned Sarah. "It's probably just some books I forgot to pack when I left Winchester." Then to Rachel, she added, "He doesn't mean anything, honey."

"Books?" Rachel asked as they headed toward the door. "What kind of books? Could I look at them?"

"Books?" Rocky echoed, opening the door with one hand while balancing the large box on the other. "This is more than books. Why would he be sending you books, anyway? As a matter of fact, why would he be sending you anything?"

"I don't know," said Sarah.

"Maybe there's a toy inside," Seth offered, his tone optimistic.

"That's stupid," Rachel told her brother, following him to the wagon. "Why would anyone send Sarah a toy?"

"Maybe they know she has a new little boy living with her," he answered in a manner that indicated it made all the sense in the world.

"Well, we'll find out soon enough, but for now we have errands to run with your uncle Rocky," said Sarah, her voice calm as could be. Then to Rocky, she said, "Shall we walk or get back on board?"

"We'll ride," he answered, shoving the box on the wagon's flatbed and coming around to where they stood. "I have several supplies to pick up at Johansson's Mercantile, and I intend to make a trip to the sawmill to check on some lumber prices if the weather holds out."

"Prices?" asked Sarah, curiosity apparent by the look in her glistening eyes, more blue than green today, probably due to the blue wool bonnet drawn over her burnished curls.

Rocky braced himself for what would come. "I plan to add a room to the back of the house so Rachel can have her privacy. She can't share a room with her brother forever."

Everyone stood stock-still except for Seth, who had hopped aboard the wagon in record time. Rocky offered a hand to Rachel so she could climb aboard the wagon, but all she did was stare at him with her bigger-than-life blue eyes.

Finally, Sarah broke the silence. "That's wonderful news, isn't it, Rachel?"

"Yes," the child managed. "I never had no room to myself before." With that, she placed her small mitten-covered hand in Rocky's and took the big step up to the wagon seat.

Rocky gave his wife a hurried look before offering her a hand up. The last thing he wanted or needed was oceans of praise. The house was small. He'd been intending to add onto it for some time anyway.

"Yippee, I get a room to myself, too!" Seth squealed with delight.

Rocky looked up at the lad. "Not so fast, fellow," he said, jogging around to his side of the wagon and pulling himself

119

up. "I'm moving in with you just as soon as I finish the add-on. It's too cold in that barn at night."

Seth's face dropped. "Why can't you move in with Sarah instead?"

It was an innocent enough question, Rocky supposed. After all, Sarah was his wife. Still, the awkward silence that followed signified the boy had succeeded in embarrassing them both, and Rocky was certain if the weather had been warmer, Sarah would have gone red on the spot. As it was, she sat ramrod straight and kept her face pointed straight ahead.

Surprisingly, it was Rachel who spoke. "That was a silly question, Seth. Uncle Rocky don't even like Sarah that much. Why would he move in with her?"

"I like her fine," Rocky corrected in haste, figuring he was only making matters worse by stepping in, but knowing it'd be worse to disregard the comment altogether. Finally, he shrugged. "Could we just drop the whole thing for now?"

"Yes, please," said Sarah, throwing him a silent plea over the children's heads.

He returned the helpless look. It was in that moment, as he began to lead the horses down Main Street toward Johansson's Mercantile, that another clap of thunder crashed through the clouds, closer now, and the freezing rain commenced.

The mercantile was scant with customers, most folks undoubtedly deciding it smart to stay put in their cozy cabins and frame homes. Rocky, in hindsight, wished he'd had the brains of the rest of the population of Little Hickman. Ice storms in Kentucky were nothing to wink at, and if this particular storm played itself out like most he'd seen, it would be a treacherous trip back to his farm.

 120

"We need a few supplies," he told Eldred Johansson while brushing cold wetness from his wool coat. The elder fellow hobbled to the counter.

"Surprised to see ya in this weather. What ken I get fer ya?"

"I'm needing a fresh box of nails and a new blade for my hacksaw." Out of the corner of one eye, he caught Sarah wandering the store, Rachel on her heels, and Seth in another aisle admiring a small jackknife. Had he not been so distracted by the darkening weather, he might have had it in his heart to buy each of them something. He pulled a list from his pocket and handed it to Eldred. "These are the remaining items. Can you work fast?"

Eldred looked down his spectacles at the wrinkled piece of paper and the scrawled list of words. "Well now, I'll do my best to gather 'em up," he muttered, turning around.

Just then, another piercing streak of lightning split the sky while a rumble of thunder cracked through the air, jolting the very floorboards. Eldred, arm up to procure a box of nails, turned on his heel. "What in tarnation? Don't know the last time we got thunder 'n' lightnin' in January."

Sarah gathered the kids close to her side and threw a worried glance at Rocky. He tried to reassure her with a hint of a smile.

"Can you hurry it up, Eldred?"

"I'm hurryin', I'm hurryin'," the elder man snapped. In truth, fast for him was similar to the speed of a tortoise.

Thanks to the large section of tarp that Eldred had loaned Rocky, the four of them remained relatively dry and safe on the trip back despite pelting bullets of freezing rain. They must have looked a sight with the canvas pulled over the lot of them, Rocky the only one with his face poking out to urge the unhappy team of horses on its way.

Rocky steered the horses over icy puddles. One slipped hoof could create terror with the animals, and he debated whether to pull the team to a stop and wait the storm out altogether. However, one glimpse of the nearly black sky overhead warned him of the dangers of stopping.

"Uncle Rocky, I'm scared," came Seth's muddled, weak voice.

Something in Rocky's heart flipped over, crumbled, then melted like butter at the simple admission, but he hadn't the time to ponder it. "You'll be okay," he said. "We'll all be fine in no time, you'll see."

"When will we get home?" This came from Rachel, who didn't sound much braver than her brother.

Rocky scouted the familiar road ahead. They still had a good mile to go. With the rain driving down in blinding torrents, it wouldn't be a fast trip, that was for sure.

"Shouldn't be long now," he answered, trying to maintain a positive tone.

All of a sudden, Sarah poked her head out from her end of the tarp and gave him a look he wished he could have captured with one of those new Kodak snapshot cameras he had yet to lay his hands on. Somewhere along the line, she'd removed that expensive blue hat of hers, and the sight of her wet, flaming-red hair framing large hazel eyes took him by surprise.

"What are you doing, woman? Get back under there," he ordered.

Her forehead furrowed in disbelief as she looked from him to the pelting sky.

"I wanted to see where we are," she shouted over the blustering winds that accompanied the driving rain.

"Well, as you can see, the rain is blinding and the sky is quite dark. Take cover before you turn into an icicle." Even as the rain fell, it froze where it hit, leaving a thick layering of ice on the wagon, the tarp, and the road ahead. Even his gloved hands had collected ice, making maneuvering the horses anything but a walk in the park.

"Where are we?" she demanded.

"Not far!" he returned.

"That doesn't tell me anything!" she retorted.

He took his eyes off the road ahead, trusting the horses to find their own way, and studied her, shocked to discover that for the first time in a long while, he wanted to laugh.

It wasn't that the situation was humorous. Far from it. If anything, it was perilous. Anything could happen. One misstep and a horse could slip, maybe even fall, creating panic in his teammate. Then what horrible fate would befall them? It was anyone's guess.

So why did he suddenly feel like laughing? It'd been a long while since he'd had the urge for a genuine laugh, and certainly now was not the appropriate time. Still, something in his wife's exasperated expression gave him pause. Maybe it was the fact that for all her wealth and finery, right now, at this particular moment, she was just an ordinary person, caught in a wretched storm, exposed to the elements, and showing her true colors. It reminded him of that first night when she'd had need of the outhouse and had balked when he'd insisted on walking her there. He'd filled her head with some ridiculous story about dangerous creatures hovering about, and she'd unwittingly drawn closer to him on the narrow, rutted path.

The simple recollection conjured up a smile, then fetched a chuckle that started down deep and moved straight up until it made its escape.

"Are you laughing?" Sarah asked, clearly indignant.

Her question, coming out on a high-pitched squeal, only made the situation worse for him. Once chuckling, he'd now worked himself up into a full-fledged laugh.

"Well, of all the..." But then her rejoinder ended with a half-smile, one he could see she was struggling to obliterate. She curled her lips under until they formed a straight line, but then what to do with her smiling, glistening eyes? It only made him laugh the more.

"What's so funny?" came Seth's loud question from under the heavy tarp.

"Did you tell a funny joke?" Rachel asked. "Tell us."

At this, Sarah opened her mouth in wonder and got a mouthful of glacial rain. The shocked look on her face when she clamped it shut again created more hilarity. There simply was no help for it.

It was the formidable clap of thunder and the bright band of lightning following that ended the jovial moment.

"Oh!" shrieked Sarah, and she immediately disappeared under the covering.

The laughter vanished as quickly as it came, and instant alertness replaced the moment of lighthearted optimism, as Rocky's eyes once more took to the road ahead.

 124

Chapter Eight

"Hurry, Sarah," Seth cried, rubbing his hands together, his excitement difficult to hide.

They'd made it safely home well over an hour before, and now, stomachs full from beef stew and biscuits, and dry clothing warming their chilled bodies, everyone, including Rocky, seemed eager to discover the contents of the mysterious wrapped parcel.

Sarah's fingers worked to loosen the strings that held the box together. When she came upon a difficult knot, Rocky stepped forward and, with his pocketknife in hand, sliced through the twine, freeing the entire carton. Sarah pulled the flaps apart at the top of the box and discovered an envelope lying atop a mass of newspaper. It was damp, but the heavy cardboard seemed to have protected the interior from the worst of the drenching rains.

"What is it?" Rachel asked.

"It's a letter—addressed to me," she answered, recognizing Stephen's fastidious script. She glanced across the room at Rocky.

"You want to read it in private?" Rocky asked.

"What's in the box, Sarah?" Seth asked, his tone revealing childish impatience.

"It's possible the letter explains the contents. Maybe you ought to read it before you see what's in there," Rocky said.

Something had happened to smooth down a portion of

her husband's coarseness, Sarah noted. She wondered how long it would take before that rough-edged exterior came back to rear its ugly head. He'd actually laughed on the ride home. Despite the fact she'd seen nothing entertaining about their miserable jaunt, it'd been nice to hear his carefree laughter, even if it was short-lived.

"You're right," Sarah said, clutching the letter between her fingers. "I'll read it first, but not privately. Stephen is a good friend. Whatever he's written will be perfectly fine to read aloud."

"Are you sure?" Rocky asked. "I met the man."

Sarah smiled and nodded. "He's really not such a bad person. He just comes off as very pigheaded at times."

"I'll say."

"We were very close growing up."

"But not close enough to marry?" Rocky asked, putting the question to her so that it sounded more like a challenge.

She ceased with fingering the envelope and looked across the room at him. "He was not the man I wanted to marry."

He could say little in recourse, so he merely watched her with keen eyes as she unfolded the missive and began to read aloud.

> *"My Dear Sarah,*
>
> *As you can probably envision, I put my trusty assistant to work and learned of your marriage to that Callahan fellow. I can't bring myself to say I am happy for you, but I will say I am confident you will make the most of a difficult situation. I still cannot quite imagine you as a farmer's wife.*
>
> *(Are you plowing fields, Sarah?)"*

She put the letter back and laughed aloud. "I'm not plowing fields yet. Will that be one of my jobs in the spring?" she asked her husband.

There was a spark of humor in his blue eyes. "Not unless I'm on my deathbed and the crops are withering," he answered. "Read on."

She picked the letter back up and continued where she'd left off.

"I should tell you I have proposed to Nancy Belmont, and she has accepted."

Sarah paused briefly to let that bit of information digest. He certainly hadn't wasted a minute of time. The way she figured it, he'd hightailed it to her place just after Sarah's refusal. Nancy, a sweet Christian and dear friend of Sarah's, had always been in love with Stephen despite the fact he'd never paid her much mind. Nancy came from old money, however, and since money always spoke to Stephen, Sarah suspected his reasons for proposing to her came because of Nancy's financial security. She could only pray the marriage would thrive and that God would awaken Stephen to his spiritual needs.

"We are planning a two-month honeymoon trip to Europe in May and June, after which she will settle in with me at our family home in Boston.

As I was cleaning out Mother and Father's house, I discovered these china dishes along with a note that I was to give them to you. Of course, Mother always thought that you and I would share them, but since that will not be the case, I am sure she would still want you to have them. Mother said you always commented on the lovely blue pattern, and

so I thought the set would serve as a fine wedding gift. I am including the silver dinnerware as my gift to you. I hope you will accept them with my best wishes.

I know we did not part on the best of terms, Sarah. Perhaps when the day comes that you wish to retrieve your inherita—"

Sarah stopped there and folded the letter. "I think perhaps I will finish the rest later. It's getting rather tiresome anyway. Shall we look at the dishes?" she asked.

"Is that all there is then, dishes and spoons and forks?" Seth asked, disappointment clearly present in his voice.

"I'm afraid so, Seth," Sarah answered, tousling the top of his head.

"I want to see them," Rachel urged. "They sound pretty."

Sarah purposely avoided Rocky's vigilant eyes, noting his stance hadn't changed. If anything, he'd grown stiffer, more stern-faced.

Indeed, the china dishes were as she remembered them: eighteenth-century blue and white Delft dishes imported straight from the Netherlands. Rachel released a sigh when Sarah carefully retrieved one of the plates wrapped in newsprint and handed it over for her perusal.

"I never saw dishes so pretty," Rachel whispered, laying the dish on the table to finger its delicate pattern. "My mama was too poor for dishes this beautiful." A wistful notion passed through Sarah's head that one day she might will these very dishes to Rachel.

"Yes, they are lovely. I did comment on them frequently, but goodness, I didn't expect Mrs. Alden would one day give them to me. We used to eat on them when our families shared meals together."

"Which was often?" asked Rocky, stepping closer to eye the dishes for himself.

Sarah looked at him. "Not as often as you might think. Holidays and special occasions, mostly. Both our mothers were involved in charitable organizations and societal events, which took up a good share of their time. They were the best of friends, Stephen's mother and Mama.

"Neither of our fathers was home much, what with all their business travel. Papa died some eight years ago, leaving only Mama and myself. The two of us joined the Aldens more frequently after that. Stephen's parents both perished in a train crash two years ago. It was most tragic." Sarah felt herself give way to a huge sigh. "Then, once Mama took ill, well, things changed even more drastically."

Since the topic had turned introspective, Sarah took to unwrapping the rest of the dishes, finally digging her way to the bottom of the box where she found the lovely silver dinner service.

"Oh my," she gasped, pulling out a beautiful knife and stroking the smooth floral design. "Aren't these nice?"

Rachel reached inside the box and took out a long, polished fork. Even Seth dug out a silver piece for purposes of studying it more closely.

"Too nice to use," Rocky muttered, looking around the kitchen and then the rest of the house.

"We'll use them every single day," Sarah declared, standing taller. "Silver tarnishes with lack of use. No point in allowing that to happen."

"This is not a big city where folks much care what your eating utensils look like, Sarah; it's Little Hickman, Kentucky.

And what we already have will work just fine. In case you haven't noticed, this rustic house wasn't made for china and silver." Now his voice took on a harsher tone, gaining everyone's attention. "If it is high society you want, perhaps you should go back to Boston."

"What?" Hurt, Sarah looked at Rocky and prayed a hasty prayer for patience and wisdom. "Of course, Winchester is nothing like Little Hickman, but that doesn't mean I don't like it here. And your house—it's comfortable and cozy."

Rocky laughed, but it wasn't the carefree laughter of before; no, this held a note of disparagement, even disdain. A snide reminder of their differences. "Comfortable and cozy?" His eyes swept the place once more. "Are you serious?"

She ignored his pointed question. "And once you add another room to the house for Rachel, it will be even more spacious."

He dipped his head slightly and gave her a probing look. "I don't understand you." That said, he turned on his heel and headed for the door.

"What do you mean? Where are you going?" she asked, frustrated by his change in mood.

He threw on his coat and hat. "I have to tend to the animals. I expect you'll all be in bed by the time I come back."

And that was half true. The children were sound asleep two hours later when he finally returned. Sarah, however, had chosen to await her husband's return by sitting in front of the fire, feet curled under her, Bible resting on her lap.

***

She had dimmed all the lights except for the lone kerosene lamp atop the sofa stand, and so the only thing Rocky saw when he first entered was the myriad of shadows skipping across the plaster ceiling.

"Can we talk?" she said, her voice quiet but strong, her oval face turned in his direction. The light from the lamp cast a glow upon her porcelain countenance, and he thought her quite beautiful. Yes, he imagined she did have words for him.

He'd been harsh with her before he'd left, but when she'd opened the box filled with china and silver from that Alden character, something in his stomach had knotted. Whether it had come from resentment or just plain jealousy, he couldn't say. He only knew he didn't want to eat off any of those blasted blue plates or put one of those dopey silver spoons to his mouth. He didn't mix with fine things. Sweet heaven, he didn't even mix with his own wife. The two of them were like oil to water, dirt to diamonds.

Sarah wasn't suited for the hills of Kentucky. Although she'd done a fine job of keeping house and lessening his load with the children, he couldn't imagine what motivated her to do it. As far as he could tell, she'd had everything she'd ever needed in the *charming* little town of Winchester, except for the fact that both her parents had passed on. But surely she had friends to whom she could turn.

At least, she had plenty of money. He hadn't missed the mention of an inheritance, even though she'd nearly choked on the word when she'd read it aloud from Alden's letter. Well, he'd make sure that she knew he never wanted one red cent of her wealth. In fact, he'd make it plain that he was ready to grant her an annulment. After all, there was nothing to keep them together—unless one counted the sacred vows they'd both spoken some ten or so days ago.

Rocky kicked off his boots, hung up his coat and hat, and walked to the fire to warm himself, aware that his wife watched him from the most comfortable piece of furniture he owned—a big, overstuffed chair of soft fabric, something his parents had given Hester and him as a wedding gift. Much as he hated to admit it, she did make a fetching sight, feet tucked beneath her, long hair falling in gentle waves about her face.

He found a place on the sofa situated perpendicular to her chair and plopped into it. "Say your piece," he murmured.

"My piece?" she asked, taken aback.

"You said you wanted to talk to me."

"Yes. Is it still raining?" she asked.

He doubted she wanted to talk about the weather, but he supposed it was as good a starting point as any. "It's more like a mist now, but it's still freezing. There's a thick layer of ice on the path leading out to the barn. Did you manage to make it to the outhouse with the kids?"

"I allowed them to use the chamber pot," she said, dipping her face at the mere mention of the word. He gave an inward smile at her sense of propriety.

"You may do the same if you like. I'll take care of it later."

Now she really went red as she squirmed in her chair. "Thank you," she whispered.

Settling into the sofa, he readied himself for a lecture. After all, she'd had two hours to prepare one. "What else did you have a mind to say to me? I know I left the house in a huff."

"Yes, you did. I decided you were upset because Stephen sent me a gift. Am I right?"

He felt like a weasel, but admitting it was something else

 132

altogether. "I don't like the guy."

"You should know he didn't mean to offend you with the gifts. In fact, he intended them for both of us."

"Well, I don't make a habit of eating off china. The flatware and plain dishes that Hester and I had should suffice just fine when it comes to our mealtimes."

"And what if I choose to use the others?"

Uncalled-for stubbornness swam to the surface. "It makes no nevermind to me what you and the kids choose to do, but as for me, I'll use the old stuff."

She shrugged her slender shoulders. "Let me know if you ever change your mind."

"Fine," he answered. "Anything else?"

A hint of a smile played around her full mouth, and he had to confess to being the one squirming now. Somehow, his rough-hewn nature just didn't mesh with her polished sophistication, and over the past week, he'd decided they had little in common. What was there to talk about with such a woman?

"Whether you choose to believe it or not, Rocky, I do like it here. The peace and quiet of the hillside, the glorious sunrises, the sight of a distant deer roaming just past that rise over there. I glimpsed one the other morning as I was washing the breakfast dishes. Oh, it was a sight to behold." Her large eyes went damp with emotion, and his heart stirred, not so much from her account as from the fact that she'd used his first name. "And the children are wonderful. I think they're slowly coming out of their shells."

He had to confess he'd seen a change in them, more so in Seth than in Rachel, of course, but even small steps seemed an accomplishment. He knew it was all due to Sarah's efforts.

"You've done a great job with them, Sarah." Unfortunately, he'd been stingy with compliments.

She inclined her head in a gesture of gratitude. "It wouldn't hurt for you to include them more, you know. Seth was thrilled the day you took him along to mend the fences. What if you offered again, and maybe invited Rachel to come, too?"

Sliding forward on the sofa, he clasped his hands together and let them fall between his parted legs. He'd enjoyed that day with Seth more than she knew. But looking at the kid was too much like looking into the eyes of his own boy. And now she wanted him to cozy up to Rachel as well? It was too much to ask right now. The pain of losing Joseph still burned a hole through his heart.

"I know they care for you," she urged in nothing more than a whisper.

"They came at a bad time in my life," he muttered, hating his own coldness.

Tilting her head, she gave it a negative shake. "When is a good time for children to lose their mother?"

It wasn't a fair question. He knew Elizabeth's passing had created unfathomable grief for Rachel and Seth. Shoot, even he felt the sting of her absence, although as siblings they'd never been especially close.

"I know they're hurting, all right? But I'm a busy man. It's hard for me to make time for them."

"But they're your family. They need you."

He leaned back in the sofa to rest his head and study the ceiling. A pounding ache had formed at his temples. "You've taken on quite a project with us, haven't you, Sarah?"

"Project?"

He pulled his head up temporarily to look at her. "Isn't that why you agreed to marry me? Some notion about obeying God's call?"

Her eyes sought his, so he lay back once more to avoid looking into their emerald depths, clasping his hands behind his head and staring at the ceiling.

"It wasn't a notion. It was something I sensed clear to my toes. Haven't you ever felt something so intensely that it was impossible to ignore? What began as a tiny seed of hope in my heart expanded into fervent passion. I simply knew that God had great and wondrous things in store for me, things that required much faith."

Rocky stretched his legs out in silence, prepared to hear her out.

"Before my mother took ill, I signed on as a mail-order bride. I loved the idea of Kentucky when I read Benjamin Broughton's response to my ad. It sounded like such an adventure. Of course, his being a Christian made it all seem so right."

"But you wound up with me," he said in jest, imagining a hint of a smile on her pretty lips. "Why didn't you just marry someone from your hometown?"

He felt her eyes on him and heard a round of feminine laughter. "I am almost twenty-eight years old, Rocky. Every Christian man I knew was either engaged or already married and raising his third or fourth child. I'm afraid most men assumed I intended to marry Stephen Alden, and so they thought me ineligible. I know our parents certainly wanted it. But God had other plans for me."

"So you enlisted in this marriage agency to find yourself a man," he said, lifting his head to catch another look at her.

135

"A *Christian* man," she put in.

"Then why marry me?"

She raised her chin. "Because of something you said. It stayed with me for days afterward."

"What was that?"

"You said you once called yourself a Christian...but that circumstances had changed you. I know that God is not finished with you, Rocky Callahan."

He felt his brow wrinkle in confusion. "You actually think God wanted *you* to marry *me*?" The very suggestion seemed ludicrous to Rocky. God wasn't about to give him any special treatment these days. He'd certainly been anything but obedient to Him.

"Every time I prayed about my future, God always seemed to remind me of that ad I'd seen posted in the city newspaper by the Marriage Made in Heaven Agency."

Rocky chuckled. *"Marriage Made in Heaven?* With a name like that, I'd have run the other way, Sarah. It sounds risky, if you ask me, a fly-by-night operation."

She threw up her hand to cover her mouth and smother her giggles. "They *did* go out of business not long after I signed up with them. That's why Benjamin Broughton never could reach me to tell me he'd had a change of plans."

Rocky's own laughter floated up from his throat, and so they shared in the lighthearted moment.

He figured he should be thankful for the mix-up, the agency folding before they could notify her. After all, it'd afforded him the opportunity to propose marriage to her instead. And he *had* needed a wife—desperately. Still, he wondered if it wasn't Sarah who was getting the short end of the stick. He was no match for her, never would be.

"Sorry about Ben breaking your heart."

She shook her head. "He didn't break my heart at all." She gave him a long, hard look. "Sometimes we think we have God all figured out when, in actuality, He just gives us little glimpses and nudges of the direction He wants us to go in, leading us there one step at a time. He got me to Kentucky, and that was the main thing."

Rocky nodded, and for the next several minutes they sat in companionable silence, watching the fire lose steam and listening to the sizzling, crackling embers that formed from a dying log.

At last, Rocky spoke, his voice hoarse. "Life on the farm is not easy, Sarah. Come spring, it will get even harder, particularly when planting season arrives. Maybe you should think about..."

Sarah sat straighter. "I can handle it."

He'd wanted to offer her an easy out, but she'd quickly cut him off at the pass. "If you say so," he said. But even as he muttered the words, he found it hard to believe that someone so delicate might soon have to muck stalls, feed the chickens, and milk the cows because he'd be fighting against the clock to meet planting deadlines. Hester had thought nothing of it. She'd been made of tough stuff, though. Her own family were farmers from way back.

Sarah played with the hem of her robe, her feet still tucked beneath her lean frame. "What did you mean earlier when you said you didn't understand me?" Her voice seemed clogged.

He swallowed and shrugged. "Nothing in particular. You're just different."

All of a sudden, she modified her position, drawing her knees up and hugging them close to her. "What do you mean, different?"

He yawned and stretched before dragging his two-hundred-pound frame to a standing position. "Could we talk another time, Sarah?" The woman made him nervous with her questions, made him worry that he might divulge his true feelings—that he didn't think she was cut out for living the hard life, that when the going got tough she would run as fast as she could back to her comfortable lifestyle.

How could he tell her without hurting her that he regretted this marriage? That he wished he'd never dragged her into such an arrangement?

Slanting her head to one side, she gave him a probing glance, as if to read him. "All right, then."

He inspected the room. "If you don't mind, I think I'll bed down on the sofa."

"It's probably a good idea on such a nasty night."

He actually planned to make the sofa his bed from now on until he finished the extra room. It was foolish to sleep in a freezing barn when he could be curled up next to a warm hearth. Besides, now he could tend to the fire and keep it blazing all night.

"Good night, Sarah."

"Good night." Although he might have lent her a hand while she unwrapped her legs and stood up, he clasped his hands tight together at his back, afraid that touching her might ignite some deadly spark.

Sarah would not be here forever. Best he not grow used to her.

***

Sunday morning came in a veil of blackness.

Sarah scrambled out of bed, shivering mightily when her bare feet hit the cold wood floor. The first thing she did was run to the window to peer outside. Had the ground thawed, or did the earth still lie under a coverlet of ice? It was difficult to tell with the absence of a moon.

She'd so wanted to attend Sunday services, even though she hadn't broached the subject with Rocky. It would be wonderful to see folks, even more delightful just to gather with other believers. Well, if the weather conditions prevented them from attending this week, she decided, they would simply hold a private service right in their very own living room, with songs, Bible reading, and prayer. In fact, she'd already prepared the entire ceremony in her head. Oh, it would be the perfect time for gathering together to sing and praise God—whether Rocky approved or not.

Sensing an immediate need for the privy and not wanting to use the chamber pot again, Sarah donned her warm robe and slippers.

Relief set in when she opened the door to the living room and discovered Rocky nowhere about. His blankets were folded and stacked at one end of the sofa and a low flame flickered in the lantern, and Sarah determined he must have headed for the barn. A roaring fire seemed to bid her a cheery welcome, its warmth filtering through the house.

She opened the back door and grimaced when she saw the glossy covering of ice and felt the rush of frosty air as it drove through her lungs and straight down her body. Everywhere she looked, freezing rain had left its mark. Tree branches, once spry and resilient, now sagged nearly to the ground, while others had given way to the extra weight and broken off to lie sprawled about the yard.

It was deadly quiet, save an occasional snapping of a distant twig or the faraway hoot of a sheltered owl. A hint of daybreak rose in the eastern skies, a tinge of orange and pink filtering through low-lying clouds. Sarah shivered and yanked her wrap more snugly about her before heading down the narrow path toward the outdoor facility, anxious to be done so she could begin breakfast before the children awakened.

While measuring each step with care, she scolded herself for not having brought the lantern. Not only was the path dimly lit, it was precarious at best. Therefore, she should not have been surprised when her smooth-soled slippers sent her legs in two different directions like some kind of bungling acrobat. Flailing arms could not restore her balance, and so it was that she found herself falling rearward. She flopped on her backside, stunned and appalled.

Unexpected pain soared through the back of her head, which she'd hit the hardest, starting at the base of her skull and steadily climbing like a noxious spider creeping along, intent on reaching its prey.

Dazed and uncertain, she sought to lift herself. Failing in her attempt, she lay back and fought down fear and nausea.

As unexplained drowsiness set in, she listened to her own voice mutter a whispered plea. "Dear God, please help me."

Chapter Nine

"Will she be all right, Uncle Rocky?" asked Seth for at least the tenth time that afternoon.

"She'll be fine," Rocky assured, pitching another forkful of manure into the wagon, his second wagonload that day. "But it will take some time. Doc Randolph says she has a concussion."

"What's that?"

"I've already told you half a dozen times."

"I forget."

Rocky bit his lip to keep from smiling. Or maybe it was to bite back a frown. The boy was driving him crazy with his questions. Truth was, he'd almost gone crazy himself when he'd discovered Sarah lying flat out on the ground on his way back from the privy earlier that morning.

When she hadn't responded to her name, he'd panicked. She'd looked so lifeless lying there in a heap in the middle of the path, all arms and legs. Relief had come quickly, however, when he'd swept her up to carry her into the house and heard her mumble, "I can walk just fine."

She couldn't, of course, and she'd been in no position to argue at that point.

He'd laid her on her bed, raced into Seth and Rachel's room, and, after waking Rachel, instructed her to watch over Sarah until he returned. Then he'd ridden Sparky, his pinto, to Doc's office faster than a brakeless locomotive going down-hill, despite the icy conditions.

He'd kicked himself for not having insisted the night before that she wait for him to walk her out in the morning—or at the very least use the chamber pot. Of course, discussing such things with his wife was nearly impossible. She went red as a cherry every time he so much as mentioned the words *chamber pot*. He suspected she'd never used one before she'd come to Little Hickman. Boston and most big cities in the East had introduced indoor plumbing some time ago, and with her sup-posed wealth, he suspected she'd had more than one indoor commode in her New England house.

"What's a—con-concoction again?" asked Seth, stumbling on the word, and then still getting it wrong.

"Concussion," Rocky corrected, grinning in spite of him-self. "Doc says it's like an injury to the brain."

"Injury?"

"Her brain has been hurt. But not so bad that it won't heal with time. She will have a headache, and maybe feel tired for a few days, but then she'll start getting stronger."

"Oh." The boy seemed temporarily satisfied. "Ain't it time to check on her again?"

Seth leaned his small frame against the stall gate, looking every bit the little man, worried frown and all. He had been Rocky's ever-present shadow that whole day since Sarah's fall. Rocky supposed the lad was dealing with some insecurity, and he couldn't really fault him for it. To date, every adult he'd loved (save his grandparents) had deserted him in one way or another. Guilt stabbed Rocky square in the chest when he real-ized he'd probably contributed to the kid's lack of confidence.

"Don't say *ain't*, Seth, and no, it's not time. We just checked on her half an hour ago."

When last they'd entered the house, Rachel had been sitting beside the sleeping Sarah, her face buried in a book...*Little Lord Fauntleroy*. She'd lifted her face long enough to scowl and give them both the shushing sign. Rocky figured the girl had learned plenty about nursing when her mother had fallen ill, and for the first time, he viewed her through different eyes. At seven years old, she was already accustomed to tending and protecting, and something about that revelation disturbed him.

"But Doc says we hafta keep wakin' her up," Seth argued.

"Rachel is with her right now, and we don't have to wake her up for a while yet."

"Why do we hafta keep wakin' her up?"

"I've explained that. Doc Randolph wants us to keep an eye on her condition. Waking her every so often is the best way to tell if she is coherent."

"Co-what?"

"Never mind," he answered, tossing a forkful of muck into the wagon before glancing at the boy. "Doc said she can sleep for a few hours at a time, so try not to worry, okay?"

"Who's gonna check on her in the middle of the night?" Seth asked, ignoring Rocky's offer of consolation.

Rocky sighed. "I suspect I will. Now, why don't you run in the house and see if Rachel needs anything. But be quiet while you're at it."

It was his secret ploy to get the boy's mind on something else—and out of his own hair. He'd accomplished precious little with the kid on his tail all day. Normally, there wasn't that much to do on Sunday afternoons, but he still had to tend

143

to the usual chores, milk the cows, gather eggs, and feed and water the animals. Seth's constant shadow had kept him from even accomplishing these most mundane tasks.

"Okay, but what if Sarah's awake?"

"Well, then, I expect she'll be wanting to visit with you," Rocky assured.

"Yippee!" Seth yowled, making a beeline for the house.

"Keep the noise down!" Rocky called after him, doubting that he'd even heard the order the way his short, spry legs sent him sailing out of the barn.

Rocky shook his head and resumed mucking out the last stall of the day.

***

Sarah couldn't believe her predicament. While Rocky and Rachel cleaned up the supper dishes, Seth delivering more dishes to the sink, she was helpless to do much more than fight down drowsiness and watch from her reclined position on the sofa.

Although it felt as if someone had split her head into two matching pieces with a razor-sharp hatchet, she wished to goodness she could get off this lumpy couch. After all, Rocky had married her for purposes of taking over the household chores. It was part of their *arrangement*. What must he think to find himself back in the kitchen again, tending to mundane chores, not to mention tending to her? Was he upset with the situation, perhaps even angry with her for her carelessness? He'd said few words to her all day long, unless one counted the number of times he had asked her what day it was, where she was, and if she could remember what had happened. However, when he'd asked her if she knew her own name, it was the final straw.

"I fell on the ice, Mr. Callahan; I did not fall off my rocker!"

He'd awarded her a slanted grin, skimpy as it was, and answered, "No need for crankiness, Mrs. Callahan. I'm just following Doc's orders."

She hadn't intended to be snappish, but her deplorable situation seemed to warrant it.

More than once, she'd held her aching head, touched the tender bulge at the back of her skull, and asked God to show her His purposes for allowing the accident. The only verse that came to mind all through the day, however, was a portion of one from 1 Peter, "**Humble yourselves therefore under the mighty hand of God, that he may exalt you in due time,**" and she couldn't figure out for the life of her what that had to do with anything. She decided she was already quite humbled if she considered her ill-timed circumstances. Did God really find it necessary to remind her? She'd wanted to gather in the living room that day for *church*. What possible good could come from missing that opportunity?

"Well, that's done," mumbled Rocky some time later, jarring Sarah out of another momentary slumber. "How are you feeling, Sarah?" he asked, laying a towel down and moving across the room to drop into a nearby chair, Rachel and Seth tucking their feet under them on the floor beside her. Everyone looked particularly drained, and Sarah felt responsible.

"Tired," she replied, "and helpless."

Rocky managed half a smile. "Well, there's no help for that. Doc says you're to stay in bed for at least three days."

"But that's ridiculous," she answered, grabbing her head when the sound of her own voice ripped at her nerve endings.

"I can help, Sarah," Rachel said, her diminutive voice holding undue authority, her small palm coming up to pat Sarah on the arm. "You have to obey Doc's orders if you want to get well."

Sarah blinked, awed by the girl's maturity. "I appreciate that, Rachel, but I won't have you doing all the work."

"I'll help, too, and Uncle Rocky says we can all pitch in with the housework."

Warmed, Sarah focused tired eyes on Rocky. "Did you say that?"

He broke into a leisurely smile. "I did, but just so you know, we'll be anxious to see you back on your feet. It was a bit of a letdown to have to abide my cooking again."

She managed a tremulous smile. "I thought the biscuits were—were…"

"They was kinda hard," Seth put in. "And burnt."

"Seth!" Sarah scolded.

When she looked at Rocky, he was laughing. "He speaks the truth," he said.

Sarah bit her lip and covered her mouth with the corner of her blanket. "Well, the salt pork was—tasty—and the cheese…" What could she say about the cheese?

The room went still until Rachel giggled. "Uncle Rocky found a block of cheese in the back shed. He had to cut off a big hunk of mold. It sure stank up the place!"

Rocky threw the girl a frenzied look. "You didn't have to mention that."

Under normal circumstances, Sarah wouldn't have laughed and the throbbing pain in her head warned her against undue movement, but there was no help for it. Something about his pathetic expression humored her, flat-out enchanted her. What started out as stern restraint transformed into a flicker of mirth, then outright laugher, bubbling up from down deep, uncontrolled and urgent.

Rocky stared, as did the children, and the more they studied her outburst, the more she giggled. Finally, a flash of humor sneaked across Rocky's face, setting off a rippling effect of laughter from Seth and Rachel, which must have amused Rocky the more.

At first, his laugh was low and throaty, as if he meant to hold it back. But as the merriment continued, his laughter deepened, reverberating off the walls of the little Kentucky cabin and blending with the others' mirth to create some kind of exquisite harmony.

Sarah didn't know what to make of it. She was thrilled to hear her husband laugh with such freedom, not to mention the children, and it struck her that she wished the moment could go on forever despite the pounding ache of her head.

Yet, just as all good things must end, this too finished— Rocky cleared his throat and stood, an instant of wistfulness stealing into his expression but quickly being replaced by inex- plicable withdrawal. "I best go check on the animals," he said. The abrupt manner in which he strode across the room and threw on his jacket told her he had emptied himself of his good-natured humor.

***

Hours later, Rocky lay sprawled on the lumpy couch, staring at the plaster ceiling, tossing and turning to avoid the loose spring that insisted on poking his backside.

He knew without checking it was well past midnight. Unable to sleep, he yanked a corner of the blanket up and over his exposed shoulder. Sarah's scent wafted past his nostrils with the simple movement. She'd used the same blanket today, he reminded himself, rubbing its downy edge under his nose once more for good measure.

"Don't be stupid," he muttered aloud, disgusted with the direction his mind had taken him. She was his wife, yes, but in name only. He'd do well to remember that.

He told himself again she wouldn't outlast spring planting, particularly after today. He could see she wasn't accustomed to inconvenience by the way she'd grumped at him off and on. She was probably used to having house cleaners, nursemaids, and butlers at her disposal. Well, lying on a lump-ridden couch all day with no one to tend to her but a five- and seven-year-old had undoubtedly soured her to the hassles of rural living. Of course, he'd checked on her as often as possible, but the usual farm chores had kept him from seeing to her every need.

He went over the events of the day—waking her every few hours; reheating a kettle of chicken soup for lunch, of which she'd only taken a few spoonfuls; helping her to her bedroom twice so she could see to her personal needs; then seeing her back to the couch, where she'd insisted on remaining. He knew it mortified her that he'd stood outside her bedroom door—waiting, listening—while she went about her business, but he'd be hogtied before he'd let her walk any distance on her own until her dizzy spells passed. Doc Randolph said she would be feeling poorly for several days if he were to judge the length of her recovery by the size of the knot on the back of her head. Yes, after today she'd be more than ready to head back East, where all the luxuries of private nursing lay at her fingertips.

He must have finally dozed, for it wasn't until close to two in the morning that he heard a shuffle in Sarah's room, something like a heavy book or lamp hitting the floor, and then a whimper or a moan.

In less than a second, his feet hit the floor. He passed a hand over his scruffy face to get his bearings, making sure he hadn't been dreaming, and made a beeline for Sarah's room, forgetting his trousers altogether. After giving a gentle knock and getting no answer, he flung wide the door. There she was, sprawled on the floor, reaching for the side of the bed, her ruby tresses falling across her face, her nightgown creeping up to reveal two shapely legs.

"What happened?" he asked, bending over her to help her to her feet.

"I'm sorry to be such a nuisance," she replied, taking the hand he offered and allowing him to lead her back to the bed. "I thought I could manage to walk out to the privy, but...I'm suddenly so dizzy." She sat down and mopped her moist forehead with a trembling hand. "I guess I lost my balance."

"Are you all right?" he asked, fearful that she'd hurt herself.

"I'm fine."

"What exactly did you think you were doing, young lady?"

His voice came off sounding harsh, but she'd scared him plenty.

Her shoulders sagged in quiet resignation as she gave way to a shaky sigh. "I just wanted to go to the…you know."

"Outhouse," he finished, biting back a grin, relieved to see she was okay, just shaken.

She gave a resolute nod. "I'm such a bother," she blurted.

"Sarah…" He dropped down beside her and felt the poke and jab of the old straw mattress, smelled the musky dampness of the plaster walls. He'd never minded the mattress when he slept on it, but somehow it didn't seem right that Sarah should have to lie on it. Raw, primitive emotion tugged at his soul, its edges sharp and jagged, as a stab of guilt hit him square in the chest.

Without thinking, he put an arm around her shoulder. It was the first time he'd actually touched her in any way but casual. Even the hasty wedding kiss he'd planted on her lips had lacked true sentiment. "You're not a bother," he said, hearing the quake in his own voice. "I'm sorry if I've given you the impression that you are."

A choked, desperate sigh escaped her throat. "But look at the trouble I've caused you. You haven't even gotten a good night's sleep since I arrived. And now you've had to go back to making the meals."

"You're not complaining about my cooking, are you?" he teased.

She glanced sideways in surprise, her warm breath touching his cheeks. "No."

"Well, then, you should just try to relax and do as the doctor says, take it easy for the next few days. Everything will work out fine." For the life of him, he couldn't figure out what had just come over him. He hadn't been this reasonable since—well, he couldn't remember when.

The tension in her shoulders loosened as he coaxed her closer, and when she rested her head in the hollow of his neck, he found himself drinking in the comfort of her nearness, enjoying her softness far more than was right.

And if he didn't watch himself, he might be tempted to kiss her.

"Are you ready for me to help you out to the privy?" he suddenly asked, recalling her motive for getting out of bed. "The ice has melted, but I insist on walking you there just the same."

She took a quick, sharp breath and pulled herself away from him. To his dismay, the place where she'd rested herself felt vacant and unreasonably cold. "I don't care what the doctor says," she declared, "I'm not going to waste my time lying on that couch—not when there's work to be done."

Just like that, she stood up, took a moment to steady herself, and began walking to the door. He jumped up beside her and took her arm.

Stubborn woman, he told himself.

***

The next morning Sarah felt considerably better despite the continued dizziness that forced her back to the couch. The headache had dwindled to a dull ache, which Rocky had insisted would worsen if she overexerted herself. Apparently, he'd felt it his duty to lecture her all through breakfast on the rash statement she'd made the night before about not following the doctor's exact orders.

Sarah had smiled to herself, toying with the notion that maybe Rocky was beginning to care for her. But when he disappeared to the barn after the breakfast cleanup, and then galloped away on his horse sometime later with no word as to where he was heading, she tossed the foolish thought out the window.

"Want me to read to you, Sarah?" Rachel asked at mid-morning.

"I would like nothing more," Sarah said. Her head had started throbbing again, but she thought the diversion might do her good.

"Can I listen, too?" Seth asked from his place on the floor.

"Of course!" Sarah answered. He'd been lining up a collection of "soldiers"—the toy Sarah had given him, along with various sticks and rocks—on the floor and forcing them into numerous battles and shootouts. She decided a diversion would be good for him as well.

"What should I read?" asked Rachel. "I've already finished *Little Lord Fauntleroy*."

"Would you read from my Bible?"

Knowing what a good reader Rachel was, Sarah felt certain she could easily read any passage.

"Sure." Rachel reached for the Bible Sarah handed her and snuggled her back to the couch, stocking-covered feet stretched toward the fire. Seth crawled over beside her, taking a corner of Sarah's blanket to cover up with, and the three of them nestled in together.

After Rachel had read the first three chapters of Matthew with nary a blunder, she paused and looked at Sarah. "Seth's asleep," she whispered.

Sarah smiled. "You're a splendid reader, sweetie. You must have lulled him with your soft, clear voice."

Rachel blushed, evidently unaccustomed to compliments. "My mama gave me her Bible." Her voice was soft and timid. So seldom did Rachel ever mention her mother that Sarah decided to seize the moment.

"How wonderful. May I see it?"

Rachel walked to her bedroom and reappeared moments later with a medium-sized, brown, leather Bible, its cover tattered and torn, revealing hours of use. She placed it in Sarah's hands, and for a moment, Sarah simply massaged its rough and ragged edges.

She would give anything to have a treasure such as this from her own mother, but most of her legacy consisted of earthly properties and monetary assets—things that mattered little for eternity's sake, things that mattered little to Sarah.

Oh, her parents had been Christians, as Stephen's had been, but to say they'd been exceedingly committed would be an error. The Woodward family had attended Sunday services out of a sense of duty and pretension, not devotion, and they even donated financial support to all kinds of worthy causes. Rarely, however, except toward the end of her life, had Sarah's mother meditated on God's Word. Even then, it was because Sarah read to her from her own Bible. And she'd never once caught her father, a successful oil manufacturer, studying the Word.

Perhaps that explained why, after the deaths of both her parents, nothing remained to tie her to the Boston area. Most of the friends she'd made over the course of her life, save Nancy Belmont, weren't much interested in spiritual matters.

If anything, they thought her a bit too zealous in her faith and convictions.

"Mama read her Bible every night," said Rachel, her voice a mere whisper.

Sarah lifted her head, knowing the importance of treading softly. "Your mother must have been a wonderful person. How lucky you are to have her Bible."

Rachel gave a slow nod. "She was fun—before she got sick."

Sarah rested a hand on Rachel's shoulder. "Would you like to tell me about her?"

"I don't know." Rachel tipped her face upward and revealed a glittering of raw hurt in her sky-blue eyes. "Sometimes I cry if I think too hard about her."

"I know exactly what you mean," Sarah answered, turning on her side and pulling a bit of the blanket with her, taking care not to disturb Seth's slumber. The boy had stretched straight out in front of the couch, his bare feet protruding from the oversized blanket he shared with Sarah.

"'Cause your mama died too?" Rachel asked.

"Yes. I miss her terribly." Her mother had never been much for nurturing; her societal activities, fund-raising balls, art auctions to benefit the poor, and charity luncheons always took up a good share of her time. Yet, in spite of that, Sarah always knew she was loved.

Rachel seemed to think that over. "I miss my mama, too."

Sarah weighed her words carefully. "Maybe if you just tell me about some of the good times, you won't feel quite so sad. Can you remember a few?"

The child brightened. "We used to walk to the city square.

There was a park there with swings and stuff. Mama would share the seesaw with me. She was too heavy for the other end, so she would push off the ground with her feet and then come back down, and it made me almost fly off my end." With that, Rachel actually giggled.

"Oh, I know what you mean. I once had a friend who was much bigger than I was. She loved to trap me up in the air by sitting on her end for long periods of time," Sarah said. Now they both laughed quietly. "Tell me more," Sarah urged.

"Well, once, when Seth was very little, Mama and me and Seth all went grasshopper huntin'."

"Grasshopper hunting? I thought you lived in the city."

"Oh, we never caught any, but Mama said we was huntin' for 'em anyways. We took a jar and everything. She said she used to hunt for 'em when she was little, so she thought we should practice the skill of it."

Sarah couldn't hold back her own giggle despite the nagging ache at the base of her skull. "I see! So it requires skill, does it?"

"Mama said so. She said you had to sneak up behind and make a surprise attack. They have good ears and will hear you comin' otherwise."

Sarah nodded. "And how are you supposed to catch them once you spot them?"

Rachel turned to face her. "With your hands, silly."

Sarah deliberately frowned, which made Rachel laugh. "Maybe you can show me how in the springtime," Sarah said, "provided you and Seth do the actual catching."

"Will you still be here in the spring?" Rachel asked, her eyes holding hope.

155

The question set Sarah back. Did the children expect her to desert them? "Of course I'll be here, sweetie. Now, tell me some more wonderful stories."

For the next several minutes, Rachel shared stories from her heart, stories of happy times that brought a smile to her face and an occasional giggle. Sarah resurrected a few of her own favorite memories to add to the collection, and in those quiet moments, the two began to build an alliance of sorts, the early stages of an enduring friendship.

Sometime later, while Sarah was slowly navigating around the house, tending to a few minor chores, and Seth and Rachel were playing with some toys in their room, she heard the sounds of approaching horses. When she glanced out the kitchen window, a smile found its way to her lips.

It seemed her husband had sent for his mother.

***

He didn't care what Sarah said—she needed help around the place, and he would not take no for an answer. He didn't know why he hadn't thought of it sooner, but bringing his mother over to stay for a couple of days seemed the perfect solution. It would mean he'd have to go back to bedding down in the barn, but it would be worth it to have peace of mind. He didn't trust his wife to get the rest she needed.

Fortunately, once Rocky had explained to his parents about Sarah's accident and the doctor's orders for bed rest, Frank Callahan had sanctioned the idea of lending his wife out for a few days. Had his father's health worsened, Rocky wouldn't have considered it, but as it was, the man looked as healthy and fit as ever. Having suffered one heart attack, he now had a heart condition that seemed to come and go, but Doc said he could outlive them all if he took care of himself.

"Why don't I wait outside while you go talk to your wife?" Mary Callahan suggested once Rocky reined the team in and jumped off the rig. She sat atop the wagon seat, bundled in her winter gear. Rocky led the horses to the hitching post before he looked up at her.

"Thanks, Ma. This'll only take a few minutes. I'll tend to your horses later if you don't mind." Sparky, tethered to the back of the wagon, gave a loud snort, as if to remind Rocky of his whereabouts.

"Take as long as you need," Mary prompted. "If Sarah is as stubborn as you seem to think she is, she may not take to the idea of her mother-in-law intruding. That's why your pa and I have kept our distance. We wanted to give the two of you plenty of time to adjust to each other."

"Well, it wouldn't have mattered if you'd come by, Ma. It's not as if we're living the life of blissful newlyweds."

Mary lifted her brows until they disappeared under her wool hat. "I see. In other words, you don't share a bed."

Rocky blushed in spite of the cold. Conversations such as this didn't occur often between his mother and him. "No. The arrangement was that she would look after Seth and Rachel in exchange for a place to live. It's a marriage in name only, Ma."

"Ah, and you're happy with that?"

"Ma, let's save this conversation for another time."

The lights of her eyes shifted and then she gave him a conspiratorial wink. "I don't think we'll need to discuss it further. Things will iron themselves out, son, you'll see."

157

It would be senseless to argue the point, so Rocky merely gave a quick nod and headed for the house.

When he opened the door, Sarah was sitting on the sofa. She gave the appearance of having been sitting there for some time, but he knew otherwise. The kitchen looked considerably tidier than when he'd left it, and there was a steaming tea-kettle on the stove. Seth and Rachel seemed to be entertaining themselves in their room.

"Where's your mother?" she asked. The question threw him. So she had seen them come up the drive.

Prepared to do battle, he pulled back his shoulders and walked straight across the room to face her head-on. "I'll have no arguing on the matter, Sarah. It's clear you need some help around the place. You don't seem to agree with what Doc Randolph suggested as far as bed rest goes, and so I think my decision is a smart one.

"You don't need to worry about Ma intruding on your space, if that's your concern. And she certainly won't tell you how to manage the household chores. She will, however, be glad to do whatever you ask of her because she's concerned for your well-being...just...as...I am."

His sentence petered out toward the end because of the way her large, liquid eyes, more blue than green today, flashed in a familiar display of impatience. "I asked you a simple question," she said.

"Huh?"

"Where is your mother? Are you making her wait outside, just as you made the children sit outside at Winthrop's Dry Goods that first day I met you?"

Now he felt duly reprimanded. "It was—her idea. I wasn't,

well, she wasn't—sure how you would react to her—coming to stay—for a few days."

"For gracious' sake, Rocky, invite your mother inside." When all he could do was stare down at her, she quickly added, "Please." That's when he saw of glint of humor pass across her face.

"You don't mind, then?"

"Why should I mind? I will be thankful to have the company. I think it was a wonderful idea."

Relief flooded through his veins. "You do?"

Her smile broadened in approval. "Yes. Now, do I have to invite her in, or are you going to see to that?"

In the space of a second, his mood went from apprehensive to buoyant, heavy to lighthearted. Without further ado, he hurried to the door.

"Ma! Come on in!" he called. His mother looked up and quickly went about unbundling herself from her array of quilts.

"Shouldn't you go help her?" Sarah asked.

"Oh. Right."

Just as he headed out the door, he heard the excited cries of Seth and Rachel trailing behind. "Grandma? Is Grandma here? Yippee!"

Chapter Ten

*G*randma, can I help?" Seth asked the next day, pulling a chair to kneel on up to the table. His grandmother had her flour-ridden hands in the center of a huge ball of bread dough, her palms and fists aptly kneading as she'd done a thousand times before.

"Of course you can help," Mary Callahan replied, tearing off a lump of dough for her grandson and pushing it to the side, her tone so chipper that Sarah was hard-pressed not to giggle.

Although her headache and dizziness had temporarily subsided, she'd been forced to rest, moving from the trusty old couch to a kitchen chair and then back to the couch when the throbbing returned and became too bothersome. She wished she could help, but she had relented when Mary insisted it was her pleasure to take over the duties.

So far, her mother-in-law had scrubbed the sink, shelves, stove, and countertop, complaining to her son when he made an appearance that he should think about replacing the rough-hewn work surface in the kitchen. "Your bride could get slivers cleaning it."

He'd given Sarah a hangdog look before casting his mother a warning glance. "I know, Ma. Anything else?" Sarah stifled a giggle and Mary shrugged. "Well, if you want a list, I'm sure between Sarah and me we could easily come up with one."

 160

Sarah had held her breath, wondering how Rocky would handle his mother's bold offer, but he seemed to take it in stride with a nod and a chuckle. "I've no doubt you could come up with a list all by yourself, Ma. Why bother Sarah with such trivial matters?"

"Well, it's her house, son. She should have a say in such things." It was certainly true that Sarah had considered inquiring about the need for a few interior improvements, but she hadn't intended to bring up the matter until they stood on firmer ground with each other.

To that, Rocky had clearly blushed. "Well then, I suppose we should leave the matter up to my wife."

"Grandma, what should I do with this?" asked Seth, glaring down at the section of dough Mary had doled out. Sarah came out of her reverie to watch the banter between grandmother and grandson.

Mary ceased with her work. "Did you wash those hands?"

Seth turned his palms faceup for her inspection. "I knew you would ask," he said with a gleam in his eye, as if he'd fooled her with his shrewdness.

"Hmm, clean as a whistle. All right then." She winked at Sarah, and Sarah winked back, delighted at the chance to observe the unfolding drama.

"Well then, you first must flour your hands...like this," she instructed, dropping a bit of flour onto his palms and rubbing them gently. "Then you take up your clump of dough and begin to play with it."

The lessons continued, with Seth mimicking his grandmother's every move until he had worked his doughy sphere into perfection.

161

About the time Mary's large loaf and Seth's smaller one, were ready for the oven, Rachel walked through the door, her rosy cheeks and wide smile evidence that she'd enjoyed playing by herself down by the creek at the edge of the property. Accustomed to tending her younger brother, she must have enjoyed the pleasant reprieve to have a few moments to herself without the responsibility of entertaining him. Not that anyone had ever forced her to care for him. She'd just assumed that task all by herself.

"Well, would you look at what the wind just blew in," Mary declared, all smiles for her granddaughter.

"I just made a loaf of bread, Rachel," Seth cried, his little chest puffed out with pride.

Rachel shed her winter gear, dutifully hanging up her coat, scarf, hat, and mittens, and placing her boots side by side in their assigned place. A smile had etched itself into her pretty, young face. Sarah reflected on the girl's subtle changes for good. From being somewhat slipshod and crabby, according to Rocky's observations, the child had seemingly grown to a new level of maturity. Had Sarah's influence and example rubbed off on her? She wanted to think that she was making a positive impact on both her and Seth.

If only Rocky would share her hopes for the children.

"What did you do with yourself, child?" Mary Callahan asked, wiping her hands on her apron after arranging the loaf pans in the oven.

"I went looking for pretty stones by Hickman Creek."

Seth raised his head in interest. "Did you find some, Rachel?"

"A few," she answered, "but none to brag about."

"Where are they?" Seth inquired, his eyes big, as if he'd never heard of anything so intriguing as hunting for stones.

"I didn't keep any, silly. Next time, maybe I'll find some worth keepin'."

"Oh." Seth wore disappointment like a bright coat. "Can I go next time?"

She nodded at her brother then looked at her grandmother. "Can I help make supper since Seth helped make bread?"

"Gracious me! I've never had so much help." Mary's eyes glistened silver as she cast Sarah another smile. "Are they always this ready to lend a hand?"

"They've been very helpful," Sarah said, pulling herself up from the sofa and waiting for the dizziness to pass, "which is more than I can say for myself lately."

Mary studied her from across the room, pushing a flour-covered hand through her already white hair. "Now, you stay put on that sofa, Sarah Callahan."

Sarah shrugged. "But I feel so helpless."

"There is no reason for you to feel guilty for that. You've had a head injury and the doc says the best thing for you now is rest."

"That is all I've been doing," she mumbled.

Mary glanced down at both children. "You two go straighten up your rooms. I see a pile of books and a smattering of toys on the floor. I'll call you when it's time to start supper." When neither moved, she added, "Shoo! I want to talk to Sarah."

After they disappeared into their room, Mary untied and removed her apron, tossing it over a straight-back chair. Sarah slid over when Mary indicated that she was about to sit beside her.

163

The first thing she did was place a hand on Sarah's knee. With a gentle pat she said, "Now then, my son has asked me to take over the duties for a few days. Please be honest when I ask you if my presence in your home bothers you."

Sarah tipped her head to see into her mother-in-law's aged blue eyes, amazed by the compassion she read in them. "Absolutely not. I'm happy for the chance to get to know you. It's nice to know that I still have—a mother. It's just that, well, I'm afraid I'm shirking my duties as a housewife and caregiver. The children depend on me and they've had such sorrow."

Mary released a deep sigh. "That they have, but then we've all tasted it of late—you included, with your mother's passing."

Sarah appreciated the kind remark. Rocky had mentioned little about her personal loss. Would he even care that she had cried herself to sleep more than once since arriving in Little Hickman?

"You miss your mother, child?" asked Mary, not bothering to mince words.

To her great dismay, the question triggered tears, and she fought to hold them at bay.

"Now, now," Mary said, increasing the number of pats she gave to Sarah's knee. "It's perfectly fine to let it out. I daresay you've been strong up to this point, and it's time you let go of those bottled-up tears."

Perhaps it was the way Mary put an arm around her shoulder, or the smile of warmth she offered. All Sarah knew was that it was just the invitation she needed to free the tears she didn't even realize she'd been holding back. For the next few minutes she blubbered into her mother-in-law's shoulder, taking the handkerchief offered her and blowing hard, as if that would rid her of her sobs the quicker.

When the well of emotion ran dry, she wiped her eyes one last time and pulled herself up straight. "Well, I didn't mean to carry on like that."

Mary shushed her with a flip of her wrist. "I will not accept any apologies. Why, I've sat myself down for a good cry more than once. Poor Frank hardly knows what to make of me sometimes. Tears are God's way of cleansing us of our deepest hurts, so don't you be holding them back when they need to come, you hear?"

Sarah sniffed and nodded, embarrassed by her outburst.

Mary's eyebrows rose inquiringly. "Has my son been kind to you?"

The unexpected question gave Sarah pause, but she had no trouble answering it. "He's been most considerate."

In fact, he'd been more than polite—carrying her into the house after her fall and riding like the wind into town after Doc Randolph, insisting that she follow his precise orders. Even calling on his mother to help with the chores had been a thoughtful act, though she supposed his reasons for that were twofold. At least now he needn't waste time checking on her.

"Well, that's good to know. Rocky was always such a kind-hearted boy. Never gave his papa or me a bit of grief while we were raising him. It's just that now he's..." Her statement fizzled away.

"What?" Sarah urged. "Please, I want to know all I can about him." As soon as she voiced the words, she realized the truth in them.

Mary bit her lip before carrying on. "When he lost Hester he pretty near died himself, but he had Joseph to consider.

165

He wrapped everything around that boy afterward, took him everywhere, rarely let him out of his sight. Matter of fact, he wouldn't even allow Joseph to spend much time with us, and we were his grandparents.

"Looking back, I'm sure it was because Joseph was all he had, and he couldn't imagine losing him as well, so he clung as tight as he could. When Joseph died of the fever, Rocky just rolled up into himself and never came back out."

Mary's eyes took on a distant look. "My, but that Joseph was a sweet little boy." Then, just as quickly, she turned her gaze back on Sarah. "He used to love the Lord, you know, my Rocky. Never missed a single Sunday service, no sir. Now, well, I just don't know what goes on in his head. I s'pose in a way he blames God. He and Hester used to pray about everything. My, she was a wonderful Christian woman."

The older woman shook her head and patted Sarah's arm. "I don't mean to go on about Hester."

"No, it's fine. Really. I've asked Rocky about her, but he has told me very little. I want to know about her. Maybe it will help me understand your son better."

Mary nodded. "Well, there's not much to tell, except that she was a fine woman, hardworking, loved farming. Pretty little thing too. That girl spent more time outside than she did in, I think. She loved her garden. Of course, it's all but withered away by now. Rocky never tends it. He's too busy in the fields raising crops for income.

"When Joseph came along, she took him outside every chance she got. He was just a few days old when she laid him in a shady spot next to the garden so she could weed." Mary shook her head and smiled. "Don't get me wrong, she was a fine mother, very doting, but she wasn't much for staying put inside these four walls."

Sarah frowned. She was nothing like Hester, and it worried her that Rocky would always regret that about her. Had he been looking for a substitute for Hester when he'd married her? If so, he surely must be disappointed.

Mary fixed her eyes on the front window overlooking the open fields. "Rocky comes off as harsh, especially with those kids, but the truth is I think he's scared to death of ever loving another living thing. Seth is right near the age that Joseph would've been.

"I know it's rough for you now, you losing your mother and all, marrying a man you didn't even know, moving into a strange household, taking care of someone else's kids, but I can't help but feel you're right where God wants you."

Sarah patted the woman's arm and nodded. "Thank you for that. I didn't come to Little Hickman on a whim. I prayed in earnest about it, and I've no doubt that God led me here. I just had no idea how it would turn out. I came to town to marry one man and wound up with someone altogether different. But I believe I did the right thing in coming."

Mary smiled and nodded. "I believe it as well. Those children need you and so does my Rocky."

As if he'd heard his name mentioned, the door opened and in came Rocky, bringing a harsh burst of cold air with him.

"Land, it's cold outside," Mary said. "Close that door."

For a moment, Rocky just stood there watching the two women, most likely wondering why they huddled so close on the sofa. "Everything all right?" he asked, eyeing Sarah in a peculiar way before closing the door.

He looked so handsome standing there, his dark eyes searching Sarah's, his cap nearly covering his thick, brownish-black eyebrows. When he took the cap off, his eyes flickered with a gleam of awareness. Not knowing what to make of it, she averted her gaze.

"Of course everything's all right," Mary said, pushing herself up with a slight groan, her plump, round body slowing her efforts. "Why wouldn't it be?"

He shrugged. "Just curious. You two look awful serious."

Mary laughed. "Women have a right to talk about things, son," she said, shuffling to the kitchen, her back to both of them.

Rocky slung off his winter coat. A long-sleeved blue and white flannel shirt stretched across firm shoulders, ones Sarah recalled being rock solid when he'd carried her into the house and she'd leaned her head against them. His black hair fell in disarray, and he quickly finger-combed it before stepping all the way inside.

Powerful legs led him directly to the chair beside the sofa. With a sigh, he dropped into it.

"How is your day going?" Sarah asked.

"Fine," he murmured.

"Tell me what you've done so far," she urged, tucking bare feet under her.

He seemed to watch that particular movement with interest, his eyes going from her feet back up to her face. "It wouldn't interest you."

Eager to hear him talk, she countered, "Try me."

One corner of his mouth pulled up. "You serious?"

She nodded and caught Mary watching, a smile creasing her face as she bent over the oven to observe the baking bread.

"Starting around six I milked my cows and then gathered nine warm eggs from under some cackling hens," he began in practiced monotone. "Then I made a few trips from the shed where I store my hay and other animal feed and saw that the horses, cows, and hog got their breakfast. Once they were fed I saw to my own stomach." There were touches of humor around his mouth while he talked.

"If you recall, I ate in a hurry."

She nodded. "You barely took time to finish your coffee."

He looked casually amused. "After breakfast I took a few more scraps out to Fester because he never gets quite full enough."

"Fester?"

"The hog."

She giggled in spite of herself. "I haven't met him yet."

"Your loss," he said as serious as you please. "After that, I carried several buckets of fresh water into the barn and filled the troughs. Then I went back to the chicken house to repair a bit of barbed wire that one of my roosters has been pecking at in a desperate attempt to reach one of his many mistresses."

It was impossible not to laugh full-throttle at that point, even though Sarah did cover her mouth in a stifling attempt. "You paint a vivid picture," she said. In the background, she heard Mary chuckle to herself.

"You want more?" he asked, his own laugh low and throaty.

"Yes!" she cried.

He threw a large stocking-clad foot over his knee and held his ankle with one hand. Sarah noted a hole in the middle of his sock and made a mental note to find the darning tools and make some repairs. Of course, she would have to wait for her aching head to allow for the extra eyestrain.

"Armed with pitchfork, I tackled all the stalls. I muck them out pretty much every day so the animals stay warm and don't get sick. Once done with that, I throw in fresh straw. I usually only do this during the coldest period of winter. Otherwise, they stay outside, and the mucking isn't a daily chore."

"I'm sure they appreciate all you do," she said, meaning it sincerely.

His head tossed back in a fit of laughter. Even Mary looked up as if quite unaccustomed to the rich sound. She winked at Sarah and went back to her puttering.

"Well now, if they do they've never let on," he said. "If you ask me, they're all pretty demanding of my time and attention. That's why I came inside. I needed to find a bit of warmth, and to take a load off."

Sarah smiled. "It's good that you did."

All of a sudden, he dropped both feet to the floor, leaned forward, and lowered his voice. "I'd have to agree."

She met his eyes without flinching. "Your mother has a fresh pie cooling in the lean-to. If you are extra nice she might offer you a piece."

He grinned and turned his head. "That true, Ma?"

"Is what true?" she asked.

"Don't give me that innocent act," he teased. "You heard every word. You got pie coolin' out back?"

"Go see for yourself," she ordered.

He stood up and pushed his hands deep into his pockets. From where Sarah sat, he looked massive, but the sudden warmth she glimpsed in his expression told her he was harmless. "You want pie?" he asked in almost a whisper.

Her stomach took an unusual turn. "A small piece would be nice," she replied.

One eyebrow arched in mischievous fashion as his lips gave way to a smile as intimate as a kiss. He bent over her until his face came within inches of her own. "I hope you're not growing too accustomed to all this service, Mrs. Callahan." His voice seemed to caress her ears, setting her pulse to racing. "A wife could get downright spoiled."

"What? No," she said, sitting back from him, suddenly unsure.

He chuckled privately. "You worry too much" was all he said before he stood back up and sauntered past his mother to the lean-to at the back of the kitchen. About that time, Mary set to humming some unrecognizable tune.

Midway through their pie and coffee, the sounds of horses' hooves filtered through the cracks of the windows and walls.

"Someone's coming!" Seth announced with a shout, suddenly abandoning his pie in favor of jumping from the table and racing to the window.

"Seth, don't yell," scolded Rocky, placing his napkin on the table and pushing his own chair back for a look.

When Rachel slid her chair back in noisy fashion, Rocky glared at her. "Sit," he ordered. "No point in everyone jumping up at once."

The girl slumped back in disappointment while Sarah

winced at his harsh tone. What had happened to her husband's former easygoing manner?

"Who is it?" Mary asked.

Rocky hovered over Seth's small frame in the window. "Looks to be Benjamin and Liza Broughton and their two youngins."

Sarah's heart leaped with joy. They had visitors!

***

The men had excused themselves to the barn while the women worked companionably in the kitchen. Liza talked a mile a minute about the events at the Broughton farm and the awful ice storm, asking Sarah for details about her bad fall while she trimmed beans.

Mary threw together a salad while Sarah sat at the table peeling potatoes. She wasn't about to admit that her head ached. She was just thrilled to have found a useful job, even if it was simple and Mary had insisted she perform it while sitting.

Seth and Rachel were busy entertaining their newfound friends, eight-year-old Lili Broughton and baby Molly, who was coming up on her second birthday. Sarah could hear Rachel asking about school and Lili explaining how the building had burned when her stepmother was the teacher. "Now I just get my teaching lessons at home," she said, "even though I'd rather wait till school starts up in the fall. Liza keeps sayin' she doesn't want me to get behind, but how can I get behind if no one else is goin' to school neither?"

"Either!" Liza corrected from across the room. Sarah giggled when she realized that Liza had also been eavesdropping on the youngsters' chatter.

"It must have been so scary for you," Liza said, turning her attention back to Sarah, "falling in the dark like that, with no one about."

"I hardly remember it," Sarah admitted. "And Rocky came along before I knew it. I had passed out, so I don't know exactly how long I lay there before he found me."

Liza shook her head. "Oh dear. Well, we can all be grateful to God for watching over you."

"Amen to that," Mary said.

"He does look out for us," Sarah said, finishing off the last potato and arranging it in the kettle.

Mary walked over and took the pan from her before she had the chance to announce she had finished. Sarah smiled to herself at the way the woman doted. It made her wonder if she hadn't come to Little Hickman as much for her mother-in-law as for Rocky and the children. The older woman seemed to have latched onto her as if she were her own daughter.

"Well, I'm just glad that Frank drove over to tell us about the mishap, or we might not have heard about it for some time. Of course, we'd have found out eventually. I've been pestering Ben to bring me out for a visit, but he wouldn't allow it. He kept saying the newlyweds needed their space," Liza said, her eyes twinkling.

Sarah shifted nervously, embarrassed by the insinuation and trying to think of a way to change the subject. "Well, I'm glad you chose today to come. Things have gotten dull around here, right, Mary?"

"It was high time we received callers," Mary answered, bringing down the dishes from the cupboard and walking to the table.

"Oh, what beautiful dishes," Liza exclaimed. "Were they your mother's?"

Sarah regarded the dishes she'd received from Stephen, realizing she'd promptly forgotten them in the aftermath of her fall. She wondered now what Rocky would say to eating from them since he'd made such a scene about them earlier.

"Actually, they are a wedding gift—from a dear friend. The dishes came from his mother."

Liza looked faintly confused but didn't question; she merely smiled, then picked up one of the plates for her own inspection. "They're lovely. What a pretty pattern."

"They come from the Netherlands," Sarah told her. "I admired them so much as a child that my friend's mother insisted they be given to me as a gift."

"How wonderful," Liza said.

"They sure are nice," Mary added, staring at one of the plates as if to study her own reflection.

"Uncle Rocky don't like 'em," said Rachel. She came up beside her grandmother to make the announcement, followed by Seth, Lili, and baby Molly. "He says ar cabin wasn't made for china and silver."

Both of the women gawked at the little girl then stared at Sarah, awaiting some sort of reply.

"Well, it's not that he doesn't like them," Sarah stated.

"Uncle Rocky says he won't eat off 'em," chimed Seth.

"Whyever not?" asked Mary.

"Well, I suppose he will if he's good and hungry," Sarah said, feeling a smile creep across her face. She still thought it odd that her husband had reacted so irrationally over the gift.

 174

As if on cue, the door opened, and Rocky and Ben walked in. Although Ben wore a friendly smile, Rocky's expression dulled at the first sight of the beautiful blue dishes.

***

The dinner was delicious and the conversation stimulating. So Rocky wondered why his appetite had dwindled to almost nothing when he'd been forced to spoon his food atop the blue windmill-patterned dishes.

Not wanting to risk making a scene, he'd merely given Sarah a disapproving look, which she'd promptly cast off. She knew how he felt about the wedding gift, he mused. Couldn't she have insisted they use the everyday dishes and saved these others for some special occasion? Of course, if this didn't qualify as a special occasion—entertaining unexpected dinner guests—he didn't know what did.

To make matters worse, the silver flatware, a personal gift from Alden, accompanied the dishes. Further, to give the table a particular flair, Sarah had produced a linen tablecloth and matching napkins, something she'd had tucked away in her trunk, she'd said. It made him wonder what other ceremonial finery she had stowed away in that massive crate of hers.

Ben had said Rocky was a lucky guy—no, *blessed* was what he'd actually used to describe the new marriage. They'd been standing in the barn looking at some of Rocky's farm supplies. "God had His hand in this one, Rock. Who would have thought that it would turn out so well? I felt so guilty inviting Sarah to Kentucky to be my bride, and then announcing to her after she'd traveled all that way that I meant to marry Liza instead."

Rocky had nodded his head, thinking that it was all quite a coincidence. Yet, to call it a coincidence wouldn't have set well with Ben, so Rocky hadn't mentioned it. Truth be told, he wasn't even sure himself anymore about such things. Was it coincidence or God's providence?

"Hm, I haven't been this full since," Ben sat back and rubbed his belly, "since…"

"Last night?" his wife asked. "After you finished off the last of the roast beef and potatoes?" Liza picked up her water glass with exacting finesse and sipped, eyeing him over the rim.

Everyone laughed while Ben conceded her point with a humble nod and a sheepish grin, still rubbing his stomach with a look of satisfaction. "Okay, I'll admit I enjoy mealtime. Can I help it if my wife spoils me by trying out all her best recipes on me? And then to come here and be treated with a meal of equal caliber is a treat indeed."

"Oh poo," Mary cut in. "Wasn't anythin' more than a regular meal."

Ben picked up a glistening knife. "Served with the finest dishes and silver, I might add. I saw my reflection in this before I slathered it with butter. Never knew you to eat off such finery, Callahan," Ben teased. "Were these a wedding gift?"

The remark and question that followed were innocent enough, but they ruffled Rocky's feathers, reminding him of how un-befitting and out of place the dishes and silver were in his humble farmhouse. He would never have the resources to satisfy Sarah's earthly desires. A woman like her deserved far more than he was capable of providing. Had he been a smarter man, he never would have interfered with Alden's proposal.

"Yeah, well, I tried to tell Sarah how foolish it was to put the stuff on display," he said, "much less use it. I mean, look around, folks. Does this cabin look suited for silver and china? I have a door in need of new hinges, a cracked front window, peeling plaster, a floor with mismatched boards, and a house too small for four bodies. But we have china and silver."

Ben looked at Rocky as if he'd suddenly grown an extra head. It only made him more determined to continue. "Yeah, it was a gift—from her wealthy beau, no less."

"He wasn't my—beau," Sarah corrected, laying her napkin alongside her plate, pursing her lips together in a tight line.

"He wanted to marry her," Rocky explained to the open-mouthed onlookers, as if it were his duty to divulge the fact. "But I saved her from the rich clod. Imagine that. I thought I was doing her a favor." To this he chuckled, noting he laughed alone, save the baby, who giggled when she pounded a rattle on the hardwood floor.

As soon as the rash words escaped, he regretted them, even questioning where they'd come from. He hadn't meant to come off sounding so cruel. Sarah gasped as a wounded look crossed her face, and his mother nearly teetered where she sat, her own face pasty in color before turning red with obvious anger.

Anger he knew immediately he deserved.

Before anyone could offer a challenge, Sarah pushed back her chair. A smile trembled across her lips. "I hope you will all excuse me," she said, her shoulders straight with polished pride. "I'm afraid my headache has returned. I think it's best that I rest."

Rocky pushed his chair back and jumped to his feet, but the belated act only emphasized his stupidity.

The harm was done, and he might have kicked himself if his foot hadn't already been stuffed up his oversized mouth.

Chapter Eleven

*S*arah, the horses are hitched," Rocky announced from the living room.

"I'm coming," she replied, straightening her hat in the mirror and adjusting the wool scarf that hugged her slim neck.

The children were as excited about going into town as she was. She could hear their restless chatter as they waited by the door. It'd been a good week and a half since the ice storm, and the temperature had warmed enough to thaw the path.

Things had been anything but relaxed between Sarah and Rocky since his outburst at the table in front of their guests. To say he'd embarrassed her was putting it mildly. Of course, she might have avoided the whole fiasco if she'd quietly asked Mary beforehand to set the table with the old dishes, but it'd seemed so silly at the time—at least to her.

Oh, Rocky had apologized for his behavior the next morning, apparently figuring it was hopeless even to try that night since she'd refused to come out of her room. She'd accepted his apology, but his hurtful words had been driven deep, even making her question her decision to marry him. It appeared he regretted the arrangement, insinuating she would have been better off marrying Stephen Alden.

Mary had said little afterward regarding the incident, but it was clear her son had angered her. She'd stayed another two days, then headed back to her own place, saying that Frank would be missing her.

Before leaving, she'd enfolded Sarah in a tight hug.

"Thank you for coming," Sarah had said, her eyes moist with tears.

"Nonsense," she'd replied, "you're a Callahan now. No need to thank me.

"Now, don't let my son's words gnaw a hole straight through you," she'd whispered. "He didn't mean to hurt you like that. I'm plum mortified that he embarrassed you in front of the Broughtons. Sometimes he says things he shouldn't 'cause he's hurting deep down himself. Try to understand that about him if you can."

Sarah gave a quiet nod but found no words with which to respond. It would be a while before she fully understood her husband.

"We don't want to miss your appointment with Doc Randolph, Sarah," Rocky said.

It would be her second checkup with the doctor since her fall. Doc had come out to the house for the last one, but Sarah had insisted she felt well enough to meet him in his office this time. "You sure?" Rocky had asked. "No point in rushing things." Truth was she was anxious to get out of the house, feast her eyes on something other than the four walls of their small home. "I'm sure," she'd said with finality.

"I'm coming," she repeated, turning away from her reflection and grabbing up her handbag from the bedstand.

The ride into town was pleasant enough with Rachel and Seth taking up the space between Rocky and Sarah on the wide seat and filling the gaps in conversation.

It was almost February, and a hint of spring hovered in the air, subtle and delicate. Sunny skies promised the possibility of

 180

warmer air and, with it, the exultant first blooms of the mirthful crocus, dogwood, and magnolia.

Some unidentified bird warbled from afar, putting Sarah on the alert for her first glimpse of a fat mother robin. Too early, she told herself. Still, Kentucky was farther south than Massachusetts. Maybe the robin made an appearance much sooner in these parts. She wanted to ask Rocky, but his clouded expression held her at a distance.

"You feeling all right, Sarah?" Rocky asked as they drew nearer to civilization, his eyes firmly fixed on the road ahead.

She appreciated his concern, even though he'd put the question to her in a formal manner. "I'm perfectly fine," she answered. An occasional headache still plagued her, but she refused to admit it. Gazing at his profile, she willed him to glance at her. When he didn't, she continued, "It's a lovely day today. The sun is downright hot on my shoulders."

"Feels like spring might be around the corner," Rocky said.

Sarah warmed at the prospect of conversing. "I was just thinking that very thing."

He threw her a momentary glance before turning his attention back to the road. "Were you now?"

She smiled. "I love spring. It's always been my favorite season."

"Mine too," Seth announced.

Rocky peered at the boy and chuckled. "Yeah? Why is that?"

"'Cause maybe I can go fishin'." One couldn't miss the boy's hopeful tone.

"Fishing? You ever been?" Rocky asked, his manner turned casual, as he held the reins, resting his elbows on his knees.

"Sure. Grandpap took me before."

"Ah, Grandpap," Rocky said, raising his head with a perceptive nod.

"Maybe you can take me sometime," the boy said, his eyes trailing a path upward, squinting into the sun as he tried to examine his uncle's face.

For a change, Rocky didn't stiffen or grow sullen at the suggestion. Instead, he nodded. "That's a possibility, provided we get all the chores done."

"Yippee! I'll help!" the boy offered, enthusiasm running through his voice.

Rocky glanced at Sarah over the children's heads and, wonder of wonders, actually smiled.

After Sarah visited the doctor's office and received a clean bill of health, the family headed for Johansson's Mercantile.

As soon as he heard the tinkling of the tiny bell hanging over the entryway, Eldred shuffled out from behind a curtain that separated the store from his living quarters. "Well, well, if it ain't the Callahans," he said. "Last I seen you folks you was headin' fer home in that bad ice storm. See ya made it safe enough."

"Hello, Eldred," said Rocky, offering the old man a friendly nod. "Came in for some supplies. I have a list here that—my wife—put together." He seemed to falter on those two words. Sarah bit back a smile. Even she still struggled with the notion of having a husband.

Eldred took the list offered him and studied it through squinty eyes. "'Spect I can gather it all up and have it ready in a jiffy," he muttered while rubbing at his scruffy beard. "Your wagon out front?"

Rocky nodded. "We'll head on over to Winthrop's Dry Goods and return within the hour."

"Sounds good 'nough," Eldred said. "I'll have Gus here help me load up." A young boy of not more than twelve or thirteen emerged from a cluttered aisle where he was stocking canned goods. "He's been helpin' me out ever since the school burnt down."

Seth appeared all eyes at the sight of the tall, gangly boy. Rachel looked mildly interested.

"Hello there," Sarah greeted, laying her hand atop Seth's shoulder when he sidled up beside her to have a closer look.

The boy produced a shy smile, then wiped his hands on his pant legs before stuffing them into his pockets. "Hi," he managed.

When all he did was stare at Rachel and Seth, Sarah hurried to add, "I'd like you to meet Seth and Rachel Reed."

"Hi," he repeated. "I'm Gus Humphrey. I think my sister Lenora is about your age," he said, directing the remark to Rachel. Then, gazing at Seth, he added, "We seen you two come in on the stage back before Christmas. Matter o' fact, Miss Merriwether, uh, Mrs. Broughton now, let ar whole class watch from the window. We was all plenty curious."

"Where do you live?" Rachel asked, not in the least bit shy. "How old is your sister?"

"My sister's nine."

"I'm going to be eight," Rachel answered, standing taller.

"They live over in Gulliver's Hollow, just past Hickman

Creek," Rocky inserted. "I know their ma and pop."

"Can she come and play sometime?" Rachel asked, pointing hopeful eyes in Rocky's direction.

"You don't even know her," Rocky stated.

"I think that would be wonderful," Sarah said. "We'll arrange for Lili Broughton to come, too. You tell your sister Lenora to be looking for an invitation."

Gus brightened. "She'll be real glad to hear it," he said. "We all been pretty bored since the school burnt."

"Is there any news as to when they might begin rebuilding?" Sarah asked, directing her question to both Mr. Johansson and Gus Humphrey.

The older man shrugged. "Ain't heard one way or the other." With that, he turned and began reaching for items appearing on the list, apparently figuring it was past time for tending to business.

"I heard the town ain't got the money," Gus offered. "We need a new church, too, and most townsfolk want separate buildings this time around."

Sarah had talked Rocky into taking them all into town for Sunday services two days ago at the home of Clyde and Iris Winthrop, and, while the home was certainly spacious, it was clear folks needed their own house of worship. Mrs. Winthrop was a fussbudget, insisting that everyone leave boots and soiled shoes by the door and coats in their laps. Although Mr. Winthrop had been warm and cordial, everyone could see that Mrs. Winthrop worried incessantly about her lovely Persian rugs and fine furnishings. Not that Sarah blamed the woman. After all, it was the Winthrops' private home, and they were more than generous to offer it as a temporary

 184

meeting place. Still, if people were to attend in a true attitude of worship, they needed to do so with as few distractions as possible.

The notion that Sarah had the resources with which to build a new church—and school, for that matter—was a weighty realization. Yet, how could she make such a donation without creating resentment? She was the newest member of Little Hickman. Wouldn't folks think her haughty and proud, and perhaps assume she gave with ulterior motives—to earn their friendship and approval? Moreover, what of others in the town who wished to contribute? A gift the size that Sarah was capable of doling out would make others' donations appear dull by comparison.

She decided then and there to take the matter before the Lord. *Show me what You would have me do, heavenly Father* was her silent, heartfelt prayer.

The streets were abuzz with talk of Hickman's unseasonably warm weather. Folks seemed delighted at the opportunity to walk the streets more leisurely. On the trek to Winthrop's Dry Goods, they passed several clusters of people who were conversing on various topics. Folks waved and smiled as the Callahans passed, often speaking a friendly greeting, but more often gaping curiously, no doubt wondering how the strangely-put-together family was faring.

Iris Winthrop's head shot up as soon as the door opened. Whatever paperwork she was poring over quickly fell by the wayside as she moved out from behind the counter and pasted a smile on her hard-lined face. "Well, my, my," she chortled, "what can I do for you folks?"

Seeing the beady-eyed woman again made Sarah think

about the time she'd hidden behind a bolt of fabric at the back of the store while several womenfolk openly discussed her unfortunate situation. *Imagine coming all this way to marry Benjamin Broughton,* someone had clucked. *Such a waste of time,* another had ranted. Even now she soured at the humiliation of it all.

"So nice to see you, Mrs. Winthrop," Sarah offered, determined to put on her best smile.

The woman wrung her withered hands, then clasped them tightly at her rounded waistline. "Are you interested in more fabric, perhaps?"

"My wife intends to sew some curtains," Rocky told her. Then, nudging Sarah lightly, he leaned in close. "Take your time. I'm going over to Sam's Livery. Later, we'll head back to Eldred's for our provisions, then make a run to Grady Swanson's Sawmill. He's got some supplies stacked up for me."

It warmed her to realize Rocky intended to abide her wishes to improve their home's interior. Apparently his mother's prodding had paid off.

"That sounds fine," she answered.

Rocky glanced down at Seth. "You want to come with me?"

Seth's eyes brightened. "Do I!"

Rocky gave Sarah a momentary look that carried just a hint of a smile. "We'll be back soon."

And with that, he headed out the door, Seth running to keep up.

"My, they do seem like father and son," Mrs. Winthrop said, watching after the two, who were even then scooting across the dusty street.

"He's ar uncle, not ar father," Rachel said, making it her duty to clarify.

"Of course he is," Mrs. Winthrop huffed, back going straight. "But the two seem quite suited to each other. It must be nice for him to have a little boy around the house again, what with him losin' his own like that." The woman cleared her throat then angled her gaze at Sarah. "Of course, I'm sure it's a challenge, having to deal with an instant family."

Maintaining her Christian witness with Iris Winthrop was a chore, particularly when the woman sniffed, then turned and looked down her long nose at Rachel.

Sarah forced a smile, then put her hand on Rachel's thin shoulder to draw her in. "We are making out just fine, thank you."

At that, Sarah pointed the girl toward the wide selection of fabrics. "Show me what you like best, Rachel," she said, pleased when the child seemed eager to help. In the end, they chose enough material to fashion curtains for every window, a fine tablecloth, and matching napkins. Add to that the colorful readymade rugs and fresh new kitchen towels they'd discovered at the back of the store, and they had quite an assortment to haul to the front counter.

"How lovely that you are handy with a needle, Mrs. Callahan," the meddlesome storekeeper remarked, flashing Sarah a rather peculiar look as she began the job of tallying up the purchases. "Wherever did you learn the craft?"

"A dear friend in Massachusetts taught me," Sarah reported, unwilling to tell her it was the live-in housekeeper-turned-nanny. Mrs. Winters, a lifelong friend, had been more a mother to her than her own flesh-and-blood mother had.

Even now, Sarah mourned the loss of Clara Winters. When the woman had fallen ill and died shortly after Sarah's seventeenth birthday, Sarah had grieved deeply, even though her mother had taken the loss in stride, having hired a replacement within the month because she said she couldn't abide having to take over the housework herself.

Just as Mrs. Winthrop rang up the last of Sarah's items, the bell above the door announced another customer. To Sarah's delight, it was Liza Broughton and her two stepdaughters, Lili and Molly. She held tightly to the hand of the younger child, Molly, who looked eager to touch everything in sight. Lili, however, walked close beside Liza, a bright smile on her face when she spotted Rachel.

Liza's own face brightened when she glimpsed Sarah. "Hello. I'm so glad to have run into you. How have you been feeling?"

"Much better, thank you. Doc Randolph says I'm well enough to resume my duties."

"That's wonderful news. Benjamin ran into Rocky at the livery. That's how we knew to find you here." She looked over Sarah's purchases. "Rocky said you planned to make several things for the house. By the look of things, you will be a very busy lady."

Sarah laughed. "I enjoy sewing, and I intend to employ Rachel's help." At that, Rachel gave a look of delight. "Besides, you saw yourself how sparse our place looks."

Liza giggled. "I swear I didn't look that close, but I will admit that it could use a woman's touch. I'm sure Rocky let the housework slide while he was without a wife."

Mrs. Winthrop cleared her throat, eager to be included.

Liza smiled, though sparingly. "Good morning, Mrs. Winthrop."

"Good day to you," she said, forcing a smile.

While the women exchanged a few cordial words about the weather and such, Rachel and Lili eyed each other with open excitement. "I wonder if we might set up a time for Lili to come over and play," Sarah suggested.

"Oh, what a lovely idea," Liza exclaimed. "Lili's been so bored since the school burned down." Both girls' heads shot up, but it was Lili who squealed, causing Molly to shriek with open delight herself.

"And I understand she's not alone. We just spoke to Gus Humphrey at Johansson's Mercantile," Sarah said. "I suggested he let his sister know that Rachel would enjoy meeting her. He seemed to think his sister would like that."

"Oh, Lenora Humphrey is my friend," Lili chimed. "I wish I could see her again, but Papa says he don't have much time for running me back and forth."

Liza's smile widened even more, this time with sudden inspiration. "Oh, wouldn't it be fun to have a party for the children? It's been a dreary time for them since that awful fire."

Mrs. Winthrop fiddled with stacking several papers in a neat pile. "If it hadn't been for that heathen, Clement Bartel, why, the school would still be standing," she murmured.

A deep frown replaced Liza's smile. "It's true. He started the fire—after he tied me to a chair inside the school."

Sarah gasped. She'd wondered about the details of the fire, only hearing snippets here and there. "I'd heard the young man died."

Mrs. Winthrop harrumphed. "We're better off without the hooligan."

Liza pursed her lips and gave the woman a scorching look. "I'm sorry to say he was a very troubled young man. Fortunately, Rufus Baxter, one of my students, entered the building soon enough to distract Clement. A fistfight ensued." Liza's face took on another dimension, as if the simple retelling of the story were painful. "Just when I thought I had breathed my last, Benjamin bounded into the building and hauled me out, chair and all. Then he went back in for Rufus. He couldn't locate Clement, poor boy. They found him later near the back door. He was not much more than a heap of ashes by then." She shuddered and hugged little Molly close.

Mrs. Winthrop heaved a weighty sigh. "And because of that stupid boy, the town is out a school and a church. Clyde and I put in a good share of money for that beautiful school building, you know." It seemed important to the woman to make that fact known. "I'm not sure we're ready to do that again."

Sarah's heart leaped at the prospect of being able to help the town financially, but she wasn't sure her husband would approve. He still had no idea of the extent of her wealth, and if she didn't approach the subject with caution, his stubborn pride might very well stand in the way.

"Well, I'm certain something will work out one day soon," Sarah said.

Iris Winthrop unleashed another loud breath. "That remains to be seen. Not many folks have offered financial assistance, even though we've held a few fund-raising events."

"Times are rough in the winter, Mrs. Winthrop. Perhaps

when warmer weather arrives, the men will get the fever to start building," Liza said, "and the town can begin talking it up."

"Spring is planting season," Mrs. Winthrop put in, sticking out her chin.

Liza nodded. "You're right, of course. I haven't been a farmer's wife long enough to know all the aspects of farming. However, I do know that Benjamin and several other men will be willing to give of their time and energy, even if they don't have a good deal of extra money in their pockets."

That seemed to silence the gruff-faced woman, and so Sarah and Liza took up once more with the discussion of how to go about arranging for a children's get-together. "It could be a winter fair of sorts," Liza suggested with eagerness.

"Oh boy," Lili cried, "could we have a cake walk and maybe some foot races and other games?"

Sarah and Liza both laughed. "Why not?" Liza said. "We'll advertise around town. I'm sure other families will be in favor. After all, these children are used to going to school every day. No doubt their restlessness is growing wearisome for the parents."

Sarah thrilled at the idea of meeting others around the town of Little Hickman, particularly the wives and mothers. "I'll do whatever I can to make it happen," she said, looking from Liza to Lili, and then to Rachel. Much to her delight, Rachel wore a smile. It would do the girl good to make new friends.

***

Seth's chatter filled the air on the trip home. He spoke

of the horses he'd seen in the livery, all the saddles and tack hanging from the walls, and the assortment of carriages and wagons. Rocky found it hard to refrain from smiling, something about the boy's lightheartedness rubbing off on him.

On the other end of the wagon seat, Sarah held her wide-brimmed hat as the wagon jostled along, contenting herself with listening to Seth, eyes fastened on the miles of farmland on either side of them.

Ever since the episode in which he'd embarrassed her in front of the Broughtons, things hadn't been quite the same between them. Oh, he'd apologized profusely the next day, but since then most of the smiles she had doled out had been for the children.

"There's going to be a town party." Rachel interrupted Seth's nonstop prattle to make the announcement.

"Party, you say?" Rocky asked, curious. "What sort of party?"

"Don't know exactly. Mrs. Broughton and Sarah were talking about it."

"That so?" Rocky asked, angling his head at Sarah.

The chilly breeze toyed with her hair, sending strands of it flitting across her cheek. She lifted a hand and tucked them back behind her ear. Rocky coaxed the horses into a faster canter, waiting for her to speak. "Liza and I were discussing that it'd be nice to plan something for the children," she said with a touch of excitement. "Most haven't seen each other since the fire, and it will give Seth and Rachel the chance to meet some children their own age."

It sounded like a good idea. Rocky wondered if Rachel would join in the festivities or hang back. Lately, Seth had grown more independent of his sister, somewhat lessening Rachel's role as caregiver, and he wondered if that didn't contribute to her morose state of mind. Not for the first time he admonished himself for his lack of sensitivity where the girl was concerned.

"When is this so-called party?" he asked.

Drawing in a breath, Sarah said, "Just before planting season." Then, eyeing him with particular care, she added, "I volunteered our barn. I hope that meets with your approval."

The announcement set him back a bit. It'd been a good long while since he'd hosted any kind of gathering. Hester used to enjoy inviting folks over, but since living on his own, he'd pretty much kept to himself. He valued his privacy. Now his wife was planning a town get-together on his property, and he wasn't exactly sure how he felt about that.

Slowing the horses at a bend in the road, then veering them toward the final leg of the journey, he set his gaze on Sarah's hopeful expression, and just like that, he had his answer.

Casting her a smile, he said, "Now that I think about it, Mrs. Callahan, I'd say it's about time we hosted a shindig."

Chapter Twelve

*I*n the weeks that followed, Sarah and Rachel worked on the new curtains, Sarah instructing Rachel how to stitch a simple hem in one panel of curtains while she cut out material for another pair. Rachel delighted in learning the craft, and Sarah thrilled at watching her dive into an activity apart from reading. At least she couldn't hide behind her sewing in the same way she could a book cover.

Midway through stitching curtains, Sarah stopped to make the tablecloth. It was large enough to cover the entire rectangular table and still hang almost to the floor, its colorful, flowery pattern standing out against the hardwood flooring and spindle-back chairs. If there were enough material, she would make fine matching cushions for each of the chairs as well.

Together, Sarah and Rachel decided where to place the new rag rugs—one in the doorway, another in the kitchen, and yet another in front of the entryway to the children's bedroom. Pretty new towels graced the hooks over the kitchen sink, and matching potholders hung near the stove and to one side of the fireplace beside the oven.

All in all, the little Kentucky farmhouse had begun to feel more and more like home to Sarah Callahan.

Not one to interest himself in girlish matters, Seth busied himself running in and out of the house, his latest adventures feeding the two hogs at the far corner of the backyard and tending to the mewing barn cats. Sarah noticed that Rocky had taken to spending more time with the boy and was not so quick to complain anymore when Seth asked to tag along, even occasionally inviting him. It was a joy to watch their relationship develop, and she marveled at how the boy seemed to flourish under Rocky's attention.

Rachel remained mostly sullen, but even she had taken to smiling more, especially during those times that Sarah included her in preparing the meals, gathering up the laundry, sewing the curtains, or watering the houseplants. The girl enjoyed staying busy, so Sarah did what she could to hold boredom at bay. Thankful for Rocky's wonderful collection of books, including many of the classics and a few history books and geographical studies, she read often to the children, creating mini-lessons whenever possible. She'd decided that the school's closing was no reason to deprive the children of an education.

It was odd how she was beginning to think of Seth and Rachel as her own. In fact, she doubted she could love them more if she'd birthed them.

Rocky came to the door just as Sarah and Rachel had finished hanging a set of curtains and were standing back to admire their handiwork. They'd completed three pairs, with one to go. Rocky gave a smile of approval. "Looks mighty nice, if I do say so," he complimented.

"Thank you," Sarah said, appreciating the accolade. "Rachel helped. She is going to be a fine seamstress some day." Sarah put a hand around the child's shoulder and gave a squeeze. "She's a quick study."

Rocky nodded and stepped through the door, wiping his feet on the new rug. "Am I supposed to use this rug?" The

195

guilty look on his face nearly made Sarah laugh.

"That's what rugs are for, Rocky," she said.

He inclined his head at her and made a sheepish face. "I know that, but this one looks too good for wiping my muddy shoes on."

"This is your house, Rocky," she said. "You should feel at home in it."

Lately it seemed to Sarah he'd been bending over backwards to keep the peace with her. She appreciated it, but it made her wonder what she'd done to deserve it. Was he still worried about the scene he'd made at the dinner table when the Broughtons had visited?

He finished wiping his feet, then walked to the kitchen, picked up a tin cup, and poured himself some fresh drinking water. After gulping down the entire cupful, he set the cup down and turned to face her. "I plan to start the addition tomorrow morning, bright and early," he announced. For days, he'd made several trips to and from the sawmill. Behind the barn, he'd stacked boards, roofing shingles, and a variety of other supplies.

Sarah heard the little gasp of air that came from Rachel. "You're really doing it?" she asked, her voice not much more audible than a whisper.

Rocky eked out a grin for the girl. "Did you think I'd forgotten?"

She shook her head. "No, but—I—never had a room to myself before. Mama never had..." That's where she stopped.

Sarah glanced at Rocky, whose face had clouded over. "Well," he said, "it won't be anything fancy, mind you, but it'll afford you some privacy from that scalawag brother of yours."

To this, he smiled, stepped closer to the girl, and dipped his head at her. Then, patting the top of her head in a tender sort of gesture, he added, "A girl your age should have a room of her own."

It was the first time Sarah could remember him touching the child in any way but indifferently, and speaking in so gentle a tone. Had Rachel noticed as well?

Oh, Lord, it seems You've heard my prayers.

Rachel managed a shy smile and shrugged. "It will be nice to have a place to read my books."

"Just don't think of your room as a place to hide from the rest of us," Sarah hurried to say.

"That's right," Rocky said. "You should be playing outside more, maybe keeping your brother company down at the creek."

Instantly, her blue eyes went bright as a summer moon. "Could I help feed the animals—like Seth's been doin'?"

Rocky's brow furrowed, as he glanced from Sarah to Rachel. "I expect Sarah needs you in the house for the womanly chores." The girl's expression dimmed.

"I see nothing wrong with her learning the outside chores as well," Sarah chimed.

"After all, I'll be tending to the barn chores myself once planting season arrives. You said so yourself. Maybe we should both spend time with you in the barn—so you can show us what to do."

He gave her an inquiring look. "I didn't think you'd actually stay around long enough to…" Now a flickering gaze led to the beginnings of a smile. "Never mind." Then to Rachel, "I guess I could use some help feeding those critters. We'll start tomorrow morning."

197

Rachel clapped her hands in delight, as if she'd just been handed her first bouquet of roses. Giving Sarah one last undecipherable glance, he headed for the door. "Seth and I'll be back at suppertime."

Sarah advanced a step, suddenly intent on extending his stay. "Where is Seth?"

Rocky chuckled, hand on the doorknob. "Out behind the barn fashioning himself some kind of doodad with a piece of wood, a hammer, and some nails."

Sarah gasped and covered her mouth. "But—he could get hurt. Isn't he too small for...?"

"How will he learn if no one teaches him, Sarah?" Rocky cut in, his face sobering with the private memory of her earlier words. Set back, she stifled a smile, and Rocky shook his head at her. "Don't worry. It's a small hammer he's working with, one I bought for—my son."

His son. "Oh."

Opening the door in haste, he stepped into the chilly air, then paused and turned. "By the way, you set a date yet for that party you're planning with Liza Broughton?"

She'd been waiting for the right opportunity to broach the subject. "March first, Sunday after next." He seemed to ponder that. "We ladies will do most of the work," she hastened to add. "All that's needed from you are some bales of hay for sitting on, and perhaps some boards for tables. Of course, you'll want to clear a place in the middle for the dancing."

His mouth twisted into a full frown. "Dancing? You mean with music?"

She could barely control her burst of laughter. "It's a might hard to square dance without it."

Failing to see her humor, he said, "I thought this was supposed to be an event for the children."

"It is, silly. There'll be plenty of games—cakewalks, egg tosses, relays, and a three-legged sack race. And for the adults, square dancing." When he still looked doubtful, Sarah added, "And plenty of good food, of course."

He nodded. "I don't dance." The statement came with a wooden expression.

She suppressed another spurt of giggles. "I wouldn't expect you to—unless the urge so overpowered you that you couldn't hold back." When he remained glum-faced, she hastily added, "Liza tells me that Eldred Johansson is a square dance caller from way back. Ben told her they used to have barn raisings followed by square dances. Apparently, Elmer Barrington is good with a fiddle."

"I'd forgotten all about that," Rocky said, fumbling with the doorknob. Cold air snapped at Sarah's ankles. "The first time I ever set eyes on my Hester was at a barn raising." One side of his square-cut jaw flicked slightly.

Just what could she say to that? Her spirits suddenly sagged. Would he never stop mourning his first wife? Moreover, would having the hoedown in their barn stir up old memories, perhaps even demolish their already fragile relationship?

Oh, Lord, please help me show my husband that it's all right to enjoy life again.

***

Sleep did not come easily that night. Images of the day's events replayed in Rocky's head...Seth trying to construct something with that piece of wood and Rocky coming alongside

199

to offer suggestions…a simple birdfeeder? a toy boat? a handy doorstop? Every time he turned around, the kid was asking for his time—and he was giving it.

Then there was the matter of Rachel. How her face had lit at the prospect of her very own room, as if he'd just offered her a handful of gold. The kids had had so little in their short life-time. Regrets assailed him. He should have stepped forward to help when his sister was still living, and he would have, had he not been so wrapped up in his own selfish needs.

Chilled, he yanked a blanket over his shoulder and rolled over on the lumpy couch, wincing with pain when he landed on the one protruding spring, and letting go a mild curse. He missed the comfort of his own bed. Quickly, he relinquished the thought, for to get his own bed back would mean sharing it with Sarah, and he doubted she would go for that. After all, they'd agreed on a marriage in name only.

Still, there was that part of him that had started imagin-ing more.

Yes, his wife attracted him, but sorting out his feelings was another story. Hester had been pretty, but in an unsophisti-cated, earthy way. Sarah, on the other hand, was beautiful, her ramrod-straight backbone, fussy hairstyles, finely chiseled face, and fancy mannerisms putting her in an altogether dif-ferent class. Lately, he'd found himself entering the house at all hours of the day, just looking for an excuse to lay eyes on her.

She was too refined for the likes of him—forget that she seemed anxious to learn everything there was to know about the farm.

I'll be tending the barn chores when planting season gets here.

He lay there scoffing at the notion of her mucking stalls in her velvet skirt—or maybe that green satin getup, the one with the shimmery buttons that traced a straight path down her bosom.

Pfff! Best not to let his mind wander where the woman was concerned. She would be gone by April, he told himself, just as soon as she realized the work was too much for her. Moreover, he would send her off with his blessing.

But then he'd be back to square one with the kids!

He growled into the covers.

"I can't do this," he finally muttered, punching a large dent in his feather pillow and turning over his bulky body for at least the dozenth time. The beginnings of a headache knocked at his temples. "I can't allow myself to love her—or anyone for that matter. Too much risk."

"Abide in me, and I in you." He squeezed his eyes shut in the hope of blocking out the words. He used to be familiar with the Bible and had recited whole passages of it from memory as he plowed the fields. But that was before... Why did they fight their way back to the surface now? **"I am the vine, ye are the branches...for without me ye can do nothing."**

This was Jon Atkins' fault, he decided. Every Sunday his friend's well-delivered sermons seemed directed straight at him. Last Sunday, his topic was "Hope," the Sunday before that, "Faith," and three Sundays ago, "Trust." Oh, he rued the day his wife had insisted he set the example by driving the family to church.

He stared at the fire's embers, watched as the flames flickered and hissed, and asked himself how he could be expected to trust a God who thought nothing of stealing away Hester and Joseph. What would keep Him from taking Sarah or Seth or Rachel next? These were hard times. Disease sometimes swept entire communities, blotting out one life after another. He doubted he had the strength to endure such loss again.

"Be of good courage, and he shall strengthen your heart, all ye that hope in the Lord."

The Word of God kept coming back to him in bits and pieces, piercing him like sharp little arrows, sending messages of hope—lulling him into a fitful sleep.

Sometime after midnight, a whimpering, whining sound forced Rocky awake. Rubbing his eyes, he pulled a hand through his hair and sat up, taking a moment to get his bearings. Snagging the Levis he'd left draped over the end of the sofa, he hurriedly stepped into them, then tuned his ear in the direction of the sound, which appeared to be coming from Sarah's room.

"Sarah?" he whispered into the closed door after giving it a light knock. When she didn't answer, he turned the knob and pushed open the door. "You all right in here?"

Still nothing. At first, he decided his imagination had played a trick on him, for she lay still under a mound of blankets, the moon's silvery glow reflecting off her thick mass of hair lying loose across her pillow. One bare, slender leg had found its way outside of the blanket, and for a moment he just stood there in the open doorway, frozen, feeling like a kid who'd caught a glimpse of something quite forbidden.

And still she didn't move.

Then it came again—that tiny mewling sound. It became clear to Rocky that she was dreaming. Perchance he even played some part in it, he mused—the ogre, no doubt. Frowning, he determined to let her work through the dream on her own, so he prepared to turn and leave, but then her cries increased to the point of quiet sobs.

In two oversized steps, he was crouching at her bedside. "Sarah," he whispered. "Wake up." Gently, he jostled her shoulder. It was then he glimpsed the tears, gleaming like diamonds on her alabaster cheeks. Without forethought, he wiped them with the underside of his thumb, reveling in the feel of her cheek, so soft against his callous-ridden hand.

Her head shifted on the pillow, and one moist eyelid lifted slowly, followed by the other. Registering her gaze, it took but scant seconds for her to sit bolt upright, tugging her blankets with her. "What—?" Eyeballs popping, she clutched the comforter tight to her chin and jerked her smooth, bare leg back where it belonged.

"Relax."

"What are you doing?" she shrieked.

"You were dreaming." He swiped at another loose tear. "Must have been a bad one."

Her mouth dropped, and eyes once filled with alarm now cast him a faraway look. "Yes, I—my mother and I were talking and walking—down at the harbor. We used to stroll past the docks and watch the ships come and go. She was telling me she had to go away and I was—begging her to stay." She drew up her knees and hugged them to her chest, pointing her head downward as if embarrassed. "It was silly." Misty eyes sought his. "I'm sorry I woke you."

"Never mind that," he ordered, flicking his wrist, furious with himself for never having inquired until now as to her personal loss. Selfish clod that he was, he'd forgotten about his own wife's burden of grief. What kind of monster was he? In one fluid motion, he rose from his haunches, grabbed a straight-back chair from a dark corner of the room and, placing it next to her, plunked his body into it. She watched him with something like fascination.

"You miss her?" he asked.

"What? Yes, of course. But, well, as you know, life goes on."

"I don't go on with life as well as you do," he confessed.

That little tidbit produced a smile on her part, but she didn't respond.

"Did she suffer long—your mother?"

Her ginger curls glistened where they fell, and he wanted nothing more than to clutch a mass of them in his fist and test their softness.

Again, she nodded. "Yes, but her suffering drew her to the heavenly Father. God's timing was perfect—for everyone concerned."

Another time he would have shunned this sort of discussion, but not tonight. "How do you mean?"

Using her drawn knees as a place to rest her chin, she thought about her answer. "Her suffering gave her time to reflect upon her life, find her way back to God." She breathed a deep sigh before continuing. "My mother and I didn't always have the perfect relationship. Because she was so involved with her charity groups, garden lunches, library club, and museum projects, the housekeeper saw more of me than my own mother did. In a sense she raised me." She gave a lighthearted chuckle. "But that was okay. I loved Mrs. Winters, and she was really the one who told me about Jesus.

My parents attended church, but more from a sense of duty, I think, than from devotion."

The round neckline of her cotton sleeping gown fell off a creamy white shoulder, making his fingers itch to put it in its proper place.

"In the latter years, Mother and I established a closer friendship." At that, a certain brightness came into her moist eyes. "She was a very generous person, my mother, always lavishing gifts of money and goodwill on one worthy cause or another. The problem was she often neglected the people closest to her. I used to resent her for that, but as I grew older, I realized a bitter heart gained me little peace."

Rocky absorbed her words. She was right about the bitter heart. He hadn't truly known peace since before Hester's passing, and he supposed his cold heart was mostly responsible.

A bright winter moon cast its glow across the bedcovers, and Rocky watched the shadows dance about on the colorful print quilt as Sarah dropped her knees, flipped onto her side, and rested her head on her propped elbow to gaze up at him. Entranced, he sat forward, clasped his hands, and dangled them loosely between his spread knees. Mere inches made up the gap between their faces, and the notion that it wouldn't take much to lean down and plant a kiss on her full lips intrigued him plenty.

He gave himself a mental tongue-lashing. *This is a marriage in name only.*

"It must have been hard for you, Sarah, moving away from everything familiar." It seemed important to keep her talking, for the more she talked the longer he could stay and feast his eyes on her.

A tight little frown found its way to her face. "It was, but I have no regrets about coming here, if that's what you're getting at. I've told you before, Rocky, I enjoy living here. Little Hickman is a quaint place, and I'm getting used to the people and their way of life. Yes, it's far different from my life in Winchester, but I'm finding it quite rewarding." She scrunched up her nose at him, and he had the strongest urge to kiss its tip. "I don't even mind all the housework."

"The real work starts when planting season comes around." *That's when you'll be heading back East, Sarah Woodward Callahan.*

"Why do I get the distinct feeling you think I can't handle it?"

Now it was his turn to grimace. "Because farming is not for everyone, Sarah. It's downright hard work from morning till night. Womenfolk especially find it grueling unless—well, they're made of tough stuff."

"Like your Hester, you mean," Sarah said, turning down her lip.

He hadn't expected her to bring up his former wife, but since she had, he said, "She was born and raised on the farm, and yes, she was pretty tough. She also knew exactly what to expect from every passing season."

"Unlike me." Sarah flopped on her back. Yanking the quilt up under her chin, she stared with narrowed eyes at the ceiling, avoiding his gaze. "You don't think I can do it because I'm rich and spoiled."

He couldn't help his sudden peal of laughter. When she didn't join in, only angled her face at him and deepened her frown, he laughed the more. "Okay, I'll admit that's part of it."

"Well, you best give me a chance, Mr. Callahan. I may not be your Hester, but neither am I a weakling." This she said while drawing her arms out from under the covers and folding them across her chest, as if to emphasize her stubbornness.

His laughter dwindled to a chuckle, then petered out completely. "I wouldn't expect you to be like Hester, Sarah," he said, wanting to make that clear.

"Well, that's comforting to know, because, you see, after all the glowing things I've heard about her, I've already determined I could never measure up."

That did it. Without forethought, he cupped her chin in his hand and moved closer to study her face. So delicately carved, he thought—sculpted cheeks of dusty rose, exotic eyes, exquisite little nose, and that plump, tempting mouth. It was enough to drive a man crazy.

No, she was nothing like Hester. And, wonder of wonders, he liked her that way.

She lay there motionless under his perusal, her expression denoting some indecipherable emotion.

Shifting on the chair, he positioned himself so that he could angle his head in her direction and was relieved when she didn't resist. If anything, she seemed cemented in place, perhaps too shocked to budge.

He kissed her slowly at first, experimentally, needing time to explore, to test her willingness. He moved his mouth over hers, waiting for her retreat. When it didn't come, he continued the journey, cupping her slender shoulders with both hands and lifting her closer. To his amazement, she responded, her own lips moving with his, her arms coming up to encircle his back.

For the life of him, he couldn't comprehend the feelings churning up inside him. He certainly hadn't planned to kiss his wife, hadn't expected this gush of emotion, this swirling, burning aftermath of passion. It was just a kiss, he told himself. Nothing more. But even as he talked himself into believing the lie, the passion multiplied tenfold.

Lord, help me...

As if waking from a dizzy spell, he quickly drew away, setting himself straight in his chair again. This was supposed to be a marriage in name only, he chided—no touching, no emotional ties, certainly no kissing. And now he'd blown their perfect little plan right out of the water.

What must she think?

Feeling the fool, he managed to mutter, "Sorry about that. I didn't intend for that to happen. It's just that, well, you looked so..."

Wide-eyed and silent as a church mouse, Sarah seemed pinned to the mattress, her mouth still red from the force of his kiss, her arms now resting limply on either side of her. Had he shocked her with his forwardness?

Grappling for the right words, he said, "What I mean to say is—I won't let it happen again. It was wrong of—me—to..."

Still no response, just chilly, dead air. She hated him for breaking their marriage bargain. That had to be it. Why else would she be giving him that stunned expression?

He dropped his shoulders in defeat. "All right, I'll admit it; I messed up. That's the plain truth of the matter. You and I struck a marriage bargain. We agreed there'd be no physical contact, and I overstepped my bounds. So—I hope you'll—accept my apology."

She dropped her gaze and appeared to be studying her toes. "No need to apologize," she replied just as simple as you please. He stared at her. "It was no one's fault."

"No, I take full responsibility," he argued.

"Fine," she replied, setting her jaw in a firm line.

"Fine." Just like that, he stood to his feet and started retreating toward the door. "Fine," he repeated, walking backward, eyes centered on her. Best to leave while he still had his wits about him, he ruled, especially since the sight of her made his heart turn over.

She'd be gone come spring anyway. Blast! He'd make it easy for her and help her pack.

At the door, he paused and asked, "Will you be all right now?"

"Of course." Her clipped answer made his nerves clatter.

And when she put her face to the wall, he made his exit.

Chapter Thirteen

On the day of the hoedown, Sarah rose just before dawn. Several women planned to arrive by mid-morning to begin preparations for the event, and Sarah wanted to have the house ready for her guests.

Benjamin Broughton and several others had posted signs, and rumor had it that nearly the whole town planned to attend. Butterflies whirled in Sarah's stomach as she flitted through the house, mopping floors, scrubbing countertops, and wiping out the oven, where the smell of freshly baked bread still lingered. She'd been baking for days now, and the pantry shelves lined with pies, platters of cookies, and various other baked goods were clear evidence of the fact.

"You're up early." Rocky stood at the closed front door, his hand still on the knob.

Sarah jolted. "I didn't hear you come in," she said, doing her best to cover her flustered reaction.

"I didn't want to wake the household." He shook off his coat, wet from a light morning rain, and hung it on a hook.

"I see." She quickly turned toward the sink and began scrubbing the potatoes she'd hauled up from the little cellar in the lean-to. Glancing out the window, she said, "I hope the rain quits. It would be a shame if it kept up throughout the festivities."

"There're a few stars peeking out in the west. I think the storm will pass soon enough."

"I'd hate for the children's games to be cancelled due to the weather."

"It would be a trifle difficult holding races in the barn, but we'll manage."

At that, she heard him wipe his feet, and the next thing she knew he was reaching around her for a tin mug. She hastened to give him room, shivering when she felt his breath on the back of her neck.

Something had passed between them since the kiss, something sweet but incredibly delicate. She'd determined even mentioning it might make it seem less real, less sacred. Apparently, he felt the same, for neither had uttered a single word about the intimate moment, particularly since they'd both decided against its ever happening again. One might have thought it hadn't happened at all—except for the nervous tension that grew between them. At least, there'd been no move to repeat the act. Good thing, for she wasn't sure how she might react the next time. She knew they'd agreed to a marriage in name only, but she couldn't deny that part of her that longed for intimacy.

"Smells mighty fine in this house," Rocky said, moving to the stove for a cup of coffee. Steam from the hot liquid rose from the cup, performing an almost eerie, circular dance in the dimly lit kitchen. Because Sarah hadn't wanted to wake the children, she'd taken care to light only a few of the lamps around the house. Now she had the uncanny urge to set every available lamp ablaze.

Sarah continued scrubbing with a vengeance, but stole a quick glance at her husband, who had turned around to lean his bulky frame against the sink and watch her work, mug encased snugly in his oversized hands. She couldn't imagine

what he found so interesting about watching her scrub potatoes, but at the risk of allowing him to see her jangled nerves,
she scoured harder.

"By the time you're done with those you won't need to peel
'em," he remarked.

"What?"

"The potatoes."

She glanced down at the nearly skinned vegetable, hastily
peeled it the rest of the way, then dropped it into the nearby
steaming kettle.

"Need some help?" he asked after she retrieved her next
potato, this one full of grit and grime, a result of having been
wrenched from its earthen bed at the end of last season. The
question made her pause midway through her scrubbing to
stare down the drain hole.

"I bet together we could make fast work of those spuds,"
he repeated. Out of the corner of her eye, she glimpsed him
taking a long swig of coffee and wondered how he did it. Try
as she might, she could not acquire a taste for it.

"I can manage, thank you," she answered, resuming her
task and wishing he would leave her to her kitchen. Or better,
leave her to her house. "Is the barn ready?" she asked.

He chuckled. "The barn was ready last night when you
asked. Bales of hay are stacked against the sides for folks to
sit on, and Ben and I moved the worktables from the center
to make room for your square dancing. You can use those
for laying out the food later. A few minutes ago, I turned the
horses and cows loose on the north pasture. Anything else you
need?" He rewarded her with a slanted grin. Her response was
a nervous cough.

"Do you have the jitters?" he asked, tipping his head closer.

"No!" she answered too quickly, sidestepping to avoid his hot breath.

"Yes, you do," he countered, setting his coffee mug on the counter. When he sidled up next to her, brushing against her to reach for a potato, she felt the quake of her body. *Lord, how could my own husband make me so edgy?*

"Be still, my child."

The simple reminder calmed her, but, unfortunately, it was short-lived.

"No need to be nervous, you know. The folks around Hickman have already accepted you." He handled the potato for a moment before dousing it in the bucket of water and then commencing to scrub it clean.

"I appreciate that," she said. And she was grateful for his offer of assistance. However, the citizens of Hickman were the least of her worries. Plainly put, ever since they had kissed, her husband rattled her to the point of rendering her useless.

"How's this?" He held up the dirt-free potato for her inspection.

"Looks good."

"Is that all you can say?"

A guarded smile played around her lips. "You want me to compliment you for washing a potato?"

He gave her a playful nudge in the side. "I like a bit of encouragement now and then."

Was he toying with her? And did his statement hold a double meaning?

Deciding to play things safe, she threw up her guard.

"Don't you have something else to do?"

He laughed. "Are you trying to get rid of me, Mrs. Callahan?" He tossed the clean potato down and set out to rinse another one.

"And what if I were?" she asked, adding vigor to her scrubbing motion, then taking up a paring knife to make fast work of her peeling job.

"Then I would just have to assume that I'm the one who makes you nervous."

"That's foolishness," she said, swallowing a dry lump, suddenly wishing for a sip of his black coffee, never mind that its taste rivaled stump water.

"Is it? You've done nothing but avoid me these past several days."

She could say the same for him. "Would you put these in the kettle, please?" she asked, handing him three large, peeled potatoes.

He took the vegetables from her hand, brushing his fingers against her palm in the process. Whether or not the act was intentional, it was enough to create an involuntary jolt. Rocky raised a knowing brow.

"What?" she asked, annoyed with herself for revealing a piece of her emotions.

"I do make you nervous," he said, dropping the potatoes into the kettle with a low chuckle.

"Oh, stop being so high-hatted, Mr. Callahan. You do not make me nervous," she fibbed, stepping around him to put a lid on the steaming pot.

He followed her with his eyes. She could almost *hear* his irrepressible grin, *feel* it when he returned to the sink to wash another potato. And when he took up whistling the tune to "Oh My Darling, Clementine," she almost gave in to a giggle, and she might have, had it not been for Rachel's sudden appearance in the doorway.

"You guys are noisy," she grumbled. Blonde hair tousled and matted, the girl fixed them with a droopy-eyed glare, her bare feet sticking out from beneath her long, flannel nightgown. "It's still dark out. Is it time to get up already?"

Sarah shot Rocky a look of admonition, chagrined to find a boyish smile plastered across his face as he busied himself at the sink. Turning to Rachel, she said, "No, honey, go back to bed."

"But you're too noisy," she fussed.

It would be nice when Rocky finished Rachel's room, which he'd recently roughed in. At least that room would stand farther from the kitchen noises.

Hastening to wipe her hands on her apron front, Sarah walked across the room. "Come on, I'll tuck you back in."

She laid a hand to the girl's shoulder to guide her back to bed, but Rachel stopped in her tracks. "But Uncle Rocky was whistlin' some song. I never heard him whistle before."

"And you won't again—at least not until daylight. Besides, your uncle is going out to the barn," she said, flinging her head around to send him a pointed look before ushering Rachel back to bed, "—any minute now."

Rocky tossed back his head and laughed. And no matter how hard she tried, she could not erase her own smile.

***

The house bustled with the sounds of bantering women

scuttling from one table and countertop to another, and buzzing about like bees in a hive. Pies of every flavor covered the kitchen table, while trays of cakes and cookies crammed the stone hearth, saturating the house with every mouthwatering aroma imaginable. In the massive warming oven beside the fireplace were cheesy casseroles, scalloped potatoes, meat loaves, creamed and fried chicken, and a huge tray of succulent roast beef. Clearly, no one would go hungry on this day if the hearty display of food was any indication.

While the womenfolk scurried about the kitchen making final preparations to carry the food to the barn, the men and children gathered outside—the men took up a game of horseshoes, and the children raced about the yard in their usual disorganized fashion. Enthusiastic bursts of laughter pealed out from the men, accompanied by animated squeals from the younger generation.

"Goodness gracious, it sounds like everyone is havin' themselves a grand time," Mary Callahan chimed. Sarah smiled across the room at the plump woman she'd come to think of as simply "Mother C." How good it was to have her under her roof again. If only she could keep her here. Of course, she was certain Pa Callahan would have something to say about that.

"Yes, doesn't it?" said Bess Barrington, a woman Sarah had met just two weeks earlier in Sunday service. "What a wonderful idea you and Liza had, Sarah. This was just the outlet these children needed. Not to mention their poor parents."

Several of the women released a hearty laugh. "Ain't that the truth? My twins, Sam and Freddie, been drivin' me nigh to distraction," said a woman Sarah knew only as Mrs. Hogsworth. "Never thought I'd see the day they admitted to missin' school.

Matter of fact, I hear most of the youngins 'round Hickman are growing restless as young Injuns."

"My Thomas has been ailin' some, so today ought to cheer him considerably," said frail-looking Iris Bergen. She brushed a stray tendril of graying hair behind an ear and hovered over an apple pie as if inspecting it for doneness.

Mary looked up from her place at the sink. "Oh? So sorry to hear that, Iris. What's been his problem?"

"Nothing more than a plain cold so far as I can see. He's been coughin' some and complainin' of a sore throat."

Mary nodded. "It does sound like a simple cold, don't it?" Several of the women gave knowing nods.

"His pa wanted him to stay home, but Thom wouldn't hear of it," Iris added, brushing another strand of hair away from her eyes, which Sarah took as a nervous gesture.

"Erlene complained of the same this morning, now that you mention it," Bess Barrington said, her brow knit in a show of mild concern. "She sneezed and coughed a few times."

"Wouldn't worry too much," said Eleanor Humphrey. She was the mother of Gus, the lad Sarah had met at the mercantile. "These things come and go in a matter of days."

Glancing about the room, Sarah made a mental note of all the women whose names she'd learned. Besides Bess Barrington, Mrs. Hogsworth, Liza Broughton, and her own dear mother-in-law, there was Fancy Jenkins, a name Sarah thought unbefitting considering the woman looked about as unkempt as an abandoned pup.

Fluttering about and removing one dish from the oven while inserting another were Esther Thompson and Francis Baxter. From what Sarah had heard, Francis was the mother of Rufus, the young man who'd come to Liza's rescue in the burning schoolhouse. Then there was Millie Jacobs, a new mother who even now doted over her baby on the other side of the room. The infant lay tucked securely beneath a mountain of downy quilts in a makeshift bed Sarah had fashioned for her from a large cupboard drawer.

Sarah turned her eyes away from the other women to fix her attention on Liza, who'd gone to the window to peer outside. How quiet her new friend had been since her arrival. Surprising, considering how everyone else could barely wait her turn to speak.

Just as Sarah was about to inquire about her silence, Liza spun about and declared above the female racket, "Oh, I can't hold it in a minute longer!"

A blanket of calm fell across the room like the sort of eerie silence that follows a riotous storm, as several pairs of eyes made Liza the focus of their attention.

Liza's cheeks grew pink and her eyes bulged.

"You look ready to split your insides, child. What is it?" asked Bess Barrington.

Liza laughed. "Oh, I am, I am!" she crowed. "Ready to split my insides, that is. I'm about to grow as big as a pumpkin. Oh, I—I'm going to have a baby!"

In one fell swoop, women descended on Liza from every direction, hovering, hugging, patting, and poking. Congratulations rang out on all sides. Since Sarah couldn't manage to squeeze in, she watched from the sidelines, quietly awed by the splendid news and delighted that Liza had made the happy announcement right in her very own house.

"I declare, this is reason to celebrate!" cried Mary amidst

the flurry of wild excitement. "When is this little one due to greet the world?"

Liza pulled back from the crowd of enthusiasts, her face a picture of perplexity. "Well, my stars, I don't know. I've never been taught the proper way of figuring. I'm hoping Doc Randolph will be able to tell."

"Well, I suspect it won't be till fall seein's you was just married in December," came the meek voice of Caroline Warner.

Liza laid a protective hand across her belly. Was that an instinctive gesture for every woman carrying? Sarah wondered. "Yes, fall. November perhaps," Liza said with a contented grin.

What must it feel like, Sarah wondered, to know you carried a miracle within your womb? Would she ever know, or would she spend her life speculating about the marvelous mystery?

As if her mother-in-law somehow sensed her secret meanderings, she came alongside her to offer a consoling hug. "It's always good news when a lady finds she's carryin'."

"Yes, it surely is," said Sarah, leaning into the older woman's warmth, doing her best to blot out her private set of doubts.

Then, squeezing tighter, Mary put her mouth close to Sarah's ear. "Your day will come," she whispered. "You'll see. It will be just like this—women flittin' and flutterin' about. Land sakes! You'd think they was preparin' for the president himself 'stead of a baby."

Sarah blushed at the thought of ever carrying Rocky's baby. Why, they were married in name only. They'd struck a bargain, after all. And so long as he held up his end of things, all thoughts of carrying a little one were simply out of the question.

219

So why did that notion suddenly leave her feeling some-how unfulfilled?

***

As Rocky had predicted, the weather held. As a matter of fact, around noon, the sun popped out, to the delight of everyone present, dropping a blanket of warmth on the mer-rymakers.

Foot races, relays, ball tosses, and tug-of-war matches made up some of the day's activities. It seemed his wife and Liza Broughton had thought of everything—including prizes for the children. Squeals of delight rang out even now as Rocky glimpsed Sarah handing each of the children, winners and otherwise, colorful candy sticks. Not that any of them needed a drop of anything more—every single kid, includ-ing Rachel and Seth, seemed to be toting around a bagful of goodies.

Spoiling them, that's what she was doing, but blamed if there was anything he could do about it!

"Now don't run with these in your mouth," he heard her instructing, her tone soft but firm. Each one nodded perfunc-torily, then snatched the stick from her hand, some offering their thanks, others running off as if they'd just struck gold and couldn't wait to tell someone about it. One young kid, he thought it might be Thomas Bergen, rewarded Sarah with a sloppy sneeze.

Rocky couldn't help but laugh at the awful grimace she made when the youngster took off at a run. For a moment, she just stood there, her hands spread, her eyes bulging in disbe-lief. Then, just as quickly, she shrugged her shoulders, lifted

 220

the corner of her apron, and wiped away the nasty spew.

Rocky rounded the curve at the barn and leaned up against a hitching post situated behind a small cluster of apple trees where he could get a better view of her, perhaps get his fill, although he doubted the latter. Lately, he could never quite get enough of Sarah Callahan and had taken to questioning his very sanity.

Moreover, he blamed his misery on his lack of self-control. That, and his inability to sleep while he inwardly planned the next time he could take her in his arms. He was going mad with wondering what would happen if he reneged on their mutual agreement to keep things platonic. He'd already pushed her to her limit this morning when he'd harassed her for a bad case of nerves.

Oh, how it pleased him to know that he rattled her. Of course, she had an equal effect on him, but he wasn't about to tell her so. For now, he had the upper hand, and he rather liked it that way.

"So this is where you've been hiding," came a friendly voice from behind him.

Rocky smiled even before turning to acknowledge his old friend. "Hey, Ben, good to see you."

Ben Broughton whacked him on the shoulder, then moved up next to him. "Enjoying some breathing space?" Ben asked.

"You could say that," Rocky answered.

Without thinking, he again sought out his wife, discovering she'd bent to help a child tie his shoe. As quickly as she finished, the little boy ran off, delighted to be free again. Sarah watched him go, completely oblivious that her husband was watching. Warmth trickled through his veins.

"Ah," said Ben, his own eyes trailing to where Sarah stood. "Enjoying the scenery as well, I see."

Embarrassed to be caught spying on his own wife, Rocky tried to deny his actions. "Just enjoying the fresh, clean air, that's all." He hastened to turn his attention away from his wife, hard as it was. Thankfully, she'd moved on to a small gathering of women.

"She's quite something," Ben mused aloud. "It can't have been easy—all she's been through."

Rocky knew his friend was right. Sarah's plans had been crushed and her life had been completely turned upside down, yet somehow she'd triumphed. More than once, he'd had to acknowledge it must be her faith that held her together.

A moment passed before Rocky asked, "Was she very disappointed that day? When she realized you planned to marry Liza?"

"Disappointed?" Ben laughed, then leaned against the side of the barn, tipping the front of his Western hat downward to deflect the sun's glare. Considering it was only the first of March, the air was surprisingly mild, but then, spring was right around the corner. "I don't think *disappointed* would be my word of choice."

"No?" Rocky's interest doubled. "Seems to me your letting her down like that would trigger some disappointment."

Ben grinned. "I think *irate* might better describe her reaction." Now a far-off look accompanied the grin. "She seemed downright irked with me when I told her I loved another.

"'Course, I apologized until I was blue in the face, even offered her fare back to Boston, plus extra pay for her trouble, but she wouldn't hear of it. Said she didn't need my money."

Rocky nodded, trying to place the unfolding event into his own head. The notion that Sarah had preferred Ben to him never had set right. Had she entertained thoughts of how different things might have been married to his good-looking friend instead?

"What made her come to terms with it?" Rocky asked, looking down at the hole he was digging with the toe of his boot.

Ben thought a moment, calling up the memory. "She insisted that God had called her to Little Hickman—if not to marry me, then for a greater cause. Said she planned to stay and find out what it was." Ben squinted into the sun before throwing Rocky a slanted grin. "Guess you were that greater cause, pal."

Rocky guffawed. "Fine cause I was. A sorehead with two kids—kids I didn't really want, at least in the beginning."

"And now?" Ben probed.

Rocky had to ponder that. Yeah, he wanted the kids. They were still a pain most of the time, Rachel keeping her distance, and Seth lately snagging onto Rocky as if he were his real pa. It was purely suffocating at times—suffocating and gratifying. In short, his head and heart didn't always agree.

"I'd say we're doin' all right. Had some rough patches, but we're workin' our way through them."

Ben nodded, thoughtful. "You two ever settle that matter of the fancy china and silver? I meant to apologize for opening my big mouth that night, but—"

With outstretched hand, Rocky halted him. "Don't bother, and, yes, I guess we did, although she hasn't brought the dishes out since, even though I've told her a time or two to use them if she wanted. Guess she's still a mite touchy about the whole episode, not that I blame her any. I was out of line that night."

Mild laughter came from Ben. "You were the picture of jealousy, my friend," he pointed out. "You didn't like the idea that the dishes came from an old beau. Who is the guy anyway?"

"An old family friend, according to Sarah. He traveled clear from Boston for the purpose of proposing marriage," he told him, scoffing even now at the remembrance.

Rocky lounged casually against the hitching post and scanned the horizon, grinning when across the yard he caught sight of Seth running at breakneck speed around the back of the house, some little girl on his tail.

He sniffed. "Guy wasn't too pleased to discover I had the same intention. Don't mind saying I hope we never cross paths again. 'Course, it just might be unavoidable, his being a lawyer and all."

Confusion traced a path across Ben's face. "What do you mean by that?"

Rocky gave a dismissive shrug, chortling under his breath. "I can't see her surviving this way of life much longer, Ben. You and I both know farming is no picnic. A woman like her deserves fine things, none of which I have the means to offer. The time will come when she'll discover it's too much for her. That's when she'll call on the old family friend—to aid her in the annulment, and you can bet he'll come running just as soon as he gets the call."

"Anul—Don't be crazy, Rock. Give the lady some credit, for Pete's sake. According to Liza, she's made a good adjustment to life in Hickman. Besides, she seems to love those little kids of yours. Have some faith."

Ben stepped closer and gave Rocky a light pat on the shoulder. "God told us in His Word that the trying of our faith worketh patience, and that the Lord is good unto them that wait for Him, that seek His ways. He wants to bless your family, but you gotta learn to trust."

"I've done nothing for God lately that would incite His favors."

"We can't earn his favor, Rock. God's a merciful God. Sometimes He just plain blesses us for no good reason—even when we don't deserve it."

Rocky turned his attention to the rolling fields, still brown and dormant. It was hard to believe that in a matter of weeks, moist seeds would begin their speedy growth, breaking through the soil almost overnight, reaching upward like ravenous children.

"You're beginning to sound like Jonathan, you know that? Did you miss your calling?"

With a toss of his head, Ben laughed. "Hardly. I'd put everyone to sleep if I got behind a pulpit. Jon is the one with the preaching gift. By the way, it's been great seeing you in church again."

A grunting sound slipped past his throat. "My wife gives me little choice."

"Smart woman. And speaking of," Ben popped him in the arm, "did you know I'm to be a father again?"

Unsure how to react, he gave Ben a wide smile and returned a playful punch.

"Congratulations!" He was pretty sure that women squealed loud enough to hear in the next county with news of that nature. Men, on the other hand, played things much cooler. "That didn't take long," he said with a wink, even then toying with the impossible notion of fathering another child himself. Kind of a hard thing to accomplish, he mused, when all he'd managed so far with his feisty wife was a stolen kiss.

Maybe he ought to make a greater effort.

Jon Atkins stood in the center of the yard, let out a high-pitched whistle by blowing through his index finger and thumb, and bellowed in his loudest voice, "Food's ready. Come and get it!"

"You gotta have preacher's lungs to spout like that," Ben joked.

Rocky laughed in agreement, and together they headed inside the barn for the second meal of the day. After supper, several men would bring out their instruments, the women would clear the tables, and the square dancing would commence.

Chapter Fourteen

*L*ively music such as Sarah had never heard filled the barn at dusk. Folks with very small children had left for the day, but everyone else seemed hesitant to go, the day's festivities having whetted their appetites for old-fashioned fun and fellowship.

Sarah was happy to see Emma Browning ride in just as she was making a trip from the house to the barn.

She gave her friend a wild wave. "Hello, Emma! I'm so glad you stopped by."

Smiling, Emma directed her draft horses to a spot alongside several other buggies and climbed down. "I can't stay, mind you," she said. "I am expecting a new boarder late this evening, so I must prepare for his arrival. Still, I did want to stop in for a brief visit." She looked toward the lantern-lit barn where folks chattered at the tops of their voices. Every so often, someone let out a loud peal of laughter. "Sounds like everyone's havin' a good time."

The blue-eyed woman smiled warmly, revealing a dimple in her left cheek. Dressed in yellow gingham with matching bonnet and shawl, her blond hair fixed in a loose bun with several strands fallen to the sides, she was a pretty thing. Sarah couldn't imagine why she'd never married, unless it was that she simply wasn't interested. Although Sarah didn't like to listen in on hearsay, she'd picked up enough in conversations with Emma while she lived at the boardinghouse to know that Emma was a loner and liked it that way.

"Her father is the town drunk," Mrs. Winthrop once stated when Sarah was buying additional sewing supplies and Emma Browning had walked past the window.

Not wanting to appear interested in what she had to say regarding her friend, she couldn't help but raise a curious eyebrow. That was all the encouragement Iris Winthrop needed. "Ezra Browning is a no-good rapscallion who ought to be ousted from the town. You'll find him sleepin' on the sidewalk outside of that—that drinking establishment across the street most every night."

"You mean Madame Guttersnipe's Saloon and Hotel?"

"Piffle. It's a bawdy house, if you ask me. Such a disgrace it is. Someone ought to burn that awful building down." Apparently, Mrs. Winthrop preferred living with an arsonist in her midst. Sarah nearly giggled at the notion.

"Why doesn't Mr. Browning take a room at his daughter's place?"

Mrs. Winthrop dropped her jaw. "That would never do. Besides, he has his own place a mile out of town, although it's a shack. Emma wouldn't allow him in her place, anyway. The two don't even speak."

Sarah thought that bit of information odd, but since she'd already learned more than was necessary, she took up her purchases and wished Mrs. Winthrop a good afternoon.

Now Sarah greeted Emma with a gentle squeeze. "Come inside where it's warmer," she coaxed. "The barn's not heated, but with the big lanterns and everyone snuggled close, we're managing just fine."

With that, Emma followed Sarah to a vacant spot on a

prickly bale of hay. "It's not much of a seat," Sarah apologized.

"It'll do just fine," Emma replied.

"Well, if it isn't the lovely Miss Browning," came the buttery-smooth voice of the handsome young preacher. Emma made ready to move to a different spot, but Jon Atkins wouldn't hear of it, taking her by the arm and seating her before she had a chance to protest and then quickly squeezing in beside her. Sarah thought it comical the way Emma blanched in Jon Atkins' presence. Did his preacher status make her uncomfortable, or was it that the young Reverend Jonathan Atkins was so charmingly handsome?

Well, no matter—it was time she saw to the rest of the guests. Smiling at the unlikely pair, she excused herself and moved along.

Eldred Johansson's square dance call rang through the rafters, wooing folks to the center of the barn. Several couples accepted the invitation, and before long, men began handing off their laughing partners to another at the caller's orders, dust flying high as boot heels broke up the straw-covered earth, fancy fiddles blaring into the frosty night.

"Swing your partner, do-si-do,

Round and round, now here we go.

Now trade her off for another girl,

Hand in hand, now give her a whirl."

Sarah looked around for a glimpse of Rocky and found him standing with several men, most of whom she hadn't met personally but recognized as the husbands of the women she knew. As if he sensed she was watching, he turned and met her eyes. When he tipped his hat at her and winked, she gasped, wondering if anyone else had spotted the gesture.

Granting him a tiny smile in response, she hastily swiveled her body, picked up her skirts, and set out toward a group of women all gathered around the one remaining food table.

"Are you havin' fun?" inquired a high-pitched, breathless voice, stopping her midstride. Spinning around, she looked down into a red-faced Rachel.

"Why, yes I am, sweetie," she answered, patting one of her red cheeks. "Where's Seth? I haven't seen either of you for the past hour or more. And why are you so out of breath? Are you feeling all right?" A number of the children had been sneezing and coughing during the day. She hoped Rachel and Seth wouldn't catch their cold.

"I'm fine! Kids been chasin' me and Seth." Her voice rang of pure delight. "It's fun, Aunt Sarah—I mean—Sarah." The girl looked mortified to have made the blunder, so Sarah quickly set out to ease her embarrassment.

"It's perfectly fine if you want to think of me as your aunt, sweetie. In fact, I'd be tickled pink."

"Truly? Me and Seth been practicin' sayin' it in private," she admitted. "That's why it slipped out."

She bent so that the girl's face came within eye level. "Well, I think it's lovely."

"Rachel, come on!" Lili Broughton stood in the doorway, one hand on her hip, her face a picture of impatience. "We're gettin' ready to play hide-and-seek. Hurry!"

Rachel looked at Sarah with an impish grin. "I gotta go play."

Straightening, she gave the girl's hand a gentle squeeze. "Run along then."

"See you later, Aunt Sarah!" she hollered loud enough that

several people turned and smiled. She scampered off into the starry night, taking no notice when she sailed right past her uncle on her way out the door. He watched her run off, then, making eye contact with Sarah, strolled over to where she stood.

"Aunt Sarah?" A wide grin stole across his face on his approach. "That's something new."

Foolishly, her heart skipped a beat at the sound of his cavernous voice.

Lord above, am I falling in love?

Wanting to hide her emotions, she gazed at the children, who had formed a huddle. In the distance, she heard the voice of Lili Broughton doling out instructions and gesturing with her hands. *A born leader,* Sarah pondered with a touch of amusement.

"Rachel tells me she and Seth have been practicing in private."

"Ah," Rocky mused. "Trying it out, huh? Well, I guess it would make things simpler for everyone, what with me being their uncle."

She nodded, shooting a gaze at the circle of children again, trying to locate Rachel and Seth in the midst, relieved when she did. "They seem happier lately," she remarked.

The last several mornings, Rachel had been rising earlier than usual to help feed the animals with Seth. Although Rocky had tolerated their tagging along, Sarah had heard grumblings from him that he wasn't accomplishing his chores in a timely fashion anymore. "They're more important than the chores, Rocky Callahan, and they need your influence in their lives," she'd reminded, giggling softly when he'd harrumphed.

Although she'd heard little mentioned in reference to the children's real father, Rocky had once told her how worthless the fellow had been, having deserted his family when Seth was a baby, then dying shortly afterward in some sort of farming accident.

Yes, the children required—even deserved—their uncle's love and attention.

"It appears they've found themselves some friends," Rocky remarked, his own gaze traveling to the group of children clustered in the yard.

Since the musicians had announced their need for a short break, the boisterous lot of dancers began to mill about the barn, some seeking refreshment at the punch table, others joining in pleasant conversation with neighbors, the light from several lanterns reflecting off their friendly, smiling faces.

Earlier sunshine had given way to full-blown dusk and, with it, cooler temperatures. Peering through the wide-open, double barn doors, Rocky must have caught his first glimpse of the full moon just as Sarah had. Without warning, he snagged her by the coat sleeve and summoned her into the chilly night air. "Come on," he urged, moving his hand down her arm and latching onto her fingers.

"What are you doing?" Sarah cried, suddenly finding herself being pulled along, pulse-pounding excitement racing through her veins. "Where are we going?"

With purposeful strides, he pulled her across the yard and past the children. "Follow me," he called.

"Do I have a choice?" she asked, breathless, taking care to hoist her skirts up as she ran, the brisk breezes licking at her cheeks.

"None that I can think of."

Surprisingly, no one followed, not even the children, when he led her to the other side of the house and still several feet beyond the outhouse. Wading through a clump of tall, dead weeds, he stopped in a small clearing and turned her to face him, their hurried, hot breaths mingling.

"There now. We can watch it in peace."

Gaping open-mouthed at him, she snagged a much-needed breath and asked, "Watch what in peace?"

Chuckling low, he cocked a thumb upward. "That," he said, his upturned gaze indicating the moon, round and luminous. Stars flickered, still faint in the slowly darkening sky.

She caught her breath. He wanted to share the moon with her? "It is a spectacular sight, isn't it?" she whispered, tilting her head for a better view.

"Quite," he answered. "The loveliest sight I've ever seen, in fact." But when she looked back, it didn't appear he was talking about the moon at all, for his eyes had come to rest on her face.

A wild exhilaration ran through her veins at the notion that he found her attractive, followed by an unnerving sense of insecurity. Was he teasing again? She would not let him goad her as he'd succeeded in doing that morning. Glancing in the direction of the barn, she cleared her throat and said, "Folks will wonder where we've gone."

"Will they now?" The moon's soft glow reflected faint touches of humor in his vibrant blue eyes. "I should think most would think it downright ordinary for a man to haul his bride away for a minute or two of seclusion."

Several words of warning whispered in her head. *You*

mustn't let him plant a seed of false hope in your heart. There'll be no more kissing, no touching. This is a marriage in name only.

"We should go back," she announced.

"You've been avoiding me all day, Mrs. Callahan. As a matter of fact, ever since that kiss a few days back, you've been trying to make yourself scarce."

He touched a cool finger to her chin and drew her face around until she was forced to meet his gaze, creating in her a jumble of shivers. "Can you blame me?" she asked.

A faint line of confusion creased his brow. "What do you mean?"

Shaking his finger off her chin, she set her spine straight and spouted, "You understand perfectly what I mean. You provoked me this morning just to get a rise out me, and now you're at it again. You're a—a bully, Rocky Callahan!"

The smile in his eyes spread to his mouth, his warm breath creating a cloud of steam as it met with cold air. "A bully, you say? Because I questioned why I make you nervous? Can you blame me for my curiosity?"

Her chin went out in opposition to his playfulness.

"It was that kiss, wasn't it?" he challenged, coming close to whisper in her ear.

Tiny shivers zoomed straight up her spine, creating a kind of panic. She took a step back. He was doing it again, trying to break her down, catch her in a giggle or a smile.

As if finding the chink in her armor, two rough, work-worn hands went to both her cheeks and held tenderly. "Well, all right then, I confess," he whispered. "I'm a bully, and right now this bully would very much like to kiss you."

Ripples of excitement curled through her, creating more

quivers. "But—I thought we agreed…"

He chuckled in husky tones as he lowered his face within inches of hers, his warm, moist breath spreading itself across her cool cheeks like feathery rose petals. "Ah, the arrangement, yes, that is a problem." He kissed the tip of her nose before moving to her temple and kissing its tiny indentation. "What say we discuss that silly agreement later?"

Silly agreement? But…

Reluctant to encourage him, yet powerless to stop herself, Sarah moved into his strong embrace, her arms spreading the wide expanse of his muscular back, his encircling her much smaller frame.

"Sarah," he muttered, dropping tiny kisses on her earlobe, then moving to her cheek to do the same.

After a time, he pulled back slightly to link gazes with her and, giving her a hangdog grin, asked, "Whose idea was it anyway—that ridiculous marriage-in-name-only pact?" Not giving her a chance to respond, he lowered his face again and met her lips with his.

The kiss might very well have gone on forever had it not been for an unusual amount of shouting coming from the other side of the house. At first, both were oblivious to the shrieks and squeals of children and adults alike, wrapped up as they were in the pure sweetness of it all.

But then one word drew their kiss to an abrupt end—a word feared by every farmer for miles around.

"Fire!" came the fierce warning. "Barn's on fire!"

At first confused, Rocky dropped his hands to Sarah's waist and turned his eyes toward the barn. A ring of smoke floated over the house, filling the starlit sky, the stench of burning wood already clogging the air.

"Oh, dear God!" Rocky cried, the impact of the moment finally recording itself in his brain. Without a word, he sped off toward the blaze, leaving Sarah in a cloud of dust and her mind drenched in terror.

When she rounded the corner of the house, several yards behind her husband, she lost sight of him. Flames shooting upward from the back and one side of the barn had folks scurrying in numerous directions, some herding small children away from the flames, others still exiting through the wide double doors.

Sarah hoisted her skirts and darted about the yard in frantic search for Seth and Rachel, snatching looks in every direction, her heart in an uproar. "Lord Jesus," she panted, "please show me where they are."

A bucket brigade formed in the yard, starting at the well where Rocky kept a number of pails stacked for such an emergency. Once folks got their bearings, they fell into line, women and older children alongside the men, taking their turns at passing pails full of water.

"Is everyone accounted for?" someone asked above the ruckus.

"As far as we know," one man shouted. "I purposely came out last after I had a good look around."

"Faster!" a big fellow toward the front of the line ordered. "Flames are shootin' higher!"

Rocky stood at the front, heaving pail after pail of water into the gigantic inferno. Soon Ben Broughton came alongside him, and the bucket brigade moved even faster, as several more people formed a second line.

Sarah discovered Seth not far from the house, his small body hugging tight to the trunk of a young tree, his pallid face awash with fear as he watched the growing blaze devour the old barn.

"Seth!" she screamed, racing toward him, relief flooding her veins.

When Seth heard her, he dropped his hands and met her running. "I'm scared!" he cried, leaping into her open arms.

"Oh, Seth, don't be afraid. The important thing is that you're safe. Now, tell me where your sister is."

He pulled away from her. "Huh?"

Sarah quickly knelt down to hold the boy at arm's length. "Where is Rachel?"

He shook his head slowly. "I dunno. Us kids was playin' hide-and-seek. I was hidin' over there," he said, pointing to a shrub beside the porch steps. "But I don't know where Rachel went."

Sarah jumped to her feet. "Whatever you do, Seth, do not move from this spot. I don't want to have to go looking for you. Do you understand?"

He gave a slow nod. "Are you gonna go find Rachel?"

She forced a reassuring smile. "I'll bet she's with Lili Broughton. As soon as I find her we'll come back for you."

"Hurry," he said, making a sniffling sound. The last thing Sarah saw before she took off on a run was tears sliding down the lad's pale face.

***

The flames climbed higher, hissing, coiling, snapping, their fiery fangs swallowing up the walls of the barn like one

237

hundred venomous snakes. Even with heaving the water as far above the ground as Ben and Rocky's strength would allow, it seemed a losing battle. The flames fairly consumed the ancient, dry wood. Rocky's heart fell at the sight. This barn had been standing long before he and Hester had bought the place.

Everything he owned was in that barn—saddles, tools, building supplies, and so much more. He felt his shoulders plummet with the knowledge that they couldn't possibly work fast enough to squelch the fire.

"Come on, Rock, you can't give up now," cried Ben above the sounds of the roaring blaze, his husky voice indicating a parched throat. He hurled another bucket of water into the raging fire, then looked at Rocky. "Pitch it!" he ordered, looking down at the full bucket of water Rocky held in his hands.

"It's no use," Rocky said, dumping the water onto the ground. "It's out of control. Look at it." Flames chewed through the huge two-story structure, licking up the walls, roaring like a hungry lion, the intense heat becoming nearly unbearable.

Ben grew silent as he watched his friend. He raised a hand at the folks in line to indicate they should stop.

"Rocky! Rocky, I can't find Rachel," Sarah screamed, running up to the front of the line and grabbing him by the collar. Fear, stark and vivid, glittered in her eyes. "Lili says she saw her run into the barn just before the fire broke out."

Rocky dropped the bucket and ran toward the flaming barn, but when he reached the door, two hands yanked him back. "Don't do it, Rocky," said Ben. "You'd be a fool to go in there."

Ben and Jon Atkins stood on either side of him, each clasping an arm, faces sober. "He's right, my friend," Jon admonished.

"Let me go!" Rocky growled, wrenching free of their tight

hold. "My niece is in there."

"If you're going in, at least put this on," said Eldred Johansson, hastily handing Rocky a wet blanket. "It'll help block out the flames."

"I'm going with you," said Benjamin.

"Count me in as well," said Jon.

Rocky cast them both a wary glance. "I wish you wouldn't, but there's no time to argue." Draping the sopping blanket over his shoulders, he took an instant to look at several pairs of worried eyes before sprinting off.

"Rocky!" screamed Sarah from somewhere behind him. "You can't..."

Blotting out her next words, he bolted through the door and felt a hellish surge of heat. "God, help me find her," he begged. "Please, Lord."

Hunching over to avoid the worst of the blinding smoke, Rocky carefully measured each step, making sure not to step on burning embers that would quickly burn through his soles. "Rachel!" he yelled at the top of his voice, his lungs filling up with smoke, scorching his insides. "Rachel, where are you? Answer me, Rachel!"

He halted, hoping for some sort of response, but getting nothing in return save for the sizzling sounds of unrestrained fire. "God, where do I look?"

Overwhelming heat sought to knock him over, endeavoring to drain him of his last ounce of strength like the devil himself. Overhead, the now ruptured roof threatened to collapse as fireballs mounted toward the open sky, launching coils of black smoke ever upward.

"Any sign of her?" called Ben.

Rocky whirled around just as Ben emerged from a cloud of blackness, sheathed in a blanket. "Nothing yet. Why don't you go back?" he urged. "No point in all of us dying. Where's Jon?"

"The crowd convinced him to stay put. He's prayin'."

Rocky nodded before advancing a few more steps, frantic in his search. "Rachel!" he yelled again, covering his mouth with his gloved hand to keep from ingesting more smoke, pulling the sweltering wet blanket tighter around him, feeling the burn of nearby flames eating at his flesh. The urge to wretch was strong, but he continued into the firestorm, unwavering in his quest, his eyes burning to the point of blindness. "Rachel!" he repeated.

Barn beams groaned and creaked, a window exploded, its glass shattering into a million pieces, one wall at the back of the barn bowed and sagged. "Get out, Ben!" Rocky yelled. "Get out now!"

"Not till we find her," Ben answered, the toe of his boot hitting Rocky in the heel. "Rachel!" Ben hollered, his voice rough and gravelly.

"Un—cle—Roc—ky," came a weak, frail voice.

"Did you hear that?" Rocky spun around, his heart squeezing in desperation.

"What?" Ben asked.

"I heard her. Rachel, where are you?" he called out, his eyelids swollen and singed. "Say something, honey." Gripping heat threatened to steal away the last of their oxygen if they didn't move fast.

"I can't—move—" came the faint response, followed by whimpering.

 240

Ben heard her that time. "Over here," he called, running not ten feet before he spotted the little girl. "She's here."

Rocky dashed the few yards to reach them and dropped to his knees. Trapped beneath a worktable that had toppled over, Rachel lay on her back in a helpless heap, the flames inching closer and closer, her cries growing weaker with each second's passing.

"Time's running out," Ben muttered between coughing spells. "Pull her out as soon as I lift this end."

Rocky stood at the ready. "I got her!" he yelled seconds later, as Ben lifted the table high enough for Rocky to scoop her out. Hauling her into his arms, he ignored her screams of pain and took off at a run, fighting thick smoke and fallen embers along the way.

The last thing Rocky remembered, as soon as he breathed his first breath of clean air, was falling to the ground with Rachel in his arms.

***

Sarah spent the night moving from one room to the other, tending to her patients. Exhausted to the point of dropping, she refused sleep for fear either Rocky or Rachel might need her.

Although Seth slept soundly on his narrow cot, dog-tired from the day's events, across the room in her bed his sister wrestled with nightmares and pain. Besides several minor burns, she suffered from bruising and a number of cuts and scrapes. Remarkably, the fallen worktable hadn't broken any bones, but Doc Randolph said she'd be sore for the next several days. The good news was that because she'd lain on the barn floor the entire time, she'd escaped the worst of the smoke. Unfortunately, that wasn't the case with Rocky.

Rocky lay sleeping but restless, his breathing jagged after all the coughing spasms and bouts of gagging and spewing he'd endured. Sarah had stayed dutifully at his side, helping him sit up, cleaning up after him, administering small sips of water, and fretting that he might not wake up, even though Doc had said his sleeping was a natural response to the medicine he'd administered. She took comfort in Doc's remark that considering how much smoke Rocky had inhaled, his lungs remained strong. The same had been true of Ben Broughton who, from what she'd heard, had suffered fewer burns than Rocky.

It amazed her yet how the men—Rocky, Ben, and Jonathan Atkins—had linked together like brothers to save Rachel's life, with no thought whatsoever for their own safety. Of course, it'd taken several men to restrain Jon Atkins once Rocky had disappeared inside the blazing barn, their argument that the town might need a minister after the day's events driving home a good point. Sarah shivered at the heavy connotation.

"Hester..." Rocky groaned from the bed she'd given up.

Sarah jumped up from the chair she'd taken a moment to recline in and rushed to her husband's side. "Rocky?" she whispered, taking a cool, wet cloth from a nearby pail to dab at his blistered forehead.

"Hester?" he repeated, his voice croaky as a bullfrog.

Her heart constricted. The notion that he might never recover from his first wife's death weighed heavy on her heart. Would he always consider her, Sarah, a mere stand-in, someone who'd conveniently come along to relieve him of his parental duties? Worse, when he'd embraced her out behind the house

242

earlier tonight and kissed her with fervor, had it been Hester he'd imagined holding in his arms?

"Rocky, I'm here," she whispered, bending over him, smelling the stench of smoke that lingered in his hair and on his skin. Between Jonathan Atkins, Mary Callahan, and Sarah, they'd managed to remove most of Rocky's charred clothing, draping nothing more than a clean sheet over his body once they got him situated on the straw mattress. She worried that the lumpy bed might lend to his discomfort, but Doc had said the mattress should be the least of her worries. Now she wondered what he'd meant by that.

Rocky's swollen eyelids fluttered but remained shut as he tossed about.

"Try not to move, Rocky," Sarah said, leaning in close, hoping her words made sense to him.

"Stay here—Hester," he managed on a husky whisper.

"I—I will," she replied, uncertain if she'd been right to encourage his fantasy.

She took his oversized hand in hers, discovered a fair-sized blister she'd missed, and dabbed a bit of the strong-smelling ointment on it that Doc had left behind. "Put this on his burns every couple of hours," Doc had instructed before leaving for the night. "It will cool the skin, make him more comfortable." Then he'd headed for the door, leaving Sarah in a bit of a dither. Even Mary couldn't stay; the fire upset Frank so much that she'd worried about his heart. "I'll stop by in the morning," Mary had promised. "As will I," Doc tacked on.

Now Sarah worried that she wasn't doing enough for her husband, this man who'd risked his life for his niece. Surely, he loved the child more than he cared to admit.

"You were a hero tonight, Rocky," she said, smoothing down his rumpled hair, enjoying its coarse texture, amazed that more of it hadn't singed off. "I'm so proud of you. Rachel is fine. She's resting." She kept up her quiet manner of conversing, hoping to bring him awake, and drawing pleasure from the chance to dwell on his face. Burned as it was over one of his cheeks and across his forehead, he was still the handsomest man she'd ever known.

She slid a chair close to the bed and plopped into it. *If only he would open his eyes,* she thought.

"Thirsty," he muttered.

Quickly, she hastened to take the glass from the bedside stand and put it to his dry, cracked lips, aiding him by tilting his head up slightly. He took a couple of swallows then surprised her by grabbing hold of her hand at the wrist and drawing it close to his mouth. When he kissed her fingertips, she stifled a sigh. Did he still think of her as Hester? She let the question fall by the wayside, deciding it didn't matter.

"Thank you," he managed in a weak voice, dropping his head back to the pillow in exhaustion and letting go of her hand.

"You're welcome," she returned, setting the glass back on the little table. "How do you feel?" she ventured to ask.

She shouldn't have been surprised when all he did was give a slight nod before drifting back to sleep.

She exhaled and took the opportunity to settle back in the chair and close her own eyes.

Dear Lord, she prayed, *please touch this man that I've come to love; heal him of his wounds from the inside out. And, Lord, as he sleeps, would You also reassure him of Your great love for him?*

244

Chapter Fifteen

*S*omething like a dark veil shrouded Rocky's thinking, making everything a misty cloud of confusion. Like a caged, desperate cat, he clawed at his subconscious, frantic to tunnel out of the ambiguity.

"I'm here," said a honey-sweet voice. *Hester?* "Try not to move," she said.

She had a deeply calming effect on him. Her simple touch and gentle manner of speaking eased the pain of his fevered skin. "Hester," he managed, but even as he spoke the name, his mind couldn't quite settle on her identity.

His parched throat burned from lack of water, and no sooner had he voiced his need than a firm hand, the woman's, went behind his head to lift him for a sip of cool refreshment.

What had happened to cause such burning over his face, his arms, his chest? Had he been to hell and back? *Dear God, bring clarity to my jumbled head.* But the minute he uttered the prayer he slipped back into a deep, dark hole of forgetfulness.

A fallen pan roused him again, hours later perhaps, stirring him partially awake. His heavy eyelids lifted in search of something familiar. Quickly he determined he was lying in his old bed, the one he'd given up.

In the other room, a feminine form in a long, flowered dress darted about, wiping her hands on her apron front, and hurrying from table to sink to kitchen cupboard. Her auburn hair, wild and unkempt, fell across her forehead and rosy cheeks, obscuring her face.

The sweet scent of baking bread flooded his nostrils, and her quiet humming his tired senses.

"Aunt Sarah," came the voice of a child.

Rachel?

Ever so slowly, reality returned, bringing with it snapshots of last night's events. His mind reeled with images of races, games, squealing children, food, and dancing.

"Yes, darling," came the woman's sweet voice. Sarah.

"My leg hurts."

Sarah left her place at the sink and rushed to the sofa where Rachel lay. She knelt beside the child and soothed her with her voice, just as she had him a while back. What had happened to Rachel, and why was her leg paining her so?

"You'll soon be good as new. Doc Randolph said you're a very lucky little girl, but I prefer to think that God Himself spared you."

"How is Uncle Rocky?" she asked in quiet tones.

"He's still sleeping."

"I hope he wakes up soon. I want to thank him for saving me."

Saving her? Rocky's head began to throb from a barrage of puzzling thoughts, thoughts he couldn't quite piece together.

"I'm sure he will. He's been quite restless all day."

"Where's Seth?" Rachel asked.

"He's out checking on all the animals—but especially the barn cats. He counted six that escaped the fire. Seth's been feeding them, and they'll find plenty of shelter. Thank God the flames didn't reach the chicken coop and other outbuildings."

"Can we bring them inside?" Rachel was saying.

"The cats? No, sweetie, they're much happier on their own."

Fire? Flames? What was all this talk?

Rocky blinked back a sordid memory, grim and unwelcome. It was all coming back now, trickling into his brain like a slow leak. There'd been a fire. And he and Ben had gone into the heart of it to rescue Rachel. But his barn was gone, burned to the ground, along with everything he owned, save for his livestock.

To make matters worse, he'd earlier mistaken Sarah for Hester, even taking comfort in the thought that she'd never departed, that life continued as it had long ago. He'd envisioned her flitting about the house, tending to his needs, cooling his brow, and had even whispered her name a time or two. What had he been thinking? Hester was gone from him, had been for three long years. Now the wound he'd worked so hard to heal bled and festered anew.

God, what are You doing to me? Isn't it enough that You took my wife and son and then my only sister?

Old bitterness he'd labored to overcome rolled back in waves. Not more than a few months ago, the schoolhouse, which doubled as the church, had burned, too. Wasn't one fire enough for the town of Little Hickman, or did God delight in watching His children suffer through one calamity after another?

He rolled over on his side, yanking the thin sheet with him, moaning at the various pains that emerged all over his body.

"Rocky, you're awake," said Sarah, suddenly rising from

247

her stooped position next to Rachel to approach his bedside. "How are you feeling?"

Oddly, her sweetness irked him. Ignoring her question, he started to cast the sheet off him but stopped abruptly when he realized he wore nothing but his underdrawers. Impatient to see what, if anything, was left of the barn, he frowned. "Where are my clothes?"

She pulled her shoulders back and returned the frown. "You're not to move about—unless you have need of the outhouse. Doc says we need to watch for infection, and that means taking care not to break open those blisters."

He pursed his lips and stared at her, trying his best to disregard the dark circles under her hazel eyes, her look of genuine concern. Had she slept at all? "What's left of my barn?"

She bit her lower lip. "Not much, I'm afraid. Several men came over today to haul away a good deal of debris and to milk the cows and feed the horses. They took care of everything. Elmer Barrington and Sam Thompson offered to come back in the morning, but I told them I'd see to things. Herb Jacobs brought out plenty of feed and stored it in the back of one of your outbuildings. He put it on your account at Sam's Livery." She took a deep breath. "Oh, and Elmer showed me how to milk the cows. I milked one of them all by myself. Isn't that something?"

Her nervous chatter unnerved him. She'd milked the cows? That had to be a first. He craned his neck to see the clock but failed. "What time is it?"

She wrung her hands. "It's approaching mealtime."

"Which meal?" he insisted on knowing.

She raised both brows. "The evening one."

"What?" He could hardly believe he'd wasted an entire day lying in bed. There were chores to tend to, animals to feed, cows to milk. "I need my clothes." Now he did throw off the sheet, unaffected by Sarah's gasp.

For some reason he relished the blush of her cheeks. "What's the matter, Mrs. Callahan? Aren't you the one who disrobed me?"

Her face went suddenly pink. "With the assistance of Jon Atkins and your mother," she stated snappily.

"Ah," he said. "Well, since neither of them is around, you just may have to assist me with putting them back on."

She pressed her lips together in a tight line. "I'll get your clothes, but I don't know what your hurry is. The men saw to your chores."

"I want to have a look around."

After an especially long sigh, she relented. "Fine."

Then, turning on her heel, as if to imply she suddenly had a bone to pick with him, she scooted out the door.

***

"Thanks," Rocky mumbled after Sarah finished tying his shoe. Bending put too much stress on the blisters on his shoulders and back, so she'd had to complete this one final act for him.

Standing, she gave him the beginnings of a smile. "You're welcome."

"How's Rachel?" he asked, still sitting on the side of the bed, as if mustering the strength to stand.

She'd wondered when he might ask. "She's fallen asleep on the couch again. But she's doing well, considering. Thanks to you and Benjamin, she'll be perfectly fine in a matter of days."

Rocky cast a glance out the bedroom window. His dark eyes, still swollen and red around the rims, penetrated the distance. "Good. Is Ben all right?"

"Your mother stopped by this morning. She said he was making good progress."

"I'm glad to hear it. I'd hate for anything to happen to him. This town has suffered enough." His jaw twitched ever so slightly, his dark brows knit together in a show of discouragement.

Sarah's stomach tightened into an uncomfortable knot. "What about you? How are you feeling?"

His expression went suddenly bland, emotionless. "Oh, aside from the fact that my barn is gone, and my skin is on fire, everything is just wonderful."

"At least no one died," she hastened, intending the statement to cheer him. Besides, it appeared he needed reminding.

He sat forward, his face awash with brooding irritation. "And you want me to thank God for that?"

She took a deep breath for courage. "It wouldn't hurt."

Now he moved from anger to cynicism. "Oh, and while I'm at it I should thank Him for burning down my barn, right?"

"The Bible tells us to rejoice in all manner of things, not just the good. There is a purpose for everything."

A sort of growling, sneering sound rumbled up from his chest. "Your philosophy lacks reason, Sarah. If God was so bent on providing us with a happy life, He wouldn't be going around causing all this grief."

"God is not in the business of causing grief, Rocky, nor is it His job to keep us happy. He allows tragedy, but He certainly doesn't create it. Our responsibility is to trust that He has everything under control." He sat stone-faced, so she charged ahead. "If it's money you lack, well, I have plenty. I could…"

Despite the pain it must have caused, he jumped to his feet and brushed past her, knocking her slightly off kilter. "I'll make do with what I have in the bank, Mrs. Callahan. Don't be expecting me to take any handouts."

"Handouts? I'm your wife. What's mine is yours, and vice versa. That applies to whatever money I might have stored in a bank account."

He stopped midstride and turned, his eyes hooded like those of a hawk. "I didn't marry you for your money."

Now she felt her ire bump up in degrees. "I never thought you did."

For a moment, he studied her with curious intensity. "I'll manage."

"Fine."

"Fine," he said, making an abrupt turn.

When he started walking away, she said to the back of him, "Has it ever occurred to you that God might well be trying to get your attention?"

He slowly turned. "What's that supposed to mean?"

"Until you surrender everything into God's very capable hands, regardless of the circumstances, you'll continue to miss out on His marvelous blessings."

He flashed her a glacial stare, then shook his head and walked through the doorway.

251

"Uncle Rocky," came Rachel's wee voice. "I thought I heard you."

"Hey, sugar," Rocky said, walking over to the girl, who still lay half asleep on the sofa. "I'm glad you're okay."

Sarah observed from the bedroom door. It was the first time she'd ever heard him use any sort of endearment with the little girl.

"Thank you for saving me," Rachel whispered.

He bent just slightly at the waist so as to touch her forehead. "It was my pleasure," he whispered in return.

Then, just like that, he strolled across the room, heaved on his coat, and headed out the door.

Heavenly Father, Sarah prayed in earnest, *open my husband's heart to Your divine truths.*

Everyone managed to make it to the supper table that evening, Rachel surprisingly the most talkative, despite her bumps and bruises, Seth more introverted than usual.

"I thought I was gonna die in there, Uncle Rocky," Rachel said after swallowing several gulps of milk and setting down the glass. Her expressive blue eyes flashed with newfound admiration for the man who'd rescued her. Sarah's heart warmed to the sudden change, and she inwardly thanked God for the miracle.

"Not a chance," Rocky replied, taking small bites at a time, the burns along his jaw apparently making it difficult to chew. He looked exhausted, Sarah observed, but the set of his shoulders said he wouldn't be admitting it any time soon. She'd offered to bring a tray to his bed, but he wouldn't hear of it, claiming he felt better moving around. Sarah doubted the truth in that but refused to argue, especially considering their earlier exchange.

He was a hard man, she mused, in more ways than one, and his first glimpse of the downed barn hadn't helped matters any.

"Why'd you come in after me?" she asked, obviously determined to press for details.

He stopped eating to look across the table at her, and didn't speak until she met his gaze. "I never gave it a second thought, Rachel. Sarah told me you were in there, and that was all I needed to hear."

"You mean *Aunt* Sarah. Me and Seth decided that since you're ar uncle we should think of her as ar aunt."

Rocky set his eyes on Sarah. "That's probably a good idea. After all, she is my wife." There was something about the way he claimed her with his eyes that made Sarah fidget.

"Well, anyway, I'd be dead if it weren't for you," she added between chews.

"Rachel, don't talk like that," Sarah said. "Neither your uncle nor Ben Broughton would have let that happen. Besides, the whole town was praying for your safety."

"How did the fire start?" Seth asked, finally joining in. He'd barely touched the food on his plate, making Sarah wonder if yesterday's events hadn't bothered him more than he let on.

"Mr. Thompson said someone must have accidentally kicked a lantern over, igniting a nearby hay bale. Everything happened so fast."

"I should have hung every lantern rather than placed some of them on tables. I don't know what I was thinking," Rocky said.

Sarah sensed deep regret in his voice. "It was an accident, Rocky," she assured him.

"If I'd planned more carefully, it wouldn't have happened."

"You didn't know, Uncle Rocky," Rachel offered. The girl's sudden compassion for the man she'd once disliked amazed Sarah. She wondered if Rocky sensed the dramatic change or spotted the respect and admiration in eyes that once held utter distrust.

Rocky looked at Rachel as if seeing her for the first time and gave a nod.

At the close of the meal, Rocky excused himself and headed for the bedroom, claiming utter fatigue. "Thank you for the use of the room, Sarah," he said without turning.

She studied the back of him, noting strong shoulders slightly slumped. "You're perfectly welcome," she replied. Sarah imagined that besides being exhausted, he suffered emotional pain. After all, he'd lost a great deal.

If only you would see what God can do through these difficult circumstances, she longed to say to him. However, her better judgment kept her mouth clamped shut. She'd probably said enough for one day. Best to let God take over where she'd left off.

Rachel meandered back to the lumpy sofa, exhaustion evident in her face.

"Would you like me to prepare a cool bath for you, honey?" Sarah asked. "I'm sure Seth wouldn't mind staying out here while you wash up. I'll get the tub ready in your bedroom and call you when it's time."

Baths, although a chore to set up, were a once a week arrangement, twice if Sarah had her way. And she suspected they would be more often than that once summer weather arrived.

 254

"I guess that would be nice," the girl replied.

Sarah glanced at Seth, who had quietly walked across the room to retrieve a toy soldier near the hearth. "Seth will use the water when you're done."

"I don't need a bath," he bleated.

Sarah sighed. "You played hard yesterday and today. The whole yard is covered in ashes and soot, so, yes, you do need a bath."

"Okay," he mumbled, dropping to the sofa, his voice giving way to a short-lived coughing spell.

Thinking she'd give him a cup of tea later, Sarah set about getting the bathtub ready.

***

Bright sunlight filtered through feathery white clouds, mocking Rocky's gloomy outlook.

He wandered through the seared remains of his barn, bending to pick up what was left of his best saddle, then dropping it onto a pile of other scorched leftovers. In his quest to finish clearing what the men had missed yesterday, he'd found a section of rope, tools, barbed wire, pieces of an old horse blanket, corroded buckets, part of a milking stool, shingles, and traces of blistered tar paper from the collapsed roof.

He kicked a stray piece of charred wood with the toe of his boot and cursed under his breath. How was it possible? Everything he'd worked for years to build—gone in the blink of an eye.

Until you surrender everything into God's hands, you'll miss His blessings. Sarah's words chewed a hole through his heart. It was difficult to believe a blessing could be hidden somewhere in

255

the midst of all this rubble, yet Sarah seemed to believe it. What did God want from him anyway?

A wagon pulled by two horses came over the rise just as he was about to head back inside. Doc Randolph sat atop the buckboard, his graying beard blowing in the wind, the wide brim of his hat dipped low to protect his eyes from the worst of the sunlight.

"Rocky," he called out. "What are you doing up and about?"

Rocky couldn't help but grin as he waved at the older man. While Doc had a fine reputation as a doctor, most complained that his bedside manner was less than impressive, probably due to heavy time constraints and the large number of folks he visited daily.

"Just stretching my muscles," he stated. "Trying to make some sense of this mess."

Doc pulled his horses to a stop and studied Rocky from his high perch. "It's a shame indeed. But you'll rebuild. Same time next year you'll look back on the whole experience and find some good in it." He sounded like Sarah.

"Glad to see you're getting some color back," Doc continued, laying the reins aside, snatching up his black bag, and stepping down. "Rode out to check on your burns." He came close. "Hm. They're healing nicely. Your wife must be taking good care of you."

Rocky thought of how Sarah had doted on him that first night, soothing his burns with a cold cloth, sitting up with him, helping him through the worst of it. When he finally woke up, she'd brought him meals, assisted him from his bed to the outdoor necessary, and spoke in quiet tones. Whether she knew it or not, she'd brought comfort to his battered soul. But then she'd ruined all that by insisting he needed to surrender everything to God, that he was somehow missing a great blessing. He'd sneered at the remark, finding the notion absurd. The best he could figure, God was using him as a punching bag.

"She's been a fine nurse," Rocky felt forced to admit. Unfortunately, he'd been a bear of a patient, disagreeable and stubborn to boot. He hadn't even thanked her sufficiently for seeing to all the extra chores, milking the cows, feeding the livestock, gathering eggs. It seemed his wife was tougher than he thought. Still, he wouldn't blame her if she up and deserted him tomorrow. To date, he'd given her little reason for hanging around, although he suspected it was the children who kept her firmly in place.

"The rest of your family doing all right?" Doc asked.

There was a hint of concern in his tone. "Far as I know," Rocky replied.

Doc pulled at the end of his beard and frowned. "A number of children have been hit with a strange virus I haven't quite put my finger on yet," Doc said. "I thought it was a common cold, but some are running pretty high temperatures."

"You worried?" Rocky asked.

Overhead, a flock of birds sailed by, their distinctive call identifying them as geese. Probably headed for wider portions of Little Hickman Creek, Rocky mused to himself. It was a sure sign of an early spring.

"Not overly so," the middle-aged man answered. "Figure I'll give it a few more days. If we don't see some improvement, or if the thing spreads, I'll put in a call to Lexington. May end up needing an antidote."

"Antidote? You think it might come to that?"

Doc shook his head. "Highly doubtful, but it doesn't hurt to stay on guard. Don't go speaking about this to anyone. No sense in creating undue panic."

Rocky nodded. "I'll keep that in mind. You let me know if you need anything."

Doc Randolph grinned. "I won't be calling on you until you're healed, young man. I expect you to spend the next several days resting."

"Several days? I have an addition to finish on my house and then a new barn to build, Doc. You'll have to bring a rope to tie me down next time you come out if you expect me to spend more than a day or so resting."

Doc threw back his head and let go a peal of laughter. "I just came from the Broughton farm and got nearly the same remark from Benjamin. You two must've come from the same mold."

Rocky chuckled. "That we did."

Doc looked up at the clear blue sky. "Well, think I'll meander up to the house and check on that little girl of yours. She sure fared better than you did as far as the burns go, and she came out on the good side of fate with that table falling on top of her. I still can't believe no bones were broken."

"Sarah would say fate had nothing to do with it," Rocky remarked, stuffing his hands in his pockets while shifting his weight.

Doc lifted a questioning brow then nodded. "S'pose she would at that. I do know that several folks were praying hard that night. Guess we can't help but give God credit where credit's due."

Doc never had been one to attend church services, but if even he admitted God's divine intervention, Rocky suspected there might be some truth to it.

At that, the doc strolled toward the house, leaving Rocky to ponder their conversation.

***

Sarah was beginning to worry over Seth's unusual cough. Poor child. It was nearing midnight and he'd gotten little sleep. She lay on the lumpy sofa, staring at the ceiling and fretting over what else she could do. She'd already given him plenty of water, a dose of homemade lemon syrup—an old remedy she recalled having learned from Mrs. Winters—and made sure he was amply covered in quilts. Hopefully, by morning there'd be an improvement.

At least Rocky slept well for the first time since the fire. She suspected he'd exhausted himself today with all the puttering he'd done outside, disposing of debris the crew of men had missed yesterday. She'd offered to help, but he wouldn't hear of it, claiming she'd already done more than her share, referring to the milking, which she'd done before he'd even awakened, a feat she was proud of, despite her tired, sore hands and achy back muscles.

If Rocky appreciated all her efforts, he didn't say. In fact, it seemed to her he made every effort to be ornery. At times, she wanted to shake him. Did he even recall those tender moments out behind the house just before the fire started? Was he now trying to drive her away with his testiness, figuring the harsher he was, the better his chances of keeping her at a distance?

Seth's cough lengthened for a time and then quieted.

Sarah slipped off the sofa and tiptoed to his bed. Relief flooded through her when she found him sleeping, his forehead cooler. Perhaps by morning he'd be good as new.

Across the room, Rachel also slept. Apparently, her brother's coughing spells had not disturbed her. Sarah carefully covered a section of bare arm then brushed a tendril of hair away from the child's angelic face. How she'd come to love this family.

Finally, satisfied that the household slept peacefully, she meandered back to the couch. Minutes later, sleep overtook her as well.

The first ray of sunlight worked its way through a gap in the curtains, coming to rest on Sarah's face and forcing her awake. Morning shadows cast strange forms across the dark, rustic walls of the small house. She shivered at the thought of crawling out from under the blankets, but also knew the importance of feeding the fire before its flame went out. She'd gotten up once to see to it, but from the looks of things, so had Rocky. There were fewer logs in the bin than when she'd last looked. She made a mental note to haul in several more pieces after breakfast.

Seth coughed about the time she pulled herself upright. She frowned. From the sound of it, he hadn't improved. If anything, the spasms put her in mind of a barking dog, dry and hacking. She slipped into her long robe and hurried to the children's room. Rocky met her in the doorway, his black hair tousled, his eyes reflecting worry.

"The boy doesn't sound good," he muttered. "When did he start coughing like that?"

Sarah couldn't help but notice bare feet peeking out from

denim pant legs and a crop of thick chest hairs behind his yet unbuttoned shirt. Of course, she'd seen him before when she'd nursed his burns, even studied him longer than required while he slept unawares, telling herself he was not only her husband, but also her patient, and she had every right to look. Now, however, she saw him through different eyes, identifying a raw masculinity she'd ignored before.

"I noticed it yesterday," she confessed in a whisper, well aware of their close proximity.

"You didn't mention it."

"I hoped that it might be a passing germ, that he'd be much improved by this morning."

His brow went into an immediate grimace. "Doc says a lot of kids are getting sick. He's not sure what's at the root."

A tight ball of fear dropped to the bottom of her stomach and bounced around. "Did he seem overly concerned?"

"I couldn't tell. I'd say he was baffled. Said not to go speaking about it lest we cause a stir among folks."

Sarah peeked past the doorway to where the boy slept fitfully, his every breath now punctuated by a raspy moan. Without hesitation, she rushed to his side and touched cool fingers to his forehead. The shock of cold meeting hot forced her to retract, much in the way she might have reacted after touching a hot stove.

Rocky observed the reaction and immediately touched Seth's forehead for himself.

"We need to get Doc over here—now."

"I'll dress," Sarah said, turning.

Rocky caught her by the arm. "No, I'll go. You stay here and see what you can do to bring down the fever."

261

"But you're still not well enough to ride," Sarah argued.

Rocky tipped her chin up with his index finger. "I'll be fine. Just do as I say. I'll be back as soon as possible."

She gave a nod of compliance, then watched him head back to the bedroom to finish dressing. Within minutes, he was out the door, and seconds after that, she heard the clomp of horses' hooves beating a path toward town.

Chapter Sixteen

*D*iphtheria?" Rocky's gut twisted into a sickening knot. "I'm not sure I know what that is, Doc."

Doc Randolph pulled at his thick, gray beard and cleared his throat. "Well, it's a type of respiratory illness, Rocky. Spreads mostly among children, although it's been known to strike adults. Just not as likely. I've been up most of the night reading from this medical book." He pointed at the thick volume lying open on his desk. "I suspect that's what we're dealing with."

Doc sighed deeply, pushed back his chair, and stood. Rocky watched him stack papers into one gigantic pile. Once done with that, he turned and yanked his coat off a nearby hook, slipped it on, and picked up his trusty black bag. "Your nephew is not the only one sick, as I was mentioning yesterday. Seems both Gus and Lenora Humphrey are down with it, as are the Hogsworth twins. Then there's little Molly Broughton and Thomas Bergen.

"Last night Bess Barrington brought Erlene straight to my office. Wish she hadn't done that, but I guess she thought it was the quickest way to reach me. Problem is there were a couple of other folks in here when she brought her in. I'm afraid they may have been exposed."

Rocky didn't know what to make of all Doc's talk. "You think it's bad, then?"

"Describe your nephew's symptoms again," Doc said, pushing Rocky toward the door. Doc always had been good at skirting issues for which he had no answers.

"He's very restless. Has a high fever and a bad cough. Sarah's trying to cool him off as we speak. Should we be worried, Doc?"

They stepped out onto the wooden sidewalk. "It's a mighty frosty morning," Doc muttered, pulling his collar up. "I'll head over and see if Sam has my wagon ready. How about I meet you out at your place?"

A bad case of nerves coupled with the brisk air made Rocky shiver. "Doc, you're not answering my questions."

The older man tipped his face up toward the sky as if to study it for any incoming storms. "That's because I don't want to make any snap judgments, son. It's still early."

"Well, what if it is this—this diphtheria—is it dangerous?"

Doc shoved one hand through his gray hair and shrugged. "Could be. All depends on a variety of things."

"Such as?"

Doc heaved a sigh. "How advanced the cough is, whether there's wheezing or blood in the mucus…how high the body temperature is, things of that nature."

Doc started walking, so Rocky tagged along, determined to get answers before heading for his place. "What if Seth has all the worst symptoms? Can he—could he…?"

Doc trudged on, looking straight ahead. "Try not to think the worst, son."

Perhaps it was an overreaction, but Rocky took the doctor by the arm, forcing him to stop midstride. "Doc, I lost Hester to smallpox three years ago and Joseph to something name-less just months ago. Don't tell me not to think the worst."

Understanding seemed to have lit in Doc's eyes. "I know that, son, and I can appreciate your concern." He put his hand on Rocky's arm. "But for now, let's try not to jump to any conclusions. Give me a chance to examine your boy. Maybe it's just a bad cold."

"I can't lose Seth. I haven't had the chance to..." But he left the sentence dangling, unsure where he was even heading with it.

Just days ago, he'd fought for Rachel's life; now it seemed that Seth's might be hanging in the balance. He'd barely taken the time to get to know his niece and nephew; he had been more concerned with time constraints, workload, and keeping a safe distance for the sake of his own heart. Now regrets bombarded him from every direction. *Dear God,* he prayed from his very depths, *please don't let anything happen to that boy.*

Rocky pulled into the farm a few minutes ahead of Doc. After he saw to his and Doc's horses, they walked to the house, Doc quiet, Rocky's stomach a bundle of nerves.

Sarah met them at the door, her eyes pools of concern as she looked from Rocky to Doc Randolph. Rachel was hugging Sarah's side, looking equally troubled.

"How is he?" Rocky asked.

She shook her head. "He doesn't seem to be responding to the cool baths. I'm worried."

Doc moved past them and straight into Seth's room, Rocky, Sarah, and Rachel on his tail. Ironic how not even a year had passed since the doc had seen to Joseph and been forced to admit he couldn't help the child, his fever having drained him of life before its source could even be determined. Now Doc's concerns were for a different little boy. Rocky fretted history was repeating itself.

Doc bent over Seth to lift each eyelid. The poor boy lay limp and nonresistant, seemingly drained, his eyes open but lifeless, the fever taking its toll. Silently Doc went for his black bag and retrieved his stethoscope and various of other supplies. He worked quietly, probing various areas of the boy's body, assessing his heart rate and temperature, then looking in Seth's ears and down his throat with a long, thin object.

"What is it, Doc?" Rocky asked when the man finally stood to face them. Sarah squeezed his hand hard. He found himself squeezing back, drawing strength from her viselike grip.

Doc's calm eyes gave way to wariness. "I can't be 100 percent certain," he muttered in low tones, "but I'm fairly sure it's diphtheria."

Sarah gasped. "I had that as a child!" she quickly reassured Rocky. "It wasn't pleasant, but as you can see, I'm fine. I had a terrible sore throat, though, and they quarantined me for several days."

Doc raised thick, gray brows. "You've built a natural immunity to the disease, then—and before they'd even developed the antitoxin. That's good news."

Sarah bent over Seth and touched his forehead. "Don't worry, sweetheart. You're going to be just fine." Seth managed a weak nod of the head.

"Will he, Doc?" Rocky asked, keeping his voice low.

Doc led Rocky out of the room and away from inquisitive ears. Thankfully Rachel didn't follow.

"Have any coffee on that stove?" he asked.

Rocky walked to the stove where Sarah had prepared a fresh pot. He grabbed a couple of tin mugs from behind the curtain and filled both with the steaming brew.

After Doc took a couple of sips, he said, "There was an antitoxin developed for diphtheria a few years back. I'm betting that Lexington has some on hand. I'll need to put in a call as soon as I get back to town."

"Do you want me to go fetch it for you?"

"You're not strong enough yet, Rocky. I'll find some other able-bodied man."

Rather than argue, Rocky asked, "How long before Seth starts feeling better?"

Doc clutched the mug between his hands. "Unfortunately, the antitoxin will not neutralize the disease that's already in his body, but it will serve to prevent it from progressing. Only time will tell, I'm afraid."

"So you're saying Seth's ailment has already reached a dangerous stage?"

Doc took a swig of coffee, then studied the ceiling before speaking. "Seth's throat and neck are alarmingly swollen, which could impair his airwaves. And I saw some evidence of bleeding in the back of his throat. He wasn't tracking very well with his eyes, either, probably due to double vision. That, coupled with his high temperature and lethargic behavior, has me worried. I'm afraid we're going to have to keep a very close watch on him. It could be touch and go for a while."

He cast a wary glance in the direction of Seth's bedroom. "There's a chance the little girl could contract the disease as well. Best to keep her away from her brother. In fact, it'd be

267

a good idea for both you and Rachel to go to your parents' house. Since Sarah had it as a child, she's safe. But you and Rachel..."

"I'll take Rachel to my folks' house, but I'm staying here."

Doc nodded, apparently realizing the futility in arguing. "I'll start Rachel on the antitoxin as soon as it comes in. The truth is, if she isn't sick yet, she'll probably be fine, but it doesn't hurt to take precautions." Doc put down the mug of coffee. "I best be on my way. I'll come back with the antitoxin just as soon as I have it in my possession. I haven't checked on the others yet, but I'd say Seth is about as bad off as any I've seen. If many more come down with it, we may have to set up a hospital at my place. This disease usually requires weeks to play itself out."

Rocky swallowed down a hard lump. "Seth has to get well, Doc."

Doc studied Rocky with particular care. "It might not hurt to deliver up a prayer to the Almighty."

Doc's suggestion set Rocky to thinking. Lately, he'd been giving more thought to prayer. Was Sarah right? Had God been trying to gain his attention? Worse, was He using Seth to get to Rocky? He couldn't bear the thought of Seth suffering on his account.

"Thanks, Doc."

Doc Randolph gave him a light pat on the shoulder. "You take care of yourself. I'll be back soon as I can."

Moments later, Rocky heard Doc's horses gallop off the property.

***

In the days that followed, Seth's condition remained unchanged, even though Doc had returned that same night to administer the antitoxin. Talk was that people all over the country, mostly children, had contracted the awful illness, leaving one child dead in a neighboring community. Sarah could only imagine the fear in homes around Little Hickman as news of the illness spread like wildfire. Since she and Rocky stayed confined to their cabin, their only means of attaining information came from tidbits they acquired through Doc's daily visits. Last they'd heard, the Hogsworth twins were recovering nicely, as was Gus Humphrey. Lenora Humphrey, on the other hand, had grown more frail by the day. Sarah had been lifting up prayers daily for the girl, praying for her even as she held to Seth's small hand and prayed for him.

Then there was baby Molly Broughton, so young to be so sick, and yet Doc said her little body seemed to be fighting the illness with a vengeance. Sarah could only pray that the rest of the Broughtons would remain healthy, particularly Liza, pregnant with her first child.

From what she could gather, Doc was holding his own and managing to maintain his patient load, but she feared by the look of his haggard face today that he was pushing himself to exhaustion.

"Do you think it's time for setting up a hospital, Doctor?" she asked after he had finished checking Seth's heart with his stethoscope and had tucked the instrument back into his front pocket.

"I'm holding off as long as possible," he whispered, leading her away from Seth's bedside. "So far, the quarantine seems to be working. There've been no new reported cases in two days."

Sarah breathed a sigh of relief. "That's good, right?"

He gave a slow nod. "I'm cautiously hopeful."

The two adults stood silent for a time, Sarah contemplative, Doc assuredly weary. "I could help you, you know. Since I had diphtheria as a child I'd be in no danger. You're looking mighty tired, Doc."

Doc smiled, aged wrinkle lines etching themselves around his inky eyes. "I thank you for that, young lady, but you have your hands full. I've learned of a couple of others who also had the illness some years back. They've offered their services if needed. You have enough to do what with a sick child and a still rather slow-moving husband. How is Rocky doing since the fire?" Clear concern swept across Doc's face.

Rocky and Sarah had been taking turns sitting with Seth, cooling his fevered brow with damp cloths, administering small sips of water for his parched throat, and comforting him with quiet words. Sarah marveled at how Rocky hovered over the listless boy, haunted no doubt by memories of having lost his little Joseph months before. Still, the truth was he was in no shape for sitting up with the lad hour after hour. Although his burns were healing, he still coughed frequently, a result, Doc said, of having inhaled a good deal of smoke and ash. Rest was essential to prevent any onset of pneumonia.

"I convinced him to go lie down for a while," Sarah said. "He's exhausted from looking after the boy. We take turns, but it seems he can't relax. I'm sure he's reliving the events of the past."

"Little Joseph, you mean."

Sarah nodded. "He doesn't talk much about his son, but I'm certain he's afraid of losing Seth now," she whispered. Thankfully, Seth slept soundly. Rocky had managed to feed the boy nearly half a bowl of chicken soup, and so far, his stomach hadn't rejected it.

Doc looked toward the bedroom where Rocky rested. "It was a sad thing, him losing his wife and then his boy. And now, on top of everything else, he's lost his barn. It doesn't seem quite fair, does it?"

Sarah shook her head. "God never promised any of us that life would be fair, but He did promise to give us necessary strength for hard times. If only my husband could believe that."

Doc cleared his throat. Sarah had no idea where the doctor stood with his faith, but she wasn't about to excuse her words.

"I'm sure your example of trust will rub off on him." He glanced out the bedroom window. "How are you managing with all the chores? You must be exhausting yourself, young lady."

"Me? Oh goodness, I'm fine." She was so tired her nerves throbbed, but Doc Randolph would be the last to find out. "I've learned how to milk the cows, a feat in itself. But Rocky has reclaimed many of the chores, even though I've told him I can handle things."

Doc nodded, then followed the gesture with a quiet laugh. "Your man is a stubborn one. Be patient with him."

Sarah winced at the term "your man." Aside from giving her hand an occasional squeeze or dropping a simple touch on her shoulder, Rocky hadn't approached her on a romantic level since the night of the fire when he'd kissed her so tenderly, and that was over two weeks ago. She wondered what it would take to break down the barrier that had once again risen up between them.

"Thank you for your concern," Sarah said, deciding not to comment on her husband's stubbornness. Best not to burden the man further. "I certainly miss Rachel," she put in, following him when he headed for the door and removed his coat from its hook.

"I'm convinced she's doing just fine in your in-laws' care."

"I've no doubt about that. I just don't want her getting too comfortable over there. She belongs with us."

Doc lifted one gray brow. "I wouldn't worry there. It's plain to see the child is completely taken with you."

Sarah's heart warmed at his kind words. She hadn't realized how much she'd needed to hear them. "And I'm quite taken with her," she returned.

After promising to pay another visit the next day, Doc bid her good-bye. Sarah watched him shuffle across the yard to his wagon, favoring one leg. *Lord, go with him*, she prayed, pulling back the curtain to watch him climb atop his buckboard. *Give him strength to see to the needs of these sick children. And, Lord, would you please keep Rachel safe and bring swift healing to our dear, sweet Seth? Also, Father, please soften my husband's heart that he may see the purposes You have for him, and that he may know the greatness of Your unfailing love.*

***

The sound of Sarah's sweet voice wafting through the air beckoned Rocky awake. He opened heavy eyes and found himself staring at his bedroom ceiling—rather, his wife's bedroom ceiling. Whether they would ever share the room remained a mystery.

He blinked back the urge to prolong his nap and wondered at the time. It appeared dusk had already set in by the look of the darkening sky. Sarah hummed the familiar old hymn "Amazing Grace" as she rattled pans in the kitchen sink. Some delicious aroma filtered through the crack under the door, making his stomach rumble in response, summoning him to further wakefulness.

He yanked a single quilt off his body and pulled himself up, then ran his fingers through his mussed hair. He knew he looked a sight. He hadn't even shaved in days because the burns along his jawline had blistered and scabbed over, making shaving a problem. What must Sarah think of his unsightly appearance? He stood and worked the kinks out of his neck and back.

When he opened the door, Sarah's body bent, as she stirred the fire, was the first thing he saw. She paused to pull a wispy red curl away from her face, then set to fueling the flame with another small log. He should be stirring the fire, he told himself, even though watching her now was altogether more pleasant. He took a moment to lean into the doorframe to steal a few more glances.

She stood up and placed a hand to the small of her back, her face to the mantelpiece where she seemed to be studying a photograph of Hester holding Joseph in her arms. He wondered if she resented the picture. But when she removed it, dusted it with the hem of her skirt, then carefully replaced it, he had his answer. She was a special woman, his new wife, and the feelings mounting deep inside him appeared to be more than mere respect. He was falling in love with her.

Yet how to tell her, or even *if,* remained a question. Nothing had been easy for her since the day she came to Little Hickman, and he wouldn't blame her a bit if she left tomorrow. With the palm of her hand, she massaged her back, and a kind of raw cocoon of guilt wrapped around him. She'd been working too hard since the fire and without a single complaint. Of course, who knew what rebellious thoughts stirred in her head? For all he knew she could be waiting for Seth's recovery before announcing her plans to leave.

Lord, how will I live if she decides to go? Will Your strength be enough to sustain me? Please, Lord, help me find my way back to You; help me trust You again.

And just like that, a newfound spiritual hunger swathed his soul.

All at once, Sarah sensed his presence and looked over at him, her cheeks pink from hovering near the fire. "I hope I didn't wake you."

Rocky pushed away from the doorjamb. "It was time I got up. You shouldn't have let me sleep so long."

"You needed your rest. You've been sitting up with Seth every night."

"How is he?"

Despite obvious fatigue, her mouth curved into an unconscious smile. "His fever broke just after Doc left today. I gave him some more soup just an hour ago. He says his throat isn't quite as sore, and the swelling in his neck has lessened. Isn't it wonderful? The Lord is answering our prayers, Rocky."

"Is he sleeping now?" Rocky asked, the knot that had been lying in the pit of his stomach for days now seeming to unravel.

 274

She nodded. "He's been napping off and on most of the afternoon. I think my reading puts him to sleep."

"It's not your reading, Sarah; it's your voice. It's soft and soothing to a body's ears." He advanced three long strides until he came close enough to take up a loose tendril of her hair. He tested its softness between his thumb and forefinger. If she did walk out on him, at least he would have this memory.

He lifted her down-turned chin with a finger, and her hazel eyes went suddenly misty. Hastily she dabbed at the corners with the hem of her apron. Was she going to cry? Perplexed, he merely stared, tongue-tied. Nothing ever prepared him for a woman's tears. Hester had shed a few in the time he'd known her, and he'd always felt about as helpless as a cornered chicken.

"Got some smoke in my eyes," she muttered, avoiding his gaze.

He looked at the fire. It spit and crackled, but there wasn't a trace of smoke anywhere. Cupping her chin with his rough palm, he bent slightly at the waist to see into her damp eyes. "Smoke, huh? Might it be more worry and stress and fatigue that's causing those tears than smoke, sweet wife? You've done nothing but play nursemaid to Seth and me, tend to the chores, cook all the meals, haul in wood, and on top of that, keep a clean house." He shook his head at her and clicked his tongue. "It's time you rested."

"But I..."

Something intense flared through his veins as he moved his hands up and down her arms, pulling her closer, inch by inch. The fight seemed to have gone out of her as she heaved a sigh and melted into his arms. When he felt a damp spot growing on his shoulder, and felt a tiny shudder, he knew with certainty she was crying.

"Sarah," he whispered, rocking her gently back and forth.

He kissed the top of her soap-scented head, and with newly awakened certainty, confessed to himself that he'd fallen head over heels in love. Was it presumptuous to believe she might feel the same?

They stayed that way for several seconds, her sniffing and sagging into his embrace, arms wrapped loosely around his back, he reveling in her softness until she finally tipped her face upward. He might have kissed her in that very moment had it not been for the pair of gazing eyes they simultaneously sensed.

"Seth!" Rocky exclaimed at the sight of the lad standing in his bedroom doorway, weak and pale, but standing none-theless, nightclothes wrinkled, hair a tousled mess. It was the first time since falling ill that the child had ventured two steps beyond his cot. "What are you doing out of bed?"

Earnest brown eyes studied them intently. "Was you two gonna kiss?" he asked instead of answering Rocky's question.

On the one hand amused, and on the other disgruntled, by the interruption, for he'd come so close to confessing his love for Sarah, Rocky dropped his hands to his sides and turned toward the boy. Sarah gave one last dab at her eyes and cleared her throat. Seeming self-conscious that Seth had caught them in an embrace, she promptly sidestepped.

He couldn't help the grin that spread across his face. "And what if we were?"

Seth gave a matter-of-fact shrug and leaned his small body

against the doorframe, undoubtedly weak. "I just wondered—
'cause I never seen kissin' before."

Rocky shook his head and chuckled. "You best get back in
bed, young man. You look about ready to topple."

"I'm tired of sleepin'," he whined. "Can I come out here?"

Rocky glanced at Sarah, whose face had creased into a
sudden smile. "That sounds like a wonderful idea. But you
have to promise to stay on the couch," she told him.

Rocky walked over to the boy and swept him into his arms,
then headed for the lumpy couch. Seth gave a weak giggle.
"I'm hungry," he announced.

No question. The boy was on the road to recovery.

Chapter Seventeen

*S*arah could not recall being happier. Although the diphtheria outbreak continued to spread throughout the area, Seth grew stronger every day, having come through the worst of it, and Rachel had returned, making their family once again complete. To top matters, Rocky had been paying Sarah special attention, helping her around the house whenever possible, insisting she take some time to rest, and every so often, giving her a quick peck on the cheek when the children weren't watching.

Rocky gained strength every day, his cough having all but disappeared, and the burns on his face, shoulders, forearms, and chest healing nicely. Even the pinkish scars were fading fast. With his newfound strength came a desire to finish the bedroom addition. The quicker he did that, he claimed, the sooner he could tackle the job of rebuilding the barn. Of course, the townsmen had promised their muscles whenever Rocky gave the word, so Sarah had no qualms about that. She did wonder, however, where the money might come from, having sneaked a peek at his bankbook when he was outside working and seeing firsthand what his financial situation looked like. There was plenty of money left from the sale he'd made on the fall harvest and the few livestock he'd sold before winter, but that would go toward meeting their personal needs, as well as feeding the animals. He had invested in a small insurance

 278

policy some years prior, but it wouldn't come close to covering the entire loss, which included many farm implements, animal feed, horse riggings, and other supplies.

Once more, she'd offered to provide the money from her private funds, and again he'd refused, saying he hadn't married her for her wealth. "I never said you did," she'd argued, reacting with irritation. "What's mine is yours, remember? When we married, we became partners, did we not? I should think that would extend to our financial matters. If you would allow me to contact—."

"Your lawyer beau?" he'd finished for her, his tone heavy with sarcasm, brow slanted upward.

Would he never get it through his head that Stephen Alden wasn't her beau?

Your man is a stubborn one. Doc's words coursed through her head. *Stubborn and proud,* she'd mulled.

Because she hadn't wanted to feed the tension between them, she'd chosen to ignore the jab and go back to the task of scrubbing the heavy kettle she'd been working on.

"I'm the head of this household, Sarah Callahan. I can manage our finances just fine without your help." He seemed to think this was the end of the discussion.

The back door slammed shut, bringing Sarah back to the present.

"Somethin' smells good, Aunt Sarah," said Rachel, a basketful of eggs under her arm. She wiped her feet on the braided rug, handed the basket over to Sarah, and took off her jacket. With April mere days away, milder temperatures had set in along with bounteous amounts of sunshine.

"It's the bread in the oven," Sarah answered. "More eggs?"

she asked with a frown. "I think you're feeding those chickens too much grain!"

Rachel giggled. "All the more money we'll earn when we take the eggs to town."

Selling the eggs for measly pennies seemed ridiculous to Sarah in light of her bursting bank account in Boston, but folks did rave about the rich flavor in the small brown eggs, and there was a certain satisfaction in exchanging goods for profit.

Sarah placed the basket on the counter. "I'll rinse them off, and you can put them in the containers for me."

"Want me to set the table after that?" Ever since the girl's return to the little house, she'd bent over backwards to do her part. It seemed her brush with death and Seth's recent illness had matured the girl beyond her years.

"I'd appreciate that. I just have to take the bread from the oven and see to the stew. Then we'll call your uncle in."

"Can I call him?" asked Seth from the sofa. He laid the picture book he'd been looking at in his lap. Although he'd gained in strength, the boy's face remained ashen and his voice weak, an indication that the illness had taken its toll on his small body. Sarah's heart overflowed with affection.

"I'm not sure he'll hear you, sweetie, but you can certainly try," she encouraged with a smile.

"Why can't I go outside and get him?"

Sarah gave the boy a stern but loving look. "We've been over this before. When you get stronger you may go outside, but we're taking things very slowly so your sickness doesn't return."

Seth's face dropped in a pout. "I'll go get Uncle Rocky

when it's time," Rachel said, attempting to smooth over the matter.

Just then, the front door opened and Rocky entered. "Is someone dragging my name through the mud?" he asked, eyes twinkling as they came to rest on each one individually, lingering the longest on Sarah. He slipped out of his farm coat and hung it on a hook, then turned to face Sarah again. A tiny smile flickered at the corners of his mouth. As was usually the case, his large presence ignited a warm flame that ran the length of her.

"Seth said he wanted to go outside and get you when it was time for supper," Rachel announced, "but Aunt Sarah says he can't go out until he's stronger."

"And she's right," Rocky said. "Your Aunt Sarah is a very smart woman." He advanced further into the house, taking a moment to tousle Seth's brown hair, then giving Rachel a gentle pat on the shoulder. Both children responded with a shy smile. They were still growing accustomed to their uncle's newfound affection.

As Rocky moved in her direction, Sarah whirled toward the sink with the basket of eggs and started rinsing each one. Despite her efforts to adjust to her husband's presence, he still managed to jangle her nerves. Thus, when he brushed against her at the sink, she accidentally cracked the egg she held in her hand in two, its gooey yoke slithering through her fingers.

A low chuckle rumbled from Rocky's chest as he set to pumping water. "Concentrate, my sweet wife," he whispered, taking her hand in his and rinsing it. His blue eyes were humorous yet tender.

"I am concentrating just fine," she replied, pulling her

hand away to regain her composure, but realizing her sense of calm wouldn't be complete until he put some space between them.

"Here's the egg container, Aunt Sarah," Rachel interrupted, suddenly shoving herself in between the two adults. "Want me to put the eggs in now?"

"Yes," Sarah answered in haste.

Forced to move aside, Rocky smiled down at Rachel as she began to place each egg in the small, sectioned container. "Looks like you'll earn a fair piece in town tomorrow."

"Me?" Rachel asked. "They're not my chickens."

"Ah, but you've named them all," Rocky countered. "I should think anyone who names a critter ought to lay claim to it. Besides, ever since you came home, you've been tending to the egg collection. Seems only fair you should reap the profits for your labor."

Rachel's eyes grew double in size as she threw her arms around Rocky's middle, her hands falling far short of meeting at the back. "Oh, thank you, Uncle Rocky! Just think, my very own money!" she shrieked.

Surprise lit in Rocky's face at the child's gesture of appreciation. Slowly, he put both hands around her shoulders and drew her close. Balmy warmth seized Sarah when she realized it was the first time she'd witnessed the two in an actual hug.

"Hey, what about me?" Seth complained from the couch. "I want a job so I can earn some money."

Rocky glanced at the boy and chuckled, his hands still resting on Rachel's shoulders. "Well now, you're a bit young for earning money. Seems to me you'd do well to concentrate on regaining your strength, young man. That's job enough for you right now." Leaving Rachel's side, he sauntered across the room and sat down next to Seth. Just like that, the boy snuggled in close.

Sarah continued to watch, glorying in the precious moment. As if sensing her silent assessment, Rocky glanced up and winked at her. More warmth trickled down her spine.

Quickly, she turned her attention back to her chores.

Moments later, as Rachel was reaching for the usual mismatched dishes with which to set the table, Rocky announced from the couch, "This seems like a fine night for the new china."

Her back to him while she sliced fresh bread for the evening meal, Sarah felt her breath catch, but her better judgment told her not to react. "That would be nice," was her simple reply.

At Sarah's nod, Rachel moved to an entirely different cupboard where Sarah had stacked the new dishes. Not since Rocky's verbal display in front of family and friends had she used them. "They're so pretty," the girl cooed as she carried a stack of plates to the table. One by one, she placed each plate in its appropriate spot, then returned to the cupboard to pull out the drawer that held the tub of old, tarnished dinnerware.

As she was counting out mismatched spoons, Rocky stopped her. "Use the new silver, too. It's in that wooden chest on that lower shelf behind the curtain," he said, pointing. The girl froze in place, obviously remembering the stir the new dishes and silver had earlier created.

Barely able to contain her own gasp of surprise, Sarah ceased with her bread-cutting to snag a look at Rocky. At the same time, Seth angled his head upward to get a better view of Rocky's face. "Aren't them the weddin' presents from Aunt Sarah's beau, Uncle Rocky?"

Surrendering to embarrassment, Sarah cleared her throat, picked up the platter of bread, and carried it to the table. "As I've said before, Stephen Alden was never my beau," she stated, forcing calmness. At some point Rachel had retrieved the silver and was even now arranging each brightly shining utensil in its proper place.

Rocky eased the boy off his lap and stood. Sarah watched his approach out of the corner of her eye. Parking his hands on the back of a chair, he fixed his eyes on her. "Guess it doesn't matter much where they come from. Seems a trifle imprudent not to use them."

When their gazes met and held, he winked at her for the second time that evening.

***

Rocky couldn't seem to wipe the grin off his face as he finished the flooring in the addition. He rose to admire his handiwork, thankful that he'd finally regained his physical capabilities. The addition nearly complete, all it needed was a fresh coat of paint on the plaster walls and ceiling and a few scatter rugs for the hardwood floor. Standing back, he determined it was the nicest room in the house. If he'd been thinking, he might have designated the new room for Sarah and him and given the older bedroom to Rachel. But what was he thinking? He didn't share a bed with his wife now; what made him think a new room would make any difference?

Stretching taut muscles, he thought about his next major project—rebuilding the barn. He'd paid a visit to Bill Whittaker,

Hickman's bank president, to see about a loan. Thankfully, his credit was good, although Bill had questioned why the loan was necessary considering what he'd heard about Rocky's wife. "What are you talking about?" Rocky had asked.

"Why, I heard tell she comes from money, son. Been waitin' for her to make a hefty deposit." He'd lifted pointy brows, his shifty eyes putting Rocky in mind of a predatory fox.

It annoyed him to no end that folks seemed to know things concerning his wife about which even he had no real details. Just how much money did she have? He'd be lying to say he wasn't a bit curious. Apparently, it was at least enough to rebuild his barn. Beyond that, he couldn't imagine she had much more, and he wasn't about to drain her of all her funds. Besides, he was the man of the house, meant to be the sole provider. He'd be hanged before he'd start relying on her money for survival. He could provide just fine for this family, and he would prove that fact after life returned to normal.

"Every one that is proud in heart is an abomination to the Lord: though hand join in hand, he shall not be unpunished." The verse came from the sixteenth chapter of Proverbs; he'd read it just two days ago. It irked him now that the verse slammed itself into his thoughts like an irate bull. Pride? How did that play in?

Yes, he'd taken to reading his Bible again in private—going out to the shed in the wee hours of the morning and sitting on a stool. Some mornings he even saw his breath while he sat there in the quiet, devouring the Word once more, looking for clues as to why God had chosen him to go through hard times, wondering if he'd ever find the answers he sought. Even though he felt closer to the Father during those times, he had yet to yield his life and heart completely. Something held him back. Was pride indeed a factor?

"Sarah said I'd find you out here," interrupted a deep voice from behind, familiar for its resonance.

An instant smile found its way to Rocky's lips as he whirled around. "Well, if it isn't the Reverend Atkins." He extended a hand. "How are you, Jon?"

"Never better, especially now that the diphtheria outbreak seems to be moving on." His face darkened briefly. "You heard about the James family?"

Rocky nodded. "Yeah, I understand they lost their youngest. A year old, was she?" The family had several other young children who had suffered milder cases, but the infant hadn't been strong enough to fight the disease. They lived on the other side of the creek, a couple miles outside of town. Since hearing about their loss, Rocky's heart had ached for them, perhaps perceiving their pain better than anyone.

Jon nodded, then said, "Little Molly Broughton came through okay, as did the rest of Hickman's children, thank the Lord. Glad to see Seth is growing stronger. He even had a smile for me when I came through the door."

Rocky nodded, grateful that the ugly claws of disease had not reached Rachel and that Seth had come through them relatively unscathed. "He's a fighter, that boy."

"He's seen his share of grief for one so young," Jon said with a thoughtful air. "These are tough times."

Rocky felt a sigh rise to the surface. "That he has, and I'm afraid I haven't always been there for him—or Rachel, for that matter."

"Don't beat yourself up, Rock. You and Sarah have done

 286

the best you could. Besides, there's always tomorrow. Look on the bright side; Doc says the worst of the sickness is over. Only a few new cases have popped up around Jessamine County in the past week, and that's something to cheer about."

Rocky had to agree. "What brings you out here?" he asked, feeling the need to change the subject.

"I had to see how my old pal was faring since the fire. Given that the outbreak has slowed down, folks are moving about more now. Church services will resume on Sunday. I wanted to let you and Sarah know." Rocky's lifelong friend scanned his surroundings. "Nice bedroom addition, Rock. You do fine work. This to be for you and Sarah?"

Rocky felt unexpected heat creep up his neck. He gave a quick turn of his body and bent to pick up his hammer and a bag of nails. "It's for the girl. She's been sharing a room with her brother."

"Mighty unselfish act, you giving her a brand-new room and all."

"It's the least I can do."

Jon inclined his blond head. "You and Sarah make a fine couple, Rocky. You two doing all right now that some time has passed?"

"Sure," he replied in haste. As usual, Jon seemed to read him like a book.

"Remember when you tried to convince Ben and me you'd seen a bear out on Sunset Ridge? We were what, ten or eleven maybe? You had Ben fooled, but not me. I saw right through that red, lying face of yours." Jon's eyes twinkled.

It irked Rocky that he'd never been successful at fooling Jon. Perhaps it was Jon's spiritual training or his fundamental capacity to read others' thoughts. "So what's your point?"

Jon shrugged. "You and Sarah started out on shaky ground. Getting to know someone intimately doesn't happen instantly, even while living under the same roof. Give it time."

Rocky laughed amiably. "And what makes you the expert along those lines?"

Jon chuckled. "I suppose it did sound presumptuous coming from a bachelor."

"Not that I think you're entirely innocent when it comes to women, Atkins. I've seen you turn a few heads."

Jon gave an impatient wave. "Naw."

Rocky stepped forward and gave his friend a good-humored smack in the arm. "Don't act so surprised. You've been charming women all your life, and you know it."

Even though Jon was a man of the cloth, he had an amiable way about him that attracted most womenfolk. Even the married ones ogled over his charismatic personality. It amazed Rocky that no woman had managed to snag him in marriage.

Jon flicked his wrist. "Enough about that foolishness." He rubbed a hand along his clean-shaven jaw as his brow line pulled into a frown. "I drove out here to speak with you about another matter altogether."

He'd suspected there might be something else. Rocky drew up a couple of makeshift stools. "Have a seat," he ordered.

The two men situated themselves on the overturned crates. "What's on your mind?" he asked, curious.

Jon took a moment to formulate his words before speaking. "Well, I've been thinking a lot about our Sunday morning services. Since the schoolhouse burned, we've put a burden on the Winthrops, I'm afraid. They're not complaining, mind you, but it's clear we can't continue expecting them to open their home week after week."

Rocky nodded. "I imagine it's been a bit of a trial for the old gal." Mrs. Winthrop was not an easy woman, and it seemed the older she got, the more crotchety she became. "My guess is Clyde's the more generous of the two."

Jon shook his head. "No matter. You have to give them credit. Matter of fact, when this is over, the town ought to do something nice for them."

"When it's over? Do you see an end in sight, Jon?"

"That's what I wanted to talk to you about, Rock. I've been giving the matter serious thought and prayer." Jon swallowed and snagged a deep breath. "I'm considering selling the family farm and donating the funds to the building of a new church."

"What? You can't be serious." Rocky parted his lips in surprise. "How could you think about selling your own house? Where would you live?"

"I'm thinking on that. I'm not a farmer, Rock. Of course, Pa would beg a quarrel if he were still breathing." At that, a half-hearted chuckle erupted. "Pa always had hopes for that homestead, but as you know, he threw away his entire life on drink and women."

Rocky nodded, remembering all too well. The fool had even sent Jon's mother to an early grave. At least, that was how most folks saw it. Sadly, Jon, then a young teenager, had discovered his mother in the barn one day after school hanging from the end of a rope. She'd left a note in her dress pocket saying she couldn't take it anymore.

"I'm a pastor. I would rather devote my time and energy to my parish. The farm and all that land is going to waste, and

I sure don't need that big house. Maybe I'll stay at the board-inghouse until I can buy something more my size in town. It's clear the town can't really afford to put me up in a parsonage. They haven't even raised the money for a school yet. These are hard times."

"Yes, but—the boardinghouse? You're talking Emma Brown-ing's place?" It was a known fact that Emma Browning would have nothing to do with church. Although she was a lovely woman to look at, she was hard to the bone. Chances were good she wouldn't want the town's only minister staying under her roof.

Jon grinned. "It's the only boardinghouse I know of in Hickman."

"You should give this more thought, Jon," Rocky insisted.

"I've given it plenty of thought, but I wouldn't mind if you'd join me in my prayer efforts. I don't want to miss God's leading."

Rocky shifted uncomfortably. "It's been a while since anyone's asked me to pray for him. I appreciate your confi-dence."

One of Jon's blond eyebrows tipped up a fraction. "You went through a tough period, Rock, but lately I've spotted a crack in your armor."

"That so?" Now it was Rocky's turn to throw his friend a questioning glance.

Jon's smile lent a boyish look to his clean-shaven face, and yet there was a strength of character about him that made up for his youthful demeanor. Undoubtedly he was one of the most respected men in all of Hickman, perhaps due to his own example of suffering through adversity and coming out the clear winner.

"I've always known deep down you weren't a quitter."

Rocky scoffed. "Thanks for your vote."

"I'm serious," Jon said, running his boot along the brand-new floor as if to test its smoothness. "The loss of a barn would have been the last straw for most men, but I've seen a light in your eye that tells me you're not ready to give up the fight."

Rocky bit his lip and thought about the preacher's words. "I'll admit to being angry with God. The shock of it hit me hard. But I quickly came to realize that people are more important than things. The thought of losing Rachel in that fire put everything into perspective. Then Seth getting sick..." He swallowed down a hard lump.

"Kind of makes you realize what's truly important in life," Jon said.

Rocky nodded his agreement before casting his gaze toward the ceiling. "I've taken to reading my Bible again." The admission came surprisingly hard.

Jon patted Rocky on the shoulder. "That's where you'll find your answers, my friend."

"I can't say I've found all the answers, but at least I'm willing to start looking."

"That's a good beginning—a willing heart. God will take a willing heart."

Both men allowed a measure of silence to envelope them while Rocky pondered his friend's words. Yes. Somewhere along the line, despite his stubborn pride, his heart had grown softer, and he suspected his wife had something to do with it. Still, maybe more than anything, it was God Himself who'd finally cracked through that outer shell, which Jon referred to as his armor.

Both men pivoted when Sarah shuffled through the doorway, arms full with a tray containing cookies, linen napkins, a tall crystal pitcher, and two matching glasses. Jon stepped forward to assist her. "I thought you might enjoy some refreshment," she said, allowing Jon to take the tray from her and place it atop a ramshackle workbench. Somehow, the finery didn't quite fit the room, but Rocky wouldn't balk at a nice cool drink and Sarah's thought to offer it. Time and again his wife demonstrated her refined ways, and just as often he wondered what kept her in Little Hickman, Kentucky. The quiet, unadorned little town had to be as different as night and day from the commotion of Winchester's city life.

Rocky looked on as she lifted the pitcher and filled each glass to its rim with lemonade, taking care to top them off with a lemon slice. She offered the first glass to Jon along with a smile. Sarah had no notion of what a captivating picture she made, Rocky thought to himself—her shimmering hair braided into a neat little knot, with only a few curly strands falling haphazardly about her oval face, her light blue calico dress gathered at the middle, accenting her tiny waist. The sight made him want to pull her up next to him.

Jon gave an exaggerated bow. "Thank you, dear lady. I shall come more often if you promise me lemonade in crystal glasses." At that, he raised the glass to his lips and took several swallows while Sarah watched. After that, he flashed her a perfectly mesmeric smile and declared that it was the best lemonade he'd tasted since, well, since his mama used to make it.

"And I declare if you haven't managed to charm my wife, you scoundrel! Have you no limits?" Rocky stepped forward to take the glass Sarah had poured for him. "Pay no attention to him, Sarah," he said in a counseling tone, coming up close to nudge her in the side. "Jon here has the notion that a preacher's license somehow gives him a wider margin with the womenfolk."

Sarah gasped and covered her mouth, obviously unsure how to handle the offhanded remark. Clearly, she didn't understand the camaraderie between the old friends.

Jon turned up his ready smile a notch. "Totally untrue, madam; he's just jealous." He grabbed a cookie off the platter and spoke between bites. "I suspect he's still bitter about all those girls chasing me around the schoolyard when we were ten."

Rocky gripped the front of his shirt as if in pain. "Yeah, truth is, it's still raw." He dipped his face toward Sarah and gave her a conspiratorial wink. She giggled in response, catching the joke.

Apparently Jon spotted the look that passed between the two, for he placed his empty glass on the platter, brushed his hands together, and looked at Sarah. "And now I must be on my way. I have several more calls to make. Will I see you in church on Sunday?"

"We'll make every effort," Sarah answered, "but I'm afraid it will depend on Seth. He's still quite weak."

Jon nodded. "How about I offer up a prayer for him before I leave?"

Sarah looked at Rocky. "We would very much appreciate that," she answered for both of them.

In the living room everyone gathered around the boy, including Rachel, while Jon prayed a prayer of thanksgiving for preserving Seth's life and asked God for continued healing.

293

The heartfelt petition touched a cord in Rocky's heart, sparked a deep-set need in the center of his soul, and took him back to earlier days when he'd prayed just as freely. *Lord, forgive me for my rebellion*, he prayed inwardly. *Help me trust You, even when I don't understand Your ways.*

It was a simple request, but when he opened his eyes, he felt somehow different.

Chapter Eighteen

ut I want to go to church!" Seth's voice came off sounding weaker than normal, but at least his cheeks had regained their rosy hue.

"I don't know, Seth. It's up to your uncle," Sarah said, looking to her husband. "What do you think, Rocky?"

"Please, Uncle Rocky? I think Seth looks just fine," Rachel chimed.

Rocky chuckled. "You would say that just to get out of the house again. I guess selling your eggs at market on Friday didn't quite satisfy those itchy feet."

"It is a beautiful day," Sarah supplied. "The fresh air alone would probably do him a world of good."

Rocky raised the lad's chin with his finger. "You are getting back a bit of color in your cheeks."

Seth's eyes brightened. "So we can go?"

"What's with this sudden desire to go to Sunday service? You know you have to sit as still as a dead bug. If you make a single sound Mrs. Winthrop will stare you down with those beady eyes."

Rachel giggled.

"Rocky," Sarah said in her best warning tone.

"I want to sing to God," Seth declared weakly while lifting his skinny shoulders.

Rocky's face split into a grin. "Well then, I suspect we ought to go just to listen to Seth's fine singing voice."

So that settled it. The Callahans were going to church.

***

Sarah could barely contain her joy. There was something different in her husband's countenance; his manner seemed more relaxed, much friendlier. All the way into town, there'd been happy conversation. Even Seth joined in the repartee, seeming to perk up with the bright sunshine despite Sarah's insistence he remain calm.

In town, Sarah took the hand Rocky offered and hopped down from the wagon. Because several folks traveled a distance, most left their wagons along Main Street and walked the few blocks to the Winthrop home. Those living nearby simply walked. Thus, families came from every direction, some hand in hand, others with children who preferred to scamper ahead of their parents.

At first glance, Sarah spotted Elmer and Bess Barrington and their two children, Thomas and Erlene. All four gave enthusiastic waves. Behind them came the Warner clan followed by the Thompsons. Sarah smiled and waved in response to everyone's greetings.

"Look, there's my friend, Todd. I played with him at the picnic," Seth said. Even though he remained weak, there was elation in his voice. Sarah once again gave silent thanks to God for His protection over Seth and Rachel.

"And there's Lili Broughton," Rachel cried, waving wildly. The entire Broughton family, including baby Molly, carried by Benjamin, strode toward the Winthrop home, approaching from the opposite direction. Again, Sarah gave thanks that little Molly had come through the diphtheria looking relatively unscathed. "Can I go say hello?"

"I think it's best you stick with us," Rocky said. "There'll be plenty of time for hellos after the service."

Rather than voice an argument, Rachel looped her arm in the crook of Sarah's and kept step. "I like this day," she announced.

Curious, Sarah looked down at the child and smiled, thinking to ask her why, but Rocky beat her to it. "And what makes this day special to you?" he asked, glancing first at Rachel, then casting a wink at Sarah. The simple act sent a delightful shiver of longing up her backbone.

"I don't know exactly, but maybe it's because the sun is shining, and spring is here, and Seth is better, and we..."

When she didn't complete her thought, Rocky prompted, "And we...?"

"We seem like a real family," she finished.

Rocky reached across Sarah and gave a tender yank to one of Rachel's braids. "We *are* a family, sweetie."

Sarah hitched a breath and tried to hold her emotions at bay. They did seem more and more like a regular family and, as if to accentuate that thought, Rocky put a hand to the center of Sarah's back and steered her around the corner of Washington Avenue.

"Hey! There's Sarah Jenkins." Rachel turned her attentions to the tall girl straight ahead, seemingly ecstatic when the girl noticed her and waved. Rachel returned the greeting then tipped her head up at Rocky and Sarah. A sheepish grin swept across her mouth. "I think I like Little Hickman."

"Yeah, me too," Seth chimed, gazing at his sister. "I didn't have no friends in Ohio, but I gots more'n one here."

Sarah winced at his poor use of the English language, but smiled in spite of it. "You'll gain even more friends once school begins," she said, "if the town ever gets around to building a schoolhouse, that is."

"Town needs to raise the money first," Rocky said, looking straight ahead. "It doesn't appear to be happening too fast."

Sarah knew exactly how to get her hands on the necessary funds. A simple phone call or telegram to Stephen Alden would do the trick. But how would Rocky feel about her making such a contribution to the town? She knew how he felt about accepting money from her on a personal level. Would he feel similarly were she to offer the funds for a schoolhouse? A barn was one thing, she reasoned, but a schoolhouse—well, that affected Little Hickman's children, Seth and Rachel in particular, and who could deny the children their education?

The Winthrop home couldn't have seated another person. Either the promise of spring or the retreat of the dreaded virus had brought people out in droves this sunny Sunday morning. Folks' moods were bright and cheery, exuding an air of thankfulness to God, with the exception of poor Mrs. Winthrop, who looked fit to be tied. Dark hair pulled back into a severe bun, her arched eyebrows, and a sour expression betrayed her deep frustration. Sarah couldn't help but feel sorry for the woman. Surely, hosting the weekly service had become drudgery, and who could blame her for her disgruntled look?

Although shoes had been stacked at the door and coats lay draped across folks' laps or behind their chairs, there was still a layer of dirt and grime on the lovely marble entryway. It was clear the townsfolk needed a building of their own in which to worship. Oh, the Winthrop home was by far the largest in the area, but it was not a house of worship, and Sarah hoped the citizens of Little Hickman would soon recognize that fact.

Jon Atkins delivered a fine sermon, challenging those present to trust God in all things, using Proverbs 3, verses 5 and 6 as his text. Several amens rose up around the room as he spoke of God's faithfulness and abiding love. Sarah glanced over Seth and Rachel's heads at Rocky and discovered him focusing on Jon's words and wearing a look of contentment. It appeared a change had taken place in her husband's heart and soul.

At the close of his message, Jon offered a final prayer, gathered up what few notes he had in front of him, cleared his throat, and, perusing the worshipers with intent eyes, spoke without faltering. "And now I have one thing further to say."

Sensing something important was on the horizon, folks sat up, shushed their impatient children, and sharpened their gazes on the preacher.

"For some time now the Winthrops have been kind enough to lend us their home as a meeting place." All around the room people nodded in agreement, some turning eyes upon the Winthrops, standing at the back of the room, who appeared just as curious as the rest. "But now it's time we start building a new church. Now that spring's upon us, I'm sure you men will agree the building can begin."

"But the town ain't raised near enough money yet, Reverend," Elmer Barrington argued from the front row.

"Not one of us here would disagree we need to find a different meeting place, Jon," came the voice of Eldred Johansson, mercantile owner, "but there's the matter of the schoolhouse, too. The education of ar youngins is awful important. If we start buildin' a church, hard tellin' when we'll raise the funds for a new school. I think most folks are in agreement that we want separate buildings this time around."

Sarah heard several utterances of concurrence rise up. Oh, how she wanted to speak, but the fact that she was Hickman's newest citizen kept her silent. She glanced at Rocky and found him pensive. If only she could read his mind. Was he worried about when his barn would go up now that talk of building a new church had taken preeminence? She longed to reassure him.

"I want my children to start school in the fall. If we build the church first, is that going to be possible?" Esther Thompson piped up. On her lap, she held the newest member of the Thompson clan, a baby girl dressed in pink and wearing a matching bonnet.

More than a few women showed their agreement with nods and murmurs.

Jon raised both hands at the restless parishioners. "Folks," he cut in, "you didn't let me finish. The funds for the church have already been raised. You can now concentrate your efforts on collecting for the schoolhouse."

Echoes of shock reverberated through the house, as people whispered among themselves. Sarah looked at Rocky and found him smiling at Jon and shaking his head. He had that look of knowing written across his face.

Jon lowered his arms and fumbled with his papers, then cleared his throat. "I've talked to a few of you, my good friends Benjamin Broughton and Rocky Callahan, in particular, sought the Lord's wisdom and direction, and, after much soul-searching and prayer, have come to an important decision."

Folks sat in utter silence as they waited, stiff and unsure. Finally, an unidentified male voice from the back asked, "What might that be, Reverend?"

"I've sold my farm, and the proceeds will be more than sufficient for building a new church." When gasps erupted around the room, Jon raised his arms once more to shush the people. "Now, I don't want any protests. I've made up my mind. I don't need that big farm. You folks know I'm no farmer."

"But…that's your home, Reverend," said Iris Bergen, tears evident in her large brown eyes. "Why would you do something so generous?" Her husband, obviously taken aback by the pastor's announcement, could do little else but shake his head.

"I want no praise for myself," Jon said. "This is something the Lord has told me to do. Now, if you want to argue the decision, well, I guess you'll have to take it up with Him." To that, Jon gave an impish grin.

Sarah glanced about the room, taking in the faces of Hickman's citizens. She saw joy and astonishment written there, and wondered at the preacher's bigheartedness. Great elation showed in his expression as he faced his congregation, no doubt with relief mixed in. *Oh, what satisfaction came from trusting and obeying God,* Sarah thought. And with that came the sudden realization of what she had to do—whether her husband approved or not. It was a simple matter of obedience. First thing Monday morning, she would borrow Rocky's rig and head for town, where she would put in a call to Stephen Alden.

***

Bright sunlight filtered through low-lying clouds as Rocky

went about his morning chores, humming as he worked. Never had he felt such contentment. Even the knowledge that his barn would have to wait until after the church was built didn't dampen his spirits. He knew the men of Hickman would come through for him when the time was right. Of course, he had yet to obtain the money from the bank, but there was no point in taking out the loan until he had the manpower. Yes, he needed a barn in which to store his tools, feed, supplies, and all, but for now, his sheds would have to suffice, and the warmer weather eliminated the need for shelter for his livestock.

Overhead, birds sang in unison as the sun's warmth blanketed his shoulders, and a hymn of praise that he'd sung just yesterday in church came to mind.

"Uncle Rocky, can I help?" Seth asked, slamming the door behind him and jumping off the front porch, his face a picture of eagerness as he ran across the yard toward Rocky.

"Slow down, Seth. You're just now getting back your strength."

"But I feel good today," Seth declared, coming to a skidding stop as soon as he reached the chicken yard and pushed open the gate. "Can I feed the chickens today?"

Rocky grinned in spite of himself. Seth's color seemed to have fully returned along with his enthusiasm. "Be my guest," he said as he pushed open the creaky shed door. "I suspect your sister will be out as soon as she finishes off her inside chores. She'll want to gather the eggs." They'd moved Rachel into her new room two days ago, and Sarah had instructed her to make her bed and sweep the floor, already gritty from her traipsing in and out.

The coop housed a few dozen hens and roosters, all of

which squawked with delight at the first sight of Rocky and Seth. Rushing on both of them, the roosters in particular pecked at their pant legs, eager to claim the first of the morning feed. Seth sidled up close to Rocky, trying not to let the pesky feathered creatures intimidate him.

Rocky chuckled. "You'll get braver with practice," he assured.

"I'm brave already," Seth chimed with pride, even as he scampered behind Rocky's legs when the biggest rooster in the lot came at him.

As predicted, Rachel joined them, egg basket in hand, not five minutes later, just as Rocky and Seth were finishing up. On her tail came Sarah, dressed in her Sunday finest, including matching blue cape and fancy hat. Rocky studied her with curious intensity. "We went to church yesterday, Mrs. Callahan," he teased. "Do you plan to do the housework dressed like that?"

She blinked, then pulled back her shoulders. "I will see to my household chores later. Right now I should like to drive the rig into town if you don't mind—alone." She put special emphasis on the word.

"I can drive you to town if you have need of supplies."

She swallowed hard, lifted her chin, and boldly met his gaze. "I would appreciate the opportunity to handle the horses on my own this time. Besides, you have work to do; you said so yourself at breakfast—fences to mend, shelves to build, blades to sharpen." Every curve of her body spoke a subtle challenge. "I am not some delicate creature, you know. I am perfectly capable of driving the rig."

He felt the beginnings of a smile. Something about her unwavering deportment dazzled him. When he should have

303

put his foot down, he found himself giving in. "You want me to hitch up the team, or are you just stubborn enough to want that job as well?"

She tried to maintain her curtness. "I suppose you can do that much."

They left the children in the chicken yard and headed for the corral where he kept the horses. The wagon sat on one side of the fenced-in area. On the way there he asked, "Any reason why you want to make this trip alone?"

She paused before replying. "None in particular," she said, though he could have sworn her determination faltered just slightly. "There are some items I want to purchase."

"You sure you know how to drive?"

"I drove our carriage plenty of times in Boston, and traffic there is heavy."

He felt his eyebrows shoot up as they strolled along. "I wasn't aware. I must say I'm impressed."

She tipped her gaze at him, and behind her hooded eyes was a slight twinkle. "I daresay there's a good deal you don't know about me, Mr. Callahan."

He turned toward her, coming dangerously close to touching the tip of her nose with his own, surprised when she didn't withdraw. "Then I think it's time I learned, don't you?"

There was a certain confidence in her smile, a cheerfulness in her gait. "Perhaps," she answered, looking straight ahead.

He tossed his head back and laughed. "Why do I feel like you have something up those pretty silk sleeves of yours?"

"I wouldn't know," she replied. She appeared beyond intimidation as she tilted back the rim of her bonnet and looked at him through gleaming eyes. A vague sense of longing passed through him, but he ignored it. So far, she'd not proven to him that she shared his level of affection. He wondered if there was a way of finding out how she felt about him aside from coming right out and asking her. Of course, that would mean revealing his own feelings.

While he harnessed the horses to the wagon, he watched his wife out of the corner of one eye. She gazed silently out over the land, every so often turning her attention to the chicken coop, where Rachel was no doubt gathering eggs and Seth was talking her ear off. She had turned out to be a good caregiver to the children, he ruled, even though Seth and Rachel weren't her own. No one could convince him that her heart wasn't capable of strong feelings the way she mothered those kids.

Besides being a good mother, she'd also demonstrated her talents around the house. The way she tended things, one would think hard work had never been foreign to her—fixing the meals, washing the clothes, scrubbing the floors, and ironing his shirts. Of course, he knew better. If she came from wealth, as so many had alluded to, then she'd no doubt never needed to lift a finger until now. It had to be sheer determination that had brought her to this point. Why else would she have worked so hard to prove herself? It still never ceased to amaze him that he'd triumphed over Alden, that she'd actually chosen life in Little Hickman, Kentucky, over the affluent suburbs of Boston.

When Sarah caught him watching her, a blush ran across her face like a shadow. "You'll watch over the children while I'm gone?" she hastened.

"I'll keep an eye on them," he assured, still curious as to why she meant to take this trip alone. "How long will you be?"

305

"Oh, I shouldn't think long at all," she answered.

He felt the start of a frown behind his brow. "Like I said, I'd be happy to drive you. The road into town is pretty bumpy, if you recall. Not many women make the trip by themselves."

An irritated look replaced her earlier blush as she positioned her hands on her slightly rounded hips. "Do you think me incapable of handling the horses? I'm not a featherheaded dolt, Mr. Callahan."

He stared at her, discovering that his wife was startlingly cute when annoyed. "No, you certainly are not that. Stubborn, maybe," he teased.

Walking the horses in a half-circle, he turned them, and the rig, in the direction of town, unable to wipe the smile from his face. Sarah waited until he halted the team and laid the reins across the front. Then she hoisted up her skirts, preparing to climb aboard, her jawline firm, her eyes clearly focused on her task.

Suddenly, he took her by the elbow and turned her until they came face-to-face.

"You make a pretty picture, Sarah Callahan." Something like a marble caught in his throat, refusing to go down.

Her heavy lashes lifted, revealing blue-green eyes that sparkled in the sunlight. He couldn't say for sure, but he thought he detected a ray of hope combining with the color. "Well, thank you," she said in little more than a whisper. When it looked like she might be waiting for more, he lowered his head, wanting to move before he lost his nerve, and placed a gentle kiss across her forehead, deciding to linger there.

Gentle breezes played against their faces as he drew her into a possessive embrace, knocking her bonnet to the ground accidentally, then taking in the lemony scent of her ginger-colored locks. He wanted her to know she belonged to him and no one else.

He kissed the top of her head first, then dropped tiny kisses on her cheek as he journeyed to her full, waiting mouth. And if he'd had another second, he just might have unburdened his heart, but something stopped him—the absolute certainty that they weren't alone.

Staring up at them were two pairs of eyes, one set blue, the other brown, both curious and speculative. "You dropped your hat, Aunt Sarah," said Seth, holding it out at arm's length.

Without a moment's hesitation, Sarah pulled back, straightened her skirts, and cleared her throat. "Thank you, Seth," she said, snatching the hat and plopping it back in place.

Rocky took her elbow and helped her aboard. "Drive with care, you hear?"

Once seated, Sarah glanced down and gave a smile that seemed mostly directed at the children. "I shouldn't be long."

With that, she made a clicking noise with her tongue and whipped the horses into a safe speed, leaving the trio in the dust.

***

Later, Sarah tried to ignore the stone of guilt sitting in her stomach as she steered the horses toward home.

She'd taken marriage vows to love, honor, and obey her husband, and yet this very day, she'd made an important financial decision without his knowledge. Furthermore, she'd spoken to Stephen Alden on the telephone and made arrangements for his arrival on the Friday afternoon stagecoach, something of which she was certain Rocky would disapprove.

But what of her strong conviction that God Himself had directed her decision? Surely, that counted for something, she reasoned. The town needed money for a schoolhouse, and she had the means for making it happen. How could her husband possibly dispute that? However, she'd not included him in the process, and therein lay the problem. Moreover, when he finally discovered the extent of her assets, would it not drive an even greater wedge between them, particularly since he'd made it clear on more than one occasion that he had no need of her money?

"Are you happy, Sarah?" Stephen had asked toward the tail end of their hurried conversation.

"More than you can imagine," she'd replied, but heavy static had kept her from elaborating.

"I'll plan to arrive on Friday," he'd shouted over the lines. "Shall I hire a driver to bring me out to your farm?"

"No!" she'd replied in haste, unsure whether she would have completely ironed out matters with Rocky before Friday. "I'll check with the general store to determine the stage's arrival time, and I'll plan to meet you in town. From there we'll walk to the bank."

"Will your husband be accompanying you?"

"Rocky will..."

"We're losing our connection, Sarah," he'd interrupted. "These wretched telephones lines. I'll see you in a few days then."

"Stephen—." But the phone went dead. Frustrated with the temperamental equipment, she'd slammed the thing back into its cradle.

And when she turned to leave, she discovered Mrs. Winthrop standing in the doorway, mouth agape, beady eyes assessing her from head to toe.

Sarah had opened her mouth to explain, but closed it again. She couldn't very well tell her she'd been speaking to her lawyer. What questions might that stir up? In the end, she'd pulled back her shoulders, given the woman a pert smile, and sauntered past, determined not to cave in to her deliberate attempt to intimidate.

Sarah heaved a weary sigh just as she rounded the final turn in the two-track road leading home. *Home.* Yes, it felt more like home to her than anyplace she'd ever lived. The little white cabin, now sporting a new addition and sitting proudly on a grassy knoll, emitted a straight stream of gray smoke out its little brick chimney. Suddenly, she felt as though she hadn't truly lived before.

"Dear Father," she prayed, whispering into the cooling breezes, "give me wisdom in the days ahead, the ability to discern Your leading, and strength and courage to listen and obey. And, Lord, help my husband to accept whatever it is You may be asking me to do. Somehow, may it wind up being a joint decision."

Chapter Nineteen

*S*arah waited for just the right opportunity to talk to Rocky about her finances and to tell him that Stephen was arriving on Friday to deliver her funds, but as the days came and went, so did her prospects for speaking to him on the sensitive topic. Perhaps it was the pervading peace and happiness that seemed to be on everyone's countenances, including Rocky's, that kept her from it. Why bring an end to family harmony? Or maybe it was her simple lack of nerve. Regardless, every time she came close to asking to speak to him privately, something else took precedence.

On Monday evening, there'd been a thunder and lightning storm that required their attention. Rachel had grown frightened in her new room and asked to move back in with Seth. Without a minute's worth of arguing, Rocky had obliged the child by pushing her bed back into her brother's room, no easy task by the time he'd maneuvered it through the narrow doors. "This is just temporary, mind you," Rocky had issued. While he'd tried to exert his authority in the matter, his eyes glinted good-naturedly. "Tomorrow morning we put the bed back." Rachel gave a limp nod as Sarah put clean sheets on the straw mattress. "I didn't build that addition so we could move you in and out every time we have a storm." Leaping onto the freshly made-up bed, both children giggled with glee to be reunited, making Sarah wonder about the wisdom of giving in to her. Still, Rocky's gentle handling of the matter had impressed her.

 310

Rocky had spent all day Tuesday working outdoors, Seth following on his tail, while Sarah and Rachel had busied themselves with washing clothes, baking bread, scrubbing floors, and polishing the new silver. She'd only seen Rocky briefly during the day—when he had come in for lunch and water breaks. Each time, he'd commented on the delectable kitchen aromas and rewarded her with a warm smile, the kind that left her weak-kneed and wanting. But at close of day, everyone had appeared so tired that after bedtime stories and prayers, they had all dropped into bed at dusk, Rachel once again settling back into her new room.

On Wednesday, Rocky had taken the wagon into town for horse tack and items needed to repair a leak in the roof of one of the supply sheds, and he'd spent the remainder of the day on that task. By the time he'd come in for supper, he looked tired and a bit glum-faced, making Sarah worry that he'd heard something in town he wasn't up for discussing. Had rumors started flying about her mysterious telephone conversation? But when his spirits had lifted toward evening, she had figured her imagination had flown away with her. Still, it hadn't seemed appropriate to bring up the matter of her finances then, not when his mood had gone from glum to cheery.

Thursday was a duplicate of the days before, although this day, as Sarah toiled, she allowed the children more free time. *My, how they've changed from those early days*, she thought, particularly when she recalled having first met them on the stagecoach back in late December. Downcast and glum, they'd clung to one another like two frightened bunnies. And it hadn't helped any when, upon their arrival, they'd met their daunting uncle, big and sour-looking, although handsome (Sarah had noticed) even through that tough and callous exterior.

Because Rocky was spending the day in the fields, plowing and readying the soil for planting, he'd insisted Seth stay back. It would be a long, hard day, he'd explained after breakfast. "Some other time, sport," he'd said, smoothing out Seth's flyaway hair and glancing at Sarah for encouragement.

"Could you help me bake a cake this morning?" she'd hastened to ask.

"That's girl's work," he'd answered.

"Well then, do you suppose you could sweep off the porch for me, then help us *eat* the cake?"

To this, his eyes had brightened. "Will it be chocolate?"

"Is there any other kind?" she'd asked, knowing Seth had a weakness for all things chocolate.

"Yippee! I love chocolate cake," he'd announced in a singsong voice, grabbing hold of Rachel's hand and twirling her around the house in a silly excuse for a dance. Sarah had laughed at their antics, and when she'd glanced at Rocky, she found him watching her. He'd pulled his mouth into a crooked grin.

"You best save some of that cake for your husband, Sarah. I'll need my strength at close of day."

"I'm sure you will," she'd answered, keeping her smile.

"I can think of a few other things that might rejuvenate me besides the cake," he had said with a mischievous twinkle while moving his face in close to hers and making Sarah's head swim with delight. Was he implying another kiss perhaps, or something more intimate? He'd seemed to be peering at her intently, making her heart turn over in response. "But the cake should suffice—for now." His normally mellow voice had taken on a husky edge.

He'd pulled back and gently tapped the tip of her nose with his index finger. "Perhaps tomorrow we can plan some time together—with the children, of course. What would you think of that? A person can't spend every waking minute working."

Normally she would have agreed, would have jumped at the chance to go on a family outing. A picnic at the creek perhaps. She could take her red and white checked tablecloth and pack all her best sandwiches along with their favorite canned fruits, a freshly baked pie, and jars of milk.

Just not tomorrow.

That particular moment might have been suitable for explaining Stephen's coming in on the early stage, but as soon as she'd opened her mouth, Rocky had already headed for the door.

"Well, you give it some thought, and when I get home tonight we can discuss it over supper." At the door, he had turned the latch, then swiveled on his heel to face her. "Oh, thanks for packing me a lunch. This will save me a trip in at noon. I expect I'll have the north end plowed by late afternoon." He'd tipped one corner of his battered Stetson upward, awarded her with a wink and generous smile, and then closed the door behind him.

The children's chatter had brought her back to reality. "Can I help bake the cake, Aunt Sarah?" Rachel had asked. "Where's the broom?" Seth had asked at the same moment.

And so the morning had gone.

***

By late afternoon, Rocky had plowed the north portion of

his land and a quarter of the south portion when he decided to call it a day. Grimy with sweat, he wiped his brow with his well-used handkerchief and surveyed his work. At this rate, and provided the weather held out, planting could begin as early as the end of next week. Unhitching the horses from the plow, he led them back toward home.

The wonderful aroma of roast beef and potatoes greeted him as soon as he opened the door. Dressed in yellow gingham, Sarah looked pretty as a spring blossom. For a moment, he stood in the doorway, whiffing the fine smells and gazing at the woman. How did she manage to look so stunningly beautiful after a hard day's work? If he'd felt more at ease he might have planted a kiss on the back of her creamy neck. As it was, she barely acknowledged his presence, merely giving him a hint of a smile, and then proceeding to dish up the food and issue orders to the children to wash up and help finish setting the table. If anything, she looked as jumpy as a cat in a dog pen.

Throughout the meal, the children babbled nonstop, losing Rocky in most of their silly prattle. Sarah seemed to take every available opportunity to leave the table, first to dish up more potatoes and replenish the meat tray, then to refill everyone's water glasses, all the while avoiding eye contact with Rocky. When they were finished, she took to clearing off the table, washing dishes, and leaving him to deal with the children's chatter.

"What do you think, Uncle Rocky?" Rachel was asking.

"Huh?" he asked. "About what?"

Rachel scowled. "Weren't you listening?"

He gave a helpless shrug, leaned back in his chair, and

folded his arms. "I'm afraid you caught me," he admitted with a smile.

The girl heaved an impatient sigh. "Me and Seth want to go fishin' sometime. Can you take us?"

"Fishing?"

"Yeah, Uncle Rocky. I know you gots some fishin' poles 'cause I seen 'em hangin' on the wall in one of yer sheds," Seth confessed, his eyes big as saucers.

Rocky's gut twisted briefly when he thought about the few times he'd taken Joseph down to Little Hickman Creek on a fishing spree. At one time, the memories might have kept him from such a venture, but now he marveled at how appealing the whole idea sounded. "Fishing, huh?"

"Can we?" Seth asked.

"Yeah, can we, Uncle Rocky?"

Unsure what Sarah was thinking because she'd failed to join in the conversation, Rocky went out on a limb. "Well now, fishing sounds like a mighty fine way to spend the day tomorrow. What do you say, Sarah?"

At that, she whirled around to face the three of them, her face a picture of bewilderment. She put a soapy hand to her throat, leaving a trace of suds on her chin. "It's—awfully short notice."

Rocky pushed back his chair and stood, the soapsuds demanding attention. When he advanced on her, she quickly turned her face to the sink. "Short notice?" he asked, walking up behind her. "Did you forget about my suggestion this morning to take the day off tomorrow?" This he whispered in her ear, drawing close enough to inhale her delicious scent. With a quick swipe of his thumb, he removed the dab of lingering soap and didn't miss the slight shiver his touch provoked.

Oh, it pleased him that his closeness riled her, and so he put a hand to the back of her neck and played with the fine tendrils that had fallen from their loose chignon. He wished she would wear her hair down as she'd done when he first met her, even though it'd been prone to fly every which way, as abundantly lush and curly as it was.

He leaned in closer yet, feeling her shoulders go taut. "We could pack a lunch and eat it on the riverbank," he whispered, "provided the weather continues its sunny, mild pattern."

"I don't..." At a loss for words, she did not finish her sentence.

"Can we go fishin' tomorrow?" Seth asked from the table.

"Shh—can't you see they're discussin' it?" Rachel issued. "If you beg too much they won't take us."

Rocky noted a tiny smile peek through on Sarah's shapely mouth. "I suppose we could go first thing in the morning, but I'd need to be back by noon."

"Noon? Why so early?" Rocky asked. "I thought we'd make a day of it." He turned her around to face him.

Even then, she avoided looking straight at him. "There are—things—I need to tend to," she returned in a soft voice.

"Things?" He dipped his head to her level, which forced her eyes to meet his. "What sort of things?"

"Well, I, um, need to make a trip into town, for one thing, some errands to run. It shouldn't take me long, however. You three could keep fishing, and once I returned we could resume our outing, perhaps have a picnic." Her eyes went bright with hope, as if her idea for breaking up the day was the best she'd ever had.

Still, something in her manner didn't feel quite right. "And I suppose you want to make this trip to town alone—again?"

When she gave a slow nod, he felt a scowl crimp his face. Not wanting to make an issue of the matter, but puzzled by her sudden yearning for independence, he merely tilted his head and perused her face. "Any particular reason?" he asked.

She slanted her face upward, and the glow from a nearby lantern mirrored itself in the flecks of her blue-green eyes. "Reason?"

He shook his head, knowing the children had sharpened their ears to hear every word. "Never mind. I suppose we can work around your schedule. We'll all set out for the creek right after breakfast and see what we can do about getting us a bucket of fish for supper. While you're in town, ahem, running errands, the three of us will pack a mouthwatering lunch. I expect you'll be arriving back shortly after we've finished with that, and then we can all go back out and find a nice shady spot for eating our spread. How does that sound?"

"Yea! That's perfect," Rachel cheered.

"Can we play games, too?" Seth asked, jumping to his feet and spinning circles.

Rocky glimpsed Sarah, whose face had softened with—what was it? Relief? A smile formed on her lovely lips, and she clapped right along with the children.

"I don't know why not," he replied, finding it hard to conceal his own eagerness.

Sarah had something up her sleeve, Rocky decided. Well, he'd let her play her game for now, but, by gum, before the rooster crowed day after tomorrow, he'd somehow cajole her into sharing the big secret.

***

"I got me a fish!" Seth screamed early the next morning.

Everyone gathered around to observe the line on Seth's bowed fishing pole. "Hang on to him, boy," Rocky coached. "Nice and easy now."

"He's a big one," Seth announced, his little chest puffing out with every twist of the spool. "Am I doing it right, Uncle Rocky?"

Rocky smiled over the boy's head and steadied him with both hands. "Couldn't do better if I was holding on to the rod myself."

"Seth's catchin' a fish, Aunt Sarah," Rachel whispered.

"And a big one at that," Sarah returned.

As the reeling continued, Rocky lent encouragement. "Don't quit," he urged, just as the fish made a giant leap from the water. It looked to be a good foot long by Sarah's estimation.

Another five minutes passed while Seth and Rocky worked together to haul the oversized rainbow trout onto the bank, its body flapping and rotating to show its complete dislike for the outside world.

"Is it gonna die?" Seth asked while staring at the slimy creature.

Rocky chuckled. "I hope so. I'm not too fond of fish that move around on my plate."

Seth continued gawking, hands shoved deep in his pockets. Rocky bent over the fish to remove the hook, then slipped his index finger through the mouth and gill and lifted it up for all to see. "Mighty fine catch."

"What are ya gonna do with it?" asked Rachel with a somber face.

Rocky exchanged a smile with Sarah before answering the girl. "Well, I was thinking to put him in this bucket of water. Later, I'll show you how to scale and filet him." Both kids wrinkled their noses. "What?" Rocky asked. "You two aren't going all soft on me, are you? Believe me, he's going to be a tasty fellow." Rocky held the flapping critter high, forcing the kids to examine it more closely.

Sarah giggled low in her chest, understanding their dilemma. They'd wanted the experience of fishing, but now questioned the notion of actually eating their catch.

"I never tasted fish before," Rachel said, her nose still crumpled.

"Me neither," Seth exclaimed, suddenly pale. "Do we have to eat him?"

"What?" Rocky's eyes moved from Rachel to Seth then landed on Sarah. They seemed to dance with merriment. "Isn't that why we got up at break of dawn?" he drilled. "So we could catch us some supper?" Rocky put the squirmy creature out in front of him.

"Don't we have other stuff to eat for supper?" Seth asked.

At that, Rocky let out a great peal of laughter. "So what you're saying is you want to let this critter go."

"Well," Seth seemed to put the matter to deep thought, "what if he has a wife?" Rocky's face flickered with interest. "If Sarah got caught by Indians or robbers or somethin', wouldn't you want them to let her go?"

As if understanding had suddenly dawned, Rocky bent at the waist and peered into the boy's eyes, mouth quirking. "Put like that, it makes a great deal of sense to let this guy go." And just like that, he walked to the river's edge and dropped the creature into the water with a splash.

Near noontime, the foursome headed home, fishing poles hoisted high, Rocky carrying the tackle box and empty bucket. Along the way, a carefree kind of banter filled the air.

When they reached a wide-open clearing about half a mile from their cozy farmhouse, Seth blurted, "Let's race to that big tree over there." He pointed to a distant, leafless oak in the middle of a stark meadow.

Rocky halted his steps and gave the lad a slanted gaze. "How fair would that be? Look at everything I'm left to carry."

Sarah giggled. "But you have longer legs than we do," she stated. More to the point, they were firm as tree trunks, she observed when he wasn't looking. Furthermore, there was that powerful set to his shoulders, the way the muscles strained against his flannel shirt as he strolled along.

"Plus, you're big and strong," Rachel supplied. Sarah looked at the child. Had she read her mind?

"And fast," Seth added.

Rocky tossed back his head and chuckled. "Why do I suddenly feel like I'm being baited—just like that poor fish Seth caught a bit ago?"

"We let him go, remember?" Seth said.

"Yeah, but you still caught him, made him look pretty silly hanging from that fishing line."

"Come on, Uncle Rocky, let's race," Seth begged.

Rocky flashed all three of them a spirited grin then rested his gaze on Sarah. "Are you up for a good race, Mrs. Callahan?"

Sheer giddiness coursed through her blood. "Of course. The question is, are you?"

"Oh," he said with lowered tone, "now there's an appealing challenge."

In a desperate attempt to escape his captivating grin, Sarah put one bent leg in front of the other, lifted her skirts a few inches from the ground and, with no warning, screamed, "Ready, set, *go!*" taking off on a run well ahead of everyone else.

"Hey, wait for me!" Seth yowled. But all Sarah could do was focus on the large oak yards away, her utter resolve to outrun everyone transporting a rush of adrenaline through her veins.

She ran as fast as her legs would carry her, Rocky's thundering footsteps trailing close behind, gathering momentum the closer she came to her goal.

Still, she reached the tree ahead of him, huffing and puffing. When she bent over to catch her breath, hand on the trunk to prove she'd won, she sensed his nearness, heard his own jagged breathing and quiet ripple of laughter. "You think you're pretty smart, don't you?" he said, placing his hand on hers. She tried to slip it out, but he wouldn't let her go. Instead, he drew in close, caressing her face and neck with his hot breath, his massive body blanketing her from behind. "I didn't know I married a runner."

She stood frozen in place despite the beads of sweat that formed on her forehead. Out of the corner of one eye, she glimpsed Rachel and Seth. Both had slowed to a walk, their faces sagging with fatigue. Feeling a little guilty for having tricked them, she managed a weak smile for Rocky. "You let me win."

"Is that what you think?" he asked, his mouth coming ever closer.

"You could have easily caught up."

"But I was enjoying the view from my vantage point." At that, she drew back from him to see into his eyes. He was teasing her, and the gentle sparring made her blush.

"Aunt Sarah, you didn't give us a chance," Rachel said.

"I know, and I apologize. I don't know what got into me," she declared with as much innocence as she could muster.

"Can we have another race that's fair?" Seth asked.

Sarah laughed. "I don't think I'm up for it, but maybe you two could race each other home. I can see the smoke rising from our chimney up ahead."

Seth squinted to get a better view. The little house and the hodgepodge of storage sheds, chicken yard, and fenced-in corrals looked warm and inviting nestled amidst an assortment of trees and shrubbery. Horses and cows roamed freely on the hillside, nibbling at new grass. "I see it. Want to race, Rachel?"

"Sure," she said, suddenly all full of enthusiasm. "Tell us when—um, not you, Aunt Sarah. This time Uncle Rocky will say, 'Ready, set, go.'"

"That seems only right," Rocky said with a wink.

Once the children set off, Rocky surprised Sarah by taking her hand. For a time neither spoke. They just strolled and watched as the children ran through the open field.

"They seem happy as two larks."

"Don't they?" Sarah said.

"You've made it so, you know," Rocky said, giving her hand an extra squeeze. She sensed his eyes moving over her face but kept her own gaze on the children.

"You've played a bigger part than I. They love you very much."

"You made a home for them—for all of us," he said, ignoring her attempt to give him equal praise. "I don't know as I've ever thanked you for that."

She dared to look at him then and found his eyes full of warmth. "No need," she said simply. "I should be thanking you."

"Me?" He pulled her to a stop. "Why me?"

More aware than ever that the clock was ticking closer toward noon and that she'd have to set off for town very soon, Sarah resumed walking, glad when Rocky didn't impede her progress. She chose her words carefully. "I—came to Little Hickman expecting to marry someone altogether different—and found myself in somewhat of a predicament. Your offer of marriage solved my problem."

"Is that what I did for you? Solved a problem?"

She hadn't wanted to sound indifferent. "Well, yes, but it's more than that. I believed with all my heart that God had a purpose for my coming to Little Hickman."

"And do you still believe that?"

She raised her eyes to find him still watching her. There was a depth to his expression that she'd never seen before. "Of course," she answered. "Do you?"

A half-smile formed on his lips as he gazed at the children. Seth was squealing something at Rachel, who appeared to be quite a distance ahead of him. "I'm not sure I did at the time, but now..." He shook his head in seeming amazement, "I look at those kids and wonder how I ever doubted that they belonged with me—with us," he amended.

Sarah nodded her agreement. Briefly, she wondered if they were reaching a milestone in their marriage. Now would be a good time to speak of her financial assets, she ruled, and her reasons for making the trip into town. Yet she worried about breaking the wonderful spell of peace and contentment that had fallen over them. Surely there would be ample opportunity later, perhaps tonight after they'd put the children to bed.

"I'll hitch up the horses for you," Rocky said as they drew nearer the house.

"I appreciate that."

Once again, she felt his eyes. "You sure you don't want me to drive you?" he asked with quiet emphasis.

A wave of panic rose in her stomach. "I'll be perfectly fine," she hastened. "Besides, you promised to pack lunches for our picnic."

He leaned toward her as they walked. "You best not be keeping any secrets from me, Sarah Callahan. Secrets don't bide well in a marriage, you know."

A bitter taste like bile collected at the front of her mouth, and she loosed a nervous laugh. "I'm merely picking up some supplies and running a few errands," she said. "It shouldn't take me long at all." *And meeting my lawyer,* she might have added.

"You're not planning to run off, are you?" Something in his tone drew her up short.

"What—do you mean?"

"Nothing! That was a stupid thing to say."

Sarah couldn't help but feel relief when she caught sight of

Seth's approach, for it would mean an end to their conversation.

"Aunt Sarah, Uncle Rocky," Seth called out, "Rachel beat me, but I came awful close to catchin' her! Did you see what a fast runner I am?"

"That I did," Rocky said, dropping Sarah's hand and walking to meet the boy, but not before he lowered his voice and added in a huskier tone for her ears only, "I suspect you and I will be talking soon about your streak of stubbornness, Sarah Callahan."

***

Rocky paced the floor of the little house, his patience running thinner by the minute. "Where is she, Uncle Rocky? I thought we was goin' on a picnic," Seth said in a complaining tone. It wasn't the first such grumble he'd heard from Seth that afternoon as they'd waited for Sarah's return. "Ar sandwiches are gonna be soggy."

Rocky forced a smile and tried to appear undaunted. "She said she'd be here, so she will. You need to find something to do while you wait. Why don't you have Rachel read to you?"

Rachel, who sat on the couch, was perfectly content to bury herself in her latest book, one of Rocky's many classics. She glanced up at the mention of her name. "Come here, Seth," she said, patting the place beside her. "I'll read a chapter to you."

Rocky threw the girl an appreciative look. Just then, he heard the sound of an approaching wagon and headed for the window. It would be at least the dozenth time he'd peered out over the landscape, hoping for Sarah's arrival. He didn't know why he couldn't throw off this overwhelming sense of concern. Seth hastily ran to his side. "Who is it, Uncle Rocky?"

Rocky squinted to get a better view. "Looks like your grandma and grandpap."

"Yea!" Seth squealed and ran to the door to swing it wide. Rachel jumped up from her seat, threw down the heavy book, and ran out the door ahead of Seth.

Rocky found himself leaning in the doorway watching as Frank and Mary Callahan exited their wagon, Frank going first so he could offer his wife assistance. His father had grown frailer, Rocky noted, but he still had that glow about him. Rocky suspected it came from living with Mary, always a positive and cheery influence.

On their way to the house, the children flanking them, Rocky's parents waved a greeting. "Hello, son. I hope we're not intruding," Frank said. "Your mother insisted the weather was far too nice for wasting. Talked me into taking her for a drive. Somehow, we wound up here."

"Glad to see you," Rocky said. "Come on in. I can offer you a glass of lemonade."

"We won't stay long," Mary said with a warm smile, pulling her son down to her level so she could plant a kiss on his cheek. "I want to say hello to your pretty wife. I brought her the recipes she's been asking for."

"She's not here right now."

Mary's eyes roamed the house as if she didn't believe him. "Not here? Where on earth is she?"

"She drove into town."

"My goodness! Alone?" The idea seemed to strike Mary Callahan as absurd. All her life she'd depended on her husband to drive her most everywhere, although she had driven the wagon to Rocky's house on rare occasions. Apparently she couldn't abide the notion that some women had a pent-up desire for independence.

"We just came from town, but we didn't see her," Frank said, a frown forming on his already wrinkled brow.

Rocky motioned for them to sit, feigning nonchalance. "That's not so unusual."

"Little Hickman is just that, son—little. Can't very well come away from there without namin' all and sundry's whereabouts and the purchases they made. I can even name everyone's horses I saw hitched today, not to mention whose wagon is whose. Didn't see yours, though. Nope."

Rocky chuckled. His father's narrative of the tiny community was true enough. It seemed a place where few secrets went unshared. It did make him wonder why they hadn't spotted Sarah. Still, he wouldn't let on that it bothered him. He walked to the kitchen, Rachel on his heels. The girl reached for five glasses without his even asking her. Apparently she'd spent enough time watching Sarah to know the ins and outs of hospitality. When she went for the pitcher of lemonade on her own, he decided to let her finish the chore.

"Stage came into town today," Frank muttered half-heartedly.

Rocky dropped into a chair across the room from his parents. "The stage?"

"Yep. Folks was complainin' 'bout it bein' late. Guess it dropped a wheel midway. Driver had to send a horseman out for help."

Rachel handed glasses of lemonade to her grandparents,

327

then returned to the kitchen. Rocky watched her with pride before turning his attention back to Frank. "You don't miss much, do you, Pa? Bet you can even describe the passengers."

His father grinned. "Only because I heard a couple of 'em complainin' about the finely dressed Boston lawyer who rode in with them. Guess it bothered the man plenty when the wheel come off. Big inconvenience for the city fellow." Frank har-rumphed. "Don't know what Hickman needs with a lawyer."

An unnerving thought surfaced then froze in Rocky's brain.

Stephen Alden.

Impossible, he thought. Still, it would explain why Sarah had insisted on going to town alone. If she planned to meet up with her former beau, she wouldn't want her husband interfering. But this was Sarah. Surely, she didn't plan to leave them now, not after all they'd been through together. Hadn't she just confirmed this morning that God had led her straight to him and the children?

Suddenly, he knew what he had to do. "Ma, Pa—would you mind awful much—um, staying with the kids while I go into town? I should probably see what's keeping Sarah. For all I know she's run into some sort of trouble."

"Didn't mean to worry you none," Frank said. "But it couldn't hurt to check. 'Course we'll stay with the youngins."

"What about our picnic?" Seth protested. "When will you be back?"

Rocky rose and went to the boy, patting him on the head for assurance. "We'll be back before you know it." He could only pray he spoke the truth.

 328

Chapter Twenty

Sarah fumbled with her handkerchief, swiping every so often at her sticky brow and casting nervous glances in both directions as she and Stephen took the wooden sidewalk to Emma Browning's boardinghouse, where Stephen had booked a room for one night's stay. Oh, she hoped no one had seen her go into or leave the bank with Stephen. The last thing she wanted to do was give rise to false rumors. Bill Whittaker, the bank president and the man with whom they'd done their business, was enough to worry about, his beady eyes bulging with astonishment when Stephen had explained Sarah's financial position, her wish to open an account for the new schoolhouse, and her plan to put the remainder of her assets into multiple accounts using her and her husband's names. Of course, the banker had maintained an air of professionalism, but she couldn't help but wonder how much of it was genuine.

"I should think this will cancel out your husband's need for a loan on that barn," he'd stated from behind the big oak desk that separated him from Sarah and Stephen.

"That is entirely up to him, Mr. Whittaker," she'd replied, annoyed that he should bring the personal matter up in front of Stephen.

The stuffy little man cleared his throat. "Of course, of course."

"Are we done here, Stephen?" she'd asked, anxious to leave

329

the small office, whose windows exposed them to the rest of the bank and its incoming customers.

Stephen closed up his briefcase and stood, extending his hand across the desk. Sarah took that to mean they were indeed finished.

"Thank you, Mr. Whittaker," Stephen had said. "I should think you won't need my services after today."

Mr. Whittaker's chest puffed unduly when he shook Stephen's hand. "I believe I can handle things from here, Mr. Alden."

At that, they'd left the place, Sarah taking care to keep her face pointed downward, unsure of just who was in the bank at the time to watch their departure.

"Thank you for all you've done, Stephen," Sarah said as they climbed the steps to Emma's porch. "You've been a wonderful friend to me. I'm sorry about the grief you had to go through getting here. It couldn't have been pleasant for you disembarking that stage and waiting for three hours along a dusty road while they repaired the wheel."

He gave a casual shrug. "It's the least I can do for someone as special as you, Sarah Woodward Callahan. Hmm, your name has a nice ring to it now that I've grown accustomed to the idea of your marriage."

She couldn't help but laugh. "You'd better say that since you're about to claim a wife for yourself. You're very blessed, you know. Nancy is a wonderful woman."

His face creased into a full smile. "I'm coming to love and appreciate her more with every day. Perhaps I should thank you for that."

"Why me?"

"When I finally reached the conclusion that there was no hope for a future with you, my eyes opened up to other possibilities. That's when I discovered Nancy Belmont. To think she was right there under my nose most of my life!"

"And what of your faith in God, Stephen?" Sarah had learned long ago that the only way truly to reach Stephen Alden was to go straight to the point.

His expression stilled, grew more serious. "It's been an interesting journey.

"Nancy is a woman of great faith, as you know. I'm humbled when I think that she would love me in spite of my spiritual weaknesses. It seems I have quite a distance to travel to catch up to her level of spirituality, but I've discovered that God is faithful and patient. Although this may sound odd to you, I've come to lean on both Nancy and God for my spiritual lessons. Imagine me leaning on a woman, Sarah!"

She burst out laughing. "Oh, Stephen, I can't even picture it."

Their laughter mingled for a time before Stephen moved to the wicker swing on Emma Browning's porch and motioned for her to sit beside him.

Sarah wasn't at all sure of the appropriateness of such a move, especially in light of how late the hour was getting. Her family was waiting for her. *Her family.* It sounded so right. She pulled back her sleeve to look at her watch. "I should be leaving soon."

"We haven't had much time to talk, Sarah. Just give me a few more minutes. I want you to tell me more about your husband and these children."

"Oh, well, I suppose a few minutes couldn't hurt, but then

I must be going. We're going on a little family outing this afternoon. I'm sure Seth and Rachel are growing anxious for my return. I had told them I wouldn't be long at all, and then with your delay, well, at least I was able to make all my purchases while I waited for the stage to come in."

"You're rambling, Sarah. Come and ramble beside me."

She laughed. "All right, but fifteen minutes is my limit."

He nodded. "Sounds perfectly fair to me."

***

Rocky dismounted his horse and tied him next to his wagon, which he'd found parked behind the bank. No wonder his parents hadn't spotted it earlier. He could think of no reason why Sarah would have parked the rig back here unless it was to keep out of sight, which he found unlikely. What could his wife possibly have to hide?

He thought about the Boston lawyer his father had mentioned and the absurd notion that Stephen Alden might have returned to claim Sarah for himself. "Ridiculous," he murmured. There had to be some other logical reason for her coming to town alone.

"Mr. Callahan!" He turned in time to discover Mrs. Winthrop lifting her skirts in a hurried approach, a look of consternation etched into her already hard-lined face.

"Mrs. Winthrop, what can I do for you?" Something told him she had plenty on her mind, what with the way she marched across the street, her skirts whooshing to and fro.

"I wondered when you might put in an appearance."

"That so?" Rocky pushed back a wave of irritation. "Why is that?"

"Why, to tend to your wife, of course. Word has it she is cavorting with some dapper lawyer from Boston. I saw them together in the bank myself tending to some transaction or another. Of course, I stayed cleverly hidden."

The bank? "Well, I hardly think cavorting is a fair choice of words, Mrs. Winthrop," he answered in a clipped tone. It annoyed him plenty that the woman seemed to know more about his wife's business dealings than he did.

"Pfff!" she scoffed, her wrinkled countenance revealing displeasure. "I should think you would have escorted her yourself rather than allowed her to meet with that smart-looking young man from Boston. Why, I fear the rumors will fly, Mr. Callahan."

"I'm sure you'll see to that," he mumbled between his teeth, lifting his hat and swiping a hand through his hair.

"Pardon?" she asked.

"Nothing. Did you happen to see which way my wife headed?"

"Of course. She and *that man* have gone to Emma Browning's boardinghouse. Sitting right there on her porch for all to see." Mrs. Winthrop clicked her tongue in disgust. "They might have at least had the decency to conceal their improper behavior."

Rather than qualify her remark, Rocky tipped his hat at the woman and turned on his heel.

Uncommonly bright sunshine filtered through afternoon clouds, lending warmth to the early spring air. Rocky walked along, his boot heels clicking on the wooden sidewalk as he made his way down Main Street. Folks passed him and nodded, withholding their opinions, he was sure, for they weren't their usual friendly selves.

What is Sarah up to? he wondered. Had she indeed connived with Alden to make her way back East? But if that were the case, why hadn't she told him? Weren't they on better terms than that? Or were there things about him that intimidated her? He knew he hadn't always been easy to live with. Still, he'd never forced her to stay; matter of fact, he'd offered to send her back if life in Hickman proved too much of a hardship and had even tried to convince her that she wasn't cut out for farm life. Now he regretted those words. What would he do if she left them?

Suddenly, Sarah's laughter carried over the gentle breezes, followed by Alden's deeper chortle. Rocky stopped short and found himself hunkered down behind the trunk of a budding oak, spying like some scheming adolescent on the two who sat together on Emma's porch swing, acting as if they hadn't a care in the world. Had she completely forgotten about her promise to hurry home? Did it mean nothing to her that Seth and Rachel waited eagerly for her return? A heavy dose of irritation played at his nerves.

Stephen Alden was as Rocky remembered—short and willowy, lacking much of a muscular build, no doubt a result of having spent his days behind a desk pushing a pen. His well-dressed manner exuded professionalism and wealth, as did the gold chain adorning his lapels and the fine-looking hat he held across his lap. His slicked-back hair, neatly parted in the middle, had not one strand out of place despite the spring breeze. Rocky hated to think how much grease it must have taken him to set it in place. Rocky raked a hand through his own longish hair and mentally scolded himself for not paying a visit to the town barber.

"It's been wonderful seeing you again," Alden was saying.

Rocky's gut twisted into a tight knot. He wanted to march onto the porch and haul the guy away by the nape of his skinny neck. How dare he talk to his wife in such an intimate manner!

"I've felt like such a heel," he said. "It was a nasty way to part in January."

"That's over and done with," Sarah said. "We can be friends from now on."

Just about the time Rocky intended to interrupt the pleasant conversation, the front door opened and Emma Browning appeared. Rocky fitted himself behind the tree once more, worried that Emma would spot him for sure if she planned to leave the boardinghouse.

"Could I interest either of you in a glass of lemonade?" she asked, innocent as you please. Did she not think it strange that a married woman was entertaining a man on her front porch?

"None for me, thank you," Alden answered.

At that, Sarah studied her watch. "Oh my, I must be getting back."

Now there's an interesting thought, Rocky mulled to himself.

Just then, footsteps from behind alerted him to the fact he wasn't alone. When he turned he discovered Jonathan Atkins breathing down his back.

"Spying on your wife, are you?" Jon whispered, highly amused.

"Shh," Rocky hushed, yanking his friend up next to him, miffed that Jon had come across him, yet angrier with Sarah that she'd put him in this awkward position.

335

"What are you doing, Rock?" Jon asked in a loud whisper.

"I was looking for my wife."

"It seems you've found her. Why are you hiding?"

"She's entertaining her previous beau. Doesn't that strike you as odd?" Rocky hissed.

"Not until I've heard her reasons for it."

"It can't be good."

"Why do you say that?"

"Look at them huddled together on that—that fancy swing."

"They're not huddled."

Something caught Emma's attention, for she glanced from the porch and spoke loud enough for all to hear, "Isn't that the reverend hiding behind the tree?"

Rocky squeezed his eyes shut and gave a low moan. All of a sudden, Jon moved into clear view, pulling Rocky with him. "I wasn't hiding. Matter of fact, I was enjoying my daily stroll when I came upon my friend here." He whacked Rocky in the arm, knocking him off kilter. "Afternoon, folks."

A loud gasp escaped Sarah's throat. "Rocky! What—are you doing here? Where are the children?" Her wide eyes held confusion and shock.

Filled with new resolve, Rocky approached the porch, pure annoyance bubbling to the surface. "The kids are fine. Ma and Pa are with them. As far as what I'm doing here, I might ask you the same question."

"I—I can explain everything."

Stephen Alden rose to his feet. "Well, Callahan—we meet again." The scrawny fellow stepped forward to extend a hand, but Rocky refused to take it, so he turned his attention on Jon. "And this is the preacher?"

"Hickman's one and only," Jon answered, shaking Alden's hand as if they were old acquaintances. "Name's Jonathan Atkins. Jon will do. And you are?"

"Stephen Alden. I practice law in Boston, back where Sarah hails from. She and I are dear friends. In fact, we've just been rehashing old times—all quite innocent, I might add." The man's eyes carried a twinkle that Rocky would have delighted in gouging out.

After offering the shyster a distracted nod, Rocky eyed his wife with suspicion while addressing the lawyer. "Is that so? I can't imagine why she didn't inform me you were in town."

"I'm sure she'll be happy to inform you later."

"What's wrong with right now?" Rocky asked, his temper flaring. He noted Sarah's mouth remained open, her eyes unblinking.

"I believe you'll want to speak in private," Alden replied, his tone surprisingly controlled, throwing Rocky for a loop, considering his initial impression of the fellow had been that he was a hothead.

Rocky gave Sarah his full attention. "Did you forget about our plans for a family picnic?"

A flicker of apprehension flashed in her eyes. "I wouldn't forget something as important as that." She took another hasty peek at her watch as if to reassure herself. "There's still plenty of time."

"The stage was delayed," Stephen put in. "If Sarah is tardy it's only because she was waiting for me."

"Is that supposed to make me feel better?" Rocky

sputtered. "My wife tells me she has errands to run, and when she doesn't arrive home in a timely manner and I begin to worry, I discover that she's been keeping company with her former beau."

"Unfortunately, I was never her beau," Stephen put in.

"Of course, it was Iris Winthrop who pointed me in the right direction," Rocky said, ignoring Alden.

"Oh dear," Sarah gasped. "I'm sorry."

"Of course, that was *after* she informed me she had spotted you at the bank together, making a transaction." It was hard not to sound angry.

Sarah's shoulders dropped. "I can explain all that."

"You couldn't have enlightened me earlier?"

"I didn't—that is, I wasn't sure—" She stopped when Jon cleared his throat.

"Uh, I think perhaps I'll be on my way," Jon said. "Miss Emma, would you care to walk with me?" Rocky sensed the invitation had a twofold purpose: one, to escape the awkward situation; and two, to discuss the possibility of taking a room in her boardinghouse.

"Me?" Emma Browning clutched her throat in obvious surprise.

As far as Rocky knew, the young woman had never set foot inside a house of worship, much less associated with a man of the cloth. A part of him wished he could tag along to eavesdrop on the tête-à-tête, but right now, he was too distracted to care much what transpired between the two.

Jon gave a low-timbered chuckle. "Someone tell her I promise not to bite."

"He won't bite," Rocky mumbled.

Emma's brow furrowed. "I guess a bit of fresh air couldn't hurt."

Jon looped his arm for her, but Emma snubbed the offer, sticking her hands in her pockets instead. Another day Rocky might have laughed.

Everyone watched as the two strolled toward town. Stephen broke the silence when he stretched and yawned. "I don't know what anyone sees in this town, but I'm pleased that Sarah seems happy." That said, Alden actually smiled. "I suppose I have you to thank for that, Callahan."

A little of Rocky's anger was defused on the spot. He rested one foot on the first porch step and stared at the man. "You haven't tried to talk my wife into going back East?"

Alden threw back his head and laughed. "You can relax, Callahan. Your wife is staying put. I only came to offer legal counsel and, well, as I said earlier, this is something you'll want to discuss in private."

A wave of relief washed over him, but he refused to show it. "I see." Actually, he didn't see, but he supposed he was willing to listen to reason when the time came for talking. One thing was certain—his wife had a bit of explaining to do.

***

The return home was anything but pleasant. Rocky had hitched his horse to the back of the wagon and taken over the reins. Sarah sat rigid beside him, waiting for him to speak, noting the set of his stubborn jaw, where every so often a muscle quivered, observing out of the corner of one eye his fixed gaze on the road ahead.

She had expected a tongue-lashing but had received a

339

blanket of silence instead. In her mind, she tried to prepare what she would say when questioned, but she couldn't for the life of her formulate anything that sounded reasonable. Any rationale she may have had for keeping her financial resources a secret now seemed foolish. Surely, her husband wasn't so prideful that he couldn't allow her to use her wealth to help the town and him. Still, as the minutes ticked on and he continued to hold his tongue, she began to doubt herself. Perhaps even now he was wishing Stephen Alden truly had come to take her back East.

Just as the first signs of smoke rising from the cabin's little chimney came into view, Sarah chanced a bit of conversation. "I'm sure the children are anxious to commence with our picnic."

For the first time, Rocky turned his unspeaking gaze on her. A chill ran the length of her as his icy blue eyes drilled straight to her core. "I believe you and I have some talking to do first."

"Can't that wait until afterward?"

He shook his head. "We'll tell them that something has come up and send them out to play."

"But they'll be so disappointed."

His lips puckered with annoyance. "You should have thought of that when you were dallying with Alden."

"Dallying?"

"What would you call it?"

"We had business to conduct."

"On Emma Browning's front porch?" His tone was heavy with sarcasm.

Sarah sighed. "You know what I mean."

 340

Like a streak of lightning, disbelief flashed across his face. "No, Sarah, I do not. When you left today, you said you had a few errands to run and some supplies to pick up. You gave no indication that you intended to meet up with Alden. How do you think it made me feel to arrive in town only to discover you had been seen with him? What am I supposed to think, Sarah?"

Realizing too late it was time for to lay things on the table, she sent up a silent prayer for wisdom. "When I took the rig into town on Monday, I spoke to Stephen on the telephone. We made arrangements then for his visit."

He looked frustrated. "I don't see why you couldn't have told me."

She gave a resigned shrug. "I didn't think you would understand."

As they drew nearer the cabin, Sarah spotted her in-laws' wagon. They would want to know where she'd been.

Just then, Seth sailed out the door and off the front porch, setting off on a run in their direction. "Aunt Sarah, Uncle Rocky!" he squealed with great enthusiasm. "You're back. Can we go on ar picnic now?"

Sarah winced, knowing that Rocky was about to burst the boy's bubble. Worse was the knowledge that it was all her fault.

"Go back to the house, Seth," Rocky said with great control when the boy came within hearing range.

Frank and Mary, along with Rachel, stepped out onto the porch and waved. It was a regular welcoming committee, Sarah mused. Seth spun and ran back to the house, jumping on the porch to join his sister and grandparents, while Rocky maneuvered the wagon down the path toward home.

A knot the size of a boulder lay in the pit of Sarah's stomach, rolling over and over until she felt ill. *Lord, please help me explain things so they sound reasonable.*

But no great sense of peace followed her prayer.

Chapter Twenty-one

*F*rank and Mary Callahan boarded their wagon and left as soon as Rocky thanked them for coming. Something in his expression must have spoken volumes, for they didn't linger, only hugging Sarah and saying they were happy she was safe.

Rocky chased the children outside, much to their chagrin, and announced there'd be no picnic today. He supposed he could have informed them in a less harsh manner, but he wanted to finish his conversation with Sarah, and the sooner the better. The children's feelings weren't first on his mind. Even Seth's tears of disappointment and Rachel's look of despondency hadn't swayed him.

"Are you two havin' a fight?" Rachel asked while yanking a sweater off the hook. The afternoon sun had dropped behind the clouds and ushered in cooler air. Attentive sister that she was, she handed Seth his jacket.

"Sarah and I have a matter to discuss—in private," he added for emphasis.

Rachel looked from him to Sarah, her eyes dancing with apprehension. "Does it have somethin' to do with Sarah comin' home late? Are you mad at her?"

"This doesn't concern you, Rachel," he snapped.

Something wistful and worrisome flashed in her eyes. "My ma and pa used to fight a lot," she confessed.

When he might have responded with reassurance, Rocky instead blurted, "We're not your ma and pa."

Sarah let out a quiet gasp and stepped forward. "What your uncle means is…"

Rachel's shoulders straightened, and her jaw jutted forward. "He means he's not our pa," she declared, "and he's glad of it." When Seth's tears fell harder, Rachel pushed him out the door. "We didn't want to go on some dumb picnic anyway. Come on, Seth; we're not wanted here." With that, she slammed the door, something Rocky clearly would not have stood for any other day.

"Why did you have to say that? You hurt their feelings."

"I didn't mean it the way it came out," he protested. "I just meant we're different from their parents. It came out wrong. I'll set things right with them later."

Out the window, Rocky caught sight of the pair marching toward the chicken yard. He released a loud breath and headed for the coffee pot. "Want some coffee?" he asked, raising the pot to her after filling a tin mug.

"I don't especially—like coffee," she announced.

Temporarily speechless, he stared at her for several seconds, brows arched. "No? You could have told me."

She shrugged, then walked to the window to watch the children. Rocky plunked his mug down on the table, irritated, and pulled out a chair. "Come and sit down, Sarah," he said. "You have some explaining to do."

She turned from the window and faced him, her expression a picture of newfound resolve. This was the stubborn woman he remembered meeting that first day in Winthrop's Dry Goods. "I'd rather stand," she retorted, her pert little chin jutting forward, her green eyes glinting with ire.

Gritting his teeth, he sought to settle the turbulence. He wagged a finger at her in invitation and pointed at the chair again. "Come on. It'll be much easier if we both sit. I promise to listen with an open mind."

Looking like she didn't believe him, she slowly unfolded her arms and walked to the chair he still held for her. Once she finally sat, he plopped into a chair on the other side of the table. "Start at the beginning," he said, leaning forward, elbows on the table. "Why'd you send for Alden?"

She chewed on her bottom lip for at least a full minute while Rocky set to tapping lightly on the tabletop. Finally, she inhaled deeply and lowered her lashes. "I am a very wealthy woman," she more or less whispered.

He didn't know why her confession made him want to laugh outright. Maybe because he'd expected something a bit more enlightening. "I gathered that much."

His teasing remark made her lift her head, meet his gaze. "No, Rocky, I'm quite serious. I am the sole beneficiary of my parents' estate."

"Okay."

She made a clicking noise with her tongue and grimaced. "We're talking—about a lot of money—and property." Again, she lowered her eyes, then drew an invisible pattern in the tablecloth.

He sat up straighter. "Your wealth aside, I asked you about Alden. What made him come all the way to Hickman? Couldn't you have conducted your—your business dealings—whatever they amounted to, over the telephone?"

She drew in a long, measured breath. "He preferred to meet with our banker in person when the transfer of funds took place, and to aid me in any financial or legal questions I may have had."

It took great concentration not to interrupt her, not to ask why *he* hadn't been included in this important matter. But then he could guess her reasons for excluding him. She'd pretty much been living with a bear these past months—an unreasonable, quick-tempered one at that.

"When my mother died she left a will that stated I must marry before I could collect on my inheritance. When Stephen came in January, he handed me a letter my mother had written him before she died. In it she stated her wish for him to marry me. He thought it would be enough to convince me, particularly when he learned I hadn't married Benjamin Broughton." She gave a sullen smile. "My mother thought the sun rose and set on Stephen Alden. I don't think she realized that Stephen loved my money more than he loved me, the person."

Rocky shook his head as if to rid himself of his building confusion. "So you married me in order to claim your assets? Is that it?"

She blinked. "Certainly not. My marrying you had nothing to do with that. In fact, earthly possessions hold little value for me personally. I grew up in utter affluence, Rocky, and have since learned that it is no substitute for peace and happiness. No, my marrying you went far deeper than any desire I might have had for claiming my inheritance. As soon as I met those children, I—well, I saw a need that I could help meet."

A tremor touched her smooth, full lips, and suddenly he remembered what it felt like to kiss them. He pushed the memory aside and asked, "So why lay claim to your fortune at all if it means nothing to you?"

Her shiny eyes took on a life of their own, glistening with a sheen of purpose, while a few strands of her burgundy hair fell loosely about her neck, creating in Rocky a river of need to reach out and touch it. "Although I am not interested in my money for what it can do for me, I am aware of what it can mean to others."

Instantly filled with curiosity, he urged, "Tell me what you mean."

She swallowed hard, then nervously fingered a few stray curls. "Are you sure you want to know?"

"I wouldn't have asked otherwise."

Bracing herself, she blurted, "I would very much like to provide financial backing for the new school."

Unsure how to respond, he gaped wide-eyed. Seconds must have turned to minutes. "Is that right?"

Nervously, she shifted in her straight-back chair. "I happen to think it's a good idea," she asserted, drawing back her shoulders. "It's not as if the folks of Hickman are rolling in money right now, Rocky. I daresay life is a struggle for most of them, but I've come to appreciate their diligence.

"When I discovered that Reverend Atkins had decided to sell his home to erect a new church building, I was flabbergasted by his generosity, not to mention his passion for Hickman's dear citizens. I knew at that point that if he could make such a sacrifice, surely I could do my part. I know that I should have consulted you on this matter; we are, after all, in this marriage together."

"That we are," Rocky answered, enamored by her explanation.

"And we should have made a decision of this magnitude jointly," she added.

He nodded. "Again, you're right."

"I don't know how the townsfolk would react to a newly arrived citizen making such a donation," she rambled, "so for that reason I'd like this offer to remain anonymous, if possible."

"The town will no doubt speculate where such a hefty donation came from," Rocky replied, "but I'm sure we could arrange for Bill Whittaker to keep his mouth shut, particularly once he discovers that a mere slip of the tongue could land your account in State Bank of Lexington. Bill's too fond of his money to nourish rumors that might jeopardize his future."

Biting her lip, she looked out the window toward the vacant space where the barn had once stood. "I know I've said it before, but there is more than enough to put up a new barn. A grand barn," she tacked on. He revealed a hint of a smile. It amazed him how much he'd mellowed since inviting God to regain control of his life. Still, he wasn't quite ready to let her off the hook.

"And I told you before I don't need your money."

"Why do you have to be so stubborn?" she asked in a rush of words. "It doesn't make sense to borrow from the bank when we have enough to build a hundred fine barns."

Rocky's eyebrows shot up of their own accord. "A hundred?"

"More than that," she answered with no emotion.

"Just how much money do you have, Sarah?"

A shamefaced look moved across her face. "I'll show you my financial papers if you're interested."

Rocky sat back in his chair to stretch out his long legs and cross his arms over his broad chest. "File the papers away for now, Sarah. I'll study on them later when I'm more in the mood."

"Are you very angry with me?" she asked, voice dropping to a hoarse murmur.

Angry? There were emotions to sort through, of course, but he wouldn't say they involved anger. Awe, maybe. Naturally, it surprised him to discover just how wealthy a woman he'd married, and it pleased him to learn how willing she was to give up a portion of that wealth to erect a schoolhouse for the citizens of Hickman. What surprised him most, however, was his own reaction to the news. Shoot, he was even envisioning a fancy new barn—paid for in full.

If he were honest with himself, he'd have to admit to having harbored some resentment, perhaps even outright hostility, when it came to Sarah's wealth. Deep down he'd feared it would drive a wedge between them, particularly once she grasped the vast differences in their backgrounds and realized that life in Hickman was a far cry from Boston. He'd been certain that when she came to terms with their dissimilarities, she would jump the next train back East. That hadn't been the case, though, and as if to prove him wrong, she'd seemingly grown accustomed to the tough and taxing way of life, making him love her more than ever.

"I'm not angry, Sarah. Just a little puzzled."

She cleared her throat and stirred. "Puzzled?"

He pulled in his long legs and pushed back his chair. Rising, he walked around the table and extended his hand to her. Placing her palm in his, she slid gracefully out of her chair, their bodies facing. "I still can't quite believe you chose us, Sarah, but I'm grateful," he murmured, hands now on her slender waist. "I'm beginning to believe God really did send you to Hickman." He leaned close and whispered. "I'm a slow learner."

He loved the sound of her lighthearted giggle.

"God has been working on me, Sarah. I was a bitter man after losing my wife and son, but I have a new family now, and I don't want to blow my chances at that. Yes, there've been a few setbacks—the fire, almost losing Rachel, and then Seth's illness—but who am I to question God's plan? I'm determined to lead this family by example, and I'd appreciate your help." He bit his lower lip until the pain gave him courage to continue. "There's something else."

"Yes?" Her misty, sea-green eyes explored his face.

Eager to kiss her completely, he moved his hands to her shoulders and locked gazes with her. "You've come to mean a great deal to me in these past months. I know I've been remiss in showing you just how much." At a loss for words, he bent at the waist and kissed her briefly on the mouth. Pulling back, their eyes met again, hers warm and forgiving, lending him courage. "My feelings go much deeper than friendship, Sarah."

"They do?" she asked, a smile growing on her rosy mouth.

He cupped her cheeks with his hands, and a kind of joy, like a freed eagle, threw wide the door to his heart.

As Rocky opened his mouth to declare his love, Seth's yelp of alarm and pounding footsteps on the porch stopped him short. "Uncle Rocky!" the boy squealed from the open door, "Rachel says she's goin' to go live with Grandma and Grandpa." Wheezing, the boy bent at the waist to catch his breath and gripped his chest. "She wanted me to come with her, but I told her—we had better ask you first. So then, she left without me—said you guys don't never wanna be ar parents. She's madder 'n a hornet."

Seth straightened his small body, his big brown eyes filling with hurt and need. "I like Grandma and Grandpa Callahan just fine, Uncle Rocky, but I wanna live with you guys." His searching eyes went from Rocky to Sarah, and without a moment's hesitation, Rocky walked to the boy and wrapped his arms around him.

***

Mary Callahan stood on her front porch, her arms folded at her plump waist and her skirt blowing in the wind, as if she knew they'd be arriving any minute. She put a hand to her brow to shield her eyes from the afternoon sun, then stepped forward when they drove into the yard.

"Where is she?" Rocky asked after he helped Sarah off the wagon and reached the porch.

"In the house, sittin' on your pa's lap, bawlin' her eyes out. Keeps sayin' she wants to live with us. I do believe she ran her little legs off getting here. Whatever did you say to her?"

"I guess it's what I didn't say that matters most."

Mary leaned forward. The closed door would prevent Rachel from overhearing. "For some reason, Rachel seems to think she's not wanted at your place."

"She's wanted," Rocky said, firm as could be.

"I think she's feeling a mite insecure. She still misses her mama somethin' fierce, whether she wants to admit it or not."

"Of course she does," Sarah interjected. "Losing a parent is an awful burden to carry. It's difficult enough for adults, but when you're young, well…"

Rocky stepped past his mother and opened the front door. His father sat in the family rocker in the living room, Rachel's curled-up body snuggled against his chest, his weary eyes connecting with Rocky's over the top of the girl's blond head. Rocky walked across the room and knelt on one knee so as to meet Rachel's nearly hidden eyes.

"Rachel, do you suppose you could come out on the porch with me? I'd like us to have a little chat."

She opened the eye that was visible to him, and he noted the redness surrounding it. For one who'd lost her mother just months ago, she'd rarely shed a tear. Tending to Seth's every need, remaining brave through her pain and loss, she must surely have nearly caved under the weight of it all. And what had he done to make her load easier? Guilt ran over his soul.

When she made no move, he extended his hand, hoping and praying he hadn't lost what little trust he'd managed to build with her. Frank nudged the girl forward, and although she threw Rocky a wary look, she took his hand.

He smiled, and the two walked to the porch.

"Give us a minute," he whispered to Sarah. She nodded and followed Mary into the house.

Rocky led Rachel to the porch swing. Once they were seated, he pushed off with one foot and gazed out over his parents' farmyard. Chickens roamed freely, poking in the ground in search of seed. Two milk cows and a horse hovered near the fence, watching, dipping their heads for grassy nutrition every now and then, seeming more interested in what went on at the house than in their meager meal. The old red barn sagged in the middle, showing its age, the late afternoon sun peeking over the roof like a lazy cat.

"I'd miss you if you decided to move in with my folks," he told her.

Rachel gave him a sideways glance. "Seth could keep you company. I don't think he's very keen on movin'."

"Seth would miss you something terrible. He relies on you an awful lot, and I hate to think how Sarah would feel. She's grown very attached to you."

A tiny glint of pleasure burst into her eyes, then quickly dissolved. "She would probably forget about me in a week or so."

"Are you kidding? On the way here, she talked about all the wonderful ways you help her around the house—reading to Seth, collecting the eggs, washing the dishes, lending a hand with the meals, sweeping the front porch. I could just tell by listening to her that she'd be lost without you. We're a family, Rachel, and families stick together."

"Grandma and Grandpa are family."

"Sure, but they don't live with us. I'm afraid we'd never see you if you moved in with them. My pa's getting older, you know. He might not feel like driving you over to see your brother as often as you'd like."

She seemed to think that over. "Grandma and Grandpa don't fight like my ma and pa used to—and sometimes you and Aunt Sarah..."

There it was—the fist in the gut. He supposed he had it coming. "Rachel, Sarah and I weren't really fighting earlier; we were discussing an issue, something that happened in town, but I think we've managed to resolve it."

"Is she gonna stay at your house for always?"

A hard lump formed in his throat when he read the insecurity in her eyes. "Yes, I believe she is." He glanced down at her and winked. "I won't let her leave, if you want the truth. She means too much to me." She gave a half-smile and Rocky

353

placed his arm along the back of the swing, giving her shoulder a tender squeeze. He weighed his next words carefully. "If you're worried our home won't always be a safe place, you can stop fretting about it this very minute."

At that, she looked him full in the face, some of her stubbornness having fallen away. "Will you be like a real pa to Seth and me?"

He smiled. "I'd like to give it a try."

"I don't remember much about my real pa 'cept for his yellin'. He died before Seth was born." She swatted at a tiny pebble with the toe of her shoe, sending it flying. "A horse kicked him to death."

"I know that." He wondered if Rachel knew her father had been drunk when the accident happened. Matter of fact, from what his mother had told him, the jerk had rarely been sober. It was unfortunate the way he died, but if the horse hadn't killed him when it did, his drinking habit soon would have.

Rachel's lips started to form a word, then closed back up, as if what she had intended to say needed more pondering. Rocky gave her time to shape her thoughts.

"I hate when people die. What if somethin' happens to you or Sarah?"

Across the yard, Seth emerged from the barn, three kittens tucked under his arm. He plopped himself into the dirt with the trio of felines and started playing with them, oblivious to Rocky's watchful gaze.

"Some things in life cannot be controlled, sweetheart, but I can tell you something I've learned." Her expression sparked with curiosity when she raised her face to look at him. "Life isn't always fair," he murmured, "and sometimes the things that come

 354

at us are cruel—like you kids losing your ma, and me losing my wife and son. But God loves us all—and He never changes. He's there to offer comfort and strength if we just let Him." It was somewhat of a shock to hear these words coming from his own mouth, and he thanked the Lord that he could say them honestly. He casually brought his hand to rest on her small shoulder.

She moved a bit closer to rest her head against his side, and the simple act set his heart in motion. "Do you think I could have my old room back?" she asked, the question throwing him.

"What? Why...?"

"It's too big for me, and I get kind of lonesome in there 'cause I can't hear Aunt Sarah when she's workin' in the kitchen."

So she'd decided not to live with her grandparents after all. He smiled. "Well, I guess we could arrange that."

She pulled herself upright. "It's not that I don't like that new room, but I was thinkin' that you and Aunt Sarah could have it, and Seth could have the room Aunt Sarah sleeps in, and I could have the old room Seth and me used to sleep in, and..." He seriously doubted the girl understood the implication of her words. Then again, in many ways, she'd surprised him with her insightful nature.

Just then, the screen door opened with a squeak and Sarah emerged.

Immediately, Rachel made way for Sarah's slender body to slide in between them.

After Sarah snuggled into Rocky's side, he put an arm around her and set to massaging little circles into the curve of her shoulder. "Rachel just announced she wants her old room back," he stated matter-of-factly, shoving off with his foot again.

The trusty old swing swayed, whining and screeching with each lift. Without missing a beat, he added, "She seems to think you and I could take the new room, Seth could have the one you've been sleeping in, and she could have her old room."

Sarah's eyes darted upward with the assertion and he smiled down at her. "It's a pretty good idea, don't you think?"

As if realizing the adults needed their privacy, Rachel wiggled her way off the swing. "I'm gonna go see what Seth's doin' with them kittens." At the bottom step, she paused and turned.

"I'd rather live with you guys," she announced with matter-of-fact clarity.

"Well, I'm glad that's settled," he remarked, watching her set off at a run, her calf-length dress blowing in the breeze, her blond braids bouncing off her back. He beamed with pleasure, then tipped his face close to nuzzle his whiskered jaw against Sarah's cheek. Her flowery scent had his mind wandering in several different directions. "You know I love you, don't you, Sarah?" he whispered, his voice suddenly gone hoarse.

"Did you know I love you back?" she queried.

He turned her chin with his finger and grinned, suddenly overcome with tenderness. "I was hoping."

Leaning down, he pressed a kiss to her waiting lips, devouring her softness, sealing their newfound love. After several moments, she pushed away and angled her eyes at him. "I've been thinking that I might like to have a baby," she announced.

He felt the beginnings of a silly grin. "Hm," he said, chuckling low and fondling a piece of her hair. "So much for our marriage in name only."

About the Author
Sharlene MacLaren

*B*orn and raised in western Michigan, Sharlene MacLaren attended Spring Arbor University. Upon graduating with an education degree, she traveled internationally for a year with a small singing ensemble, then came home and married one of her childhood friends. Together they raised two lovely daughters. Now happily retired after teaching elementary school for thirty-one years, "Shar" enjoys reading, writing, singing in the church choir and worship teams, traveling, and spending time with her husband, children, and precious grandson.

A Christian for over forty years and a lover of the English language, Shar has always enjoyed dabbling in writing—poetry, fiction, various essays—and freelancing for periodicals and newspapers. Her favorite genre, however, has always been romance. She remembers well the short stories she wrote in high school and watching them circulate from girl to girl during government and civics classes. "Psst," someone would whisper from two rows over, and always with the teacher's back to the class, "pass me the next page."

Shar is a regular speaker for her local MOPS (Mothers of Preschoolers) organization, is involved in KIDS' HOPE USA, a mentoring program for at-risk children, counsels young women in the Apples of Gold program, and is active in two weekly Bible studies. She and her husband, Cecil, live in Spring Lake, Michigan, with Dakota, their lovable collie, and Mocha, their lazy fat cat.

The acclaimed *Through Every Storm* was Shar's first novel to be published by Whitaker House. *Loving Liza Jane* and *Sarah, My Beloved* are the first two books in the Little Hickman Creek trilogy.

You can e-mail Shar at smac@chartermi.net or visit her website at www.sharlenemaclaren.com.

357

An Excerpt from Sharlene MacLaren's next novel,

Courting Emma

Third in the Little Hickman Creek Series

~ Chapter One ~

July 4, 1896

Emma Browning's boot heels clicked out a rhythm on the wooden sidewalk as she strode purposefully toward home. She'd just spotted Ezra, her galoot of a father, staggering in her direction, and if she didn't get out of sight soon, he'd be sure to make a fool of her—again!

Emma halted when she heard a commotion up the street. Everyone's gazes alighted on the staggering, heavyset man, dirty trousers sagging below his protruding belly, one suspender keeping them from sliding to the ground, a bottle of booze swinging from one hand. Singing at the top of his lungs, he slurred each word so terribly that no one this side of the Tennessee-Kentucky border would have been able to decipher a single phrase.

Emma put a hand to her throat. It was what she'd feared. Disgust and shame roiled in the pit of her stomach. How could Ezra Browning keep doing this to her—mortifying her in plain daylight—especially when it seemed the entire town had shown up for the holiday festivities. Someone ought to shoot the miserable, tanked-up, tangle-footed jug head, she thought, then heave him facedown into Little Hickman Creek's deepest waters. If she weren't afraid of the consequences, she'd do it herself.

Hauling in a heavy dose of air, Emma mopped her damp forehead with the back of her hand. "Guess I should get him off the street."

She knew what she'd like to do. "I'll stick him in that old tin tub out back. He can lay there til he sobers up."

***

Emma looked up from her bread making. It was just past nine-thirty. Her shoulders slumped as she heaved a sigh. Jon Atkins was helping old Ezra out of the tin tub, and from the sound of things, her father wasn't too happy for the help.

Why couldn't the reverend mind his own business?

~ *Chapter Three* ~

Lemme go," Ezra screeched, both hands flailing. "I don't need no help."

"I beg to differ, old man," Jon argued. "You can't even stand up on your own. Look at you."

Jon caught sight of Emma Browning bounding off the boarding-house back stoop, skirts flaring with every step, wisps of blond hair coming loose from its tight little bun and falling in damp ringlets around her oval face. Her blue eyes sparked with a mixture of anger and confusion as she marched with purpose in their direction, Luke Newman on her heels.

"What do you think you're doing, Jon Atkins?" she asked.

"I'm about to take this odorous fellow to the bathhouse."

Emma fixed him with a perplexing stare and set her jaw in a firm line. Jon paused, one arm around Ezra to keep him from toppling. "Why would you want to do that?" she asked, lifting a hand to shade her eyes from the early morning sun.

"He could use a bath, don't you think?" The man's stench was enough to knock over a horse.

"Don't need no bath," Ezra grumbled. "Had one already."

"When? Last spring?" Jon asked, trying to make light of the situation. It had been at least a week since the guy had even shaved, let alone bathed himself.

Ezra coughed and spat, just missing Jon's boot. It was all Jon could do not to set the oaf back down in the tub and let him sleep awhile longer. But he'd determined to get involved in the fellow's life—actually,

God had prompted him to get involved—and so here he was defending himself to the drunken fool's daughter.

"Won't do you any good," Emma said. "Matter of fact, you'd be wastin' your time." Her eyes skittered over Ezra's slouched frame. She crossed her arms and stuck out her obstinate little chin. "He's nothin' but a drunk."

Jon took a moment to study Emma's stance, spine straight as a pin, jaw tense, eyes hard and proud. She'd learned that stance from years of struggling to survive, he was sure of it. "When was the last time you saw him sober?" he asked.

Emma laughed, but there was no warmth in the sound. "Well now, that'd take some recollectin', preacher." Preacher? Jon? Reverend Atkins? Which was it? She'd known him all her life, but since his return to Hickman a little less than a year ago, she didn't seem to know quite how to address him. Furthermore, she was determined to dislike him.

Ezra swayed and Jon got a firmer grip on his arm. The bum was still so liquored up he didn't even know he was the topic of conversation.

"Come on, old man," he said, turning Ezra around and pointing him in the right direction, slanting his face away from the worst of Ezra's overpowering odor.

"You w-want some h-help?" asked Luke. Up until now, he'd been the silent observer. Matter of fact, Luke spent most of his time on the sidelines watching life go by. Jon wondered if the boy didn't know a whole lot more about living than most folks gave him credit for knowing.

"That'd be real nice, Luke. You take the other arm."

Luke stepped forward and Emma's frown grew. "There's no hope for Ezra, Jon. You might as well accept it." Ah, so now he was Jon again.

He paused and smiled at her. "Oh, there's hope, Emma. As long as there's a God in heaven, there is hope."

She made a scoffing noise. "You'd best save your sermonizin' for your congregation."

His grin widened as he tilted his face at her. "I will if you promise to come hear me sometime."

He detected the slightest hitch at the corner of her mouth. "Now, why would I bother comin' to hear one of your sermons?"

"To please me maybe?" She gave him an odd look, and how could he blame her? She'd be blown away by the knowledge that he was attracted to her, had been since he was a snotty-nosed kid. Of course, his attraction made no sense. He was a pastor, for crying out loud. He needed a wife, yes, but a good *Christian* wife, someone to support his ministry, not someone like Emma Browning who openly admitted she had no use for God.

He gave himself a mental scolding.

Ask her about the room, Jon.

The nudge was as strong as if Jupiter, his horse, had plowed straight into his side. *I've asked her plenty, Lord. She's made it clear she doesn't want me under her roof.*

Ask, Jon.

"You rent that room to anyone yet?" he asked.

She gave him a stunned look, probably still mulling over his invitation to come to church. "What? No." Her arms remained crossed, except now she hugged herself more tightly and added a scowl to her pursed lips.

"I'm still in need of a place."

Ezra belched loud enough to scare the birds from their perches. Not only that, it carried a deadly stench. Emma lifted a hand and batted the acrid air to ward off the worst of the smell.

"Oh, for crying in a bucket! If you get him out of here, you can rent a blasted room."

Jon grinned. It was a victory grin, he knew, so he tried not to let it grow to extremes. *Thank You, Lord.* "That's a load off my shoulders, Emma. Tom Averly, who bought my place, will be pleased to know I'm finally moving out."

He and Luke started hauling Ezra out of the yard.

"Rent's $12 a week, but my long-termers pay by the month," she called to his back. "I'll expect you to pay the first month's rent on the day you move in. Thereafter, rent's due the first of every month. And if you get behind, there'll be no mercy."

Jon waved, hiding his victory grin. "I always pay my bills on time."

"And I won't stand for any of your preaching, either, you hear?"

"Will you sit for it?"

She didn't respond to that, just made a grumbling noise.

He was still grinning when they passed Winthrop's Dry Goods and he caught a glimpse of Iris Winthrop through the glass, her wide-eyed, gaped-mouth reaction when she saw Luke and him escorting Ezra through the center of town only adding to his satisfaction.

The bath was no easy affair, but when finished, Ezra Browning did smell as nice as a field of daisies. Of course, he'd sauntered in the direction of Madam Guttersnipe's Saloon shortly thereafter much to Jon's dismay and not in the least bit grateful for their help.

"Let me take you back to your house, Ezra," Jon had offered. "Luke and I'll help you clean up the place then fix you a decent meal." But Ezra had shaken his head and mumbled something about needing a drink instead.

"I guess h-he don't like ar cookin'," Luke had said while they stood there next to the bathhouse watching Ezra amble off, Jon's arm looped over Luke's hunched shoulders.

Jon slanted his head at Luke. "He doesn't know what he's missing. I cook a mean bean soup."

Luke shot him a twisted grin. "Me and Pa like bean soup, but Miss Emma don't n-never make it. She says she don't dare m-make b-bean soup for a houseful of r-rude men."

At Luke's remark, Jon clutched his stomach and bent over laughing.

***

Emma dusted with a vengeance. Now, why had she gone and offered her vacant room to Jonathan Atkins? Hadn't she just been telling herself she neither wanted nor needed the company of a preacher in her establishment? So why was it that when he'd looked at her with those powder blue eyes of his, she'd crumbled like a month-old cookie? Was it because he'd taken old Ezra off her hands? It seemed a likely excuse. After all, one good deed deserved another, and Lord knows she wasn't about to take her father to the bathhouse herself, much as the old codger did need a bath. But then she had to confess there was more to it than that.

Emma dusted faster. Truth was, she wasn't willing to delve much deeper into her reasons for relenting. All she knew was that the town's young preacher was about to make his home in this very room, and she'd best get it ready for him. She lifted a lace doily from the chest of drawers, gave it a little shake and replaced it, smoothing down the corners with care. Then she glanced up at the ancient picture hanging crooked above the chest and righted it.

Standing back, she made a sweeping assessment of the room. Clean sheets on the old four-poster bed, braid rug freshly beaten, gingham curtains laundered and pressed, and the cracked leather seat of the old wooden rocker wiped clean. She had no idea when Jon Atkins planned to move into Mr. Dreyfus's old room, but at least it would be ready for him when he did.

She dropped her hands to her sides and felt a bulge in her apron pocket. Stuffing her hand into her pocket she withdrew the lone wool sock she'd found under Mr. Dreyfus's bed, the one she'd darned for him on numerous occasions. More than likely, he hadn't missed it yet, but come winter he'd be wondering what had become of it.

Fingering the woolen fabric, an unwelcome memory poked to the surface. *Blustery winds sneaked through the cracks of the poorly heated cabin, the pile of firewood next to the stone fireplace dwindling down to almost nothing. Papa staggered through the door, eyes watery red, snowy boots leaving a trail of white on the just swept rug as he stomped his feet. An icy look on his round, whiskered face matched the frigid temperatures. Emma shivered in the straight-back chair and drew the wool blanket up closer around her neck, tucking the book she'd been reading beneath its folds.*

"What you doin', girl?" he growled, slamming the door shut behind him,

bloodshot eyes narrow and suspicious. "How come I don't smell no supper cookin'?"

"We're outa most all the food, Papa. All that's left is some flour and oil and a few cans of beans." She drew her knees up close to her chest, hoping he wouldn't find her book. He'd accuse her of laziness for sure. No matter that she'd spent the afternoon sweeping, dusting, and shoveling a narrow path to the rickety old outhouse. Her ten-year-old muscles felt sore and fatigued.

"Then cook the lousy beans, missy."

"We've had beans three times this week, Papa."

As soon as the words left her mouth, she wanted to reclaim them. Papa didn't take nicely to backtalk. He reached her in two long strides and gave her the back of his hand. The force of the blow was enough to knock her off the chair, sending her precious book of Bible stories in another direction.

With his beefy hand he retrieved the book and held it at arm's length. Papa couldn't read, but he squinted at the words as if in doing so he might be able to make out its title. "What's this nonsense?" he asked.

"Miss Abbott gave it to me," she confessed, her cheek still burning like hot coals where his hand had struck it. She wouldn't mention the book's contents.

"That old lady what runs the boardinghouse? How many times I gotta tell you to stay away from that religious crazy?"

Emma pulled herself upright. "Can I have my book back, Papa?" she squeaked out, ignoring his remark. Miss Abbott was as close as Emma would ever come to having a mother, or a grandmother, for that matter. Nearly every day after school she took an extra minute to swing by the older woman's board-inghouse to receive a warm hug and, if she was lucky, cookies and a tall glass of milk.

Papa took one look at the fireplace, its flames died down to a few red embers. Without a second's hesitation, he tossed the treasured volume into the fire, ignoring her sudden gasp. A puff of black smoke climbed the chimney until the hard cover of the book took hold, reigniting the flames to a rich orange-red.

The sound of trudging feet coming up the stairs dragged Emma's sullen thoughts back to the present. She took a gander at her watch and

 364

found it near suppertime. Gideon Barnard glanced inside the open door on his way past then halted and backtracked. "You lookin' for somethin', Miss Emma?"

She jammed the wool sock back in her apron pocket. "Just cleanin' out Mr. Dreyfus's old room, makin' way for the next boarder."

Gray eyes slanted under a crinkled brow, lending credence to the older gentleman's perpetual frown. "Yeah? Who's movin' in?"

"The Reverend Atkins." She purposely kept her answer short, not wanting to elaborate. Bending, she picked up the bucket of water she'd used to mop the wood floor, gathered up the dusting cloth and a few other items, and headed for the door, hoping to slip past Mr. Barnard without further incident. But it wasn't to be.

"That so? The preacher?" He moved aside to let her pass, then, rather than go to his room as he'd earlier intended, he followed a few paces behind her. "That mean we have to clean up our talk around here?"

"I've been askin' you hooligans to do that for some time now. Don't imagine a preacher will have any more success at it than me." On the way down the hall, she stopped, set the bucket down, and with her free hand righted another picture, then ran her fingers along the top of the frame, pleased to find it dust-free.

"I ain't cleanin' up my mouth—or my actions, for that matter."

She sniffed. "Fine. Now, if you'll excuse me I need to be checkin' on my supper." She picked up the bucket and resumed her steps.

When she turned to take the stairs, Gideon Barnard was muttering something under his breath.

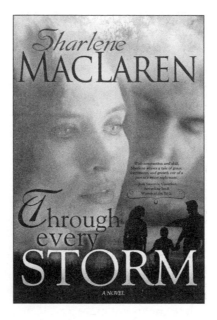

Through Every Storm
Sharlene MacLaren

When tragedy strikes, can love survive?

Struggling through the tragic loss of their child, Maddie and Jeff Bowman experience the immense pain and grief caused by a broken heart and a marriage so severely strained that a divorce seems imminent. Will life ever be normal again? While still overwhelmed with feelings of complete hopelessness and loneliness, they are additionally faced with having to care for a precocious little boy. Maddie and Jeff must learn how to overcome their problems. But together they may find a joy and happiness that they had never known before.

ISBN: 978-0-88368-746-8 • Trade • 368 pages

WHITAKER
HOUSE
www.whitakerhouse.com

Loving Liza Jane
Sharlene MacLaren

Liza Jane Merriwether had come to Little Hickman Creek, Kentucky, to teach. She had a lot of love to give to her students. She just hadn't reckoned on the handsome stranger with two adorable little girls and a heart of gold that was big enough for one more.

Ben Broughton missed his wife, but he was doing the best he could to raise his two daughters alone. Still, he had to admit that he needed help, which is why he wrote to the Marriage Made in Heaven Agency for a mail-order bride. While he was waiting for a response, would he overlook the perfect wife that God had practically dropped in his lap?

ISBN: 978-0-88368-816-8 • Trade • 368 pages

WHITAKER
HOUSE

www.whitakerhouse.com

1	31	61	91	121	151	181	211	241	271	301	331
2	32	62	92	122	152	182	212	242	272	302	332
3	33	63	93	123	153	183	213	243	273	303	333
4	34	64	94	124	154	184	214	244	274	304	334
5	35	65	95	125	155	185	215	245	275	305	335
6	36	66	96	126	156	186	216	246	276	306	336
7	37	67	97	127	157	187	217	247	277	307	337
8	38	68	98	128	158	188	218	248	278	308	338
9	39	69	99	129	159	189	219	249	279	309	339
10	40	70	100	130	160	190	220	250	280	310	340
11	41	71	101	131	161	191	221	251	281	311	341
12	42	72	102	132	162	192	222	252	282	312	342
13	43	73	103	133	163	193	223	253	283	313	343
14	44	74	104	134	164	194	224	254	284	314	344
15	45	75	105	135	165	195	225	255	285	315	345
16	46	76	106	136	166	196	226	256	286	316	346
17	47	77	107	137	167	197	227	257	287	317	347
18	48	78	108	138	168	198	228	258	288	318	348
19	49	79	109	139	169	199	229	259	289	319	349
20	50	80	110	140	170	200	230	260	290	320	350
21	51	81	111	141	171	201	231	261	291	321	351
22	52	82	112	142	172	202	232	262	292	322	352
23	53	83	113	143	173	203	233	263	293	323	353
24	54	84	114	144	174	204	234	264	294	324	354
25	55	85	115	145	175	205	235	265	295	325	355
26	56	86	116	146	176	206	236	266	296	326	356
27	57	87	117	147	177	207	237	267	297	327	357
28	58	88	118	148	178	208	238	268	298	328	358
29	59	89	119	149	179	209	239	269	299	329	359
30	60	90	120	150	180	210	240	270	300	330	360

town's new pastor, Jonathan Atkins, takes up residence in the boardinghouse. The whole town will witness the miracle as Emma begins to experience God's transforming power at work.

Trade • ISBN: 978-1-60374-020-3 • 368 pages
Available Spring 2008

WHITAKER HOUSE

www.whitakerhouse.com